Praise for *USA Today* bestselling author
Rebecca Forster and her electrifying novel of
suspense . . .

HOSTILE WITNESS

"An enthralling read, with colorful, well-developed characters and the unique atmosphere of the California beach communities."   —Nancy Taylor Rosenberg

"Blending complex psychological character portraits with spot-on accurate courtroom drama, Forster's riveting legal thriller keeps the plot twists coming until the last, satisfying page."   —Alafair Burke

"*Hostile Witness* punches all the right buttons for a must-read legal thriller. Rebecca Forster delivers fascinating characters, realistic courtroom theater, and a complex, fast-paced plot. This novel is the perfect blend of an emotional, heartfelt story and a beautifully conceived whodunit. I will eagerly await her next legal thriller."
—David Ellis

. . . and for her previous novels written as R. A. Forster

"[A] riveting legal whodunit."   —*USA Today*

"As the lives of her characters unfold, the reader has the pleasure of watching a master storyteller weave her powerful tale. . . . One of today's best writers of legal thrillers. With a cast of characters as real as your own next door neighbors, and an easily identifiable story, the book is impossible to put down."   —Under the Covers

"[Forster] does what one expects of a good writer of legal thrillers, i.e., drives the plot through unexpected twists without overstretching the bounds of credible law. But Forster adds a bonus by transcending the flat stereotypes of the genre and creating, instead, diverse and realistically drawn characters."   —*Publishers Weekly*

SILENT WITNESS

Rebecca Forster

A SIGNET BOOK

SIGNET
Published by New American Library, a division of
Penguin Group (USA) Inc., 375 Hudson Street,
New York, New York 10014, USA
Penguin Group (Canada), 10 Alcorn Avenue, Toronto,
Ontario M4V 3B2, Canada (a division of Pearson Penguin Canada Inc.)
Penguin Books Ltd., 80 Strand, London WC2R 0RL, England
Penguin Ireland, 25 St. Stephen's Green, Dublin 2,
Ireland (a division of Penguin Books Ltd.)
Penguin Group (Australia), 250 Camberwell Road, Camberwell, Victoria 3124,
Australia (a division of Pearson Australia Group Pty. Ltd.)
Penguin Books India Pvt. Ltd., 11 Community Centre, Panchsheel Park,
New Delhi - 110 017, India
Penguin Group (NZ), cnr Airborne and Rosedale Roads, Albany,
Auckland 1310, New Zealand (a division of Pearson New Zealand Ltd.)
Penguin Books (South Africa) (Pty.) Ltd., 24 Sturdee Avenue,
Rosebank, Johannesburg 2196, South Africa

Penguin Books Ltd., Registered Offices:
80 Strand, London WC2R 0RL, England

First published by Signet, an imprint of New American Library,
a division of Penguin Group (USA) Inc.

First Printing, February 2005
10 9 8 7 6 5 4 3 2 1

Copyright © Rebecca Forster, 2005
All rights reserved

For John A. Czuleger

Prologue

Archer shot the naked woman at nine thirty in the morning; the naked man was in his sights five minutes later.

Three more shots: the front door and address, the woman's car nestled in the shadows of an acacia tree, the man's car parked in front of the house as subtle a statement as a dog pissing to mark its territory. That was when the camera choked, caught and started the rewind whir. Deciding he had enough to satisfy his client that the missus wasn't exactly waiting for him to hightail it home, Archer reloaded, stashed the exposed film in his pocket and let his head fall back against the car's seat. Cradling the camera in his lap, he let his body go heavy as his eyes closed. He was tired to the bone and not because he had another couple of hours to wait before Don Juan decided to pack up his piece and take his leave. This tired was in Archer's soul. This tired crept way deep into his heart and made it hard for that muscle to pump enough blood to keep him going.

He moved in the seat, put one leg up and tried to stretch it out. There wasn't a comfortable place in the rental for a man his size. Archer missed his Hummer but it was too noticeable to use on surveillance. He could live in that baby if he had to. His brain was another matter. A rental, his car or his home, Archer couldn't find a comfortable place in his mind for the thoughts that had been dogging him these many days. Maybe spying on wayward wives was making him uneasy. No self-respecting cop would be doing this kind of work even if the wronged husband was paying big bucks.

But, then, Archer wasn't a self-respecting cop anymore. He was a part-time photographer with a penchant for solitary trips to Mexico, a retired detective, a freelance investigator and a man who was running on empty when it came to making ends meet this month. And then there was the anniversary. Archer didn't want to think about that either but it was impossible not to when California autumn had come again, a carbon copy of a day he would just as soon forget: bright sky-blue up high, navy in the deep sea, a nip in the sunny daytime air, downright cold at night. Lexi, his wife, was so sick. And then there was Tim.

Tim.

Archer stirred and held the camera in the crook of one arm like a child. His other one was bent against the door so he could rest his head on his upturned hand. He moved his mind like he moved his body, adjusting, settling in with another position, another thought until he found a good place that felt almost right.

Josie.

There it was. The thought of Josie was always good. She had saved him from insanity after Lexi died. They'd hit a little rough patch lately, but that would right itself. It always did between them. Sleep was coming. What was happening in the house was just a job. The other was just a memory. Josie was real. Josie was—

Archer didn't have the next second to finish his thought. The door of the rental was ripped open, almost off its hinges. Archer fell out first, the camera right after. Off balance already, he was defenseless against the huge hands that grappled and grasped at his shoulders and the ferocity of the man who threw him onto the asphalt.

"Jesus Christ . . ." Archer barked just before the breath was knocked out of him.

"Shut up, fuck face."

Archer grunted as the man dug his knee into his back and took hold of his hair.

Shit, he was getting old. The guy in the house not only made him, he got the drop on him. That was damn humiliating. Don Juan was a suit. One-seventy tops. He should be able to flick this little shit off with a deep breath.

Hands flat on the ground, Archer tried to do just that, but, as he pushed himself off the pavement, he had another surprise. It wasn't Don Juan at all. The man on Archer's back was big, he was heavy and he wasn't alone. There were two of them.

While the first ground Archer's face into the black-top, the second found a home for the toe of his boot in his midsection. Archer bellowed. He curled. He tried to roll but that opened him up. This time the kick clipped the side of his face, catching the corner of his eye. The blow sent him into the arms of the first man who embraced him with one arm around his shoulders, the other at his throat. Archer's eyes rolled back in his head.

Jesus, that hurt.

His eyelids fluttered. One still worked right. He looked up and stopped struggling. The guy who had him in a headlock knew what he was doing. If Archer moved another inch, and the man adjusted his grip just so, Archer's neck would snap. As it was he was doing a fine job making sure Archer was finding it damn hard to breathe.

His eyes rolled again as pain shot straight through his temple and embedded itself behind his ear. Archer tried to focus, needing to see at least one of them if he was going to ID them when—if—he got out of this mess. They could have the car. No car was worth dying for—especially a rental. But he couldn't tell them to take it if he couldn't speak, and he couldn't identify them if he could barely see. There were just the vaguest impressions of blue eyes, a clean-shaven face, a checked shirt. Archer's thoughts undulated with each new wave of pain. Connections were made then broken and made again like a faulty wire. The one that stuck made sense: These guys didn't want his car but they sure as hell wanted something. Just as the choke-hold king tightened his grip, and his friend took another swipe at Archer's ribs, one of them offered a clue.

"You asshole. Thought you got away with it, didn't you?"

That was not a helpful hint.

Roger McEntyre took the call at ten thirty-five without benefit of a secretary. Didn't need one; didn't want one. He kept important information in his head. If he shared that information, it was because he wanted to. If Roger wasn't in his office, couldn't be raised on his cell, had not told his colleagues where to contact him, then he didn't want to be found. That was how a company guy did business. He worked under the radar; he delivered what the company needed and was rewarded with the knowledge that the company appreciated it. Because Roger was so good at what he did everyone had tried to hire him away: Disneyland, Magic Mountain, Knott's Berry Farm. He was never tempted. A company man was loyal, and Roger McEntyre was loyal to Pacific Park, the oldest amusement park in California. Most of all Roger was loyal to the man who had given his father a job when no one else would; faithful to the man who treated him like a son when his own father passed away.

Now Roger was about to deliver a piece of good news the company, and the man who ran it, needed badly. That made him proud, though it was difficult to tell because Roger's smile was hidden behind the fringe of a walrus mustache. That was a pity, since he actually had a pleasant, almost boyish grin when he thought to use it.

Leaving his small, spare space off a long corridor, Roger McEntyre passed two others where his colleagues worked. One was ex-FBI, the other a product of New York's finest. Roger was Special Forces. Honorable discharge. Fine training.

He walked through the reception area of building three and gave the girl at the desk an almost imperceptible nod as he passed. He walked with purpose and didn't mess where he wasn't supposed to. If he had been another kind of man that little girl would have been in trouble.

Roger pushed through the smoked-glass doors and put his sunglasses on before the first ray of light had a chance to make him wince. Thanks to the year-round school schedules the park was busy even on a mid-October morning.

Roger dodged a couple of teenagers who weren't looking where they were going, stopped long enough to oblige a woman who asked him to take a picture of her family and noted that the paint was peeling on the door of the men's bathroom near the park entrance.

Roger took a sharp right, ducked under a velvet rope and walked through a real door hidden in a fake rock. The air-conditioning hit him with the annoyingly prickly cold Isaac preferred. He walked down a small hallway, through another glass door, across another reception area and into the executive suite. The woman behind this desk was of a different caliber. Slick. Stylish. Sexy.

"Mary."

"Is he going to be happy to see you?" she asked as Roger passed.

"Yes," he answered without stopping.

Roger opened one of the double doors just far enough to slip through, then stood inside the office, arms at his side, posture perfect as always. Isaac's office was nice. Very adult. Very sophisticated considering the kind of business they were in. The silver-haired man behind the mahogany desk was on the phone. That call wasn't as important as Roger. The receiver went to the cradle but Isaac Hawkins held on to it as if he were bracing for bad news.

"They got him. It's out of our hands."

Isaac's shoulders slumped ever so slightly in his relief. Roger moved closer to the desk just in case he was needed. Isaac looked ten years younger than he was, but even that would have been old.

"The district attorney made the decision," Roger reminded him as the old man got up. "We just gave them what we had."

Isaac Hawkins walked up to Roger. He took him by the shoulders, looked into his face and then drew him forward into a hug of gratitude and relief.

"Your father would have been proud. I'm proud. Thank you, Roger."

"Don't worry, Isaac," Roger muttered, happy the old man couldn't see how much this moment meant to him.

"I'm glad we did the right thing. Let me know how it goes from here. You'll do that, won't you?" Isaac held Roger back, searching his countenance for reassurance.

"I will," Roger assured him before turning away, satisfied he had done his work well.

Of the five attorneys, five secretaries, two paralegals, receptionist, mailroom boy, suite of offices in Brentwood and shark tank, Jude Getts was proudest of the shark tank. True, it was a cliché, but in his case the cliché worked. Getts & Associates was not the largest law firm but it was the leanest, most voracious plaintiff's outfit in Los Angeles. Lose a leg? A lung? A life? Jude's associates put a price tag on everything and collected with amazing alacrity. They didn't so much negotiate with defendants as hold them hostage until they coughed up the big bucks; they didn't try a case as much as flay it, peeling back the skin of it slowly, painfully, exquisitely. And, of all the attorneys in the firm, Jude Getts was the best.

Bright eyed, boyish, his blond hair waving back from a wide, clear brow, Jude was tall but not too tall, dramatic without being theatrical, a master of the touch, the look, the smile. He had exquisite timing, whether it was offered during closing arguments or a rare intimate moment with a woman chosen for the length of her legs or the look of her face. But what made Jude a really, really good plaintiff's attorney was that he loved a challenge more than anything else. He rejoiced in it. A challenge made his heart flutter, made him smile wider, laugh heartier and made his work even more impeccable. What he was hearing on the radio as he drove to meet his client was making that heart of his feel like an aviary just before an earthquake.

Jude passed the keys to his car to the valet and cheerfully advised him to "keep it close" before he bounded into the foyer of the Napa Valley Grill, past the hostess who was gorgeous but rated only his most radiant, thoughtless, everyday smile. Even though it was early, he gave his drink order to his favorite waiter with a touch to the man's arm and a tip of his head that indicated Jude really didn't think of him as a waiter at all but as a friend. The drink arrived at the table just as Jude was sliding onto the chair.

"Colin," Jude greeted his client as he laid the heavy white napkin on his lap.

"Jude." The other man nodded. He already had a drink. It was almost gone.

"They make a good drink here, Colin. Damn good drink, don't you think?"

"I've had two."

Colin Wren was not a man who really enjoyed life. Forcing him to smell the roses gave Jude a kick. But while he was laughing on the inside, the outside was always respectful. Colin was, after all, the client, and five months ago he brought a problem to Jude that promised a hell of a payday. Now everything had changed.

"I'm sorry I kept you waiting, but something's happened that will change the course of our business, Colin."

"I don't want anything to change, Jude. I've waited too long."

Colin pushed aside his drink, put down the glass and looked Jude in the eye. Colin's were soft brown and gentle-looking behind the wire-rimmed frames of his glasses. They were the eyes of a priest, but Colin Wren was not a priest, nor was he particularly kindly or likable, although Jude could not, in all good conscience, say that the man was unlikable or inconsiderate. Colin Wren was simply a man with an agenda.

"Well, Colin, I'm not sure we have a choice. Pacific Park has made a brilliant move. They handed the problem off to the district attorney. This is a criminal matter now, and, until the DA does what he's going to do, we don't have a snowball's chance in hell of collecting on a civil action." Jude picked up his glass again. "How's that for a surprise?"

1

"Ms. Bates, I'm going to have to be brutally honest with you. Some parents are concerned about Hannah enrolling at Mira Costa High School. Ms. Bates?"

Startled, Josie shifted in her seat. She'd been watching Hannah dutifully fill out registration forms. The girl was already behind, starting school more than a month late. There was so much against her, not the least of which were the problems in her gorgeous head, that Josie couldn't have felt more anxious if she were Hannah's mother. Josie forced herself to look away, giving her attention to the principal, Mrs. Crawford.

"I don't know why they would be concerned. Hannah didn't kill Justice Rayburn," Josie said.

"But they remember the trial. There was a great deal of publicity."

"And there was even more when Hannah's mother was actually convicted of the crime," Josie reminded her. "Her mother is in jail and all ties to her have been severed. If anyone is unaware of that, I'll be more than happy to fill them in."

"Facts seldom have anything to do with emotional perception," Mrs. Crawford said, smiling regretfully. "I know you're aware there will be gossip and innuendo, curiosity on the part of the students and their parents regarding Hannah. What may surprise you are the consequences of all that. You don't have children, do you?"

Josie shook her head. "I'm not married."

Mrs. Crawford knew that for people with children the world was a lunar landscape of deep valleys and insurmountable mountain rises. Even those born to be parents had a tough time navigating the terrain. She gave Josie Baylor-Bates a fifty-fifty chance of surviving unscathed.

"Look, I just want to be straight with you. Parents won't want Hannah at their houses 'just in case' she's a bad influence. Other students may try to take her on to see how tough she is. They'll want to see how far they can push her. . . ." Mrs. Crawford hesitated. "They may want to see if she really doesn't feel pain the way the papers reported."

"Since you are aware of what might happen, I know you'll take every precaution to see that Hannah is safe." Josie's lawyer voice covered the unease she felt at being a surrogate parent for this troubled girl who, only months ago, was her client.

"Unfortunately, I can't promise that." Mrs. Crawford sat back. "We have a lot of kids who have problems with their peers. They're targeted because of their sexual orientation, their IQ or just the way they look. We do the best we can, but Hannah is a little different. She's been to jail; she pled guilty to a murder."

"I'm assuming this is leading somewhere, so why don't we get to the bottom line," Josie suggested, trying not to worry that the morning was almost gone and she had work to do.

Mrs. Crawford took a minute to gaze through the window, too. She lifted her chin toward Hannah.

"Off the record, I think Hannah is a beautiful,

smart, well-spoken, selfless young woman. My kids wouldn't have gone to jail for me, that's for sure." She held up her hands as if helpless when she looked back at Josie. "But this is a big school, Ms. Bates, and we draw from two different districts. Hannah might do better in a smaller venue like Chadwick."

"No, Chadwick isn't an option. Hannah's had enough of really rich people." Josie left no room for discussion. Josie had enough of them herself.

"Okay, then." Mrs. Crawford nodded. "I just wanted to make sure we were on the same page. Funding cuts have left us with only one psychologist on this campus. If Hannah needs help, she'll have to understand she isn't the only one who does."

"No problem. Hannah's trial isn't going to be the talk forever. She'll deal with things, and if she can't, we'll know sooner than later."

"I hope so."

"Take my word for it, we will," Josie answered, knowing that one look at Hannah's arms would tell them if the girl was heading for the deep end. She shivered, thinking of the road map of scars on Hannah's arms. It was one thing for a child to be tortured by an adult, another to know a child's pain was so great she would shred herself to ribbons to be rid of it.

"I guess we're clear then." Mrs. Crawford put on her glasses, sat up and pulled a file toward her. "You're Hannah's legal guardian?"

"I am. Her mother signed the papers last week."

"And will Hannah need a parking permit?"

Josie shook her head. "Not yet. I'll drop her off and pick her up until she's settled."

"I see that Hannah will have to miss sixth period every Tuesday?" The principal's eyes flickered up.

"She has an appointment with her psychiatrist. I

figured since that was the PE period it would be better than missing math," Josie answered.

"I imagine she'll be making up her exercise, since you live in Hermosa Beach. Does she run?"

Josie laughed. "No. Hannah's artistic, not athletic. I don't think I'll get her running anytime soon."

"Too bad. I'd give anything to live down there. Are you a runner?" Mrs. Crawford made small talk as she filled in forms and offered them to Josie for a signature.

"That and volleyball." Josie scribbled her name and passed the papers back and Mrs. Crawford stacked them.

"Well, then, I think that does it. And don't worry. We have a fine art department. Hannah will enjoy it."

"Thanks." Josie checked her watch. A bell rang. A couple of thousand kids changed classes and made a thunderous sound. It was time for her to go, too. "So, do you need anything else?"

"Nope." Mrs. Crawford stood up. "I'll take Hannah around to the classrooms during lunch. I've arranged for one of our students to help her out for the next few days."

"I appreciate that."

Josie took the principal's hand and shook it. She hitched her purse and glanced at Hannah. Finished with her own paperwork, Hannah was looking right back at Josie with those clear spring-green eyes of hers. She was even more beautiful than the first day Josie saw her. The nose ring was gone. The tongue stud was gone. Her hair had grown back where the hospital had shaved it after her accident. Today she had wrapped a sky-blue scarf across her brow, her long black hair fell in curls past her shoulders, her dark skin gleamed and Hannah's fingers were busy touching the arm of her chair.

Josie counted along. *One . . . five . . . ten . . . twenty times.* The doctors called Hannah's behavior obsessive-compulsive. Josie had another name for it: heartbreaking. It would end. It was already better. Hannah didn't cut herself anymore, and that was a big step in the right direction. All Josie needed to do was hang in there. She dug in her purse, turned around again and handed the principal a piece of paper.

"Look, I know this is a lot to ask, but Hannah's terrified of being left alone or forgotten. If there's ever a problem . . . well, that's a list of friends—family really. If I ever get hung up and can't get to a phone to call, I'd appreciate your contacting anyone on that list. One of them will come get her."

Mrs. Crawford looked at the list before sliding it under the picture of her own family. It wouldn't be forgotten.

"That's something I can personally promise. So . . ." She put her hands together. "I guess we'd both better get to work."

Hannah didn't look back as she walked down the now-quiet halls with Mrs. Crawford, but Josie couldn't take her eyes off the girl. She wanted to go with Hannah just to make sure she was okay. That was something a mother would do—just not something Hannah's or Josie's mothers had ever done. But Josie wasn't a mother. She had taken Hannah in because there was no one else who wanted her. That decision had changed Josie's life, and she wasn't quite sure it was for the better. Archer would say it was for the worse, and Josie thought about that as she walked across the campus, crossed the street and tossed her purse and jacket in the back of her Jeep Wrangler. She swung herself into the seat, Archer and his pig-headed attitude still on her mind. Her cell phone rang. She picked it up, checked the time and didn't recognize the number of the caller.

Too early for the court clerk to be calling to find out where she was on that settlement hearing; the new client didn't have her cell number, and she was free-lancing for Faye, so no one expected her at the office. Whoever it was could wait. Josie rolled up her shirt-sleeves and reached in back for her baseball cap, but the ringing of the phone was getting on her nerves.

"Oh, hell," she muttered, and grabbed for it. "Bates."

Less than a minute later Josie was peeling down the street, laying rubber as she headed to the freeway that would take her downtown to Parker Center and the detention cell where Archer was being held on suspicion of murder.

2

Josie was twenty-seven when the call had come that her father was ill. Strike that. He had a heart attack, and that was different from being ill, but Josie wasn't going to split hairs. She had taken off in the middle of a trial despite the threat of sanctions. It almost ruined her career.

Josie left Los Angeles on the two A.M. flight to Hawaii. For five hours she had looked out the window. She didn't read or eat or sleep. Above all, Josie Baylor-Bates did not speculate. Her marine father had taught her better than that. At her destination she would kick into high gear, gather information, assess the situation, speak to the experts and make decisions to ensure her father's survival. Tears, fears, hopes and prayers would be kept behind the lines until then, but when she had arrived too late, Josie broke down. Her father wouldn't have minded. It was forgivable when a good soldier passed, when the battle had been lost. Even though all that was a long time ago, she was in marine mode again as she parked in the lot next to the fortress that was Parker Center, headquarters of the LAPD.

No stranger to the place, Josie pushed through the doors, handed over her purse to be inspected, stated her business and waited for the officer who had given her a heads-up about Archer. She didn't wait long.

"Josie Bates?"

"Yep."

She turned around as she spoke and found herself face-to-face with a cop who had a hundred pounds on her but stood two inches shorter than her six feet.

"Newell." He shook her hand and didn't bother with small talk. "I saw them bring Archer in. Didn't get a chance to talk to him, but I know you two worked on the Rayburn thing together. Figured I'd give you a call."

"Why didn't he call himself?" Josie kept her voice low as Newell steered her toward a corner of the lobby.

"Can't say. We didn't pop him." The officer shrugged slowly, as if it were tough for his muscles to work under all that skin. "We would have shown him more respect. DA investigators made the arrest and brought him here for booking."

"DA investigators? What's going on here?" Josie muttered before asking, "Did they refuse him a call?"

"Don't know that either. What went down is off the scope, but I recognized Archer right away. We were in the academy together a hundred years ago. You don't forget a guy like Archer."

"The district attorney's investigators?" Josie prodded. They'd have old-home week later.

"Oh, yeah, those idiots," Newell scoffed. "I don't know what went down. John Cooper is one DA who plays things close to the vest. If he didn't let us in on this then he's looking for the glory—or something else."

"Like what else?" Josie pushed for information, but he took her arm and pulled her farther aside as two officers lingered in the lobby.

"Payback? Maybe one of his private gigs went sour

and compromised the DA on something big. Whatever it is they probably wanted to clean him up some before they get to it. Either Archer put up a hell of a fight or these guys have it in for him, if you know what I'm saying."

Josie nodded. She knew exactly what he was talking about, and she could hardly believe it. Archer never even had a parking ticket as far as she knew, so what would make him deserving of this kind of arrest? Newell put his hand on her arm for a second. She had swayed and didn't realize it until he held her steady. Her father would have narrowed his eyes just enough to let her know it wasn't time to get girlie.

"Thanks for the call. I'll take it from here," Josie assured him.

"No problem. I'd sure appreciate someone stepping in if it was me."

"I'll keep it to myself," Josie assured him.

"No skin off my nose. I retire in three months."

"Still, you went out on a limb," she said, acknowledging the over-and-above effort.

"Yeah, well, Archer did good turns for some of us along the way. This will square things." The officer paced off a few steps but Josie matched him. She had one more question.

"Newell, who's the alleged victim?"

"Like I said, close to the vest." His shoulders swiveled. He was anxious to be away. "So, you want to see him?"

"Damn straight I do," she muttered, and followed him down the hall. Newell pointed to an interrogation room and took off. The man standing outside the door looked less than friendly; she could only guess who was inside with Archer.

"You've got my client in there," Josie announced as she approached, but the man seemed unimpressed until she went for the door.

"We're not done," he said quietly, his hand clamping over hers when she touched the knob.

"Yes, you are." Josie took her hand from under his and pulled up to her full height. Their eyes were locked. His were unmemorable. "And I don't care if the pope sent you. You're history until I talk to my client."

"He didn't call an attorney." The man wasn't going to back down.

"I don't know what they teach you at the DA's office, but you were supposed to ask him if he wanted one before you questioned him. It's kind of basic. Keeps your cases from being thrown out of court on a technicality."

"And I don't know what law school let you slip through the cracks, but you should know better than to assume. We offered. He declined," the man drawled.

Shaken, Josie stepped back and glanced through the square of glass in the door. Newell had been right. You didn't have to be on top of Archer to see that this had not been an easy arrest. Josie looked back at the investigator.

"I don't think my client had the wherewithal to understand that right, considering the shape he's in. Now, unless your boss wants some very pointed, very public questions about how the district attorney's investigative unit does its job, I would suggest you let me in that room now and get your buddy out."

They shared an unpleasant moment. When it ended Josie got her way. The man gave his partner his walking orders, knocking with one knuckle before opening the door. Slimmer but no less arrogant, his partner gave Josie the once-over as his friend announced, "Attorney" with the kind of effort it took to hurl.

The two men left, sliding along the testosterone-slicked hall until they were swallowed up by the bowels of Parker Center. Josie watched them go, her jaw tight, her eyes narrowed. Those two would melt into the bureaucratic soup, only to be fished out later and spoon-fed to a jury hungry for the particulars of this day. Those men would remember everything; Archer would remember next to nothing. Josie had to make sure it never came to that.

When they were gone Josie put one hand on the knob, the other flat against the door. She needed a second before she faced Archer. At that instant Josie was not lover or friend, not a woman who would follow Archer to the ends of the earth if he asked. Josie was a lawyer, and she cataloged what she saw. The blank room. The dark table. The four chairs. Archer sitting with his legs angled on either side of one. He had one arm on the table and his forehead cupped in his upturned hand. His shoulders were slumped so that his other arm dangled between his legs. He was hurt, possibly broken and probably afraid.

A tremor of fear spidered out from Josie's center, creeping into her arms, her legs, up through her neck until her jaw was locked, but her knees and hands shook uncontrollably, almost imperceptibly. Two shallow breaths through her nose and the vise around her lungs weakened. Another deep one filled them and she was ready. She pushed open the door, went inside, shut the door and stood against it.

Archer didn't move. He didn't look up when he said: "I don't want you here, Jo."

3

"So, I don't sleep over for a couple of nights and you go get yourself in trouble. There are better ways to let me know you miss me, Archer."

Josie moved slowly, getting a feel for the lay of this new land. They should have been home, sitting on the rooftop balcony of his place watching the afternoon crowd at the beach. They should have been at her house knocking down that back fence, the one she wanted to replace with a cinder-block wall and cover with smooth stucco. They should have been at Burt's restaurant fighting about Hannah and the way the presence of a sixteen-year-old kid was changing their lives. They should have been in bed screwing their brains out, making up once the fight was over. They should have been doing anything but this. Not this.

Archer shifted in his chair, keeping his head lowered, his face turned away.

"Go home, Jo."

"I'd like to, Archer, but we were having a fine fight a few days ago and I can't finish it alone. So unless I walk out of here with you, I'm not going." She stood beside Archer, towering over him, unsure what to do.

"The hell you are." His head came up fast, his arm went down and every muscle in his face contorted with a pain that bent him half over the table.

"Christ, Archer," Josie exclaimed.

She reached for him. Touched him. She raised his

chin. Archer sliced his eyes left, winced and pulled away. Josie looked from his face to his massive chest and the hand that lay protectively against his side. His breathing was labored; it seemed to rub against his bone like a kayak scraping bottom. Josie guessed a cracked rib. She tried again to get Archer to look at her, but he was as ornery as a junkyard dog, and caution would be the order of the day if Josie was going to get past the gate.

Gently she shifted his head. Her other hand went to his shoulder. She hunkered down, balancing on the balls of her feet to look at the mess that was Archer's face. His left eye was swollen. There was a cut over his brow. Dots of asphalt tattooed his temple. His upper lip was distended and purple and his right cheekbone was scraped raw.

"Ribs hurt bad," he whispered.

"Sounds like," Josie whispered back as she laid her open palm gently against the side of his face. His head tipped into her hand and his breathing slowed.

Finally Josie pushed up, stepped back and opened her briefcase. She pulled out a disposable camera, ripped off the foil cover and pressed the button to charge the flash.

"Don't." Archer ordered her away with a wave of his hand and a single word.

"Sit up, Archer." She brushed at his hand.

"You won't need it. It was a mistake. I'll take care of it," he growled.

"You can't fix this with the right word to an old buddy," Josie muttered. "Nobody is arrested the way you were without a damn good reason or a bellyful of hate driving it. So turn your head up."

When he finally did as he was told Josie shot the first five frames close-up: Archer's eye, his lip, the red screaming streak of raw skin across his cheekbone. Jurors reacted well to close-ups. Close-ups turned their stomachs and made the defendant look all too human. There was nothing beautiful or forgiving in cheap photographs.

Josie pointed to his shirt. Reluctantly, slowly, Archer lifted it. Time enough had passed for a fine bruise to be spreading.

Snap.

Cold with fury, Josie shifted back and shot from a few feet. She took comfort in the rote steps called for in situations like this. Without them, Jo, the woman who loved and admired Archer, would fall apart.

Click.

She took another picture.

"What in the hell happened, Archer? They say they tagged you for murder. When have you had time to murder anyone?"

"Jo, I . . ." Archer tried to sit up straight but didn't make it far. Pain zigzagged through him and exploded behind his eyes. Josie pressed the button. There was a flash. It would be a stunning picture; a perfect exhibit. She was going to make the city pay big for this.

"Leave me alone," Archer mumbled.

Josie let the camera fall. Her patience was wearing thin.

"What is it with you, Archer? Why don't you want me to help?"

"Because there are things between us. Personal things. I don't want to screw with that. This is separate from us."

"Nothing is separate from us." Josie lowered her voice, almost to softness. "You need me. You have no leverage. You're already processed through. They've got a nice bed waiting for you at the men's prison. They don't do that unless they're sure they're going to keep you. Now, tell me what's going on, starting with who they say you took out."

Archer took two more of those short little breaths. Josie was bringing the camera back up toward her eye, only to drop it again when she heard: "A kid." He took a shallow, sharp breath. "They say I killed Lexi's kid."

4

Josie's father said that when a bullet tears into you and you go down there's a whole minute where all you do is think. You know you're hit, you know you're down but you think you can get up. You try. Your arms or legs might move and you're happy for a second. Then your hand comes to rest on your head or your chest or your gut and you realize blood is pouring out of you. If that's not bad enough you realize that your guts or your brains are coming out right along with all that blood. And all of this—surprise, pain, hope, honesty—takes a few seconds. Then you do one of two things: You scream as you die or you do what you can to save yourself. But those first seconds of waiting, absorbing, associating and assessing are critical to survival. So when Archer hit her with that piece of information, Josie took the thinking time before she stuffed her guts back into her belly and got on with things.

"Now do you see why I don't want your help?" Archer asked miserably. "It's about Lexi. I don't want you to—"

"I don't care what this is about," Josie lied easily.

"You will," Archer muttered.

Josie pulled out a chair. She felt wooden, uncoordinated, off her mark as she sat down. He was right. It made a difference that this was about Archer's dead wife. Josie just wasn't sure exactly why there was a skittering of dread running under her skin. Was Archer afraid she'd find out something she shouldn't about Lexi or about him? Whichever it was, there was no turning back now. There was no other champion in the wings.

"How old was he?" Josie asked, trying to control the surprise and dread in her voice.

"He'd just turned thirteen."

Archer's voice should have been comforting. Instead it was dark like the bottom of a well where ugly things grow under the deceptive depth of crystalline water.

"I've known you a year. I would have known if you had a teenage stepson," Josie said.

He shook his head. "No, you wouldn't. Tim died two years ago in an accident at Pacific Park."

"That big amusement park off the 405 freeway?"

Archer nodded, every movement and memory causing him pain. He moved as if he wanted to get up. Josie half rose to help him, but Archer found a better place on his own. Their eyes met. There was nothing for Josie to read in those eyes of his: not assurance, not guilt, not anything.

"Tim fell off one of those rides that take you way up and drop you to the ground really fast. It was ugly. God, it was horrible. Lexi was . . ." A dry heave of a sob gripped him, and Archer paused. He bent his head, swallowed the cry and went on. "Lexi was sick six or seven months already. She had maybe three weeks left. Pacific Park was her kid's favorite place and she wanted him to have a good day. So we went. Something happened. Tim fell and we had to ride all the way down to the ground looking at him with his head broken open. There was blood everywhere, people screaming, and we were strapped onto that fucking thing like bugs. How in the hell do they make that into murder?"

Archer dropped his head. He put the heels of his hands to his eyes. Josie expected something more. When he remained silent, she asked: "Did you know you were under investigation?"

"I don't know what anybody thinks they're doing," Archer roared back, shaking his head adamantly, the fight of a wounded lion still in him. "Tim's death was an accident. I don't even know what caused it. Maybe he caused the accident himself because he was such a mess. Tim was retarded. He had cerebral palsy. He had some heart problems. The whole thing was a nightmare. It happened two years ago, and only God and the DA know why it's so damned important now."

Archer's red-rimmed eyes flashed with anger and fear. Josie understood the first; she was shocked to see the other. If Archer was innocent, there was nothing to fear. But she looked again and readjusted her thinking. Hannah had been convicted of murder despite her innocence. Only an eleventh-hour moment of clarity on Josie's part had saved her. Josie would be smarter this time. She would turn over every rock until she found the truth.

Truth.

The word reverberated in her mind, and she brushed away the possibility that she may not want to know the truth. There was one thing, though, that she needed to know right now.

"Why didn't you ever tell me about—"

The door opened before Josie could finish her sentence. A uniformed officer was in the doorway.

"Ten minutes, Counselor."

Josie checked her watch. It was a little before two.

She waved the cop away. Realizing personal things weren't relevant in this room, she abandoned her interrupted question.

Josie put her palms flat on the table, as if that would keep her on the track she was about to lay. "Look, there isn't much time, so let's get practical. No judge is going to entertain a reduction of bail if we're talking about the death of a disabled child, so I won't request a hearing. We'll suck up the ten percent on the million-dollar bond. I've got fifty thousand. You put up the paper on the apartment building and that will give us more than we need to get you out of here."

"No. I'm not going to let you lose fifty grand because somebody's screwing with me." One of Archer's hands sliced through the air to cut her off. "No bail. Let me handle this."

"How? From a cell? Jesus, you're a cop," Josie wailed.

"I'm a retired cop," Archer shot back.

"Like anybody's going to check your pension and cut you some slack once you're behind bars? Like being retired is going to make a difference where they put the shank in you? You know the two things cons hate most in the world are a cop and a guy who messes with kids. You struck out, Archer, so take my money and worry about how it's going to make you feel later."

"I'll put up the apartment building, but I won't take your money," Archer insisted. "That building's worth a bundle. It will cover the bond."

"A bondsman isn't going to just take paper. He'll want cash. I'll get—"

The door opened again. This time the uniformed officer was young and fresh faced. He sported the kind of pretty that came from razor haircuts and pressed pants, a gun that had never been fired and hands that hadn't quite dirtied themselves in the LA grit. Josie turned on him, flinging up a little grit of her own just to give him a taste of it.

"Can't you tell time? We've still got five minutes and we're taking it whether or not the bus leaves—"

"Yeah, well, the bus is going to leave without him anyway." The officer's eyes rested lazily on Josie before sliding Archer's way. "Your belongings are at the window. Pick them up on your way out."

Stunned, Josie and Archer looked at him. It was Josie who stood up first.

"I'm glad someone came to their senses." She gathered her things, talking large to hide her bewilderment. "They just came to them a little late. I'm going to make sure there's a full investigation on my client's behalf. This man should never have been arrested, much less charged. Whoever decided to drop those charges is the only intelligent person in this entire building."

She reached for Archer and helped him up. Josie hitched her bag and took the first step to the door. She never managed the second step.

"Nobody's dropped the charges, but somebody put up the bond," the young cop said. "Now get his butt out of here."

The door hadn't even closed before Josie turned to Archer. He was pale and shaking. His lips moved once, twice; then finally he answered the question she didn't need to ask.

"I don't know, Jo. I really don't."

"Okay, then," she said, and tightened her grip on his arm. "We'll just wait for your guardian angel to come to you. Right now, let's do what the man says and get your butt out of here."

Josie steadied Archer at the elbow as they made their way through the building. His ribs weren't broken; his breathing was steadying. She would have Archer checked out, get him home, then head to her place and start to work. She wanted to talk to John Cooper, the DA. Josie wanted some answers, not the least of which was who had come up with a hundred grand to secure Archer's bond?

Outside, Archer put on his sunglasses and turned his face to the sun. Josie stood beside him, smelling downtown, listening to the traffic, feeling the proximity of neighboring buildings and the oppressive bunkerlike structure of the LAPD headquarters behind them. Josie turned to take Archer's hand, but, as she did so, she caught sight of two men in her peripheral vision. She turned her head and instinctively moved protectively toward Archer.

They went around the concrete barricades quickly, these two men. The older one walked with his arms by his sides, his bespectacled eyes trained on Archer. The other had a lighter step, his arms swinging freely. His eyes were on Josie as he crossed the wide plaza with the grace of an athlete warming up for the big game.

"Josie Baylor-Bates." The younger man greeted her heartily, as if they were old friends. He held out his hand. She glanced at it but gave him only a look that said *make it good*. "Jude Getts, Getts and Associates. This is my client. He put up the bond for Archer, here. Ms. Bates, Mr. Archer, this is Colin Wr—"

If Colin had a last name it was lost in the roar that came from Archer. He lunged at the man in a fury that could only be described as murderous.

5

"That asshole was Tim's father. I don't want to be on the same planet with that fucker, much less sit across a table from him."

Josie shot a glance at the two men waiting for them. They were calm. Archer was not. They were focused; Archer was not. Josie was trying to get him there. She had managed to peel Archer off Colin Wren and convince him that, at the very least, they needed to listen to what these men had to say. It wasn't an easy task. Archer pointed out that a hundred thousand dollars bond didn't come with strings; it came with a choke chain. Josie countered, arguing that whatever Colin Wren pulled couldn't be worse than the chains that would have tied Archer down to a seat on the bus to the Men's Central Jail. Now Josie leaned against the wall and got close to Archer. On any regular day she couldn't get within ten feet of him without thinking how nice it would be to crawl between the sheets. Funny how fast things could get irregular, how quickly the seeds of caution and doubt took root.

"No, Archer, you will sit there and you will listen," Josie said firmly. "If you don't like what he has to say, fine, but I'm the one who says when we're gone."

"That's not the way I see it." Archer dropped his head back against the wall. His good eyelid drooped; the other had never really opened. He was exhausted

but not tired enough to give up. Sympathy was a lux-
ury, so Josie didn't indulge.

"Then look again, babe," she said dryly. "You
aren't going to block a road I may have to walk down
just because you're ticked off at that man. Okay?"

"That bastard can't have anything good in mind,"
Archer muttered. "He left Lexi right after they figured
out Tim would never be normal. I'm telling you he's
scum, Jo."

Josie shifted and looked past Archer toward the restaurant and their newfound friends. Little Tokyo had
been convenient; the New Otani Hotel had seemed neu-
tral ground on which to meet. Josie had never favored
the place when she worked downtown, but Jude Getts
seemed right at home. The man was slick, his suit was
expensive, every tooth was capped. He reeked of money,
as did his client. But Colin Wren's money wasn't flashy.
His money weighed him down, heavy in pockets that
opened only when there was a return to be had. A
hundred thousand dollars got Archer out of jail and
Colin Wren closer to whatever it was he wanted. Jude
Getts's money was lighter than air. Josie was sure it flew
out of his pockets as easily as it drifted in. She didn't
like the extremes of their benefactors, yet, practically
speaking, there was no choice but to indulge them.

"Okay. Colin Wren is scum. Fill me in before I get
their take on the situation." Her hand found its way
to her long fringe of bangs, longer than the hair at
the back of her neck. She pulled her fingers through
it and let it ruffle back over her brow as if that would
clear her mind. Archer was silent. He was staring at
the wall. "Archer?"

"I can't. I don't know him. All I know is that he
left Lexi alone with that kid. She worked her butt off,

scraped by to get Tim everything he needed." Archer's fist hit the wall behind him. "What kind of man does that? What kind of man leaves a wonderful woman like Lexi alone with a defective kid?"

"I don't know, but maybe we should give him the benefit of the doubt," Josie suggested. "Don't forget that somebody thinks you killed that defective kid. What kind of man would that make you?"

"I didn't kill Tim, but that bastard did take a hike. There's a difference," Archer objected.

"Perception is a crazy thing, Archer," Josie warned. "Let's not speculate. Let's have him spell out what he wants. To get him to do that I want you to sit with the man, try to keep your mouth shut and listen. That's all I want you to do."

Archer pushed away from the wall. He didn't bother to look at Josie as he tried to stand straight, only to encounter a little problem when the pain in his ribs reminded him the morning hadn't started out so well.

"He's got ten minutes to convince me I shouldn't take his head off," Archer growled.

"Fine. Ten minutes," Josie agreed. Ten minutes wouldn't get them far, but she'd take it. Archer was still in shock. His body was racked with pain. He was running on empty. She cut him some slack and touched his elbow lightly, a sign for him to move to her step. He didn't object, and Josie didn't waste any time after they sat down at the table.

"Okay, we're all ears." Josie looked from Jude Getts to Colin Wren.

"Archer, I ordered something for you. I know how you must feel. . . ." Jude offered a sympathetic grin.

"They don't have a drink for what I feel," Archer said.

"Can we just get to it, Jude?" Colin prompted softly, ignoring Archer's animosity.

"All right. We'll start with the bottom line." Jude let the grin go as easily as a balloon on a windy day. "I'm representing Mr. Wren in a civil action against Pacific Park in the wrongful death of his son, Timothy. I believe your arrest will cause the civil suit to be put on hold for obvious reasons, and we can't have that."

Jude sat back and opened his hands, offering the floor to anyone who wanted to dance.

"That's rich," Archer muttered as he let his head swing back and forth.

Josie could just imagine what he looked like full-face with his puffed-up lip making it difficult to talk, his purple eye half-closed from the bruising, his short nose and close-set eyes almost lost in the swelling. He looked bad enough in profile, like a luckless Irish boxer beaten to a pulp. Jude Getts didn't mind, but Colin Wren seemed absolutely rigid with fear, or loathing, or perhaps both. They waited for Archer to speak his piece.

"First off, last I heard you could only sue for loss of love and affection in a civil action. You could throw in loss of prospective wages but Tim could never work because he had the mind of a five-year-old." Archer tapped his head and glared at Jude before swinging toward Colin. "And, for the record, I didn't see a whole lot of love and affection coming from you when Tim was alive, so how in the hell do you think you're going to collect for losing it?"

Archer slumped in his chair as if they weren't worth the effort of civility.

"Second off, there's a statute of limitations on filing

a civil suit. It's been two years since Tim died. So it doesn't look like it matters one way or the other what happens to me because you're already screwed."

"*Almost* two years to the day," Jude pointed out. "But that's not a consideration. We're clear on the statute because we filed early enough. And the reason Mr. Wren didn't think to come to me sooner for help is because he was unaware that his son had died."

"Oh, for God's sake," Archer barked in disbelief. "Lexi wrote you even though she was sick as a dog herself. She wrote to you when she got sick and when Tim died, you bastard, and you never answered."

Half out of his chair, Archer planted his hands on the table as if he had to hold himself down. His voice was curdled by the disgust he felt for this man. But Colin Wren had his own take on the facts.

"I never got a letter." Colin's gentle priest eyes held steady with Archer's angry ones. And, like a man who understood divine right, Colin Wren leaned forward ever so slightly and told the only truth that counted— his. "I didn't know that Tim had died until the press linked his death with the boy who died a few months ago. Tim was called 'the other fatality.' Two deaths in two years at Pacific Park. That's what they said. I don't think you can imagine the shock of finding out your son—your only child—was not only gone, but killed in such a gruesome manner."

"I'm sure your heart bled," Archer drawled. "You couldn't find two seconds or two cents for your kid while he was alive, and now you're going to line your pockets with a nice fat settlement because he's dead. That is so damn rich."

"I don't have to listen to this. I've made a terrible mistake trying to help you." Colin pushed back his chair. Jude's hand went to his arm. Colin shook it off as he protested. "I told you. My ex-wife would not let me see my son."

"An interesting position, Mr. Wren," Josie said quietly. The men looked her way. "Blame a dead woman for keeping you from your son. It's the perfect argument, a creative way to maneuver around the problem that the loss of love and affection would pose for an absentee father. Was that your idea, Mr. Getts?"

"As a matter of fact it was. I find the truth is often quite effective in a courtroom. And the truth is—"

"I don't want to hear it," Archer cut him off. "Jo, you said we could walk if they pulled anything. I think this qualifies. It's disgusting."

"Don't be stupid." Jude put a hand out, almost standing, his chair pushing back as he tried to stop Archer and make him listen. "I've got information that will help you, and believe me, you're going to need it. I've already been around the block with Pacific Park. They're not going to make it easy for you. We can help each other if we deal with the here and now and figure the past out later. Lexi wouldn't want you to take a chance with your life."

Jude locked eyes with Archer, moving his gaze only when he saw the other man's body sag. He looked at Josie, the lawyer, the one who would get it, and saw that he had won. Distasteful as Colin Wren was, swooping in to feast on his son's carcass, Josie and Archer needed to listen. Jude adjusted his suit jacket and reclaimed his seat. Archer sat, too.

"We filed five months ago in superior court and we're still waiting for substantial discovery documents. Pacific Park has blocked me at every turn. Judge Bellows cited the park for willful indifference, and they were sanctioned by the court. That makes me think they have something big to hide that would make it easy for us to get a settlement. The sanctions didn't work. They dug in their heels. Then I heard about your arrest"—he nodded at Archer—"and it all made sense. Somehow Pacific Park has convinced the DA that there was a possibility that Tim was killed. Archer's conviction would exonerate Pacific Park. They would have no liability, ergo no payday for my client . . ."

"I told you not to talk like that." Colin's curt directive was barely audible, but Jude corrected himself smoothly.

". . . there will be no *justice* for my client from Pacific Park. Not that Archer's conviction would leave us without options. If he is responsible for Tim's death we can file a civil suit against him, but the settlement wouldn't make up for Colin's loss of both Tim and the bond money."

Jude smiled apologetically, as if sorry to have to point out Archer's financial limitations. Archer stayed silent. He had heard a lot in his day as a cop. He had mastered the poker face but he was out of practice. Disgust was written all over his face.

"You must be expecting a hell of a settlement if you're willing to risk a hundred grand on me." Exhaustion got the best of Archer. His hand was on his side; his eyes went to Jude. "You're telling me that Pacific Park wants to see me convicted in order to protect their reputation and their bottom line, Mr. Wren here wants a big settlement and I'm just a bump in the road that you're going to smooth over one way or another. Both of you are telling me that Lexi, the finest woman I've ever known, willfully kept you from your son. You'd like me to believe that you would have bent over backward to be a good father to that boy if only Lexi had let you?"

Archer shook his head in disbelief.

"God, you are both so sick. I quit the force so I wouldn't have to listen to crap like this anymore and now here it is, on my own back step. This all stinks so bad I can barely breathe."

Archer pushed his chair back. He started to stand, swallowed some pain and hung his head. Before he walked, Colin Wren addressed him.

"Perhaps the bond was a mistake. Perhaps I should have considered that you might be responsible for my son's death. Tim died on your watch, sir, or have you forgotten?"

Those words slid across the table and spilled into Archer's lap. Archer had been dealt better, so he left it all behind as he got up and walked out the door. Josie started to follow but Jude held his card out to her.

"Josie, you know John Cooper must have something solid. He wouldn't make a fool of himself this close to an election. Come see me. I've got some documentation that will help you get a head start if they go to a preliminary hearing instead of the grand jury, and Archer might know something that will help us. We should work together. It's a win-win, Josie."

"Then you think he's innocent?" she asked, wanting an ally so badly she could taste it.

Jude walked a few steps with her so that Colin Wren was out of earshot. He took her arm high up. Very familiar. Very tight. There was no doubt that Jude Getts meant her to listen until he was finished. His voice changed. The brightness was gone, replaced with an even, arrogant tone.

"I don't care if he pushed the kid off that ride. I just want to get on with my business. To do that, I need you to do your business fast and right. It's as simple as that."

Jude's fingers tightened, squeezing Josie's arm as if acknowledging they had reached some agreement that brought them closer, made them somehow intimate. That wasn't how Josie saw it. She shook him off and smiled ruefully. She had been a lawyer like Jude. Thank God she'd come to her senses and turned her back on that kind of practice. Luckily, she hadn't lost her senses completely. Josie took the card.

"I'll follow you. I can pick up whatever you have now."

"Nice as that sounds, I have a dinner engagement." A lazy grin spread across Jude's face. He had her where he wanted her. Jude looked at his watch, saw that it was time to play and turned a megawatt smile her way. "We'll have to make it in the morning, since the day is almost gone."

"Almost gone?" Josie breathed. "Oh, my God. Hannah!"

6

Josie didn't bother with the garage. The tires of her Jeep Wrangler squealed as she turned into the driveway, threw it into park and jogged around the corner praying that Hannah was safely inside the house. Part of her was frantic with worry because she hadn't been able to reach the girl; the other part was angry that Hannah had forgotten to turn her cell phone back on after school, and all of Josie was awash with shame that this day—of all days—she had forgotten Hannah.

Josie's step slowed, her fear abating when she saw Billy Zuni sitting on the low wall that surrounded her side patio. One of his long legs hung over the side; the other was bent so that he could lean his chin on his knee. His blond hair fell across his perpetually tan brow, and Max-the-Dog sat on the patio, head cocking with each snap of Billy's fingers. Max sensed Josie before Billy did, but as soon as the old dog struggled up and put his front paws on the low wall, Billy looked Josie's way, too.

His grin was as bright as seashells polished by the sand, his eyes sparkled with leftover specks of the midsummer sun and Josie wondered how his mother could care more about her booze and boyfriends than she did about this kid of the beach. Not that Billy didn't have folks to look after him: Josie looked after him when he ran afoul of the local law; Archer liked him despite the façade that he only tolerated the boy. The ocean loved Billy and he loved the ocean back.

"Hey." Billy slid off the wall, leaned his hip against it and ruffled Max's ears, waiting for Josie to come to him.

"Hey, Billy." Josie lifted her chin. "Is she in there?"

He nodded, his skinny shoulders shifting as his free hand combed through his long hair.

"Yeah. Hannah was really ticked off when she got home, Ms. B."

"I don't doubt it." Josie stopped and mirrored Billy. Her hip went against the wall; her hand went to Max's other ear. "Were you in school today?"

"Yeah, but I kind of skipped sixth period," he admitted with no apology. He pulled his lips tight and screwed them up to one side, as if it were his distasteful duty to point out that Josie had made a big mistake. "Hannah didn't have a way home. You could have told me. I'd have brought her home if you wanted."

"I thought I was going to be there to get her." Josie sighed. "I should have been there to get her. It was her first day."

"Don't beat yourself up. That's what my mom always says. 'Don't beat yourself up for things you can't help.'" Josie closed her eyes and prayed for patience at the mention of Billy's mother. She'd like to wring that woman's neck for making Billy believe he didn't deserve any better out of life. Luckily, he couldn't see her eyes behind her dark glasses, so he just kept talking. "Yeah, well, I was hanging with Carl and we saw her coming and she looked really ticked." Billy's hand left Max's head and he flipped his fingers like he'd just touched something hot. "She was so mad I thought she might, you know, hurt herself. So I followed her and then I stayed to watch. Just to make sure she was okay."

Josie looked at the house. It was shut down tight, all the blinds drawn. Hannah could have sliced herself into lunch meat and Billy wouldn't have a clue. Still, he'd done his best.

"How did Max get out?" she asked.

"I knocked on the door to see if Hannah was okay. When she opened it Max came out. Then she threw the leash out, too, so I took him down to the pier and came back. I've just been here. You know, kind of watching." Billy took a deep breath, his shoulders rising but his concave chest barely registering the breath.

"You're a good kid, Billy."

"Thanks, Ms. B. I figured whatever kept you had to be bad. I tried to tell Hannah that, but she didn't want to hear it."

"It was bad, Billy." Gently Josie pushed Max down and let herself through the little gate. She thought for a second and then decided there was no upside in keeping quiet about what had happened. She turned back to Billy. "Archer was arrested this afternoon. They're charging him with murder."

"Dude," Billy breathed, his face registering such disbelief that Josie almost put her arms around him.

"It's not an excuse for forgetting Hannah, but it was an emergency," Josie said, knowing she didn't have to convince Billy of anything.

"That's so foul. No way that's even remotely close to what Archer could have done," Billy whispered.

Josie's lips twitched with a wry smile. Her own sense of outrage hadn't even come close to Billy's eloquence. Indeed the day and the problem were foul.

"Thanks." She patted his shoulder and with a snap sent Max to his outside bed. "And thanks for looking after Hannah. Do you think you could see school through to the end of the day for the next few weeks? Maybe see that Hannah gets home until I have a handle on this thing?"

"No doubt," he said seriously before his brow beetled. "If Hannah will come with me. I don't think she likes me a whole lot."

"Right this minute I doubt Hannah likes anyone a whole lot," Josie muttered, sending him on his way with a nod. He would go back to the beach or to Burt's restaurant. Billy would hang out until he was sure he could sneak into his own bed without an angry word from his mother.

"Ms. B.?"

Josie turned around before she opened the door.

"Yeah?"

"I'll keep this quiet. I mean, I appreciate you thinking I'm worthy to know about Archer's trouble. I just want you to know I'll help any way I can because you always help me any way you can."

"Thanks, Billy. That means a lot. Just go to school. Keep an eye on Hannah. Go to class. That will help more than you know."

They had probably spoken more in the last five minutes than they had all through his troubles, but in those five minutes Billy Zuni meant more to Josie than he could imagine. Sometimes kids knew exactly the right thing to say to help and sometimes they knew exactly the right thing to say to hurt. Josie opened the door and stepped inside her house. She had a feeling that the hurt part was going to come at her like a tsunami.

Josie turned on the table lamp. The light was soft. It illuminated the corner of the room in which she stood and sent just enough light toward the dining

room and kitchen that Josie could see nothing had
changed since morning. The blueprints for the re-
model were still on the dining room table. Hannah
had not moved them to eat. There was no sign that
she had used the kitchen. Josie listened. There was no
sound. No music coming from Hannah's room. No
sobs. Nothing. Josie called as she walked.

"Hannah?"

All was quiet.

"Hannah?"

Josie tried the knob on Hannah's bedroom door. It
turned and she walked in. The bathroom light was
on; there was a candle burning on Hannah's desk. It
flickered and Josie's eyes went to it. Even though
Hannah had been cleared of setting the fire that killed
Fritz Rayburn, Josie was only human. The connection lingered.

In the corner was the draped easel. Hannah hadn't
been painting. On the bed was Hannah's backpack.
She hadn't been studying. In the middle of the room
was Hannah, sitting on her little red-lacquered stool,
the only thing she had brought with her from the Mal-
ibu house where she had lived those last months with
her mother. Hannah's knees were drawn up to her
chest. She rocked back and forth, her arms wound
tightly around her legs. That black hair of hers hung
down, down almost to the ground. Josie couldn't see
Hannah's face or the inside of her arms but she could
see the little dish and the paring knife that lay across
it, the apple on top of it. Not a speck of blood to be
seen. She was getting better all the time. Pain in her
heart didn't translate to inflicting it upon her body.

Josie's muscles unlocked. She hadn't realized how
scared she had been for Hannah until she walked into
the room and sat in front of her. Josie lotused her

long legs and propped up her elbows on her knees.
Her hands were clasped under her chin.

"I'm so sorry. So, so sorry." Josie's apology was
warm and heartfelt. It was the kind she would accept
if her own mother ever returned and asked forgiveness
for deserting her teenage daughter. Josie waited to
find out if it was enough.

Hannah's lashes fluttered. There was a quick tic at
the corner of her mouth, as if she had been suddenly
stung. She raised her green eyes. They were shot
through with anger and disenchantment, and she was
going to make Josie pay for her transgression with
silence.

"Archer was in trouble. I had to help. It was an
emergency," Josie explained patiently.

Hannah didn't cut her any slack. Still no words.

"Look, it's bad. They beat him up when they arrested him." Josie looked away. This was harder than
she imagined. "Archer is accused of killing a young
boy two years ago. His wife's son from a previous
marriage. I had to help him, and there were things
that had to be done, and I forgot you."

Josie couldn't be plainer than that. Still Hannah
didn't speak.

"You know I didn't intentionally forget about you.
I've never had a kid. This is new to me, and I'm doing
my best."

Josie's jaw set as the silence continued. She was
angry, not just at herself any longer, but also at the
girl who was demanding a perfection Josie couldn't
aspire to.

"Do you understand the magnitude of what I just
told you?" Josie insisted, her patience wearing thin.

"Yes. The man comes first," Hannah shot back viciously. "So, I guess you're no different from my mother after all."

Before she even knew what had happened Josie was on her knees grabbing for Hannah's shoulders. Their faces came together: the woman and the girl. One square jawed and handsome, the other exotic, dark and delicate.

"I am not like your mother at all," Josie said through clenched teeth, "and we should get that straight right now, Hannah. I was helping someone I love. The same way Billy Zuni tried to help you because he cares about me. Everyone in Hermosa Beach will come to Archer's defense when they find out about this, and that's the way it's supposed to be. I don't have to choose one person over the other; I just have to make sure I don't throw one away for the other. Get it?"

Hannah pulled away, and Josie let her go. She sank back on her heels, hardly believing Hannah had riled her like this or that she felt the need to explain herself. She had answered to no one for so long that Josie resented the position Hannah was putting her in. She resented it like any parent who—Josie stopped that train of thought. She would not go there fearing, perhaps, that she had been like Hannah all those years ago and sent her own mother packing because of her attitude.

"These are the people I love, Hannah, and I will help any of them whenever they need me. You can either be a part of this family or not. Your choice."

Josie got up, gave Hannah one last chance to speak and, when she didn't, walked out of Hannah's room and into her own. She felt drained, a shell of a person, and there seemed to be nothing in the room to comfort her: not the giant bed with the down comforter, not the leather chair in the corner where she could sit and look at the small garden dug into the patio, not the books on architecture. Slowly she unbuttoned her shirt and tossed it on the bed before she dropped her trousers and left them on the floor. The morning hearing had been missed. The new client blown off. The day was lost. Josie sat down on the bed, using the toe of one shoe to dislodge the heel of the other. She planted her bare feet on the floor, leaned over and closed her eyes. Suddenly she felt exhausted. When she finally opened her eyes, Josie found herself staring at a rough spot on the hardwood floor missed during the renovation. Funny she hadn't noticed it before. But, then, there hadn't been too much amiss in her house or her life before this.

Josie closed her eyes again but not because she was tired. She only wanted to soak up the tears that were coming. Crying never did any good. Not when her father died, not when her mother took off, not when she had seen Hannah lying near death in that hospital room. Tears wouldn't make Archer's problems go away, and they sure as hell wouldn't make Josie stronger.

Startled by the sound of a door, Josie opened her eyes. Her shoulders pulled back, her hands were on the mattress, her senses alert. It was a reflex learned after Linda Rayburn, Hannah's mother, had attacked Josie here in her own home. But there was no danger; it was only Hannah coming out of her room. She stalked by Josie's room without a second glance. She carried the plate and the knife and the half-eaten apple. From where she sat Josie couldn't see Hannah once she turned from the hall, but the sounds of Hannah's deliberate housekeeping were like nails on a chalkboard. The water in the kitchen was run full-blast, the door of the dishwasher was yanked open, the dish was thrown in and the dishwasher door banged shut. The knife was tossed in the sink like a javelin. Teenage angst manifested itself brilliantly: anger at being forgotten, being alone, not being the first thing Josie attended to. Josie was sorry. She didn't know how to be perfect for Hannah and still do what needed to be done for Archer. She would try harder. Hannah would have to let her feel her way through this strange black box of a child's dependency.

In the quiet that followed, Josie thought about apologizing again. Maybe she would take Hannah to dinner. Maybe she should just get up and do that. Yet Josie did nothing. A fog had settled over her mind. Her strength was gone; the course was unclear. All she could think about was Archer and the information he had kept from her. Lies by omission. Josie didn't have a clue what to do next, but Hannah did. She stood in the doorway and announced: "I have homework. If you go to Archer's place it will be quieter. I can study better."

Josie blinked and Hannah disappeared. The door of her room slammed but not with the force of unadulterated fury. Rather it had the ring of reticent understanding.

Fine. Josie would accept that. She got off the bed, pulled on a sweatshirt and zipped it halfway up. Sweatpants and her clogs were next. Max's old neon-pink leash was in her hands, but the dog slept peacefully on the patio where he'd been left. He didn't raise his head as she opened the gate. Josie put the leash on the wall and let sleeping dogs lie.

She crossed the wide walking street in front of her house, jogged to the Strand and crossed over to the beach. She stuck to the shore, not wanting to see anyone she knew. The low tide rolled toward her with a gentle whoosh and rolled back with a skitter. The sun set away from her. Archer's building loomed ahead: pink and old and in need of some fixing up after an especially hot summer. It used to be the best building on the beach. Now it was just an old broad standing in the midst of the new babes. But those new places just passed as homes. In reality they were merely buildings.

Josie trudged the last few yards, crossed the bike path again and walked up the three flights to Archer's place. The door opened easily, which was odd. Archer was usually so careful. Josie stepped in and locked the door behind her.

"Archer?"

Inside there was a sense of sedation, as if living had been suspended until further notice. She maneuvered through the living room, glancing at the huge rooftop deck. Archer's bicycle was there. The barbecue. The tripod. No camera. They had brought it back from the police station. Archer had it when she dropped him off right after they checked the high school for Hannah. Then she saw it in the corner. Either the damage was bad, he had lost interest in what he was doing or his injuries were worse than she feared. His pride and joy, the camera that was now his livelihood, lay in pieces on the end table.

"Archer?"

She called louder, wandering toward the bedroom only to find him in the bath. His head was back; his eyes were closed. She stood in the doorway.

"You didn't answer."

"No." He didn't open his eyes.

"Want me to go?"

He moved his head slightly. That was a negative.

Josie knelt beside the claw-footed tub. It was long and it was deep: the perfect tub for a man like Archer when he invited a woman like Josie to join him. But now, alone, he didn't seem to fill it the way he usually did. Josie let her eyes roam over the body she knew so well. His right side was black and blue and purple and red; the bruise had spread like an oil slick. Archer's hair was wet but his face was dry. Josie pushed the sleeves of her sweatshirt up, reached into the water and retrieved a washcloth.

"Why'd they come after you so hard, Archer?"

Josie dabbed at the red wound on the side of his face. He winced. She adjusted. She feathered the strokes patiently, working every last bit of dirt and asphalt out of his skin.

"It's about a kid. Nobody likes perps who pick on kids," he mumbled. "They don't like bad cops either. That's what they think I am. Jesus . . ."

"Okay, babe," she whispered, knowing he was right and knowing it pained him to speak and to imagine that he was accused of crimes he, himself, despised.

Seeing there was no help for the lip and little for the eye, Josie kissed the bruised flesh and spent some time on the cut above his brow. There would be no more questions tonight, so she finished up. Josie searched the medicine cabinet for what she wanted and bent down again. Dabbing at him with a dry towel, she then worked a salve into his cuts and scrapes.

"Come on. Time to get out," she said.

Josie steadied Archer and he leaned on her. Gently she dried him, taking a moment to put her cheek against his broad back. She reached for his robe and covered him before leading him into the bedroom.

"Are you hungry?" she asked as he eased onto the bed and lay on his back.

"No, Jo. Tired. So damn tired. Like a bad dream . . . all of it coming back . . . thought it was done . . ."

When Archer stopped talking he held out his hand and Josie crawled in beside him. Her long, athletic body stretched out against his. Her arm went around him. Archer was a big man, not unmanageable. Josie had always felt safe, as if the world could fall in and Archer would protect her. It should have been like that now. So much was familiar. Lying together. Listening to the sounds of people below, the white noise of the waves no matter how low the tide. So much was different. There was a catch in Archer's voice. He didn't hold her as much as let her lie beside him. This new Archer was as shocking as the hidden jolt of an undertow that dragged you silently out to sea. And, like an undertow, the more you struggled against it, the more frightening it became.

"Why would anyone say I did this? Why would they?" His voice spiked, then trailed off.

Having no answer, not wanting to see Archer's anguish, Josie did what women do when their men are afraid. She soothed him, she pretended that all would be well, she ignored and appeased and turned a blind eye to this horrible thing that had happened.

"Rest, Archer. Just go to sleep. Tomorrow we'll figure it out. Not now. Don't worry. Don't worry. Don't . . ."

She petted the side of his face that didn't hurt. Her other arm was crooked under her own head. When she was sure that he wouldn't cry or ask the unanswerable question, Josie opened her own eyes. In this dark, familiar place, in this bed where they had made love a hundred times, Josie was scared. They weren't alone anymore. Someone she'd never met was between them—a boy named Tim. Someone she thought was long gone watched them—a wife named Lexi.

Turning on her side, Josie looked toward the place where Lexi's picture had always stood like a blessing beside the bed. It was still there but now Josie saw a different woman: one whose eyes were slightly narrowed, whose mouth didn't quite smile, whose head was cocked as if in question. Did she question Archer's innocence or Josie's ability to help him? Maybe she was trying to tell Josie something. Beside her Archer slept. Josie shuddered and rolled off the bed. She didn't belong there. The spirits of Archer's dead family were too oppressive for her to rest, and Hannah's needy spirit called her home.

Quietly she let herself out and walked slowly down the stairs. On the bike path Josie paused. She looked back. No light had gone on. Archer didn't know she was gone. At her place Hannah wouldn't sleep until Josie was safely home. There was no bed that would feel comfortable tonight. For Josie Baylor-Bates there were two people who needed her and no one she could turn to for help.

"It's a good night in the park."

Isaac Hawkins shrugged into his overcoat. He did this more from habit than necessity as he surveyed his park. It wasn't exactly overrun with thrill seekers but it wasn't a bad weeknight for Pacific Park either.

Roger McEntyre stood beside the old man, his hands clasped behind his back as he stood at his ease. Isaac Hawkins was properly turned out as usual: His overcoat was on, his tie knotted just so, his shirt buttoned up. He'd lost his wife and his son to diseases that were usually reserved for the very old, but Isaac never lost his old-world style. Roger admired that because it came with old-world values: hard work, loyalty, determination, ritual.

They stood as they did at the end of every workday. Isaac would look around and say, "It's a good night in the park." Roger would agree. There had been only two exceptions. The days those boys died Isaac hadn't said it was a good night. But tonight no one had died, the problem of Timothy Wren was on the district attorney's desk and the gate was good.

Isaac's faded eyes looked at every young face that passed by as if waiting for one of them to notice him, say something nice about his park. When they didn't, his gaze wandered to the line at the concession stand before he squinted toward the roller coaster. It sparkled, outlined by ten thousand new red and blue lights. Roger looked, too, but his gaze was sweeping and he looked for different things: the wrong hand in the wrong pocket, the teenager with the sharp edge of a troublemaker, the middle-aged man alone in the park eyeing the little girls. When the silence stretched and Isaac didn't offer his usual good nights, Roger knew there was something on his mind.

"We did the right thing, Roger."

It was a question disguised as a statement, so Roger answered it.

"Of course, Isaac," Roger said quietly. "The district attorney said so."

"It is a man's life we are talking about, you see." Isaac's right hand drifted up like a teacher trying to ascertain whether the pupil truly understood the deeper meaning of a critical equation.

"Questions were raised. We couldn't make the call, Isaac. It wasn't up to us."

"So we did the right thing?" This time Isaac asked outright.

Roger put his hand on the old man's arm and made no further move. The connection was enough. They both understood it was a sign of affection.

"Not a problem, Isaac. Go on home. Sleep well. It's been a long day. I'll see you tomorrow."

"Yes." Isaac hesitated. Roger waited. The old man looked at the crowd. "There are a lot of people here, Roger, and probably none of them will know one another their whole lives. They won't even remember who they came to Pacific Park with on a cool night in October. That's sad. That makes me miss your father. He was a good friend during his short life." Isaac turned and smiled. "As are you, Roger. You are a good friend for life. Like a son to me, Roger."

With that the old man walked through the throng of people who waited in lines in front of rides that were designed to stop their hearts just for the fun of it. They had forgotten that people died at Pacific Park. Those had been freak accidents, nothing more. Even Isaac would have forgotten by the time he got home. Age and familiar surroundings would lull him to sleep, keep him dreamless. So Isaac Hawkins dissolved into the night, leaving Roger McEntyre to weigh the worth of life, money, friendship—things. In the end Roger didn't spend much time on it all. He decided that pretty much everything was equal in the end. Everything except friends. Those were worth a lot, and he and Isaac didn't have many to spare.

Colin Wren did not go back to work after his meeting with the two lawyers and . . . that man. He didn't go back even though work had sustained him through

many a trying time. Most people would find this difficult to understand because Colin Wren's work, while
lucrative, was not very interesting. He owned a factory
that made things people didn't think about. His factory made knobs that were used for car radios and
kitchen appliances and wall heaters. He made levers
for toasters. Some had serrated edges, some were
smooth, some were big and some were small. The levers came in five colors and two thicknesses. They cost
pennies to make but, because they were sold by the
hundreds of thousands and because Colin's factory
worked lean, making knobs made him a lot of money.

When Colin was younger, he had taken pride in the
amount of money he earned. As he grew older, and
life did not go as planned, money no longer mattered
as much. He had made bad choices; he admitted it.
But in the last years, money was a means to an end,
and that end was to find his son in order to start
over again.

Then, one day, as he ate his spartan meal in front
of the late news, Colin Wren found out exactly what
had happened to Tim. Knowing he could no longer
help his son in this lifetime, Colin went after the people responsible for his death. Pacific Park would pay
for their negligence because someone had to.

That had been the plan until Colin found out about
Archer and Jude pointed out the logic of helping him.
Colin bought into it. Pacific Park had been the object
of Colin's hatred for so long, all he could imagine was
a settlement so large it would ruin the place. That
thought had driven him to post Archer's bond.

But then Colin sat across from Archer, a brutish,
low man who had not acknowledged Colin's pain or
shared in his anguish. That was when Colin started to
have doubts. Perhaps Jude, in his lawyer's greed, had

pushed Colin too fast, too far. It was to Archer Lexi entrusted the care of their son. It was Archer who now stood in the way of Colin's plan. It was Archer who was there the moment Tim died. Archer had brought a new dimension to the plan. He had soiled it and had derailed Colin's thinking.

So, instead of going to the factory and losing himself in work, Colin Wren went home. He watched the news, ate his dinner and changed into his nightclothes. Colin laid his head upon his pillow and pulled the covers up to his chin, then made a quarter turn as he prepared to sleep. The last thing Colin did was look at a picture of his son. He stared at that poor little vacant face. It was the only picture he had of him.

Unable to see much without his glasses, Colin blinked at the picture as if wishing it good night. Then he closed his eyes and let the new information run through his head like a production schedule. Lexi had remarried. She had married a man so totally opposite Colin it was an embarrassment. The man she married wasn't sorry Tim was dead. Lexi's choice was an insult, her decision deadly wrong.

As sleep came, Colin Wren decided to see how things unfolded. He would watch the players and, in the end, he would have exactly what he wanted: revenge and atonement. When he knew how to accomplish that, no one would stand in the way. Not Jude. Not that woman lawyer, and definitely not the man who might have killed his son.

7

Hermosa was awash in gray as if overnight it had taken sick. Colorless and dense, a haze curtained the early morning sun; fog blanketed the water, swirling uneasily across the shore before seeping toward the horizon and spilling over. The sand was cold, the surf lethargic, and all of it had weighed Josie down as she ran. Finally, unable to muster the energy to finish the last mile, Josie had slowed to a walk. Hands went to her hips. Her head was down. The air intake needed to balloon her lungs was deep. The day felt as if someone had died, and the sense of sadness was heavy. Finally Josie stopped and looked toward the buildings lining the Strand, half expecting to see them ringed with the weeds of mourning. It was Archer's building she saw, Archer's place that caught the eye. The old building appeared to sag, but Josie knew it was only a trick of the feeble light, its backbone bending as it tried to cut through the gloom.

Josie had looked toward the ocean as if it would wash away her melancholy, but the sea was no more uplifting than the town. No one was in the water. The surfers did not sit their boards, no children kicked at the shore, no girl raised her skirt to her knees and laughed at the cold.

Josie checked out the pier. Two people walked the length of it a hundred yards apart, both hunched into their jackets. Life as minimalist art.

Josie scanned back to the bike path but her attention wandered. She was at odds and ends, sixes and sevens because her schedule was off. Since Hannah's arrival even the most basic parts of her life had changed. The time Josie ran, the time she showered, the time she sat down to work. The two of them had been close to finding a rhythm. Then school started and everything changed again. Josie had to drive Hannah to school and that meant her run was half an hour late, and like a house of cards, the rest of the day fell in on itself. She would get used to it. She just was not used to it yet. Nor was Josie used to the heaviness in her that harbingered some sort of grand cataclysmic event gathering on the horizon, in the gloom, just past the haze where Josie could not see. Finding no comfort, no inspiration, no answers to her questions, Josie had turned her back on the beach and picked up the time as she ran home, away from the gathering storm.

Now, glancing at the clock, Josie saw she was only forty-five minutes off on what used to be a set-your-watch-by-it schedule. She was dressed, her appointments canceled for the day, and she had fifteen minutes before she was due to meet Archer. Still she was off her mark. The night had been restless, the morning silent, as she and Hannah kept their thoughts private. Her run hadn't worked out the kinks in her body or her psyche. The walk to Burt's did not lessen the rough edges of unease. Her restlessness turned to trepidation when she opened the door and found Burt behind the bar hunched over the morning paper.

"Hey." Burt raised his head, greeting Josie without his usual smile.

Josie gave him a halfhearted one as she slalomed around the mismatched tables, stopping to pick up a napkin that had been missed in cleanup the night before. She put her large bag on the bar, slid onto a stool, planted her elbows, laced her fingers and cradled her chin on her doubled fist.

"Got coffee?"

Burt shook out the newspaper, laying it on the bar as he turned to get her a cup.

"Archer's in a shitload of trouble. He made the front page." Burt lifted the newspaper slightly. Josie tilted her head and pulled the coffee toward her.

"I saw it," she said.

"Probably doesn't tell you anything you don't know." Burt shook his head and clicked his tongue against the place where his tooth was chipped. "I don't know what I'm more surprised at: you taking on something big like this again or Archer having this grief. Man, life is so fucking weird."

Josie cupped her hands around the mug. The coffee was black; she preferred it with cream. Burt had forgotten. This morning black would do.

"Weird enough for me, but I can't imagine how you must feel after all these years, Burt," Josie mused.

"How long have you been with him, Josie?" Burt glanced at Josie as he straightened and folded the paper.

"A year. We were going to celebrate our anniversary before all that stuff with Hannah. Now this . . ."

Josie drew one hand through her short, short hair, looked at Burt and wondered if he saw the change in her. The shock of yesterday was lodged like shrapnel behind the deep blue of her eyes. Either Burt didn't see it or he simply accepted that bad things changed people. If you were alive after a bad thing, cool. Life according to Burt.

"Yeah, well, let's see," Burt mused. "I think I've really only known Archer about two years."

Josie raised a brow. There were more surprises, and that alone should not surprise her.

"I thought you guys went way back."

"For Hermosa Beach we do." Burt chuckled and grinned. That chipped front tooth of his made him look boyish despite the sun-leathered skin, the hard-living creases on his face. He folded the paper in half and in half again as he spoke. "Archer and Lexi moved here right after this thing with the kid. I just didn't know that, and I didn't know about the kid. I guess I figured they sort of landed in Hermosa like all the rest of us and decided to stay."

"Just like the rest of us," Josie murmured.

She ran a finger around the top of her cup, disappointed in both Archer and herself. He hadn't actually lied to her about anything; she had erred in her assumptions about his life. What Archer knew about Josie was what she chose for him to know; what she knew about him was what he decided to tell her. They had reveled in their independence and now she knew that was a mistake. Understanding that made her feel lost. It was natural for a lover to believe she knew everything—intuitively, instinctively, intimately—about the man she had committed to. Wasn't it?

"So, Archer shows up two years ago. Did he tell you why they moved? Where they came from?" Josie asked this as if her surprise were minimal, her hurt minuscule. Burt, though, wasn't fooled. He made no jokes. He scratched his chin and thought hard.

"Somewhere in the Valley." Burt shook his head. "Man, can you imagine Archer in the Valley? I'd kill myself if I had to spend more than five minutes in the Valley."

"Burt," Josie admonished.

"Yeah, well, I would," he insisted. "Anyway, I met

Lexi first. She was one of those people you just knew right away. Like she walked in one day and by the time she left we were cool. Know what I mean?" Burt's question was rhetorical. He was oblivious to the glint of envy that sparked in Josie's eyes as he admired the other woman in Archer's life. Burt was too busy chuckling to notice. "She was a spitfire, that one. Always had an opinion about something and said it straight out like it was fact. And she was just funny. Really entertaining. Not like . . ."

"Me?" Josie asked.

"Come on, Josie." Burt shrugged. "You're different ladies. You're more serious but you're straight like Lexi. She was always straight. I can say that for her. . . ."

Burt's voice trailed off as he disappeared into the kitchen. Josie heard him yelling something but couldn't quite make it out. He came back carrying a tray of glasses that shivered and tinkled as he put them on the bar.

"So she tells me that she was married to a real asshole before Archer. She doesn't mention the kid, by the way, or how sick she is. She was one of those people who always talked but only gave you what she wanted to give you. So I knew she was married before but that's about it." Burt lost interest in the glasses and scanned the booze inventory behind the bar. Ducking down he came back up with a bottle of tequila, wiped it off with his shirttail and asked, "Did you know she was a paramedic?"

"Nope."

Josie had both hands around her cup as she hunched over the bar, hanging on his every word. Burt had hung loose his whole life, making it through high school before turning pro on the volleyball circuit, settling in with the restaurant after a motorcycle accident broke every bone in his body and ended his athletic career. His chipped front tooth, a souvenir of those hard times, was a reminder to everyone who knew him that shit happened. Shit was definitely happening to Josie and Archer.

"Yep, and old Lexi thought she did a hell of a job." He chuckled again and checked out the bourbon while he talked. "She was working on a domestic violence call when she met Archer. He wanted to call the coroner because he could see how exhausted Lexi was. Besides, the woman was dead. But Lexi wanted to try everything. That Lexi, she believed in miracles."

"Or she thought she was God's gift," Josie remarked, only to regret it in the next instant. She covered her tracks with a shrug and an explanation. "I mean, I've seen first responders act like that. Like if they try harder they can pull it off."

"I think Lexi just didn't like to throw in the towel. That's the feeling I got."

Burt finished his inventory but took one last look at the bottles stacked behind the bar anyway.

"So was it love at first sight with Archer?" Josie asked, hating that she sounded like a schoolgirl wanting to know if her boyfriend still pined for the one who got away.

"Something like that. She told him to have some respect for the dead. Seems he used the toe of his shoe to lift the sheet over the dead woman when Lexi finally gave up. Guess Archer was impressed that she wasn't thinking he was some big man because he was a detective."

"Archer?" Josie snorted, amused until she gave it another thought.

Archer probably did have an attitude back then

when he was the guy in charge. In fact, he had an attitude when Josie met him, and that was part of the attraction. She hadn't been immune to the charms of the pursuit, because the pursuit had been honest. Taking that photo of her on the beach, the one where she was pissed because she'd blown an easy put-away, missing the spike and losing the point. That photo had opened the door. He had come to the pro-am tournament and made himself known even when Josie was clear that she wasn't interested. But Josie had been interested because Archer was different. He didn't pursue the way most men did, leading with their mouths and letting their minds tag along. He presented himself. Big, sure, solid. Josie appreciated that; Lexi probably had, too. Josie found herself smiling and then realized that Burt hadn't noticed her distraction. He was still talking.

". . . that's according to Lexi, naturally. She said she made it tough for him, but, in the end, she had to admire a guy who hung in there, especially when she was such a bitch. She said she was a sucker for loyalty and persistence."

"I can understand that," Josie answered. "I met her ex. I don't think he was exactly the kind of guy who thought of others first."

"No kidding?" Burt pushed back his long hair, gray mixing in with the perpetually sun-bleached blond. "Man. History is just so strange. It's got a way of showing up when you least expect it, huh?"

"That's the truth." Josie set aside her coffee. Somehow it had cooled even though it seemed Burt had just poured it.

"You hungry? I can get the stove heated up. I've got some eggs and toast. No bacon. It would make you feel better."

"No, thanks. I appreciate it."

"I should probably think about adding breakfast to the menu, huh?" Burt mumbled, then answered his own question. "Naw, maybe not. Too much competition around here as is."

"I think you've got it knocked with lunch and dinner, Burt." Josie shifted on the stool, not ready to leave the topic of Archer and Lexi behind. "So why didn't Archer come here with Lexi?"

"Never really thought about it. Never asked him." They stayed silent for a few minutes; then Burt said, "Maybe she didn't want him to. Maybe she just wanted some time by herself. We'd talk a little; then Lexi would take her coffee and go sit on the wall and watch the beach. Now that I know about her kid, I guess she was taking some time to think about him."

Josie looked out the window and saw what Burt had seen. Lexi. Small, wiry, scarf over her head, a face that had earned its character. Josie imagined Lexi pondering the end of her life, wondering why God had visited such sadness on her. Tim was already gone and Lexi was next up. Josie wondered if knowing that you were about to die, that you were going to leave the person you loved, hurt as much as that person simply vanishing the way Josie's mother had. Probably. It didn't matter how the person you loved was lost; it mattered only that they were gone. Josie turned back to Burt.

"Do you think Archer refused to come with her?"

"Naw." Burt shook his head. "I mean, it wasn't like I didn't see him. I knew they were together. Sometimes he'd walk his bike down with her, then go for a ride and come back. They'd hook up again. But most mornings it was just her walking. It was always just Lexi who came in."

"So when did you and Archer get to know each other?" Josie prodded.

"Couple of weeks after Lexi died he came in and told me she was gone. Archer told me Lexi felt like Hermosa was home because of me. That was a nice thing for him to do. I liked him right off for that."

"He can do nice things." Josie took a deep breath and cradled her chin on her upturned hand. "So what else did Archer say?"

"You mean about him and Lexi?"

Josie nodded.

"Nothing. I figured he'd get around to telling me his life story eventually."

"Did he?"

"Nope. He just kind of disappeared. I thought he'd left town. I didn't know about Mexico then. You know, those trips to shoot pictures?" The trips to Mexico. Yes, she knew all about them. Didn't she? "I guess that's where he went. I figured he was gone for good. Then he showed up again. But that made sense. I mean, why stay away after Lexi left him that prime bit of real estate?"

"The apartment building? That was hers?" Josie's coffee never made it to her lips. Slowly she set it back down.

"Oh, man, I'm sorry, Josie, I thought you knew?"

Josie shook her head. "I figured he bought before the market went nuts."

"Naw, Lexi got it in her divorce settlement," Burt said.

"And Archer told you about that but not about the accident with the kid? That sounds kind of chatty to me," Josie mused uneasily as the columns of this balance sheet weren't adding up.

"Lexi told me she was leaving Archer really well

fixed for the beach babes. It was kind of sweet, you know. It was like Lexi was looking out for him." Burt ran some water in the sink and added a spritz of detergent. "She'd sure as hell be happy to know you're here for him now. She'd be happy he didn't sell the building."

Burt was gone again, called by some chore in the kitchen. Josie heard him speaking to someone in Spanish. A deliveryman at the back door, somebody needing a handout. When he reappeared with another tray of glasses he had a smile on his face and a thought in his head that turned Josie cold.

"Or, you know, maybe we've got this all wrong. Could be Archer's been keeping to himself so much because of this thing with the kid. Wouldn't that be something if he really did it and he was hiding out? Hey, Josie, who was that guy that murdered his whole family? He was like an accountant and he laid 'em all out and then went away and got a new wife and everything? Who was that, Josie?"

Burt dropped to the floor and rummaged in a low cabinet as he filled the ensuing silence with his chatter, spinning conspiracy theories, amused at his own imagination while Josie sat stone still. What Burt implied was stupid and thoughtlessly uttered. Yet she had not instantly dismissed the idea that Archer could have done just that. Even now Josie found no quick voice to stop Burt, and so he went on.

"John Wayne Gacy? Naw, he was the guy who dressed up like a clown. . . . Killed boys . . . I think that was him. . . . But the other guy . . . What was that guy's name?"

"Burt, stop. That's ridiculous. You don't really think Archer could have done anything like that."

Burt raised his eyes. He rested his arms on one of

his knees as he balanced on the ground with the other.
He opened his mouth, but before he could answer,
someone else joined the conversation.

"Did you really need to ask that, Jo?"

Slowly, Josie turned her head. Archer stood behind
her, taking up more space than she ever remembered.
Archer removed the sunglasses he wore despite the
unremarkable day. Burt stood, and Josie heard the
tinkle of glass as if Burt backed into the bottles on
the bar, shocked when he saw the damage to Archer's
face. But it wasn't the bruising and cuts Josie saw. She
was looking Archer in the eye. Those eyes—once level
playing fields—were now hard and desolate and as
uninviting as the tundra.

8

"How's Hannah?"

"She's okay. She's in school."

"What did she say about me?"

Josie rested her arm on the back of the chair. They had moved from the bar to a corner table. More coffee for Josie. A first cup for Archer. From the looks of him he had breakfasted on aspirin, and that, it seemed, had been a less than satisfying meal. His face was a bright and shiny palette of purple and red, black and teal, the skin stretched tight as the tissue beneath swelled to unnatural proportions. His left eyelid had the look of patent leather; the cut above it had scabbed. All in all, Archer was not a pretty sight, so Josie stared out the window until he insisted she pay attention.

"Did Hannah say anything about me, Jo?"

"Nothing." Josie lied easily, reluctant to add to Archer's misery.

"Bullshit," Archer responded. He drank his coffee with one hand wrapped around the cup, the handle turned inward. When he drank, he stared over the rim at Burt.

Josie crossed her arms on the table and tried hard not to show how annoyed she was. Burt's joke had been in poor taste, his speculation completely ridiculous, yet Archer hadn't seen it that way. He had turned his back on Burt, his good friend, and now he was bullying Josie into some loyalty game that smacked of destructive, macho self-pity. It was the last thing she would have expected, and she dealt with it the only way she knew how.

"Okay," Josie said flatly. "Have it your way. Hannah said I should be careful. She said I should have learned that adults can do bad things to kids. She said there was always a chance you could be like that. Does that make you feel better?"

"Out of the mouths of babes," Archer said sarcastically as he hung his head, putting his hand on the back of his neck. "You took in a damn expert on freaks who hurt kids."

"What would you expect, Archer? You didn't exactly welcome her with open arms when she moved in with me. You can't expect her to come to your defense."

"Hey." His hand came down hard on the table and the coffee cups jumped. "You didn't exactly ask if I wanted to be part of the Brady Bunch. I respected your taking her in, but I didn't think she would change things the way she did. I didn't want anything to change. I didn't think you did either—"

Josie cut him off, tired of the old tune he was singing.

"What's happened between us because of Hannah isn't in question, Archer. I just want to point out that you shouldn't expect any sympathy from her until you earn it."

"I don't want it," Archer snapped. "I don't want any from you either."

Josie stiffened, hearing a whole lot of frustration talking that had nothing to do with his arrest. It was Hannah and had been Hannah since Josie announced the girl was going to live with her. Conceptually, it had been a fine and noble move. Reality was another matter. Archer argued that Hannah had seen more in sixteen years than Josie had seen in forty. She could fend for herself. Josie wondered why she should have to. Archer countered, pointing out that Josie couldn't make peace with her own mother's desertion by pretending she was Hannah's. He might as well have slapped her with that one. To his credit, he apologized for crossing that line, so Josie chalked Archer's basic objections off as selfish and male and assumed he would come around. Now she had to wonder if there was more to his desire to be rid of Hannah than met the eye. Maybe Burt had hit on something. Just maybe Archer had something to hide. Perhaps Hannah, with all her knowledge of sordid human behavior, saw something in Archer Josie didn't. That, Josie decided, was plain idiotic.

"Okay, sorry. I'm as edgy as you, so let's forget Hannah." Josie reached into her bag, got her tape recorder and put it between them on the table. "What about Tim Wren, Archer? Was there any love lost there or is it just Hannah you object to?"

"You don't need that thing." Archer's voice was ice. His head jerked with the insult of the recorder.

"I do if I'm going to defend you," Josie answered sharply. Just as sharply she looked at him, sending a warning. No more games. They didn't have the time. "Be truthful and it won't matter what's on this tape."

"Fuck you, Jo," Archer whispered as he leaned away from her.

Josie was quick, punching at the small recorder and turning it off with one hand as she grabbed Archer's arm with the other. Her grip was tight and hard, her nails too short to dig in. She bent forward, close enough to smell the ocean on him and see that his arm was sunburned where he leaned it out the window during his surveillance. Any other day, these things would have endeared him to her. This wasn't any other day; this wasn't even Archer.

"Don't you ever say that to me," she hissed. "And don't make me work so hard to help you. You can be angry because you don't like Hannah being at my place, you can be mad because I don't squeeze the toothpaste out right, but there is no you and me when it comes to this. There is no assumption of truth or innocence just because we sleep together."

Slowly Josie sank back in her chair, easing her grip just a bit.

"You're not thinking straight, and I'm not exactly top of my game, so I will use whatever helps. If I say it's a tape recorder, then it is a tape recorder. I'll call the shots and I'll ask the questions. Any other attorney would do the same thing, but no one else will care as much as I do about finding out what in the hell is going on. Nobody."

The hand that had held Archer was shaking as she let go of him; her voice had trembled and that shamed her. If she was going to help Archer, or stand up to an ugly truth, then Josie had to be as tough as her talk.

"Do you want to start again or do you want me to walk?"

The minutes ticked by. Archer didn't speak. A woman came in asking to use the bathroom. A boy dropped a stack of *The Beach Reporter* newspaper on the floor with a thunk. She felt Archer's anger hot as the August sun and realized that it wasn't just the recorder that set him off; it was his own impotence.

The cop was now the perp.

Finally he picked up the recorder. It looked so insignificant in his big hand, so unworthy of the scrutiny he gave it. Josie heard the click. The recorder was back on the table.

"Tim Wren was nothing to me."

9

"I didn't love him. I didn't *not* love him," Archer admitted. "Tim was thirteen when he died. He wasn't like his mother at all. He was big and Lexi was so small. He was dark. Lexi was light. She was so bright and smart and that kid was just broken. Nothing worked right on him. How could a woman like her have a kid like him?"

Briefly Archer put the palm of his hand to his brow, as if that would help him think. His fingers curled as if his head hurt. He breathed deep through his nose and then continued.

"Tim had a degenerative muscle disease. Some problems with his heart and his lungs, but it was his mind that was really screwed up. That big, hulking kid who went through puberty early and fast had the Goddamn mind of a five-year-old. I couldn't stand listening to him or watching him jerk around knowing there was no way to stop him. Every time he jerked or threw a tantrum or drooled it killed Lexi. Just destroyed her. I could see it on her face."

Archer's fist pounded the table lightly, underscoring his long-ago frustration and aversion to Tim's disabilities—reactions a jury would see only as callous. His chair was close enough to the window so that he could rest his head against it when he tipped it back. Archer looked at the ceiling, at the business cards that people had tacked up there over the years, but Josie knew the only thing he saw was Tim Wren.

"Why didn't you tell me about him?" Josie asked.

"I haven't told you about a lot of things." Archer lowered the chair to the floor and slid his eyes toward Josie with a look she could only describe as pity that she had misunderstood. "Wasn't that part of the deal between us? Our time started when we met. I had pictures of Lexi. You asked about her. I told you. You never asked about Tim."

"I asked why you never had children," she reminded him. "You didn't talk about Tim then."

"I didn't lie, Jo. I said if Lexi and I had had kids, they would have been beautiful. Bottom line, he wasn't ours. Why should I want to talk about him when he represented a terrible time in my life? I didn't even think about Tim again until yesterday. But Lexi? I've thought of her every day since she died. Every damn day."

Josie toyed with her cup, feeling her own anxiety but unable to detect any from Archer. He touched her hand and stopped her fidgeting. Time and memory and Josie's attention were softening him. Or, like a good actor, Archer knew when to change the pace and the tone to draw his audience into the web of his fiction. Either way, Archer would make a fine witness if it came to that.

"Jo, you're looking for me to say Tim was like a son to me, but I won't lie. Tim was so damaged it was impossible to have a relationship with him. I didn't grieve for him when he died, but I hurt because Lexi hurt. That's not a bad thing, Jo. It's an honest thing. It's what I did. It's who I am. You know that."

Josie eased her hand from under Archer's. Okay.

She believed him, but Archer's explanation wasn't good enough. Josie detected half-truths lying dormant, waiting to be brought to life by a prosecutor.

"It must have been hard to live with this boy if he was as bad off as you say. You must have been frustrated. Were you angry all the time, Archer?"

"Lawyer tricks, Jo? Christ, I haven't been retired that long." Archer laughed in disappointment. "If you want to know if I was ticked off enough to do something to that kid, ask me."

"Were you?" There. It was on the table. Archer sent it right back at her.

"No. And if I was I wouldn't have waited five years to take him out. I wouldn't have done it in an amusement park with ten thousand people around to watch and his mother sitting right next to him. There would have been better ways, easier ways, to get rid of him."

"Then tell me what it was like to live with a boy who couldn't control his body, who couldn't carry on a conversation, who probably needed to have his diapers changed even though he was almost as big as you," Josie insisted.

"It sure as hell wasn't as peachy as having Hannah hanging around," Archer scoffed. "Tim needed twenty-four/seven care by the time he was seven, so he didn't live with us. Colin left Lexi when Tim was three, when they figured out he was never going to be normal. What a pisser, a guy like him making a buck off a kid he hasn't seen in what, ten years?" Archer's bottom lip disappeared under his teeth for the briefest moment. When he spoke again his voice was steady but still colored by bitterness. "Lexi worked her butt off to pay for a place out in the Valley. She went to see Tim every week. She took him out as often as she could. She didn't ask me to go with her until the kid started getting too big for her to handle. She never asked for Tim to live with us because that would have been a deal breaker. I told her straight out I wouldn't marry her if that's what she wanted."

"Did she resent you for that?"

"Lexi was practical. She married me hoping I'd have a change of heart but she knew I wouldn't. She lived with it," Archer said matter-of-factly.

"Then why would the district attorney think you killed Tim Wren?" Josie pressed.

"I don't know." Archer threw up his hands. "Christ, Jo. I swear, if I knew I would tell you."

Archer's admonition was the cry of an animal suddenly wounded by a hunter he did not see, the one he failed to smell, the one he couldn't outrun. Josie saw Burt reflected in the bar mirror. His hand was on the phone. He was ready to call for help if trouble came. Josie tore her eyes away from the mirror, needing to see every flicker and tic in Archer's face when he answered her next question.

"Did you know you were under investigation?" Josie lowered her voice; Archer followed suit.

"I would have heard something, seen something if it had been going on for any length of time. No." His voice skidded into a harsh whisper as the heel of his hand went to his good eye. "Whatever went down, it was fast. If Lexi were here she could tell them I didn't do anything. If Lexi were here . . ."

"But she's not. I am."

Josie laid out the obvious like she was fanning a deck of cards. *Pick one, Archer. Her. Me. The truth. Lies. Your pride or my hurt.* All of it could be compromised and that was where the skill of the game came in. Josie couldn't force Archer to be honest; she could only hope she wouldn't be blinded by her feelings for him. Archer's life before her had been held so close she didn't know it still clung to him. His secrets may have been kept out of consideration for her, a need to leave a hurtful past behind, or it could have been something else. Something sinister. Archer's reticence could have been the self-serving silence of a man with something to hide.

Josie turned off the tape recorder just as Burt flipped on the television above the bar. Startled by the sound of the TV, Archer let his eyes go to it and then scanned the rest of the place as if he weren't quite sure where he was. Josie collected herself. It was time to go. The day would happen but in Hermosa Beach it would have to happen without her. She gathered her things. This was just the beginning, not even the tip of the iceberg. There was a lot to do.

"I have an appointment with Jude Getts. I'd better hit the road if I'm going to get to Brentwood before noon."

"I don't want you to go, Jo." Archer stopped her.

"I have to. You'll be fine here. Stay with Burt for a while," Josie directed as she palmed her keys and looked at Archer one last time. "I'll be back as soon as I can."

"I didn't mean it like that," Archer said. "I mean, I don't want you dealing with that bloodsucker: him or Colin Wren. I'll sign over the apartment building to him. I'll pay back every cent of the bail money, but I don't want to be beholden to either of them for anything. Do you understand?"

Josie hesitated. Above her the air-conditioning had kicked in and the draft of cool air tickled her bare neck. It was as annoying as Archer trying to tell her her job.

"Don't be a fool, Archer. If Jude Getts has information that will help us, I want it. Your ego isn't going to get in the way of that. It's not good business; it's not good lawyering, and if we come up with something that will help him, I'll reciprocate."

She got up and slung her purse over her shoulder.

"When I get back I want a detailed account of what happened the day of the accident. From the minute you got up that morning to the minute you brought Lexi home. Do you understand?"

Archer's petulant silence gave Josie pause. Pushing her chair out of the way she leaned over the table. Defiance, hurt and anger, every bad thing Archer was feeling was directed at Josie as if she had brought this on him. It would take a whole lot more than that to make Josie bend, but it was just enough to really tick her off.

"Do you understand me, Archer?" Josie asked.

A muscle in Archer's jaw quivered. Finally he nodded. Josie wasn't going to ask for more.

An hour later she was walking into Jude Getts's office. She hoped Archer was at home reconstructing that fateful day. He wasn't. As a matter of fact, Jude and Archer were doing the exact same thing. They were tuned in to the noonday news, and Archer was the headline du jour.

10

Jude Getts's office was nice. Leather furniture, smooth and soft as a baby's bottom. Plants lush and green. Carpeting thick as a Southern whore's accent. Josie took a minute to miss what she'd left behind when she abandoned her high-stakes private practice a few years ago when it occurred to her that not everyone with money to pay for it deserved a defense. But a minute was all she took. The price paid to get and keep a place like this was just too damn high. Ridiculous billable hours. No time to call your own. Clients who turned your stomach or broke your heart or tugged at your conscience. Colleagues who wanted everything you had and more. Lovers who faded into oblivion in the face of a trial that lasted longer than a relationship ever could. Being sought after, smart and rich made for a tough life. Only a few were cut out to make it big, and it was evident that Jude Getts was one of the anointed. Josie could feel his energy before she even crossed his threshold.

"Here you are. The DA's having a field day." Jude greeted her as if she were just in time for cocktails. He motioned to a client chair.

"Who's that with him?" Josie asked as she took a seat.

"That's Sharon Flaggerty, the Pacific Park spokesperson."

"Turn it up."

Josie wiggled her fingers at the plasma screen embedded in the wall. Jude touched a button somewhere
on the desk and the sound went up. It was a wonderful
toy, and the exquisite color and clarity did Sharon
Flaggerty's blond good looks justice. What was coming
out of her mouth was equally slick. She was a well-
spoken, businesslike young woman who seemed to
have mastered the art of the spin, and it was spiraling
toward John Bogert, the *Daily Breeze* reporter.

"Of course it's been difficult for Pacific Park to remain silent and endure the charges of willful miscon-
duct and negligence levied against us by Mr. Getts.
We are a family-owned, family-oriented business, and
it hurts that some people think we participated in a
cover-up. As you now know, we could not release
information relevant to a civil trial while we were
cooperating with the district attorney on a criminal
matter. Pacific Park was dedicated to getting justice
for a young boy, even if our own reputation suffered."

"Are you going to take any legal action against the
judge who sanctioned you for withholding evidence?"
someone called.

"No, of course not." Sharon Flaggerty feigned
shock with practiced grace. "There's no reason to af-
fidavit the judge for doing his job. It is now clear to
Judge Bellows that we would have compromised the
DA's investigation by complying with Mr. Getts's request for information. The judge has rightly granted
a motion to formally stay the civil case pending the
outcome of this criminal action."

"Damn!"

Jude's hand hit the arm of his chair, but a glance
told Josie he wasn't as much upset at the ruling as he
was getting a kick out of the park's strategy.

"Shh," Josie admonished as the next reporter asked the question of the day.

"If you knew it was murder, why not hand over the evidence two years ago?"

"It wasn't until Mr. Getts brought the civil action that we reexamined the information we had on Tim's accident," she said with sincere regret. "Seeing the evidence in hindsight made us reevaluate our initial conclusion that Tim's death was an accident. Even after that reevaluation, we weren't sure there had been any wrongdoing. That's why we relied so heavily on Mr. Cooper, the district attorney. He followed up, and it was his decision to pursue this as a criminal matter."

There was a hue and cry as everyone asked the same questions. What tipped the balance? What made the DA sure he could get a conviction? Could she be more specific regarding the evidence against the suspect? No, Ms. Flaggerty said, but John Cooper could. Graciously she stood down, and John Cooper stepped up to the microphone. His wonderful voice, his seamless delivery, his perfect choice of words made John Cooper seem more intelligent than he was. He talked so long without saying anything that some of the reporters began to drift away. Jude Getts had the DA's number, too. He turned down the sound before John Cooper finished his first compound sentence.

"So." Josie turned toward Jude. "What's she talking about? What evidence?"

"Haven't got a clue. Pacific Park fought us tooth and nail for months and now they're holding themselves out to be conscientious citizens—saints, no less. Incredible." He swiveled toward her, simultaneously turning off the television. Jude paused, then tossed the remote on the desk. "No problem. I'll get my PR guy on it. Archer's had a long, solid career as a detective. Who can hate a guy who cared so diligently for a sick wife? Those things will go a long way in the public's perception of Archer. We'll taint the jury pool with good thoughts. By the time they're seated we'll have them eating out of our hands."

"And I think we're not going to do anything even remotely like that," Josie informed him. She had expected more than smoke and mirrors. "I don't exploit my clients or their victims. It's not the way I work."

"Well, it is now, Josie. It is now."

Jude rested his head against the back of his chair. A small spotlight in the ceiling was positioned so it created a halo of light around him. The connection Josie made was laughable.

Saint Jude.

Funny.

The saint of lost causes.

That was rich.

Archer was no more a lost cause than this runway model with a law degree was a savior.

"So you've still got a little fire in the belly, do you, Josie? That's good." Those fingers waggled and Josie wanted to rip them off. Instead she listened, taking her medicine so she could get the candy he had promised. "But my research department is as good as my public relations guy. That kid you defended recently—what was her name?"

"Hannah Sheraton?"

"Yes, of course. Hannah Sheraton," Jude murmured, and unclasped his hands. "Wasn't that just a little fiasco. You actually lost that case. It was the mother's stupidity that let you save face and kept an innocent from a life sentence. You're rusty, my girl, and I don't think you want to polish up your skills on this particular matter. There's just a little too much at stake."

"First," Josie said coolly, "I'm not your girl. Second, I didn't lose that case; I quit when Hannah asked me to. When I knew the truth, I took matters into my own hands."

"Yes, you did. But that doesn't alter the fact that you were working with limited resources that kept you from knowing the truth sooner. This time around you're going to need more than a wing and a prayer. You're going to need me."

With one hand he pushed a manila folder her way.

"The few documents we managed to get out of Pacific Park before they started playing games do not look good for your client. There was nothing mechanically wrong with the Shock and Drop ride, so blaming a technical problem for Tim's death is going to be iffy unless they're trying to bury something."

Jude let that little bombshell explode at Josie's feet. She stared at the folder, fearful that if she looked inside she would find herself outflanked before she even got to the battlefield.

Jude gave the folder one last nudge. He never took his eyes off her as he opened it and slid documents her way in long, sensual movements. He teased her, and that tease proved so seductive Josie couldn't resist the invitation. One by one Josie looked at the documents, getting a feel for the overview, ignoring the detail for now. Spread in front of Josie Baylor-Bates were engineering schematics, diagrams and reports. Jude provided the voice-over.

"The three of them were strapped into the proper position. Archer was on the right, Lexi on the left, Tim in the middle."

Jude pushed another schematic her way.

"The locking mechanism on the harness was in the middle of Tim's chest."

And another.

"The ride went up slow. It was designed to have a hesitation of one and a half seconds before releasing and dropping the riders to the ground at twenty miles an hour. There's a slowing curve about four stories up. Tim Wren fell from his station to the ground before they hit the slowing curve. Whatever happened, it was perfectly timed. He was catapulted to the ground because of the speed. Had he fallen two minutes later there might have been a chance for survival."

Josie's eyes moved in clicks, resting on each piece of paper as Jude slipped one past her line of sight and replaced it with another. She didn't want to touch them. She was already second-guessing herself. Maybe Jude had been right. Hannah's acquittal had been a fluke, a mistake on the part of Hannah's mother instead of the brilliance of Josie's advocacy. Maybe Josie was rusty and Archer's defense would suffer because of it. Could she risk that? Could she live with herself if hubris kept her from following Jude Getts's advice? Not a chance. She was up to defending Archer, and it was time Jude Getts knew it.

"The ride could have hit something just before that curve," she said. "Something unexpected may have been on the rail: bird droppings, something airborne that nicked the steel, something that caused the mechanism to hesitate or skid."

"You're quick. That's nice," Jude said smoothly. "But the inspection reports are all in order. . . ."

Jude stopped talking long enough to eye a stunning woman who came into the office as if it were her own. Her hair was chin-length and as dark as her eyes. Her suit fit like a glove. Josie nodded as she served coffee, took a report from under her arm and handed it to Jude. When she left Josie's eyes followed and Jude read her mind.

"She's an associate. Top of her class at Yale. Someday she's going to be earning this firm a lot of money, and I want to say that I was the one who saw past her obvious attraction." Jude was smiling when he looked up from the papers at Josie. "And, just so you know, I'd bring her coffee if she needed it."

"That's democratic," Josie mumbled. Chagrined to find her thoughts had been so transparent, she reached for her coffee cup and held it in both hands. "Those documents could have been doctored. I'll have them looked at by experts."

"That's what Amelia was doing." He held up another sheaf of paper. "This is the last report and it has been authenticated. This inspection was completed right after the accident."

He tucked that one away in the folder and gathered up the rest.

"If you don't mind, I'll have them rechecked." Josie put her coffee back on his desk. "But I don't want to jump ahead of myself. Right now I'd like to take a look at the files from the first civil trial. Who handled Lexi's claim?"

"Well, there you have hit on an amazing thing." Jude looked like a kid who had just stumbled across twenty bucks lying on a long, lonely road, no chance of getting it back to its rightful owner. "There was no settlement on Lexi for Tim's death. If she had collected, it would have been near impossible for me to settle on Colin's behalf. Not that I couldn't have pulled it off eventually, mind you. It's just that a wrongful-death claim two years after one parent was compensated would have been an uphill battle."

Expressionless, Josie looked at Jude without really seeing him. She didn't see the lush greenery in the atrium behind him or notice his smile or the gleam in his eye. Josie's visual field had shrunk to focus on a pinpoint of color on the collar of his shirt, a hatch print of delicate navy, beige and gray lines intersecting on a white background. Desperately she tried to make the bits and pieces of information fit into a pattern as neatly as the tattersall boxes separating the white ground of that shirt. No mechanical problem. No civil action after the accident. No reason for Archer to commit a crime. No evidence that a crime had been committed.

"I don't get it," she mused. "Even if there wasn't a mechanical error a case could have been made for operator error. If that didn't fly, Pacific Park would have paid out if Lexi made the right noises just to keep her from talking publicly about what happened. Sidestepping any appearance of wrongdoing would be worth a bundle."

"Maybe you should ask your client why his wife didn't file," Getts suggested. "But for now it's all a great mystery. If we work together we'll solve it sooner than later. I think you know that, Josie."

Josie cast him a harsh glance.

"Do you think patronizing me is going to get your hands in Pacific Park's pockets any sooner?"

"Do you think insulting me is going to make me change my mind?" Jude laughed back. "Look, let's get something straight. I'm not ashamed of what I do. Believe it or not, this isn't all about money. I help people who need my help, and Colin Wren needs it."

"You've got to be kidding. A man who ignored his son for ten of his thirteen years? He's the kind of client you want to help?" Josie demanded.

"You only have Archer's word that Colin was a creep," Jude reminded her.

"That's good enough," Josie assured him.

"And I have Colin's word that he wasn't," Jude replied. "And to me that's good enough."

"Keep talking. You'll convince someone that Colin Wren deserves to profit from Tim's death."

Jude shook his head, then planted his hands on the arms of his chair. Fun and games were over.

"You're obviously a good lawyer, Josie, but buying into your client's point of view so wholeheartedly isn't all that smart. You don't know Colin Wren, you don't know me and none of us knows what this case is really about. If you take everything your client says at face value then he has a fool for a lawyer. Argue his point of view but don't own it until you know it's the right one."

"Thanks for the advice." Insulted by the lecture she pointed to the file. "Is that for me?"

"Copies of everything we have. Xeroxed just for you." He handed it over with a smile.

"Thanks." She took the folder and held it against her chest. "I'll take it from here and you can get back to whatever other business you have on your calendar."

"I don't think so, Josie. You and I are going to be joined at the hip for a few months, so you might as well relax." Jude's expression was mischievous, and his cavalier attitude was not making her happy.

"In your dreams, Jude. I don't like the way you work."

"I think I've been fairly efficient so far." He feigned hurt before his expression melted into resolve and he crossed his arms. He was tired of sparring. "Without me your boy would still be in jail. Without me you wouldn't be one step ahead now. Without me, you'd be running just to catch up. And without Colin, Archer would be an ex-cop in jail. Not a pretty place for him to be."

"Okay, I'm impressed with the theatrics and your secretarial staff and Colin Wren's deep pockets," Josie agreed. "But I'm having a real hard time with you. This isn't funny, and money is secondary to the fact that a boy is dead and a good man is accused of killing him. You seem to think this was all conjured up to amuse you."

"Believe me, I know this is no joke," Jude insisted, and Josie saw the steel of Jude Getts behind the polish. "But I won't apologize for thriving on the challenge. When I smile it means I'm revved. I smile because without some levity I would fall into a black hole of despair when I realize how many wrongs I can't right. But most of all, my attitude is just reflective of the fact that I love what I do." He leaned forward, picked up a pen and pulled it through his fingers. "And I'm anxious to do it with you."

"Double entendre not intended," Josie shot back, unimpressed.

Jude laughed outright and tossed the pen away.

"You're not my type. Love the legs but I prefer a little more hair to run my fingers through. Blond, not brunette."

"Fine. I'm not your type. You're not mine professionally or personally. So let me get on with my work, because I work better alone."

"And I don't intend to work at cross-purposes," Jude warned. "We want the same thing, just for different reasons. It doesn't make sense not to put our incredibly smart heads together on this."

Josie opened her mouth to object just as her phone

rang. A half turn afforded her some semblance of privacy while she took the call that would finish her conversation with Jude Getts.

"That was Ruth Alcott's office. She's the deputy DA who caught this case, and she's got time to see me now." Josie raised the file in her hand. "So thanks for the information. I'll handle it from here. I don't need any more of your help."

While Josie filled him in Jude rolled down his shirtsleeves, grabbed his coat and rounded his massive desk. With a friendly pat on her back as he passed, Jude said, "Don't be ridiculous. Of course you do."

It wasn't just the way he looked that made people on the Strand give Archer a wide berth; it was the way he moved. He walked with his arms by his sides and his chin thrust out. His powerful body was propelled forward like a missile seeking a target. Archer moved as if he would not, could not, stop for anything or anyone. He moved dangerously, and people watched him pass with more than a little curiosity and a great deal of relief that he had not stopped to notice them.

His pace did not change when he turned in to his building and took the stairs two at a time. Ignoring the pain that shot through his ribs and the incessant pounding in his head, Archer made it up three flights in sixty seconds flat.

The key caught; the lock gave. He slammed the door open and walked straight onto the balcony . . . and back in . . . and back out again. Three times he did this. Once he hesitated near the tripod. For a millisecond he thought about screwing the camera on, refracting his rage through the lens, calming himself

by framing the ocean, the sky, the birds, the beach-
goers.

Fuck it.

That notion shredded in his mind like a past-due
bill he couldn't pay. What was the use of trying to
feel better about any of this? Archer stormed inside
and outside and in again. There would be nothing to
see through that lens that he couldn't see without it.
A gray day. A doomed day. Nothing to recommend
it just as there was nothing to recommend him anymore. The district attorney and that woman from Pacific Park had seen to that.

The newspaper accounts had been bad enough, but
voices speaking against him, using his name in the
same sentence as murder, was unconscionable. He was
defenseless against the impact of that news conference. Archer had seen his future in the faces of the
two men having coffee at Burt's. They kept their eyes
northwest like the pointer on a faulty compass but
couldn't help flicking his way to check him out. There
had been doubt in Burt's eyes, too. Burt who never
gave anyone shit was suddenly cautious, wondering if
it was good for business to have Archer sitting alone
looking so damned scary in the back of the place. So
Archer left. He paid his bill and he left, and as he
passed Billy Zuni, Archer wondered if he had been a
coward not to stop and look the kid in the eye when
he called. But Archer couldn't stop because a kid alive
and well was the last thing he wanted to see.

Archer was on the balcony again, shaking under the
weight of his fear and anger. With a great cry he
brought his hands down on the balcony wall, gripping
it as if it were the only thing keeping him from falling
off the edge of the world. Beads of rough stucco bit

into him, punctured the skin of his palms before he marched through the house again looking for something to put him out of his misery. Booze. Pills. Not his style. Never even thought about it until now. His service revolver. His revol . . .

Archer headed toward his bedroom. He would find it. He would touch it. He wouldn't use it but he needed to know the option was there. Five more steps. Hard and heavy on the floor. He didn't get far because he stumbled at the sight of Lexi's picture, the small one he kept in the living room up on the bookshelf. Without thinking, reacting to its mere presence, he let loose with another bellow, grabbed it and threw it against the wall. Archer didn't know how long he stood there, his arms akimbo, his breathing labored, but it couldn't have been long. The sound of the shattering glass still rang in his ears, the sight of Lexi's face crumpling in the cheap, twisted frame the only thing he could see. With no glass to protect her, no frame to hold her straight, no shiny gold metal to make her pretty, Lexi looked back at him as if he had punched her down then and there. He might as well have killed her and left her body lying on his living room floor for all the grief he felt.

Falling to his knees, Archer picked up the photo and ignored the small cut that bled when he brushed the glass against the wall with his bare hand. Sitting back on his heels he cupped the photograph in both hands. Lexi still smiled but her eyes looked through him, stoic in her acceptance of what he had become. There was a gash on her cheek where a shard of glass had cut through the color to the white paper beneath. The way the picture had crumpled and creased aged her.

Slowly Archer got to his feet, cradling the picture

in his hands. Ignoring the frame and glass at his feet he frantically tried to smooth the wrinkles, work the shreds of paper to cover the cut. It was useless. The more he tried, the more insistent was the thing welling inside him. It felt like a cry. It felt like something living. A huge thing that was growing and bringing with it a sense of doom. Archer wanted to be rid of that awful feeling, the premonition that his life had caught up with him. Maybe if he didn't look at Lexi, maybe he could put that feeling away, too.

Turning her face away, Archer wiped the photograph on the side of his hip, cleaning it up before he slipped it between two books on the shelf.

Better?

Not yet.

Carefully Archer tapped the picture in until he couldn't see even the edge of it anymore. He had made a little tomb, buried Lexi one more time, and this time it was easier. In a minute or an hour or a year Archer wouldn't even remember where he put it.

Better?

No, it was too soon. He knew Lexi was in there, damaged by his hand, exiled because of his fear, wedged between two books. In the dark. Alone. Archer put a hand on those books; then his head fell onto his hand and his lips moved. The words reverberated in his head and he hated himself for speaking them, thinking them, meaning them right at that moment.

"Damn you, Lexi. Damn that kid."

11

Ruth Alcott went back to college before her third marriage. She graduated law school in time to handle her own divorce from a husband who had settled neatly into a routine she found boring. Now fifty-four and independent, Ruth made just enough money to keep herself in elastic-waist pantsuits, sensible shoes and yearly trips abroad to check out medieval churches—the kind of adventure her third husband had despised.

Ruth Alcott was a deputy district attorney who had no illusions that she would ever actually amount to anything under the generally accepted guidelines for success. She would never be the district attorney—not enough media appeal. Private practice was out—not greedy enough. She would never marry again—too selfish. She was, however, a fine deputy because from nine to five, fifty weeks a year, Ruth Alcott was a rabid good guy. She believed that if the cops brought it to her, and there was the slightest appearance of cause, it was her duty to pursue that matter to the bitter end. For Ruth that end usually resulted in a conviction. Today Archer was the bad guy and Ruth was seated high on the white horse of justice. In fact, that horse was so high she couldn't seem to hear a thing Josie Bates was saying.

"Look, Ruth, you guys have been messing with Archer six ways from Sunday."

Josie stood up and planted her hands on Ruth's desk. She thought about swiping the desk clean to make Ruth sit up and take notice. Instead, she lowered her voice and picked up the pace of her argument.

"Using your own investigators to make the collar was bad enough, but it's been more than twenty-four hours and there hasn't been an arraignment. This whole thing stinks, Ruth."

"I don't remember that class in law school that said prosecutors had to lay out their case for the defense within twenty-four hours," Ruth said, unfazed by Josie's indignation. "Your client was advised of his rights. . . ."

"After your people ground his face into the street . . ." Josie objected.

"And he was told he was being booked for the murder of Timothy Wren, and he did not request an attorney. We followed procedures to the letter."

Ruth finished as if Josie had never spoken. Josie threw up her hands, simultaneously chancing a glance at Jude. He was sitting quietly, watching closely. Josie gave him credit. It seemed he could play well with others when it was called for.

"If I didn't know better, I'd think that you were helping John Cooper do an old friend a favor." Josie went after Ruth again. "Everyone and his brother knows that John's first job as a teenager was at Pacific Park. That little bit of folklore is standard media chatter when he's trying to pretend he's just a regular guy at election time. And it's no secret that Pacific Park reciprocates with a nice fat check every time he gives them the free publicity. So if this doesn't look like there's a whole hell of a lot of back-scratching going on, I don't know what does."

"That's good, Josie, but it won't fly, so don't try to get this office to recuse itself," Ruth clucked. "First off, John isn't prosecuting this case; I am. For the record, I never worked at Pacific Park. I couldn't fit into those cute little costumes even when I was sixteen."

"But John isn't keeping his distance. He spoke at the press conference," Josie pointed out. "He didn't give one good reason why my client's been arrested, much less charged. So either step back and apologize or you give me that one good reason right now."

Ruth, full of energy, happy to have this glorious work to do and someone to do it with, was in her element.

"No problem, Josie. I'll share one with you and your cohort. You are still with us, aren't you, Mr. Getts?"

"Most definitely," Jude answered, gracing Ruth with a truly magnificent smile.

"Excellent. Then I'll get to it," Ruth said, amused that he seemed to be trying to charm her.

Josie sat next to Jude and crossed her long legs. She cocked her elbow on the arm of her chair and put a finger to her lips as she watched Ruth. A cheap television set with a built-in VCR was propped on a stack of reference books on her credenza. A Starbucks coffee mug and a brown paper bag shared the space along with dog-eared files, souvenirs of Ruth's travels and two new case boxes. One was completely filled; the other was not.

Ruth took a videotape from one as if she were pulling a rabbit out of a hat. She put it in the machine and with a little flourish hit play, stepped back and gave her elastic-waist pants a snap for good measure.

The images were instantaneous, cued in anticipation of showing it.

Shot from a stationary security camera, the lens panned a wide angle of Pacific Park. The crawl of the San Diego Freeway could be seen in the distance. The San Bernardino Mountains were snow-tipped and sparkled brilliantly in the southern California fall. In the foreground was the Shock & Drop: a huge, hulking mass of steel columns and pulleys, levers and cogs, bright paint, grease and rust. Small platforms were attached three across to the outside of the structure. Neon bright. Happy, jarring colors. The kind of colors that would make a heart race just to look at them. Colors that would make children scream out for dibs.

Dibs on red. No, yellow. Blue. Blue! No worries. Pick one just for you.

The platforms were narrow: wide enough to accommodate all sizes of feet, small enough to feel precarious if you were the one standing atop them. Webbed safety harnesses were wrapped over the shoulders and strapped the rider tight to a backboard of what looked like Plexiglas. A huge medallion—the locking mechanism—lay on the middle of the rider's chest like a badge of courage. Pacific Park patrons reached up for handholds that forced the body into a rigid, upright position.

So fun. So safe. Something to hold on to. Something to stand on. Something to strap on. No worries.

Suddenly, there were people in the picture. Three teenage boys laughed and joked, hollering at each other. They scrolled through the screen in an excruciatingly slow crawl. Questions raced through Josie's mind. Who were they? Friends? Acquaintances? Strangers sharing only the anticipation of the ride? Did they have anything to do with the day Tim died?

How old were those boys? Sixteen? Seventeen? It didn't matter. This moment was long gone. They were older now. Tim Wren was not.

Far in the distance a plane glided into the frame and out again.

The gears of the Shock & Drop rotated.

The boys had been so joyous and, with that realization, Josie took note.

Something wasn't right. Something was missing.

Sound.

There was no sound. They were watching a silent movie. Josie blinked; her head jerked. Jude had touched her. One finger pressed against her arm, warning her not to give anything away to the opposition, not even an expression of curiosity. Josie moved away from him but took heed. Her expression was impassive as the boys on that platform were pulled out of the frame. Josie was left staring at the main track of the Shock & Drop—but not for long.

Suddenly the three boys shot past the camera. Their mouths were open, their jackets were flying and on their faces were expressions of abject terror. In that split second they learned a grown-up lesson: Life hung in a balance. Without the platform, the harness, the handholds, all was lost. The camera followed to a certain point and went no farther. The film hiccoughed. It ran another minute, maybe less. It would be important to know the split-second timing between the drop and the next riders, but Josie couldn't even formulate the question before the stars of the show appeared on the screen.

Archer staring straight ahead, looking ludicrously large. His barrel-chested body was held back by a crisscross of fabric; his huge hands dwarfed the safety holds. He was not having a good time.

Lexi in life. She was ill but still the kind of woman Josie would have been drawn to. No frills. Having a good time without being giddy. Wanting to share the moment. Too far away from Archer so she shared it with her boy.

Tim Wren was big in a way Archer wasn't. He was soft. He carried too much weight at his middle. Baby fat, muscles soft from lack of discipline. On his upper lip was the soft down of a young man's mustache. Puberty was upon him. Even on the tape she could sense his strength and his unpredictability, his damage. Tim would have been a good-looking boy if his features had not been rearranged by nature to reflect the defects of his body and mind.

His head moved in a slow wave pattern; his eyes were half closed. His lips were lax, not quite open, perhaps ready with a word but less able to form a sentence. His hands gripped the safety holds loosely, one arm slanted at an odd angle. His fingers jerked as if his grip were unsteady. Tim bent at the knees in a sequence that might have been meaningful to him or simply the irresistible reaction to the impulses of his poorly wired brain.

There was so much to see in him, so much to analyze, and yet the one thing Josie knew for sure was that Tim Wren was just a kid and Lexi loved him. It was there in the way she let go of her handholds to pat his arm, the way she looked at him and smiled, tipping her head, trying to make eye contact with her son. Josie saw Lexi mouth the words *I love you* as they were drawn heavenward together.

And then they were gone like the boys before them. The ascension was complete. The silence was deafening in Ruth Alcott's office. The air was close; Josie thought she might not be able to breathe. She reached for Jude's arm, barely aware she was doing so. He moved just enough to let her know that he was there, and before they made contact, Archer, Lexi and Tim shot back through the screen.

Three of them for a moment; then there were two.

Josie saw it. Jude saw it. Ruth Alcott had seen it before and was pleased with her little surprise. She rewound the tape with incredible precision and played it again. This time with a voice-over.

"Your man's hand was on the safety latch and then the kid fell," Ruth pointed out at the appropriate time, freezing the frame to underscore the point. "Want to see it again?"

"No."

Josie had seen enough. In the blink of an eye Archer's hand reached across Tim Wren. The boy's hands came down. Lexi's arm near Tim was thrown up in shock; the other was across her mouth. As the tape torturously tracked the descent of the platform, Archer looked down, his face expressionless. Lexi turned her head away; her eyes were screwed shut, her mouth clamped so that it pulled the lower half of her face into an awful look of unbearable pain. The camera tracked only so far. Josie shut her eyes. Her stomach turned and her heart bled for Lexi. There was nothing for that woman to do but wait to be delivered to where Tim lay dead.

Ruth turned off the video. There was a heartbeat of silence and then she was at it again.

"I have one of these for you. I figure you're going to want to watch it a couple of times and get creative on an explanation for the whole thing. You can have it checked out to make sure it wasn't tampered with but it's a waste of money. We already know it's the real deal." Ruth busied herself with the cardboard sleeve and then held it out to no one in particular. "Kind of hard to argue with something like this, don't you think?"

Jude remained still, waiting for Josie to speak. When she didn't, he looked and saw that Josie was pale, her body quaking; she was shaken to the core. Unaware of the dynamic, Ruth was gaining speed, delighted by the sound of her own voice.

"Eric Stevens, the ride operator, still works at the park. You'd think he would have quit after something so traumatizing. But he says since he didn't do anything wrong his conscience is clear. He also told us something very interesting. He tells us your client insisted on handling Tim's restraints himself. Stevens says no one before or since has ever insisted on doing that.

"Without the tape, of course, you could argue that Archer made a mistake while strapping Tim in. But with the tape, you can infer that he did something to make it easier to release the safety. It looks awfully suspicious, I'd say."

Ruth opened her hands, holding them to the sky in mock amazement, so darned pleased with herself.

"There could be a hundred reasons why Archer was reaching for that boy," Josie objected. Her voice was shredded on the edges but she was regrouping. "Archer could have noticed something was wrong and tried to help. That tape doesn't prove anything, and the fact that he assisted with the harness doesn't prove anything either—not without a motive."

Ruth chuckled and reminded her, "First off, Josie, he didn't assist with the harness; he took over the job. Second, as you well know, I am not bound to offer a motive."

"But you know you'd better produce one if we go to

a jury." Jude moved into the conversation smoothly, standing up so that he stood shoulder-to-shoulder with Josie. "The fact that Ms. Bates's client was reaching for the release doesn't mean he pulled it. Without motive I think you're going to have a very hard time convincing a jury that he intended to harm that mentally challenged boy. They won't want to believe it."

"They especially won't want to believe it of a man like Archer." Josie took up the argument. "There can't be a motive for something like this. Tim Wren was a thirteen-year-old boy and Archer was a seasoned cop. He never hurt anyone—not even the bad guys. Check his record."

"I have. And I know he was a man who had issues," Ruth answered cryptically. "As we all have issues, Josie. Just know that I have enough to prove reasonable cause in the prelim, and I'd bet my bottom dollar that in the end I've got enough to put your guy away for a good long time."

"Then I can't wait to see who you've been talking to, Ruth."

"I'll just bet you can't, but I'm not releasing my witness list to you."

"That's absurd." Josie bridled at Ruth's coy smile. "Release it or we'll be in court so fast you won't know what hit you. A judge will understand that I can't investigate without your witness list. My client has the right to know who's accusing him."

"Not if I am concerned about what might happen if I release that information," Ruth countered. "Your man is a trained investigator and he's not shy. If I give you contact information on my witnesses, I'm opening them up to possible intimidation."

Josie rolled her eyes. "Don't be ridiculous. Do you

think I'm going to send Archer out to break some legs? Please, this isn't the Mafia."

"I don't like to take chances," Ruth insisted.

"Great. If you want to make a fool of yourself, let's take this to a judge. You tell him you're afraid a retired cop with no priors is going to go on a rampage."

Ruth considered this. She put a finger against her lips, choosing her battle, ready to accept a draw in return for expediency.

"How's this? I'll release the names. No home phone or addresses before the preliminary hearing," Ruth offered. "Take it or leave it."

Josie and Jude looked at each other, their thoughts running on the same track. The only chance Josie would have to make this whole thing go away would be to challenge the defense witnesses during the preliminary hearing. In the long run, taking the list and running down the contact information was more efficient than actually trying to get a court date and an order to make Ruth release it.

"I want that list by tomorrow."

Josie put her card on Ruth Alcott's desk, turned on her heel and almost made it to the door before Ruth called her back.

"Didn't you forget something?"

Josie looked over her shoulder. In her hand Ruth Alcott held Josie's very own limited edition of a film she would rather not have seen.

Roger McEntyre drove like an old woman. He kept to the speed limit. He stopped behind the line at crosswalks. He used his turn signals so Archer knew well in advance which way he was going, and all the while McEntyre seemed oblivious to the fact that Archer was following him. A Hummer in your rearview mirror for more than a quarter mile should have been worth a look, but then Archer remembered who he was dealing with: a security guy, not a trained cop. Archer had to assume that once he left work, McEntyre left his vigilance behind.

Archer was wrong.

Ten seconds after McEntyre pulled into his garage and closed the door he was opening the passenger door of the Hummer. Archer hadn't seen him coming, couldn't figure out how Roger got to the street before he even killed the engine, and had to work hard to hide his surprise when McEntyre took a seat as though he were settling in for a friendly chat.

"You worked undercover." Archer figured he had failed to recognize a brother in blue.

"Special Forces. Two tours in the Gulf and then some," McEntyre said. "Next time you want to talk, make an appointment."

"Like you'd see me?"

"I'd have called our lawyers first. I'm a cautious man. Maybe you should follow suit. Next time bring the family car and maybe I won't make you if you want to spy on me. Following me in this thing makes me think I have to protect myself."

"From me? That's a laugh."

Archer shook his head as if the idea of it were too far-fetched even to consider. It was a poor ploy. McEntrye would not be charmed; nor would he be convinced by a change of tone, an unthreatening stance. Archer lifted his chin. He looked out the front window, thinking the interior of the car was getting warm. They were both big men. Archer was taller and broader, but McEntyre was pure muscle, younger by a few years. It was body heat he was feeling, and McEntyre's cool scrutiny was adding fuel to the fire.

"So now that you're here, what can I do for you?"

"I want to know what's going down. I need what you know."

Archer put his arm over the back of the seat, arranging himself so he could look straight at Roger McEntyre. It was like looking in a mirror. McEntyre's face gave away nothing, and Archer offered nothing to read in his own.

"I know that your friend Colin Wren stirred up a hornet's nest when he came after us and you got stung," Roger said. "Other than that, I can't help you."

"That's crap and you know it. Whatever the district attorney has you gave them, because you're the one who handled this mess from beginning to end," Archer scoffed, surprised that McEntyre wanted to play games.

"You forget, I got there after the kid died. I walked your wife through the paces, I made sure the body was transported and I got you in touch with our lawyers. But the beginning? I didn't see it. Maybe other people did, but not me."

"You debriefed your people, and I'd bet everything I've got that you're the only one who liaisoned with the DA. You said it yourself: you're cautious. You must have a good idea who they talked to and why they think I could have murdered that kid."

"And I can't give you that information even if I wanted to. The DA will work with your attorney, but I won't compromise my standing with the company." Roger's eyes never left Archer's. He seemed to take no pleasure in the other man's frustration; nor did he offer any sympathy for it. "You wouldn't do it if you were still a cop. Go home. Wren's got some deep pockets and he's willing to dig into them for you. Let the lawyers work it out. Other than that, I can't help."

Roger put his hand on the door latch. It clicked softly, then opened. The fresh air did nothing to ease the heat inside the Hummer. Archer made a move to reach for Roger. McEntyre reacted, snapping his arm into a defensive move, relaxing only when Archer backed off.

"I haven't got anything for you, my man," Roger said quietly. "Nothing except a piece of advice. Back off. Stay cool. You'll be okay."

"I don't need much. Point me in the right direction." Archer tried to negotiate, but there was a plea in his voice, and he could see McEntyre lost a notch of respect when he heard it. *Tough.* Archer would beg if he had to. "We are the same. Whatever you had to do, it was part of the job. I'm not asking you to lay it out. Just point the way so I can find out what I'm up against. What goes down here, stays here."

Roger considered this. He checked out Archer. The talk had been straight but it wasn't enough for him. He got out of the car, then, as if having second thoughts, turned back.

"Just tell the truth. That's the only thing you can do. Do you understand that? The only thing. Tell the truth and see how it washes."

With that, Roger McEntyre closed the door, showed his back to Archer and walked into the house that he shared with no one. He turned on the light in the living room, picked up the phone and walked to the window as he dialed directory assistance and asked for the number for Josie Baylor-Bates, attorney-at-law. The Hummer was still there. He couldn't see Archer through the tinted car windows but he knew the man inside was wounded and scared. He would be no trouble. Still, it didn't hurt to lock him down. When the operator came back on, Roger committed the number to memory and dialed without looking. He got an answering machine. Bates's voice wasn't the most provocative but there was a tone of intelligent confidence in it.

"This is Roger McEntyre, head of Pacific Park security. Your client has been to see me. I would suggest that he work through you if he has questions. No problem this time. There might be if it happens again."

Roger disconnected the call and stood where he was. Something had changed out there. McEntyre's battle senses were honed; his antennae were up. He could feel Archer looking at the house. He could feel Archer vibrating with a need to act. His wounds were closing over as he got strong with a second wind. Even from this distance Roger understood what was happening because, if it were him, he would be doing the same thing. But he wasn't out there feeling his way in the dark and he wasn't the one who had to watch his step, so Roger McEntyre forgot about Archer. He went to the window and drew the drapes.

He had done everything he could do and then some.

12

"Are you okay?" Jude asked.

"I'm dandy. Why?" Josie snapped.

"I thought maybe you were walking so fast because you were upset." Jude pulled up short and Josie shot ahead. Finally she slowed to a standstill and waited for him to catch up.

"It's bullshit. You know that, don't you?" The minute Jude came alongside, Josie pivoted and picked up speed again.

"Do I?"

"Of course you do. That tape is so damn bogus it's not even funny. Archer couldn't have done anything to that boy. You paid his bail. You should know. You should—"

Jude sprinted, grabbed Josie's arm and twirled her toward him. He was strong and he wasn't grinning anymore.

"Josie, I don't know anything about Archer. Colin paid his bail. He expects a return on investment. It was a business deal, remember? We wanted to keep the criminal fuss to a minimum. Remember?"

His dark eyes searched her face. He saw the trembling at the edge of her mouth, the hot tears in her eyes. That was when he finally got it.

"Oh, God. Archer's not just a client, is he?" Jude chuckled humorlessly and let her go. "Well, that's just great."

"What's that supposed to mean? Don't you think I
know the difference between personal bias and appropriate advocacy?"

"Oh, please. Intellectually you know it all. Emotion-
ally, you're going to handle this differently because
you're personally involved. I dare you to deny it."

"Okay, I deny it." Josie pushed past him, but Jude
stayed close like he had her on a leash.

"Hey, hey. I'm not saying you're incompetent. I'm
just saying this is a whole new ball game and I don't
know if you can play first string. You haven't even
thought about the pressure this is going to put on you
or Archer, have you? You haven't even given yourself
a minute to work this through. You've just been a bull
in a china shop because you're too scared to analyze
the situation, and that's plain stupid."

"Screw you, Jude. Just screw you," Josie hollered
just as she reached Jude's car and threw herself at
the door.

She pulled at the handle. She yanked and grunted.
It was locked. She pulled harder, and when that didn't
make a difference Josie slammed her hand on the roof
of the car and bowed her head as Jude went around
the other way.

"It's all I've thought about, okay? I don't expect
you to understand. This isn't a game where the one
with the most tricks wins. Maybe you should think
about the fact that I'm responsible for Archer's life,
and you"—Josie raised her head and glared at him—
"you're just talking about money, you prick."

Josie's insult echoed through the subterranean garage, and it proved Jude's point. Those emotions he
was so worried about were showing like a red slip
under a black dress. Rolling away from him Josie
crossed her arms and put her backside up against the

car. Jude thought for a minute and then took pity on her.

"Okay. Okay." He sighed. "I'm sorry I had to push you, but we've got to get to the truth."

"Or skirt around it," Josie mumbled.

"Yes. Sometimes we do that even when we know the truth." Jude propped an elbow on the roof of the car. "We're advocates. Our job is to win, and sometimes that's tough if your client or your cause means something to you."

"It's supposed to be about justice when people's lives are at stake," she said.

"And where money is at stake, too," Jude reminded her. "Justice is justice, Josie."

"It's different when it's money."

"No, it's not. Someone wins and someone loses and someone's life is changed even if it's about money. And if you're blinded by your emotions you lose your objectivity, and that's the worst thing an attorney can do. If you lose that, you might try to hide a piece of evidence, you might push it aside because you know it will be bad for your client. Josie, there's a reason doctors don't operate on their relatives. Get it?"

Josie's head fell back. She listened but didn't hear. Above her was the ceiling of the garage. But it was also the floor of a building. The floor held up a structure that housed hundreds of people; the ceiling protected the cars below. If the floor gave way, the ceiling caved in. If the ceiling cracked the floor did, too. It didn't matter which was at fault; the result was the same: People died, cars were destroyed, a building was brought down. Above her, then, was the epitome of that proverbial fine line. According to Jude, lawyers walked that fine line every day whether or not they acknowledged it.

Lawyers didn't ask if they were protecting the guilty or fighting for the innocent. Lawyers tried their cases, took pleasure in the twists and turns of the law and then went on to the next challenge. They paid little attention to the building in which they dwelled because it was designed by others. Lawyers didn't make the law; politicians did. The people did with their votes. Justice was perception, and each man perceived it differently. It didn't matter if Archer was innocent or guilty; the system only wanted someone to make the decision, and all Josie had to do was make her case. But there was something weighing on the legal system's fine line, and that weight was Josie's feelings. Those feelings could create just enough pressure to crack the floor, to cave the ceiling, when there was no other reason it should collapse.

"Do you think that's wrong?" Josie finally asked. "I mean, am I wrong if I don't try to figure out whether Archer is guilty?"

"How should I know?" Jude's incredulous laugh sounded harsh. "We can't ever be one hundred percent sure about our clients, but we'd better work like we are. I mean, what if we're wrong? What if we judge them and find out we were wrong? I'd rather err doing my best to win than find out I've failed someone who truly deserved my help. And my best is pretty good. I'm looking at a ninety percent win rate. I'd say my bases are covered."

Jude smiled, he teased, he wanted Josie back so they could get to work.

"I would have expected a higher percentage," she muttered.

"I'm not perfect." Jude grinned.

"I'll quote you on that."

"So? What about it? Are you okay with this case?

With that?" Jude nodded to the tape she still held in her hand.

"Any good defense attorney can make mincemeat of this tape." Josie put it in her purse. "And I'm a good defense attorney."

"Yeah, but what kind of woman are you?" Jude asked. "Are you going to turn out the light when this is all over and wonder if Archer could have killed that kid, or are you going to pack the doubts up when this is over?"

"All you need to know is that I'm not going to let this get past the prelim. So I would suggest you do your homework, Jude. You're up next. You and Colin and a shot at all that money."

Jude cocked his head. He pushed a button and released the locks with a mechanical chirp. Josie opened the door and got in. They caught the traffic on the 10 freeway but didn't spend the time getting to know each other any better. Josie was busy trying to rip off that psychic sleeve where she had so brazenly worn her heart and her insecurities. She did a pretty good job by the time they arrived in Brentwood. When Jude dropped her at the Jeep, he only had one thing to say: "Clear your calendar tomorrow. There's someone you have to meet."

"I don't have to do anything." Josie swung her legs outside the car and dragged her briefcase behind her. Jude leaned across the passenger seat she had just vacated. He looked up at her, eyes bright, so annoyingly sure of himself Josie could hardly stand it.

"You're right. But if you decide to go this alone, I swear I'll roll right over you if I think it's in Colin's best interest."

He gave her a name, an address, waited for her to close the door, and then he hit the gas without looking back. Jude Getts disappeared into the subterranean garage of his Brentwood building. The Jeep had been valeted. Josie paid the fee, noted the information Jude had given her and, as soon as she had her car, headed home. She took surface streets all the way to Hermosa. It was a long drive, and the notion that the videotape in her purse was the real deal dogged her all the way.

When Josie got home, as she walked to the front door and let herself in, when she petted Max and saw that Archer was sitting on the patio waiting for her, the thought that the tape was big trouble didn't go as far away as Josie would have liked.

13

"Can I be excused?"

Hannah asked permission of Josie, Josie looked at Archer and Archer didn't bother to acknowledge either of them. It had been an uncomfortable dinner and, from the looks of Archer and Hannah, refusing permission for Hannah to bolt wouldn't make it any more pleasant.

"Sure. Go ahead."

"She should do the dishes. At least clear the table," Archer complained as soon as Hannah was gone. It was a picky, suburban, married kind of comment, and it made Josie testy.

"I don't think who clears the table is high on the list of things I worry about these days, Archer." Josie fingered the bowl of her wineglass, picked it up and finished what was left. Trying to be patient she offered Archer a closed-lip smile. "Are you feeling better?"

"Aspirin's helping with the swelling." Archer's answer was accompanied by a shrug. "Work will take my mind off all this. I've put in calls to a couple of buddies of mine. They're going to get me my arrest report and Tim's accident report. I need to refresh my memory about that day. It's been a long time and I—"

"Okay, Archer." Josie shoved her wineglass away and crossed her arms on the table. "Haven't you already screwed up enough by going to see Roger

McEntyre? What was that? Following him, for Christ's sake. Archer, he could have brought charges."

"But he didn't," Archer objected sharply before retreating reluctantly. "Look, I'm sorry. It was stupid. I just did it. I waited for him outside his office; I couldn't think of what to say to him and he got away before I could figure it out. I just followed . . . and . . ."

Half listening as Archer tried to rationalize his behavior, Josie reached for the wine and refilled her glass even though it was the last thing she wanted. Archer stuck with beer, and he twirled the bottle like he was trying to dig a hole in the table. Hannah was big on water and light on food these days. Josie would have to talk to her about that when all this blew over. For now, she would talk to Archer, and it didn't matter that she cut him off midsentence. If she didn't control him now there would be no controlling him.

"Why didn't Lexi file a wrongful death suit, Archer?"

"What purpose would it have served?" A question posed to a question bought time—a trick of someone with something to hide—and Josie knew enough to nip that in the bud.

"Let's not get philosophical," she countered. "You and Lexi knew a hundred lawyers who would have handled a wrongful-death suit for you. Why not let one of them file?"

Archer lifted his beer, took a long pull. The refrigerator hummed and twitched. Max slept, snoring, yelping once as he dreamed of something urgent. Outside, they heard voices. Archer cocked his head as if waiting for the people to pass before he confided in Josie. Josie waited. They were pretending to talk; both knew this was an interrogation.

"What good would it do to have a lawyer sucking the life out of her for thirty-three percent when cancer was doing such a good job of it?"

It was a good question, and Archer didn't notice Josie flinch at his disparaging remark. He didn't really notice Josie at all. He was thinking about Lexi and decisions and death.

"Nope, Jo, a couple of continuances, Lexi would be dead and I wouldn't have any standing. Tim wasn't my kid. Nobody was going to touch that kind of action. Does that answer your question?"

Archer's eyes slid toward her. In the dim light his bruised face looked evil. Josie wondered what she would hear if she didn't fill the quiet. What she heard was Archer speculating.

"Is that what they're saying, Jo? Are they saying I killed Tim because I thought I was going to share in some big payday?" Archer let his head roll to the side. He let out a sound that seemed like a laugh, a moan, an utterance of disbelief all in one. "Christ. That's a damned stupid motive."

His sigh of disgust pulled out like taffy until it was so thin Josie hardly heard it anymore. She dropped her eyes. Archer swept the bottle of beer up again and found it empty. He let it dangle from his fingers. The kitchen clock ticked. Music came from Hannah's room—something dark—drums that put an irregular heartbeat into the house.

"You know, Jo, maybe Tim's accident was a blessing. With him gone Lexi could deal with her own dying." Archer put a big hand over his eyes and drew it down his face as if that gesture helped him come to grips with the past. "Lexi wouldn't have survived as long as she did if she'd had to worry about what was going to happen to Tim. She needed her strength.

Maybe it wasn't a bad thing that he died. Not a bad thing . . . in the end."

Josie's stomach turned. No matter how much Archer valued Lexi's life, to say Tim's death was a blessing—even to Josie—was incautious at best and damning at worst. She pushed back her chair and stood abruptly. She stacked the dinner plates, keeping her head turned away so Archer couldn't see the stain of doubt in her eyes. In the kitchen Josie put her hand on the faucet and said, "Don't say that ever again, Archer. Not to me. Not to anyone."

Josie rinsed the dishes and put them aside, only to stop halfway through her chore. Her hands cupped the lip of the sink. She hung her head and hunched her shoulders. That tape was an albatross around her neck; Archer's comments were tightening the noose that held it.

Suddenly Archer's arms were around her waist. He pulled her close. Josie wasn't sure she wanted that, but she also knew she was powerless against him. Instinctively Josie leaned against him, her hands covering his. It still felt so right.

"We'll be okay." Archer buried his lips in the small space behind her ear. His chest rose and fell against her back. Archer was steady as an innocent man would be. She believed in him, but it was easy to doubt. His lips moved to her brow and back to the fringe of hair near her ear. "Once we hear what the DA has I'll call in every marker I've got. I'll make this go away. I promise, Jo."

Josie turned in his arms. She put her hands flat on his chest. It was enough to make him back off. Josie's life hadn't been easy. Archer had fought through a couple of hells himself, so she didn't believe all would be well just because Archer said it would be. Life didn't work that way. Not for people like them.

"Save the markers, Archer. You're not going to be tracking down anything."

"That doesn't seem too smart, Josie," Archer said quietly. "This is what I was trained to do. I promise I won't screw around. No more tailing anyone, no more confrontation. Straight-out questions, Jo. Aboveboard investigation."

Josie slipped away. Curious, Archer followed her into the living room. She reached for her purse, holding it close before she pulled out the video.

"You can't chase down what they've already got. The DA doesn't want you intimidating witnesses and, if McEntyre chooses, he can make a whole lot of trouble for us by filing a harassment complaint. Jesus, Archer, if you had just waited for me to come home before you pulled a stunt like that I could have told you it was dangerous to try to run down witnesses."

"Fucking A, Jo. What witnesses? To what crime? There was no crime." Archer threw up his hands. Their quiet time was gone. Their rope bridge was swaying under their feet and only Josie saw that it was already beginning to unravel.

"There is a list of them, Archer." Josie hunkered down and slipped the tape into the deck. Her fingers hovered above the button. She spoke just before she pushed it. "You're in a whole lot more trouble than you know."

The show started. The light from the television illuminated Josie's face but not the corner where Archer stood watching. Slowly he came forward, close enough now that she could have leaned back against his legs. She heard him catch his breath as he saw Lexi. Another intake as Tim fell.

"Again," Archer whispered when it was over.

"Archer, you don't have to—"

"I said play it again. I want to see it again," Archer commanded.

Josie replayed the tape. This time she didn't watch. Instead she looked over her shoulder and up at Archer. His eyes glittered; his body was rigid. When he spoke his lips barely moved.

"They're going to use that piece of shit against me?"

"The ride operator says you put Tim into his harness." Josie looked up at him. "Did you, Archer?"

"Yes. I did. And if anyone bothered to ask me I would have told them that Tim was strong as an ox and big for his age. He could be belligerent and impatient and dangerous when he thrashed around. I wasn't going to trust some kid with Tim. I was doing the right thing, and you're telling me that operator said I sabotaged the damn harness?"

Josie stood up, eye-to-eye with Archer.

"Calm down," she ordered. "I won't know until I talk to him. Luckily he won't be too hard to find, since he still works at Pacific Park. At least I got that much out of Ruth Alcott."

"Well, we'll just get a whole lot more from that lying little sack of—"

Archer stopped short. Josie looked at him quizzically and then she felt it, too. There was a vibe in the dark room. They weren't alone. Both of them turned and both of them saw Hannah. A shadowy slip of a girl whose presence was invasive, whose existence they had forgotten. The look she gave Archer trailed suspicion and anger with it. When her eyes moved to Josie questions and curiosity came along.

"I needed some help with my English." It was a request that shut out Archer.

"Okay." Josie busied herself, ejecting the tape, getting up and turning on the light near the couch. She wondered how much Hannah had seen.

"I'm going." Archer hesitated as he drew alongside Josie. "And I am going to help. My life, my case, babe."

"No, Archer. Your problem, my case," Josie answered evenly. She included Hannah in the next sentence. They were a family—they were supposed to be a family. "You can help by getting Hannah to school in the morning. You can keep track of the information the DA is going to drop on my doorstep. That's how high your profile is going to be on this thing."

Archer glanced at Hannah and back to Josie, clearly unhappy but equally clear that he wasn't going to spend any time arguing about it in front of the girl who cut into his time. She wasn't a part of them, and Archer would never let her be.

"Right." The word seeped out through his swollen lip. "I'll pick her up at seven thirty."

The door closed behind him but Josie and Hannah weren't really alone. Archer's antagonism and bitterness lingered.

"It isn't you, Hannah. It's the whole situation," Josie explained, but neither of them believed it.

In a split second Hannah was out the door. Josie followed, hovering near the gate when she saw Hannah had caught up with Archer fifty yards down. They were bathed in the yellow light of the city fixture. Hannah had hold of Archer's arm with one hand. Her face was tipped up; the breeze pushed her long curls in her face and she pushed them back with her free hand. They were too far for Josie to hear what Hannah was saying but she could see that Archer was listening. When she was finished, Hannah stepped back and, without a word, Archer continued on his way.

Gratitude tugged at her heart as Hannah strolled back, oblivious to Josie's scrutiny. Her fingers tapped the top of the low wall Josie had built around her house. Tapping twenty times, indulging herself in her counting, thinking she was alone until she was brought up short by the sight of Josie. They considered each other. Josie smiled.

"Thanks for whatever you said to Archer," Josie said.

One finger tapped against the stucco wall. Hannah's head was doing that cocky thing that warns adults to back off because they may not want to hear what's coming next. But Josie couldn't read the signal. She was too new at the mother thing.

"I was just telling him he didn't have to pick me up in the morning. I'm going to walk to school." There was a split second before she finished cruelly, the way teenagers can. "I didn't want to be in a car with him just in case he could have killed a boy who couldn't defend himself."

The edges of Hannah's lips twitched; her eyes were unreadable. When she had given Josie enough time, when she found Josie's confusion annoying, Hannah went past her. The perfume of youth trailed her and suddenly Josie felt old without being wise. Hannah turned around at the front door, giving Josie one more chance to demand an apology or an explanation. When it didn't come Hannah put a hand on her hip, pressed her luck and dared Josie to get in her face, choose Archer over her.

"Are you still going to help me with my homework?"

14

Very few things surprised Josie Baylor-Bates. To be precise, there were very few things Josie reacted to with surprise. Bad news, strange things, coincidences, accidents—she seemed to take these all in stride. Even accepting responsibility for Hannah had been handled matter-of-factly. It was understandable that Josie believed the cure for her empty heart was in proving that she was nothing like her mother, that she was as capable as her father.

That unflappable sense of what was right and wrong drew people to Josie. But the exception to the rule of Josie's composure was Wilson Page. Josie was honestly surprised when she saw him.

Josie had seen fat, she had seen portly and she had seen big-boned. Josie had even seen obese, but she had never seen anything like Wilson Page. A good five inches shorter than Josie, he carried four hundred pounds on a frame put together like an Erector Set. Wilson was made up of right angles, blocks upon bulges. Legs, torso, arms, neck and head. His range of motion was limited to up and down. *Around* didn't seem to register with Wilson Page's joints. The hand that grasped Josie's was like a baseball mitt. Josie, who could palm a volleyball, felt almost childlike as he closed his fingers around hers. He spoke with a sharp intake of breath every third word.

"How are you?"

Breathe.

"Nice to meetcha."

Breathe.

"Have a seat."

Breathe.

"Over there. No . . ."

Breathe, breathe.

". . . there."

He directed Josie to a couch and then a chair and finally settled her back on the couch with a flick of a sausagelike finger. There Josie sank into a very distinct pothole in the upholstery. Wilson, it seemed, had a preference when he sat on the couch because Jude, watching with amusement, sat a good three inches higher than Josie.

Wilson settled in a huge chair, custom-made so that it kept him at the proper angle to maximize his breathing. Still the top half of him pushed down on the bottom half until, neck to groin, he was an accordion roll of flesh. His massive torso filled up the chair; his legs stuck out straight on a footrest.

"So." Wilson's voice was exceedingly pleasant, his delivery smooth now that he did not have to move. "Jude, whatcha say? Time to tell the tale? I mean, you want me to tell, right? This is a lady who's interested in Pacific Park, right?"

Jude smiled at Wilson the way an old friend does, a friend who sees past the obvious, finding something inside Wilson Page to admire. Josie found that expression far more attractive than Jude's blinding grin.

"Jump in, Wilson. Josie? You all here?"

"Yeah, sorry. I was just . . . daydreaming."

"That's all right." Wilson chuckled. "We know what

you were doing. You were trying to figure this out, weren't you? Jude and me. Beauty and the Beast. Jabba the Hut and Han Solo, Orson Welles and—''

"Oh, God, Wilson. Please." Jude groaned. "Enough."

Josie watched, she listened, she wondered what secrets lay buried behind Jude's pretty face and winning ways, she wondered how they matched the maze of hurt encased in Wilson's massive body. She had felt their closeness the minute she walked through the door, and she felt something else, too—a whiff of loving resentment. Josie just couldn't tell if it came from Wilson or Jude.

"Okay, I'm curious. I doubt you two play racquetball at the club," Josie said.

Wilson laughed and said, "That's a good one," before he told his story with relish.

"Jude's hard drive went down the night before a big case. Meant a ton of money to you, didn't it, Jude?"

Breathe.

"So Jude starts calling around at two in the morning trying to find someplace that will fix the thing because all his exhibits are on it. He gets me . . ."

Breathe.

". . . I tell him I'll fix it. He's talking, trying to cut a deal on the cost like he thinks I'm not going to be honest, and I tell him it will cost what it costs. So he brings it right over here. Poor Jude. I thought he'd pass out when he saw me. He's holding his computer like he's afraid to give it to me. Maybe he thought I'd eat it and him, too. . . ."

Breathe. Chuckle. *Breathe.*

"Come on, Wilson," Jude said affectionately. "Everyone is surprised when they first meet you. That computer had sensitive information on it, and the way you work does not exactly inspire confidence. I mean, look at this place."

Wilson's big head lolled in agreement. This time the breath was drawn through his nose.

"Point well taken, Jude. To make a long story short, he gave me the computer. I recovered the files on the hard drive and, in the process, found it had been tampered with. Someone on his staff did not hold Jude in high esteem and had tried to ruin Jude's very hard work."

"To make a long story even shorter, that person was let go and Wilson and I became friends," Jude cut in. "Now, can we please get to the matter at hand?"

"But"—Wilson held up his hand as if to request a point of clarification—"we didn't become real friends until Jude got the bill. He was so impressed I didn't take advantage on the back end that he put me on retainer. It's been good years with you, Jude. Nobody finer, Ms. Bates. I don't care what anyone says about this plaintiff's attorney. He's the finest man. Whenever I need anything he . . ."

Breathe.

"And if you don't stop Wilson he'll talk your ear off. Time is money, Wilson."

Jude cut in quickly. Josie saw the color rising in Jude's cheeks. Could it be she was seeing the soft underbelly of a shark? Fascinating that it should show itself for this lump of a man. The science of attraction, friendship and affection was mysterious. Josie thought of Archer and missed him and loved him. Then she forgot him. Time was short. Jude was anxious and Wilson felt it.

"Fine. Fine. Well, enough of that. On to bigger and more important things." Wilson licked his lips, then

drew three fingers over them as if adjusting his mouth
so the words would come out right. Finally he folded
his hands together and rested them on his massive
belly. "Don't you worry, Ms. Bates. I'm not going to
let those people railroad your client."

"Wilson has issues with Pacific Park. Little did I
know that would come in handy someday," Jude informed her.

"It wasn't always that way, though. I loved Pacific
Park at one time because it was so different from all
those corporate monstrosities. Pacific Park was user-
friendly, or it was until they decided they didn't like
me anymore. You see, I was large as a child. Then I
got to be bigger, and when I was eighteen—it was
eighteen, right, Jude?"

"That's what you told me, my man." Jude nodded
comfortably. "Eighteen."

"Yes . . . that was . . . let's see . . ." Wilson put
one huge finger to the place in his face where his chin
should be. "That was, oh, now, six years and two
months ago. I could tell you how many hours and
minutes if you want, but I don't think it's relevant.
Jude?"

Jude shook his head. That was all it took for Wilson
to move on.

"Well, anyway . . ." *Breath.* ". . . okay. So you don't
need the absolute specifics. Just generalities. You want
me to get to the point. Okay."

This time two deep ones that sounded shallow, like
they never quite made it to the bottom lobes of his
lungs. Josie tried not to look worried, since Jude
looked concerned enough for both of them.

"I used to go to the park two, three times a week,"
he said, smiling with the memories. "Wonderful to get
out, get some fresh air, some exercise. Walking from

ride to ride is good exercise for a big man like me. Even standing in line burns calories when you carry some extra weight."

"Wilson, can you fast-forward a little?" Jude prodded gently, and sidestepped the obvious understatement.

"Sure, Jude. Sure. No problem. Went to the park. To the park," Wilson whispered, sucking a bit of oxygen through his teeth as he tried to find his place. When he got it his small bright eyes focused on Josie. "I was there one very nice day. I stood in line forty-seven minutes and thirty-two seconds before it was my turn for the Hanging Glide. I'd been there all day and been on all the rides except the Hanging Glide."

Deep breath.

"Well, the ride operator insisted the Hanging Glide would not hold me, but she was wrong. I knew the weight capacity of every attraction in that place. The Hanging Glide handles a maximum weight of three hundred and sixty-three pounds. At the time, I was three hundred and fifty-eight and three-quarters of a pound. I explained that to the operator. . . ."

Breath. Breath. Breath.

"Wilson went to Cal Tech when he was fourteen. He knows whereof he speaks."

Jude slipped that little bit of information into the conversation, covering for Wilson until he could go on.

"Thank you, Jude. I do, as you say, know my stuff." Wilson inclined his head graciously. "Always have. And I had made it my very serious hobby to catalog and understand each and every thrill ride at the park. I understood the engineering limitations, minimum and maximum safety parameters regarding weight, height, G-force stress. There was absolutely no danger to me or other riders if I were to be strapped into the

Hanging Glide. Not to mention the fact that it was illegal for her to refuse me if she did not weigh me. There were no public warnings, no signs that indicated the ride operator had that discretion based on her unqualified assessment of my weight. There was, of course, proper and legal signage that indicated service could be refused based on height. You see, height is a completely different matter from weight, as evidenced by the warnings. . . ."

"Wilson," Jude warned.

"Yes, of course. Back on track, Jude," Wilson agreed. He took a moment. "There were the natural warnings for pregnant women, people with heart trouble, et cetera, et cetera, so on and so forth."

Wilson waved that fascinating hand of his. It seemed to move independently of his arm. He was a resting Buddha, the Cheshire Cat sitting lazily in a tree.

"But weight? No, no. There was no notice of that, and I would have respected it if there were a sign or some such. I assured the operator—who was one of those perfectly darling little girls with blond hair who looked very cute in her uniform but had the IQ of a hot dog"—*breathe*—"that I was willing to assume the risk. I also assured her that the hydraulic harness's design was beyond compare and would hold me quite securely and I would not fall at her feet and splat like a large water balloon if she would just let me on the ride."

Wilson's voice rose to a soprano pitch as he recounted that horrible day. There was that hand again. This time it was at his chest.

"I assume she didn't let you on," Josie suggested quietly, hoping to calm him. Wilson blinked. It seemed he had forgotten his guests as he relived the moment of his mortification.

"No, indeed, she did not, Ms. Bates. I was very unhappy." Wilson breathed deeply again. His eyes glittered. Not with malice but, rather, Josie thought, with tears. It was hard to tell, since they were so deeply set in that huge, kind face. "In fact, I was sad, and true sadness is a terrible emotion. But there was more humiliation to come. That little wiener-brained girl called security." This time the intake of breath was punctuated with amazement. "They were going to 'escort' me from the park, but what they did was worse. They expelled me in a most degrading way. I don't know what that little cheerleader told them, but I can imagine. Her excited utterances probably ran along the lines of a really, really fat guy was giving her trouble and they'd better send storm troopers to get him. I doubt she had the vocabulary to go any deeper than that. I've told you, Jude, how humiliating that was, haven't I? They sent four men. Four!"

Wilson's head rotated to Jude and they shared a moment of commiseration. Wilson's nostrils flared. He reached up and touched the corner of his eyes. Wilson Page sighed and talked to the floor beneath Josie's shoes.

"I understand that I am not the norm. I understand that people might feel uncomfortable around me. But to be treated as if I were a threat when all I was trying to do was educate the young woman, to take responsibility for my own actions, was beyond shame. It was degradation. I could not let it pass."

This was followed by gentle breaths, as if he were sucking in his sadness and somehow it would be digested by his heart, sent away as waste, forgotten. Suddenly Wilson looked up and smiled. He tried to raise an eyebrow but succeeded only in moving the folds of his face. "Oh, I haven't offered you refreshment. I have soda. Some cake? Would you like some soda or cake?"

"No, thanks," Jude said as he cocked one leg up on the couch, one arm on the back so he could talk to Josie. "Basically, Josie, Wilson doesn't take such treatment lying down."

"So to speak," Wilson added with a chuckle. "Actually, I never lie down. I recline in this custom-made chair that Jude—"

"I don't think you know Josie well enough to get that personal, Wilson." Jude laughed and the big man chuckled back, the sounds of it riding the wave of Jude's segue.

"Anyway, when Wilson feels that he's been treated unfairly he educates others through the Internet. In this instance, Wilson has a Web site that investigates and makes public the failings of Pacific Park."

"This is not done with spite, Ms. Bates," Wilson broke in with his qualification, but then amended that. "Well, there was just the smallest bit of spite in the beginning. But I will tell you that I have never fabricated any of the information that I make public. What started as a simple Web page to air my grievance and explain the engineering facts to ordinary people suddenly became a much bigger project than even I had imagined. I found hundreds of people who did not find Pacific Park the joyous experience they had anticipated."

"Wilson, you should point out that most of the problems you've uncovered are trivial," Jude reminded him.

"Oh, yes, to be fair, Jude," Wilson huffed. "You know, the basic items: food that was cold, drinks that were warm, long waits in the lines—what did they expect?—problems with the aesthetics of the place.

Those gripes were of little consequence to me. But there were other things. Bad things. Injuries. Negligence. Those things people should know about."

Wilson raised one foot slightly as he tried to adjust his weight on the chair.

"I monitor bloggers, I infiltrate the ranks of the employees and find those who have complaints against the company, suppliers who aren't happy, and I follow up on rumors. I promise, everything I make public has been checked out in excruciating detail and back and forward again. Truly, Ms. Bates, I quite simply do not lie. I live for facts, and those are the facts."

"That's good, Wilson, because that's what I'm looking for, too," Josie assured him.

"Excellent." Wilson beamed.

Jude rearranged himself so he could plant his feet on the ground and his elbows on his knees and said, "Now, can we look at what you've got, Wilson? I know Josie is going to like it."

Wilson gave a grin, and even Jude's could not hold a candle to it. Josie smiled and they began in earnest.

"Well, then, here it is. Pacific Park's problems have not been limited to two fatalities in recent years. Jude?"

Jude reached behind the couch and retrieved some papers from a bookshelf. He handed one to Josie.

"When Mr. Wren came to Jude for help, I began my research. What you have there is a list of every single accident over the last twenty-four months. You'll note that there were two serious accidents that resulted in broken bones and another that sent a young girl to a plastic surgeon for lacerations on the face and upper body as well as a sizable crack in her skull. She's recuperating after brain surgery."

Breath.

"One of the accidents was the result of an outright mechanical problem. The other two are being investigated, and there is a difference of opinion as to whether the rider caused the difficulty or it was caused by a mechanical failure."

Wilson seemed to choke. Jude tensed and watched his friend critically, determined Wilson would be all right and waited out Wilson's spasm. When it was over Wilson cleared his throat and went on after a quick "Sorry about that."

"Four other accidents have resulted in lawsuits. Two were due to improperly made repairs. On top of that, there were fifteen near misses that were a result of operator error, poor maintenance or cost-cutting maneuvers.

"Of the two fatalities, the most recent appears to have been caused by the rider. In the case of Timothy Wren, the records simply list his death as accidental and assign no blame."

Wilson was finished for the moment. He breathed rhythmically through his nose, adding a lung filler every now and again as Josie studied the report. Times, dates, specifics on the injuries, ages of those injured, phone numbers and addresses. Many of the victims were children. In those cases, Wilson had listed their parents or guardians, their prognosis and, every once in a while, character studies of the children and speculation on their culpability in the accident.

"This is great stuff," Josie murmured, then put the paper aside. "But if all this has happened in the last two years—plus the two fatalities—then why hasn't there been more press attention?"

"Two reasons," Jude answered. "First, you probably didn't pay any attention to the coverage. If there were shark attacks on surfers in Hermosa Beach you'd be all over it, but I'd guess it's been a while since you've been to a theme park. People pay attention to what's in their sphere of interest."

Josie inclined her head. "Point well taken."

"The other reason is that Pacific Park isn't a news maker," Wilson explained, rested now and anxious to be a part of the conversation. "California has a plethora of choices for those of us who are avowed theme-park rats: Knott's Berry Farm, Magic Mountain and, naturally, the eight-hundred-pound gorilla, Disneyland. It's sexier to report on accidents that happen in any one of those places. Pacific Park is the oldest, just not as sexy. It's got a loyal following but attendance is not on the same level as the others, nor are the attractions quite so cutting-edge."

"So you're saying the press just didn't cover these accidents?"

"Public relations works two ways, Ms. Bates," Wilson cautioned. "I'm saying Pacific Park did a good job of keeping their problems quiet. But when someone dies the press takes notice. Tim Wren's death was reported; it just didn't have legs. There was no lawsuit. The mother wouldn't talk to the media. But everybody's fighting about the second death. The victim's family wants a lot of money. Since the general public has an insatiable appetite for death or dismemberment, Tim Wren's death was brought back as a sidebar. It made the current story more ghoulish, sold more papers, got better ratings for the broadcast media."

Wilson shrugged as if to say such was the way of the world, and his breathing took on a little flutter of regret.

"But what do we learn from all this? We learn that there are problems at Pacific Park. Looking further into the situation we can infer that the problems can be traced back to the age of their equipment. Maintenance keeps it nicely painted, but Pacific Park buys a lot of their equipment secondhand and refurbishes it. Much of it, anyway."

"You mean their equipment is second-rate?" Josie asked incredulously.

"No, no, no." Wilson waved his large hand again, a gesture that was quickly becoming a barometer of how he felt. He was winding down, but he was hanging in there. "Good stuff, but previously owned. Already used up when it comes to the depreciation schedule. The old man, Isaac Hawkins, he makes sure all those rides are maintained. He's very strict about that. What he doesn't understand is that you can't maintain good enough to account for metal fatigue, wear and tear, ancient designs—yes, the flaws could be in the designs, not the actual working parts. I have to wonder if Isaac considers that, given the number of mechanical failures on that schedule I gave you."

"Okay. Great. Thanks. This is something to work with. More than I ever expected." Josie included Jude in her gratitude. "What about their payout? All of these incidents may not have gone to court, but money changed hands."

"Sure. They had money to burn for a while. Overhead isn't as high as it is on a park that reinvents itself every season," Jude explained. "Pacific Park isn't producing movies and tying in advertising. There are no retail stores, books or videos so they have more of a war chest than most. They settled appropriately and they stayed out of court."

"But it's not going to last forever. Those pockets aren't as deep as they used to be," Wilson reminded him. "Not at all. Don't even think that. Deep does not mean bottomless. But here's what we must consider. Not many people know about this, but I do. I do because I listen, because knowing everything there is to know about Pacific Park, it is my—"

"Life," Jude finished for him. Even Jude had a limit of patience for his friend. "Come on, Wilson, tell her or I'm going to drop it."

"Okay. Okay. Okay," he said, "Here it is. Ms. Bates, Pacific Park needs to make Jude's lawsuit go away because they can't afford the kind of payment they would have to make to Mr. Wren if Jude wins. They will have to settle the most recent fatality, and Mr. Wren's action on top of that would push them into bankruptcy. Isaac Hawkins can't have that. He's an old man, this is his legacy and, personally, Isaac is sucking eggs, so to speak. He doesn't have time to rebuild if that happens. And, the icing on the cake, Greater United Parks is thinking of acquiring Pacific Park. If lawsuits suck all the dough out, then all Pacific has to sell is old equipment. They won't even have any goodwill left on their balance sheet, and Greater United Parks won't want to make a deal. Isaac can't afford to fight two wrongful-death suits at the same time. One for the kid who died three months ago is okay. But if they have to deal with the one for a kid who died almost two years ago—a disabled, retarded boy at that—they're ruined."

"Oh, my sweet . . ." Josie sighed. "This is good. But it still doesn't explain the tape. There's a video that seems to show my client doing something to the boy's harness. Is that possible, Wilson? Could Archer have unhitched the harness on the Shock and Drop?"

"Yes. Possible." He gathered his thoughts and paced himself. "The Shock and Drop showed up about 'ninety-seven, and it was already ten years old. With that kind of harness it's possible that your client could have pulled the release easy as a car seat belt. But to make the boy fall, your client would have to intervene somehow. Instinct would make a rider hold on tighter or lean back or something."

"Maybe not with this kid, Wilson," Jude mused.

"But wouldn't there be backup safety measures?" Josie pressed.

Wilson shook his head.

"That harness wasn't hydraulic. The rider wasn't swinging free; the weight wasn't held at the shoulders. The design is a bad one because it relied on the cooperation of the rider. Tim Wren was standing on a platform; gripping the handholds kept the posture straight. That harness was just holding him back and still. I won't swear, Ms. Bates. I won't swear at all that it was possible or not possible for your client to undo the harness until I see the machinery."

"Then I'll make sure we all take a look at that ride, and this time you're going through the VIP entrance, Wilson," Josie said, and asked for the phone.

Wilson pointed her in the right direction. He grinned as she had words with security at Pacific Park. When she hung up Jude was already putting on his jacket and helping Wilson as he struggled to get off his chair. They both stopped when they saw the grim look on Josie's face. Hand still on the receiver, Josie said, "Forget it. They won't let us in. They refused us permission to look at that damn ride."

15

"Have I told you that you look particularly fetching today?"

"And may I say you are exceedingly full of it today."

Josie and Jude walked in lockstep toward Department Fifty in the civil courthouse, where Judge Carl Smith waited to hear arguments on the motion for inspection that Jude had filed a week earlier.

"Okay, then, have I told you you're brilliant? I think between brilliant and beautiful you really should think about coming to work for me."

Josie rolled her eyes but took no offense. Jude's flirtations and energy were taken in stride. She no longer wanted to be rid of him, understood his information had cut her prep time in half and she had, in fact, grudgingly come to like him.

"Thank God for the brilliant part or I might just fall for your line, Jude." Josie pulled up just before they reached the courtroom. "You're ready for this, right?"

"Piece of cake, Josie. We expected you to get shot down when you requested an order of inspection from the criminal court. I'm just sorry you thought of skirting the issue in civil court before I did."

"There would be no living with you then." Josie put her hand on one of the double doors leading to the courtroom. Jude grabbed the other. She said, "Let's do it."

Together they walked into the courtroom, only to split off as Josie took a seat in a wooden pew behind the bar and Jude stood aside, waiting until the judge finished with the attorney before him. A minute later one unhappy lawyer left the courtroom and Judge Smith turned his attention to Jude.

"Mr. Getts. Always a pleasure."

"Your Honor." Jude pushed through the swinging gate, offering a deferential nod as he took his place behind the plaintiff's table like he owned it.

"Mr. Hillerman?" The judge waved the defense attorney up with a papal gesture.

"Here, Your Honor."

An older man who wore gray well came forward and had barely settled when Judge Smith began.

"Well, Mr. Getts, I've read your motion and, Mr. Hillerman, your response. Naturally, I could give you my thinking straight off, but I'm running ahead of schedule today. So why don't you two lay it out one more time for me—just in case there's anything that I missed." Casually Smith sat back, ready to be entertained. "Tell me a story, counsel."

"Judge, I represent Colin Wren in a wrongful-death suit against Pacific Park, and I am simply seeking an order of inspection for the Shock and Drop amusement ride, which my client's son was riding at the time of his death. Such an inspection is not only appropriate but critical to my case."

"Your Honor," Mr. Hillerman interjected, his voice that of experience and wisdom. "I'm afraid Mr. Getts is being overly anxious. There is a stay of the civil proceedings pending a resolution of a criminal trial in the matter of Timothy Wren's death. There is absolutely no reason for Mr. Getts to inspect the park's ride at this time. In fact, the issue could possibly be moot. An inspection would be a waste of Mr. Getts's time, as well as Pacific Park's, if the criminal action is resolved in the manner we expect it to be. I would ask the court to remind Mr. Getts that patience is a virtue."

Jude grinned, happy that this would be more than a formality.

"All true, Your Honor. This has become a complicated matter except that, as we understand it, the machinery in question is in a storage area that is open to the elements and has been for almost two years. If the criminal matter extends to a year or more, there is no telling how that machinery might further degrade. Should that happen, vital information will be lost to the plaintiff. The worthiness of the machinery is at the very heart of our case."

"Has the defense attorney in the criminal matter requested an inspection?" Smith asked of either one of them.

"Yes, Your Honor, but the motion was denied," Jude answered. "In that matter it was ruled that Pacific Park was simply the place where the crime occurred and not the focus of the action as perpetrator of the crime. As such, Pacific Park has the right to refuse entrance to the park and access to the equipment as they see fit. They have refused the defense right of inspection, citing privacy concerns, and the criminal court agreed. They also stated that the district attorney has all pertinent information in that trial and Pacific Park, as a third party, is under no obligation to be forced to grant inspection by the defense.

"In the civil matter, the victim must be represented

against the park, not defended from the people. We have a clear right to inspect for defects in that machinery. Moreover, we have the right to do so in a timely manner. Before the criminal matter was established, Pacific Park was less than forthcoming with information that might affect the representation of my client and had been cited for contempt—"

"Your Honor, that judgment was reversed when Judge Bellows realized that we were only doing our best to assist the district attorney in a very delicate criminal investigation," Mr. Hillerman objected.

"And that, Mr. Hillerman, has no bearing on my decision here today," Judge Smith reminded him.

"Then, Judge," Hillerman went on, refusing to be put off so easily, "consider this. To hold Pacific Park to civil discovery standards makes no sense, because we are not talking about an accident. Mr. Getts is effectively out of a job, since Tim Wren was murdered."

Judge Smith held up his hand.

"As the contempt citation has no bearing here, neither does the criminal action, Mr. Hillerman. Murder has not been proven, only alleged. In fact, it's my understanding that no one has been arraigned for the crime of murder after any factual finding. Until there is a trial and a conviction, no one really knows what we are talking about." The judge paused. He thought. He crossed his arms on the bench and inspected his wedding ring as if that gave him inspiration. Looking up, Judge Smith said, "I respect the stay in terms of Mr. Getts getting his wrongful-death matter heard, but I also know that the criminal outcome is not a foregone conclusion. Mr. Getts may very well be back on the docket tomorrow for all I know. So, in the matter before this court, I see no reason not to allow Mr.

Getts and his team into the park to inspect the machinery in question."

With that, Judge Smith neatened a stack of papers and handed it to his clerk as he wrapped up his findings.

"Mr. Getts, you and your designated representatives are free to inspect the theme-park ride called the Shock and Drop. You are to be admitted to Pacific Park and carry out that inspection in a timely manner and with appropriate notification. You are to inspect only the ride known as the Shock and Dr—"

"I would also like to inspect the grounds where that ride stood before its removal," Jude interrupted charmingly to ask for more. David Copperfield couldn't have done it better.

"Mr. Hillerman?" Judge Smith looked to the older man.

"I see no purpose in that, Your Honor. It's been almost two years since that ride was moved to storage. Another attraction with a completely different configuration has taken up the space; new landscaping is in place. There would be no basis in fact for comparison to the Shock and Drop at the time of the accident."

"I agree," the judge answered. "We'll limit the order to an engineering inspection of the machinery itself. Mr. Getts, I would like you to work through Mr. Hillerman. Mr. Hillerman, you will designate a liaison at the park if you cannot be present."

"Very good, Your Honor." Mr. Hillerman inclined his head, grateful to have a small victory to bring back to Pacific Park.

"And you will make it clear to whoever it is that meets Mr. Getts's party that they are to afford them every courtesy. I don't want to be the next court citing Pacific Park for contempt."

"Yes, Your Honor." Hillerman inclined his head.

"Excellent. We're done, then, unless either of you has any more business before this court."

Neither man did. Not one to waste time, Judge Smith had his clerk call the next matter. Jude and Hillerman were already forgotten by the time they walked out the door. Hillerman kept going. Josie joined Jude.

"So?" Jude asked.

"I'm not going to fall all over you for a slam dunk," Josie noted dryly, refusing to give him kudos no matter how pleased she was.

"Love the way you show your gratitude." Jude chuckled. "I did all the work."

"It was my idea. You were just a pretty face." They had reached the elevators. Jude punched the down button. Josie thought aloud as they waited. "Wilson can't do the inspection. He would be useless as a witness without the proper credentials. Not to mention his obvious bias against Pacific Park and the fact that I'd worry he'd have a heart attack if he tried climbing on anything higher than a step stool."

"Already taken care of," Jude assured her. "We have a professor from MIT. He's done a couple of stints as an expert witness, but not so many that he'll seem tainted. Works for his expenses only, which, in and of itself, makes him suspect in my eyes."

"Always a bottom-line guy, huh, Jude?' Josie noted. "So, when's he available? I want to do this ASAP."

"Day after tomorrow? Latest, Friday. I want to make sure we've got all the bases covered before you and Ruth go at it," Jude answered.

"Fine. I'll tell Archer." The elevator doors opened. Josie took the first step in, only to have Jude pull her back.

"Unh-uh. You're not going to bring him, Josie. Don't even think it," he warned.

"Not very friendly of you," Josie said. Jude let go but stayed close when he followed her into the elevator. "And you're not thinking smart. Ruth made it clear she doesn't want Archer around any of her witnesses, but there's no restraining order keeping him out of the park. Judge Smith said your team could inspect. Archer is now officially part of the team. Or have you forgotten that this hearing was just an end run for the criminal defense?"

They were on the first floor again, battling past those who were trying to get in the elevator while they tried to get out. Josie made it out first and looked to make sure Jude was behind her.

"Archer is critical to the inspection, Jude. He's the one who was on the ride. He's the one who needs to remember what happened that day. Maybe seeing that thing will jog his memory or give us some insight regarding the procedures taken after the accident. . . ."

Jude jogged a step and got in front of her. Josie feinted left, then right, but Jude would not let her pass.

"What?" she demanded.

"That's a bunch of crap, Josie, and you know it. What you're doing is dangerous."

"That's absurd." She tossed her head, saw that people were looking, then lowered her voice. "What possible harm could there be in having Archer along?"

"You're intentionally antagonizing Pacific Park, getting in the DA's face, putting your client in an untenable position, and, above all," Jude pointed out, finishing his litany on a high note, "having Archer there could kill you, Josie."

Josie looked away; she gave a little click of antipathy with her tongue against her teeth.

"You are so good, Jude. Just this side of melodramatic, a little anxiety about the status of my case thrown in and top the whole thing off with a pitch for your very personal concern about my feelings. Very nice. Very sweet."

"Stop it," Jude ordered. "You're not that hard-assed and you know exactly what I'm talking about. What's going to happen when Archer remembers doing it? Or what if he's known it all along and he's been playing you for a fool? What if he looks at that machine and you look at him and see guilt?"

Josie's eyes were flinty. She knew there was something to be said for Jude's objections. She understood the risks and that the consequences would affect her and Archer. Given that, there was only one thing to do. Josie pushed Jude aside and said, "Archer's in."

16

Josie drove with the top down, her baseball hat on, her sunglasses cutting the sharp, cold wind as they sped down the 405 freeway. The ragtop was down by choice, not neglect. Sitting cocooned under the top with someone wound as tightly as Archer was, angry at her for every little thing because he was too proud to admit that facing the past frightened him, would have made her crazy.

Josie ran the back of her hand across her nose. It was so cold it hurt to touch it. She shifted, rotating her neck to work out the kink that ran from the base of her skull to the knob of her spine. Archer wasn't the only one hanging on by a thread. Josie was none too keen on this whole trip either, not since she had decided that Jude was right on the mark about her motives.

The realization had come in the middle of the night while she lay awake next to Archer. Their naked bodies held no allure for each other; their minds were in complete control. Neither wanted to be the first to seek solace in lovemaking for fear there was no more reason to love. Both were terrified that they would share only sex and the emptiness that came with the act when there was no other connection.

Fear was a new thing between them. So were apprehension, tension and any other word that described the relationship between two people who suddenly felt

as if they didn't know each other yet had no one else
to turn to. There was ground they couldn't tread upon,
questions Jo the lover couldn't ask but Josie the lawyer must. There was the slight intake of breath before
an answer was given; the barely audible exhale when
the answer moved them forward and not back, cleared
up a point instead of creating suspicion.

Now the cold air, the speed of the car and the gathering twilight gave Archer and Josie reason to keep
their own counsel as they drove toward Pacific Park,
where they would meet up with Wilson, Jude and the
engineer. When they saw the park in the distance Josie
loosened her grip on the wheel and instinctively
reached for Archer. He didn't move away when she
slid her palm over the back of his hand and entwined
her fingers with his. There was an instant of resistance,
that moment when he was afraid of showing how
much he needed her, and then Archer squeezed back.
It was enough. They were together.

Satisfied, Josie let go and used both hands to maneuver off the freeway. She took the off-ramp ten
miles too fast and felt the old Jeep shudder as she
pulled to a stop, yielded to traffic and then got in the
queue to enter Pacific Park.

"There." Archer raised his hand and pointed to a
huge sign that indicated section E of the sprawling
parking lot. Josie nodded and broke off from the flow
of traffic, trolling as they looked for a space.

"That's Jude's car." Josie raised her chin. Archer
looked.

"Predictable," Archer mumbled as she parked two
spaces away. Pulling himself out of the Jeep, he dusted
himself off as he gave the eye to the champagne-
colored Mercedes.

Josie joined Archer and took his arm, aware of but

not surprised by his insecurity. The champagne-colored car represented every threatening thing in Archer's life: money he didn't have, freedom he didn't have, Jude's youth and looks that Archer could never have. So he dissed Jude's car and it translated to questions for Josie. Did she still love him? Had she been seduced by someone who understood her business, was closer to her age, was a man who didn't bring a pack of trouble with him? Josie heard him and answered the only way she knew how.

"You okay, Archer?" She put pressure on his arm. He nodded. She smiled. "Okay, then. Let's do it."

She let go of him and stuffed her hands in the pockets of the ancient leather jacket her father had treasured. She kept her hat on. The glasses she ditched. Archer walked with a determined stride beside her, like a man with nothing to hide. That was good. What wasn't good were the butterflies in Josie's own stomach, the sense of impending doom, the very unlawyer-like emotion that seemed to make her falter.

Then she saw Jude and all was well. The suit was gone, replaced by jeans, a dress shirt open at the neck, a jacket that looked like cashmere. Hiking boots. His gaze never wavered. Josie kept her eyes on Jude but her hand reached for Archer. Roles were reversed, but not loyalties. Archer had been her rock; she would be his.

"There you are," Jude hailed them as they joined his little group. "I was beginning to worry."

"There was a backup on the transition at the 710," Josie said. "Have you called security?"

"I did when I saw you coming," Jude answered. He turned to Archer. "Are you going to be okay to go in there? If not, let us know now."

"I'll just do that when I feel myself getting the shivers," Archer answered, his breast feathers ruffling at the audacity of this new cock.

"Just covering the bases." Jude backed off gracefully, so Archer gave an inch.

"I'll be okay."

"Great." Jude put out his hand, Archer took it, and Jude drew him into the circle. "This is Wilson Page."

Archer shook the big man's hand and looked him in the eye.

"Appreciate you being here," Archer said.

"Wouldn't have missed it for the world, so to speak," Wilson answered gently. Josie looked askance, noting Wilson's pallor, still not used to his labored breathing. Wilson did the honors, introducing the tall, thin man next to him. "This is Dr. Hart, a fine engineer. He's just what we need here. Just what we need right now."

Everyone said their hellos courteously, in subdued voices that spoke of the seriousness of their task. Josie was about to engage Dr. Hart when suddenly, from the shadows of the employee entrance, Colin Wren emerged like a ghost, his priest's eyes trained on Archer and only Archer. He was pale; his thin hair blew in wisps around his head. The bulk of his corduroy jacket did nothing to hide the slightness of his figure, and his glasses and demeanor did not disguise his wariness. Neither Archer nor Colin acknowledged each other, and Josie watched them with interest. There was a new charge in Colin's eyes, as if irritation had given way to antagonism. Josie pulled Jude aside.

"You should have told me he was going to be here. I don't think it's appropriate," she said.

"Do I have to remind you that the only reason you or Archer is making it through the gates is because of Colin?"

"The only reason there's a criminal action is because he started this in the first place," Josie shot back. "You should have at least warned me."

"He didn't make up his mind until the last minute. This is going to be very rough on him, and I expect you to have some sympathy for that," Jude said.

"Like it's going to be a piece of cake for Archer?" Josie pointed out. "Like—"

"Just control Archer," Jude said under his breath.

"I don't know that Archer's the one we have to worry about." Josie looked over at Colin, sizing him up, trying to put her finger on what was different. "What's going on with him? I thought he wanted to help us. I'm getting a vibe that isn't good. Is there something I should know?"

"He's just on edge. This is like visiting the site of a plane crash. Dredges up all sorts of conflicting emotions."

"No, it's something else." Josie didn't buy it. "What was he doing hiding like that?"

Jude looked over his shoulder. "Good Lord, Josie, he was standing out of the wind."

"He hasn't moved an inch. He hasn't taken his eyes off Archer. It's like he's goading him."

"Look, this whole night is going to be stressful; don't make this worse than it is by imagining things. Come on, time to put on a team face. The games are about to begin." Jude took her arm. Roger McEntyre was bearing down on them. He stopped just outside the gate.

"Mr. Getts?"

Jude's group closed ranks.

"Yes."

Roger McEntyre's eyes barely moved but Josie knew he could testify about the color of the buttons on Jude's cuffs if he had to. His gaze swept over everyone else as he handed them their badges in turn.

"Dr. Hart, Mr. Page, Ms. Bates and Mr. Getts. Mr. Wren." The man was good. He'd done his homework.

"You're missing one." Josie stepped forward.

"No, I don't think I am. The park was directed to admit Mr. Getts's team for inspection." Roger's eyes flicked to Archer. "This person is a criminal defendant. We have the right to refuse admittance to anyone we deem necessary per the ruling requesting inspection that was denied in the criminal action."

"There were no limitations placed on Mr. Getts," Josie countered, admiring McEntyre for covering all the bases. "The order of the court was broad. It did not specify the number or the makeup of the inspection team, nor did it specify any exclusions."

"I disagree, but I'm not an attorney." Roger was polite like a bouncer at the corner bar is polite just before he breaks your head when you push too far. "However, I'll be happy to contact our in-house counsel and have him run down the judge for clarification. Unfortunately, the hour is late and it might take some time."

"Mr. McEntyre," Jude interrupted, "we are within our rights per the order, and, since the inspection will be supervised, you'll see that Ms. Bates's client will only watch the proceedings. He won't be allowed to touch anything or speak to your personnel. He will remain within view of your representative at all times. And, if that isn't satisfactory, I'll be sure to ask that you, personally, be held in contempt for not honoring a court-ordered inspection."

McEntyre's mustache twitched in annoyance but he gave no ground. He looked at Colin and saw a spark of approval in the man's eyes. While he found that reaction interesting it was Jude he engaged.

"Because Pacific Park's motives have been misunderstood in the past, I want to err on the side of caution. I doubt any judge would find that contemptible. I have been instructed that Ms. Bates's client is not to come into the park. I will honor those instructions until I'm told differently."

Roger eyed Archer. Josie braced for mention of Archer's indiscretion but none was forthcoming. They did, perhaps, have a friend in Roger McEntyre. Then, in the next instant, Roger McEntyre showed his true colors, and they belonged to Pacific Park.

"I think I'm stretching the bounds of our hospitality by allowing Ms. Bates into the park as it is. So you're free to argue with our attorney and to find a judge willing to listen to you, but you will have to wait in the parking lot until I'm satisfied that I am legally bound to let this man through the gate. Your choice."

Satisfied he had made himself clear, he looked from Josie to Jude. McEntyre knew where the power was; he just wasn't quite sure which one had more of it.

"All right. Those conditions are fine with us."

Josie spoke up. Someone had to make a decision. Jude's expression remained impassive. Colin looked triumphant, and Archer uttered a small sound of contempt that came just before confrontation. Josie took hold of Archer's arm, steering him away from the group and talking fast.

"It was a long shot at best—"

He interrupted with the same alacrity.

"This is crap. . . ."

Josie held his arm tight. He tried to shake her off. She would have none of it.

"It was a long shot at best," she reiterated firmly. "They have the right. They could argue that their patrons would be spooked at the sight of you wandering around the park."

"Like any of those people in there would even recognize me. Come on, Jo," Archer complained, jerking his head toward the park.

"If they can convince a judge that letting you through that gate is akin to letting Jack the Ripper through a brothel door then that makes theory reality. Besides, we don't have the time to argue. Their lawyer could take all night making the case to keep you out, and, in the end, McEntyre might decide to mention the little visit you paid him. The hearing, the motion, it will all be a waste of time that we can't afford to lose. I need this inspection before I walk into the prelim." Josie moved in, her body close to his, her head turned as if they were dancing. She whispered. "Please, Archer. Be smart now. I will make this go away. I promise, babe."

Archer's eyes closed. Degradation, disgrace, humiliation piled atop him like sand on a buried man. A grain here or there could be brushed off; buckets of the damn stuff started weighing him down, hurting his heart, crushing his spirit. Josie took his shoulders in both her hands.

"I'll be back in an hour even if they aren't done. I'll be back for you, Archer, and we'll wait together if you just let me go in there long enough to check the place out."

It seemed like an eternity, but finally he nodded his agreement. Josie let her hands drop. She stayed close for a second, then rejoined the men at the gate.

"He'll stay."

"Good." McEntyre waved to a man standing nearby

and spoke loud enough for Archer to hear: "I'll leave a guard at the gate to make sure your client doesn't forget the rules."

Josie's gut tightened at such condescension, but it was the sight of McEntyre's self-satisfied grin that proved her second thought had been the right one. They had no friend here. McEntyre had just poured another bucketful of sand on Archer. With a prayer that it would not be the one to crush him heart and soul, Josie followed the men into the playland that was Pacific Park.

17

Josie and Jude followed Roger McEntyre through Pacific Park. Wilson and Dr. Hart brought up the rear. Wilson looked pale with the exertion but determined to walk all the way on his own. Colin walked by himself, connected to no one, uninterested in his surroundings, eyes forward, steps measured. He seemed to fear falling off his imaginary line. He was a curious, concentrated man, and Josie could not imagine how Lexi could have loved him and Archer both. Archer's emotions were worn openly, Colin's hidden behind a stoic mask. If Josie had to pick who to stand and fight with, Josie would have chosen Colin Wren. He was the kind of man who strategized, moved carefully and with purpose to a designated end. He would never let emotions rule his—

"Cool, huh?" Jude walked beside Josie like a kid on a free pass.

"We're not here to have fun." Josie walked faster when McEntyre made a sharp left without so much as looking back.

Jude stayed behind to make sure Wilson and the doctor saw the change of course. Colin was in between. Strung out, making progress at different rates, the caravan reunited far from the boisterous crowds.

Roger McEntyre waited until they were all present, drew back a flap on a huge canvas structure and went inside. The canvas was passed from person to person as Jude's team followed. Once there, they fanned out, lining up against the side of the canvas wall and looking around. They were in an enclosed space without a roof. The canvas walls simply shielded the Shock & Drop from prying eyes.

Initially no one moved. Then their heads twisted, turned upward, their eyes roamed right and left, to the ground and up again. Eventually, they were drawn to the tower of metal and wire, plastic and pulleys. The Shock & Drop was massive, impressive, treacherous as a monster playing dead, ready to reanimate at the slightest touch, the softest tread.

"My goodness." Wilson breathed out and then in again so that the hiss of the S became a whistle.

"Damn straight," Jude agreed.

Colin stared at the monstrosity.

Josie looked through it until she was ready to look at it.

Dr. Hart was the first to take action.

He did so decisively, walking to the base, finding an appropriate point of operation and opening his bag. From it he took measuring instruments and pads of graph paper, magnifying equipment, things Josie would have to learn about if she was going to examine him effectively on the stand.

Suddenly, as if Dr. Hart had given permission to begin, there was a flurry of activity from the men. Wilson found a place to set his bulk and fell easily into strategy discussions with Dr. Hart. Josie shied away from them, only to find herself assaulted by Jude's questioning of Roger McEntyre. She moved on, skirting the periphery of the action, keeping her distance, wanting simply to look at the thing that had wreaked such havoc on Archer's life. She backed away, her gaze skimming over the ride until she found herself staring at Colin Wren through a maze of metal. He was not looking at the Shock & Drop. Rather, Colin was lost in a discussion with Roger McEntyre until, quite suddenly, he paused. He pivoted. He felt Josie's curiosity and searched the compound for the source. His eyes were so naked, his hurt so raw, his anger so deep that, when their eyes met, Josie stood accused just by her association with Archer.

Unable to breathe, unable to look at him, Josie ducked out of the housing structure and walked head-long into the mess of people that kept the money coming into Pacific Park.

She charged through the crowd, aware of the lights, the noise, the smiles on the faces of the children she passed. She danced aside when the little girl in front of her dropped a toy made of plastic and wood. Josie bent to pick it up. She put the toy into the girl's palm but forgot to let go.

Ten if she was a day, the girl stirred something in Josie. Maybe it was her eyes, or the set of her jaw, the way her hair was pulled up so that half was caught in a ponytail and the rest hung long down her back. Maybe it was the pretty clothes worn uncomfortably, a tomboy dressed to a mother's specifications. It wasn't until the girl tugged at her toy and Josie let it go that the sense of familiarity became comfortable. The girl ran away and pulled Josie into the past as she did so.

Jolted by the surprising clarity of her memories, Josie sank onto a bench shaped like a daisy and painted the pink of a Hermosa Beach sunset. Swinging her head up she checked out the now-dark sky, smiled and waited for the beating of her heart to calm. As memories went, this was a real good one, probably the last good one she had of the mother who took a powder when Josie was thirteen.

But that day Josie was eleven and Emily was the perfect mother, doting on her daughter at the Funland. She laughed at Josie's jokes, shared a pizza with her daughter. They sat together on all the rides, close enough for it to feel like they were hugging. They had their picture taken.

They had their picture taken.

Josie put her hands on her knees and thought about that as she pushed off the pink bench. She walked slower, smiling to herself, wondering what happened to that picture. Even now Josie remembered exactly what it looked like: Josie and Emily, their arms flung high, laughing through their screams as the roller coaster tipped them over the last, terrifying drop. Emily had been dazzled by that picture. *Where was the camera?* she asked. *How did they develop the pictures so quickly?* she wondered. *Aren't we gorgeous?* she cooed, and Josie believed that Emily really thought Josie was beautiful, too.

Josie laughed out loud. Kids could convince themselves of anything. Now that she was older Josie knew that day was special because Emily wanted it and not because Josie needed it. Sidestepping two men, oblivious to their admiration, Josie wondered where that picture was. Destroyed? Given away? Lost? Perhaps it was packed away. . . . Maybe Josie would check her dad's stored boxes. . . . Maybe . . .

"Daddy!"

"Hey, lady. Shit, you can't just cut in line. . . ."

The expletive was followed by a compelling jab of a sharp elbow. A man in a T-shirt espousing the extermination of mothers-in-law was protecting his turf.

Josie looked around, amazed to find herself wedged
between people 'who were standing in line for the
roller coaster. She hadn't been on a roller coaster
since that day with her mother, and Josie had no intention of getting on one of those things again. With
muttered mea culpas, she pushed through the line and
cut left, her eyes still trained on the Perilous Peaks
Coaster.

It was a marvel of engineering, as frightening to
hear as it was to see. Packed into tiny cars linked in
lines of eight, riders were hauled up right angles, shot
through double loops, dropped like pinballs down a
chute and shot back up to the heavens again. Everyone screamed—everyone—even guys with obnoxious
T-shirts. Most held on to the metal lap restraint. That
and gravity kept them in their place. Some brave souls
raised their arms; others buried their faces in their
companion's shoulder. But every face . . . every . . .

Their faces.

Josie stepped a little closer to the coaster.

Pictures.

Josie's head snapped left, then right, and that was
when she saw it—the huge board where pictures were
posted. Everyone who rode the Perilous Peaks
Coaster had their picture taken, developed as the cars
ground to a halt and posted as they wobbled through
the exit. The picture would be taken from two different angles, just the way they were the day Josie and
Emily went to Funland. They had been given a choice:
one picture shot head-on, the other taken from a
three-quarter view.

Excited by the idea taking root in her brain, Josie
minced her step, jockeying to get through a break in
the crowd that surged forward toward the interior of
the park. She put her hands out to block a woman

who had stopped midstride, then squeezed past her, searching for the cameras. Cameras. Josie was positive she would find more than one.

Finally Josie punched through the crowd and threw herself against the long, low security fence. People were behind her, close to her, around her. They shouted to be heard over the deafening noise of the roller coaster, but Josie was oblivious. She was close to the tracks, concentrating on the configuration of the ride. To her right, parallels of steel ribboned over a wooden infrastructure that rose skyward. To Josie's left the track skated into a double loop and, right in front of her, the line of cars plunged into a little valley before shooting up again. Gravity defying, death defying, terrifying. Josie leaned on the railing. She heard the shrieks merge into one frantic scream as the cars crested the rise. Before Josie could think, the train of cars whooshed by her, leaving a wind in its wake that made her crinkle her eyes against the kickup of dust and dirt. The train was gone as fast as it had come, voices were nothing more than a vapor trail, faces were forgotten. Tall enough to keep one foot on the ground, Josie strained as she leaned over the railing. Now only inches away from the track Josie Bates saw what she was looking for.

Cameras.

There were at least two. One hung high on a light pole on the south side of the ride; the other was mounted on the ground a few yards from her. Pressing her hips tighter against the railing, Josie bent her torso over the top, straining to see into the interior of the structure. Above her she heard the scraping of metal on metal, the grinding of gears. Another train was being towed up the far side of the angled track. There was a hesitation, a gigantic, mechanical stillness, a second when all sound ceased. Then the rush of air, the squeal of metal wheels and the cacophony of terror-filled voices. In her peripheral vision Josie saw the car hurtling toward the valley. She couldn't pull back now. There was another camera . . . on the opposite side. Josie had to see if . . .

Suddenly there was nothing but the sound of the train, the blast of air as the cars rushed by and the feeling that she was floating, her feet not quite on the ground. Josie Bates grabbed for the railing and tried to hold on but her fingers slipped off. An arm clamped around her waist, knocking the breath out of her and Josie heard someone growl, "What the hell do you think you're doing?"

Archer sat in the Jeep, his chin buried in the collar of his jacket, his hands stuck deep into the pockets. The front seat was reclined and the heels of his shoes were on the dash. A flat-white shine came from the incandescent industrial lighting that pocked the parking lot. The night was just beginning, and it ticked Archer off royally that he was sitting in the car like a kid waiting for his parents to come fetch him. Dropping his feet he sat up straight, took his hands out of his pockets and cocked one arm on the door. He stayed that way for a second. In the next he threw open the door, got out of the Jeep and checked out his friend at the gate. The guard was still there.

Idiot.

Archer flipped the door shut. The damn thing sounded tinny compared to the Hummer, and it just made Archer all that more irritated. He rested his leg against the fender. It would have been a good time for a cigarette if he still smoked. It was a better time for an idea, and he just happened to have one.

Casually Archer moved around the car, snapping the ragtop into place, making sure the guard saw him. He paced the length of the Jeep, feigning boredom. Archer ambled up the aisle of section E, checked out the cars, stretched his legs, passed the time. He turned at the end and walked back again, hands in his pockets like a good boy. Archer was within six car-lengths of the Jeep when he saw his opening. The guard at the gate had lost interest in him. A woman with three children had a question; the rent-a-cop had a long-winded answer.

Well and good.

Archer's timing was impeccable as he slipped between two cars and ended up in section D. His pace didn't change; he didn't look over his shoulder to see if the guy at the gate had caught on. Archer was cool, and it would take a better man than that imbecile to figure out that he was not in the same place he had been a moment before.

One more time Archer walked the length of the parking aisle, turned to walk back and saw his mark. A van filled with people had just pulled into a space in section C. A casual glance assured him he was not on the guard's radar. Archer made the pass between two minivans and landed himself on the next aisle. He was a knight, and Pacific Park's parking lot was his chessboard: two over and one down, one down and two over. Archer moved methodically, keeping his mind on checkmate, knowing the guard at the employee gate would assume he had climbed back into the car. At least that was what Archer was counting on as he looked inside his wallet, puzzling over it just long enough for five kids and two adults to pile out of the van next to him.

Chatting and talking, joking and laughing, they all

headed for the park entrance. Archer fell into step with them. He knew not to walk ahead or lag too far back. He knew enough to turn his head and smile and look interested in one of the kids, like he knew him from way back. Archer also knew enough to back off when said kid looked like he was getting nervous about the big guy with the fading bruises hanging a little too close. At the right time Archer broke ranks and was absorbed by the larger crowd congregating near the main entrance. There were enough of them to hide a herd of Archers.

During the next three minutes he waited politely in line, flashed his auto-club card, handed over two twenties and was welcomed with a discount admission to Pacific Park.

Archer was in, and he was damn well going to stay until he had what he wanted.

18

"Stunts like that can get you killed. Or haven't you heard that Pacific Park has a problem with people dying because they do stupid things?"

Roger McEntyre let go of Josie Baylor-Bates and stood back. It wasn't far enough. McEntyre was like a wall. Josie couldn't go through him; he wouldn't let her go around. She waited for his signal. It came as he turned and cast her a sidelong look that said he expected her to fall in.

"I wasn't that close," Josie objected, wanting some conversation to keep from feeling as if he were leading her to the gallows. "I wasn't going to get hurt, unless you count windburn."

"I didn't know you were an expert on what constitutes a danger in a theme park." Roger turned sideways and held out an arm. Josie hesitated, half expecting a trick. Finally she walked ahead, pushing through the migrating mass of people. Roger followed. When she came out on the other side she was alone, surrounded by the crowd but not a part of it.

"It's a movement-pattern phenomenon," McEntyre explained as he joined her. "People move in groups, leaving an oasis of space now and again. We can track it; we can manipulate it with the right sounds and smells, the proper placement of an attraction. It keeps people from turning into human bumper cars."

"So all this fun is a science," Josie noted.

"It's a talent of the creator of the park," McEntyre responded, "enhanced by science and common sense."

"I'm not sure I've seen the common sense part."

"Your little trick over there by the Perilous Peaks? That's a nice little example of the lack of common sense." McEntyre pulled a thumb over his shoulder. Josie looked in that direction briefly but kept walking.

"Maybe it wasn't the best example for the kids. . . ."

"That's an understatement. Didn't your mother ever tell you there's a reason why fences are built?"

"My mother didn't believe in fences," Josie said.

"Mine did," McEntyre said casually. "There is usually a good reason for them. They kept me out where I wasn't welcome, and in where I was. Fences protected me from things that could hurt me."

McEntyre raised his hand slightly. The ice-cream pavilion was deserted on this chilly night. Roger sat on one of the little round red stools, four to each round yellow table. Josie sat on another. McEntyre didn't offer to pop for a cone. He just kept talking.

"So there's a reason we have fences around rides, and there's a reason why they are posted in specific areas. For instance, let me tell you about that fence you were leaning over. You chose a particularly vulnerable point. The cars are traveling at forty-five miles an hour. The plan is to hit the dip smooth, shoot up into the loops and go on to the next rise. It's a lot of physics you don't necessarily need to understand. What you do need to know is that, once in a blue moon, the cars jump the tracks, and where do you think they have the greatest probability of doing that?"

"As they come down that first slope?"

"The one where your head was sticking out? Why, yes, you're right."

Roger unbuttoned his jacket and drew it back. He put his hand on his hip. Josie saw the shine of a buckle, the deep mahogany color of the leather belt. He carried no weapon at his waist, but Josie wouldn't swear he didn't have one somewhere. She looked at his face again.

"I'll take my chances," Josie said. "According to you guys, there's no such thing as mechanical error, so I figure I'm pretty safe."

"Then let's talk human error. You know what these people do any chance they get?" McEntyre raised his brows; he touched his mustache and looked at all the people in the park as if they were not held in particularly high esteem. "These people do stupid things. They lean the wrong way, they stand up, they throw stuff. You wouldn't believe the shit they think is funny. Once we had a kid who took a rock up on the Peaks and threw it from the top to see which would hit the ground first, the car he was riding in or the rock. The rock landed on a baby stroller. Imagine that."

Josie didn't want to hear what came next. He told her anyway.

"Luckily the mother had just picked the baby up because it was fussing. The woman was hysterical, the stroller was crushed and the kid on the ride was kindly asked never to come back to Pacific Park again. The parents sued us. They said since no one was hurt there was no reason to keep their precious little boy out of the park. That incident cost us a small fortune to defend. Luckily, common sense won the day. A judge agreed that kid didn't deserve to come back."

"Okay." Josie propped her elbows on the table. "I was wrong. Leaning over that fence wasn't the smartest thing in the world to do."

"It wasn't even close," McEntyre said. He put a hand on the table. He didn't fidget. He was a very calm man. "What were you looking for?"

"It's what I was looking at. There are two cameras pointed at the coaster. I think there was a third in the middle area," Josie informed him.

"Did you want your picture taken?"

Josie propped her elbows on the yellow table, rested her chin on one upturned hand and said, "No, I want to know how many cameras were pointed at the Shock and Drop. We only have one tape. Where are the rest of the tapes, Mr. McEntyre?"

Josie swore she saw just the hint of a smile underneath the straw-colored mustache. It might have been a trick of the light, though, because Roger McEntyre didn't seem particularly amused or interested in the question.

"We looked through all our old files and turned everything we had over to Mr. Cooper as soon as we had questions about the tape. That one is all I had in the archives."

"So you're telling me there are multiple cameras on the Perilous Peaks but there was only one camera on a ride as big as the Shock and Drop?" Josie asked incredulously.

Roger shrugged and stood up. He buttoned his coat. People had changed their mind and suddenly ice cream was very popular. The man didn't like crowds so they were walking again.

"That was then; this is now. It was an older attraction, so I don't know how many cameras were on it. The roller coaster is newer, we've put more money into it and the footprint is three times that of the Shock and Drop. Three cameras are not excessive. If you'd like me to arrange a meeting with our park planning engineer so he can explain the ratio to you, I'll be happy to do that."

"I'll just bet you'd be tickled pink to do that," Josie said amiably.

He was giving her the company line, but confrontation would accomplish nothing. Josie would wait until she had something more to work with, and hopefully she'd have that in time for the preliminary hearing. They walked toward the back lot, where Jude and his team were still working.

"Why didn't the park get the Shock and Drop up and running again if there wasn't a mechanical problem?" Josie asked.

"Why are you reaching for straws?" Roger shot back. Then he saw that she was not going to let it go. He sighed. "That attraction was due to be phased out, so it was no problem to shut it down in anticipation of Tim Wren's mother filing against us. When she didn't, we just kept it out of commission. The plan is documented. I'm sure Mr. Getts has that information."

"And you know that Mr. Getts didn't get all the documentation he asked for."

"I heard that was a problem. There's a high turnover in our administrative staff. It's hard to find good help these days," Roger lied, straight-faced. "I'll check it out."

Josie stayed quiet for a moment, admiring Roger McEntyre. She recognized the tone, the walk, the posture. She recognized him. He had seen service, and that meant he was a good soldier. His loyalty was to this place. Josie talked to him plainly, the way her father had spoken to her.

"Just so you know, I don't believe a word you say. I won't believe the engineering reports. I'll take every piece of information you feed me and rip it apart piece by piece until I understand exactly what went on here. I'll look for information you don't want me to have. I'll talk to people you don't want me to talk to."

"I'd do the same thing." His eyes glittered sharp and dark. He saw everything around him, what was going on past him and things so close they would blur for anyone else. "Do what you have to do. You're not going to find what you're looking for here. And, just so you know, you can't count on me being around to pull you back if you ever get in trouble again. Not here. Not anywhere."

"I figured as much," Josie said, her eyes never leaving his even when he moved a step closer and lowered his voice.

"And if you make too much trouble, I'll have a restraining order issued against you and everyone you've ever said hello to."

Josie inclined her head.

"I can live with that, but if you know something, if you're covering up, you'll be an accessory to wrongful death when I file—"

Josie didn't finish her sentence. Roger's phone rang; he whipped it out of his pocket and walked away from Josie Bates.

"McEntyre."

Josie moved close enough to hear him say, "I got it covered."

"What's going on?" Josie asked, but McEntyre was already headed out. Josie tried to stop him with a hand on his arm, a question thrown his way.

"There's a disturbance on the east side of the park. It's nothing that concerns you."

"Hey, boss, we've got a red code." A man in plain

clothes was on the run past Josie and Roger. He paused, waiting to see if Roger needed assistance.

"I'm there." Roger yanked his arm away from Josie. She took a few steps forward and called after him.

"What's going on out there, McEntyre?"

Roger ignored her as he looked over his shoulder and spotted another man to his left.

"It's Eric. Go. Fast." Roger's head whipped back to Josie one last time. He was angry to find her near. He pointed. He gave an order. "Finish up, get out and stay out."

With that he was gone. Josie sprinted inside, where Jude's team was working on the Shock & Drop.

"Jude," she hollered. "I'm going to the east side. Don't wait. Call me later."

Jude's head popped up but Josie was already gone, running through the crowds without a care for the stares as she passed, carrying with her an awful feeling that whatever was going down would be a hell of a lot worse if she didn't get there fast.

Jude rushed to the hangar entrance. He could just make out Josie's head as she bobbed and weaved through the crush of people. Colin Wren came up beside him, silent as a ghost.

"Are they done?" Jude asked Colin, even though he was still looking after Josie.

"Almost. They're packing up," he answered.

Jude nodded and turned back, suddenly anxious to be away from this place. Ten minutes later they were ready to go. They had everything they needed. Everything except Colin Wren.

19

The news of trouble was like a stone skipped on a pond.

There's been an accident.

A shooting.

Something awful!

Oh, God! Where?

People were drawn to trouble because it was human nature. They stopped. They turned. They searched for it, stared and passed the news in excited whispers and frantic calls.

Where are the kids?

Something is wrong with the Reeling Rotator.

But they didn't have to talk about what they could see. Against a black sky feathered with the glow of Pacific Park's lights, the buckets attached to the massive spokes of the humongous wheel of the Reeling Rotator hung motionless. The buckets were painted purple and green and red. The cages that enclosed the riders were made of steel mesh. Neon lights speckled the machinery and stuttered on a controlled blink. People were strapped to a bench and locked inside to keep them from being thrown around as they were turned up, down and sideways while the gargantuan wheel rotated. Faster and faster, twisting and turning, it was a most horrifying ride made even more terrifying now that it was at a standstill. On the ground, park guests fell silent as families drifted, pulled toward the bloodcurdling screams and pleas for help that came from the sky.

Josie slowed but didn't stop. She went around those who seemed rooted where they stood. Half of the buckets were upside down. Three of those were in the highest position. Others were sideways and only two were upright. The lights on the buckets twinkled and flashed like an SOS. On the hub of the wheel a huge neon spiral of colors pulsated to the sound of computer-generated music.

Josie pushed through the people, scanning for any sign of Roger McEntyre. She found him moving through a group of teenagers like they were the enemy. McEntyre was closer to the ride entrance, but Josie was taller. She saw what was happening and it sent a shock of panic through her. Archer had a young man in a Pacific Park uniform thrown up against the wall of the operator's booth. The operator was screaming for help and Archer was screaming back. Frantically, Josie fought her way forward, trying to reach Archer before McEntyre, but McEntyre was a pro and jumped the fence.

"Archer!"

Josie screamed, unable to move any faster. He didn't hear her warning. She jostled left and right. Suddenly there was a clearing and she saw McEntyre clamp down on Archer's shoulders and yank him to the ground. Archer hit hard and tried to roll away but McEntyre was fast. He bent over and jerked Archer up, whisking him away before Josie could reach them.

On the deck three men closed ranks: One hustled the ride operator away, two others smiled as they took over the operation. Josie tagged three more working the crowd, calming everyone. A thousand heads turned east as the Reeling Rotator came to life with a grating, mechanical groan. The lights blinked off, then on, and slowly those who had been stuck in the sky were lowered to the ground. Josie didn't wait to see the first two people come out of their basket, pale and shaken. She knew everyone would be fine now—except the one person she cared about.

"Miss? Miss?"

Someone tugged at Josie's arm just as she was about to go after Roger and Archer. Startled, Josie looked at the girl who wore Pacific Park pink and a grand smile. She had the overt brightness of a child told to go kiss Great-aunt Maude and like it.

"Miss? Were going to have to shut down the Reeling Rotator, but Pacific Park would like you to have two free tickets to—"

"Where's the security office?" Josie demanded.

"I just wanted to give you—Hey, you can't do that . . ." the girl stammered as Josie grabbed her by the shoulders.

"Where is it?" Josie screamed. "The security office. Where is it?"

"Over there." Flustered, the girl flung one arm out and the free tickets scattered. "Near the Western Wheels restaurant . . . I mean behind it."

Josie took off with a "Thanks" thrown over her shoulder. She jogged in the direction the girl had pointed. She danced to her left, thinking she saw something. She moved a man out of the way with her hands on his shoulders. An objection died on his lips when he turned and saw she was in no mood for anything he could dish out. She ran a few more steps, then fell back again. McEntyre was about fifty yards on, pushing Archer ahead of him like a POW. Josie kept her eyes on the men as best she could, but they traveled in the shadows on the edges of the park, while she waded through the crowds. She reached the side gate a few minutes after they did and saw the flash of a rotating red light. McEntyre and Archer weren't alone.

"Wait! Hey, hold it!"

Josie held up her hands as she ran toward the cops who were pushing Archer into the backseat of a black and white. McEntyre stood by, indifferent to Archer's fate. Archer's head was pushed down; his wrists were cuffed. The cop who had custody of him slammed the door. His partner was already behind the wheel. The engine purred. They were ready to go.

"Officer. Hold up," Josie bellowed, wedging herself between McEntyre and the cop. "I'm this man's attorney. I want to talk to him."

"You can see him after he's been booked," the officer answered.

"Has he been read his rights? If . . ."

The uniformed officer gave Josie the once-over, then waited on Roger McEntyre. Something passed between them and the officer was satisfied. He planted himself in the car and slammed the door. They pulled out fast enough to force Josie out of the way. Furiously, she whirled on Roger McEntyre.

"You could have stopped them. I saw the way he looked at you. You could have made them give me a minute."

"And you should have left your client behind when you came here. This is my place and I won't have him in my park. Now get the hell out of here before I have you arrested as an accessory to assault." McEntyre turned his back as if she were of no consequence.

"That's bull and you know it." Josie stepped in front of him. She dogged him, insisting he listen. "I left Archer in that parking lot. It's not my fault that your guard is incompetent. And if you're implying that I planned this—"

"You want to play?" McEntyre was in her face. "Do you? Because if you do, I can make a damn good case that you conspired with your client to intimidate my employees and our guests."

McEntyre let that thought sink in. He squared his shoulders; he put a hand on the back of his neck. Finally McEntyre had it together again. When he spoke, whatever he was feeling had been packed away, and Roger McEntyre offered Josie Baylor-Bates a bit of advice.

"He's dangerous. Maybe it's time you admitted that to yourself."

When Josie screamed for them to wrap it up Jude had turned to Dr. Hart, Wilson had looked at Jude and the three of them went into overdrive. The scramble was on to get what they needed before Roger McEntyre cut them off. None of them thought about Colin Wren and none of them had noticed when he walked away toward the Reeling Rotator. Once there he was invisible, but Colin Wren saw everything and everyone. He saw the glitter in people's eyes—young and old—as they waited for the worst. Maybe even hoped for it. No one looked away. No one had that respect. It was bloodlust, pure and simple.

Colin saw Archer on the platform, his big hands around the neck of that young man. That boy, whose job it was to push a lever, who wanted to go home when his shift was over, whose eyes were like those of an animal caught in the headlights and knew it was about to become roadkill. Colin Wren saw the dispassionate expressions of the men who took control, assessed the cause of the fray and calculated the effect of their actions on the waiting crowd.

Colin Wren saw it all and realized that, in a way, he was watching his son's death: the cries, the fear, the cleanup. Both times Archer was in the middle of the fray. Colin had followed along as they spirited Archer away. He had stayed closer to the shadows than McEntyre and paid more attention than Josie Bates. He avoided them all. He saw the police and rejoiced that Archer was getting what was coming to him this night at least. He had heard Roger McEntyre say Archer was dangerous, and now Colin believed it heart and soul. Not because McEntyre said it with greater conviction than the district attorney but because this time Colin had seen Archer in action. This time it occurred to him that maybe something needed to be done about Archer—not Pacific Park.

20

"That was the dumbest thing you've ever done. I can't believe how stupid you are, Archer. What in God's name were you thinking?"

"I was thinking I wasn't going to sit in that car like some freaking little girl and wait for you to solve my problems."

"Oh, that's just great. You got yourself arrested because you don't want me to show you up? I ought to walk out of here right now."

Josie's hands chopped the air. She threw them up in despair as she paced the small room, too disgusted to look at Archer. He was no less angry, no less frustrated than she, but, damn it, he had created this mess and now he was making it worse.

"May I point out that you do need me, given the fact that you haven't done a real fine job of solving your problem either, Archer? What you did was just plain idiotic."

"What I did was smart. They were stupid. They put a guy on the side gate and let me walk right through the front. They're such sorry sons of bitches they can't even keep me out of an amusement park."

"Archer," Josie wailed. "Who is it that's locked up? Who was dragged out of Pacific Park like a dog?"

Archer's chin went up like he'd been clocked. He licked his lips and swallowed his fury.

"I'm just saying that they have holes in their operation. If they've got holes in that then there's holes in other things—like their case against me. Or hadn't you thought of that?"

"Gee, no, Archer. And I hadn't thought that beating up a kid with a high school education was going to prove anything." Josie taunted him, furious that he would betray her. She had vouched for him. She had promised to return. She was standing up for him and he was spitting on her.

"I wasn't . . . going to . . . hurt him."

Archer grabbed the back of a chair and yanked it away from the table. Raising it he brought the back legs down hard on the floor and turned his head away from her before whipping himself around to sit down. For a minute he jerked this way and that, wrapped in a seizure of exasperation until, tired and humiliated, Archer put his elbows on the table and bent his head.

"He's not a kid. He's twenty, maybe older."

"He's a kid who didn't know what hit him," Josie said under her breath. "He works at a theme park and thinks that's a profession, Archer. You've got thirty years on him and fifty pounds. Come on. No contest."

"And he's telling the DA that I screwed with Tim's harness," Archer said. "I just wanted him to admit he lied, but he wouldn't even look at me. I just wanted him to see what he was doing to my life. Then he wouldn't, and I don't know what happened. I was just going to make him tell the Goddamn truth."

Archer threw himself back, defeated. His arms fell to his sides and his broad chest seemed to cave under the pressure of the day. Josie pushed away from the wall; the fight was gone out of her, too. She sat in the chair next to him. Between them was a curtain of antipathy so tightly woven she couldn't have reached through it if she wanted to.

"Nothing he told you tonight would have mattered, Archer. There were no witnesses to anything except assault. Even if he said you jumped off the ride and tried to save Tim, I couldn't have used it in court. All you've done is dig yourself a deeper hole."

She let that hang there so Archer could admire his handiwork. Finally, when Josie couldn't help herself, when the question in her brain began to burn, she asked it.

"What were you going to do? Beat him until he told you what you wanted to hear whether it was the truth or not?"

Archer cast her a look so ugly and mean it was hard to imagine she even knew him. The raised welt above his eye was still red and raw. It reminded Josie that there were people who thought he was a killer, that there were grown men who were afraid of him.

"You know me better than that," Archer rasped.

"I knew a man who was patient when I was trying to make a new life for myself. I knew a man who stood by me when I was fighting for Hannah's life and never once raised his voice, much less his hand. I knew a man who used to bide his time, face the truth, act without prejudice. That's the man I knew."

"Fuck it, Josie, that's who I am and you know it!"

Archer shot out of his chair, half standing as he grabbed for her, grasped her, his hands tight on her lean arms as he lifted her toward him. Their faces were close, inches from each other. His was crimson with rage, hers white with shock. In a crackling minute Archer realized what he was doing, froze and slowly fell back into his chair. The hands that had held Josie shook as he let her go, and he wrapped his arms around his own body, fearful of what he might do to her.

"Oh, Jesus, I'm sorry. I'm sorry." He raised one hand and buried his face in it. "I am so scared, Jo. So damned scared."

Josie's gut wrenched. She had seen angry men, men who accepted their fate, men who fooled themselves and refused to accept the obvious. But she had never seen a broken man, and to see Archer broken was brutal. This was God's miserable joke. He had given Josie someone to love, a man who was her safe and constant companion, then asked her to watch as he took away everything she found honorable in Archer. To make matters worse, it seemed God and Archer had combined to take away her compassion.

"I don't know who you are, Archer. You lied to me about everything." Josie raised her head, lifted a hand up as if to ward off the pain an objection would cause. "Selective truth telling doesn't amount to much in a relationship, and in the courtroom it will hang you."

Archer's eyes narrowed. There was little left to see in them but bitterness.

"You don't know shit, Jo. You've never even seen a real death. Your mother took off and you don't even know if she's alive."

"Jesus," Josie breathed, "Archer . . ."

"Your father was laid out all nice in that hospital by the time you got there, wasn't he?" Archer demanded. "Well, I saw my wife writhing in pain through the stupor of medicine that was supposed to stop it and never did. I saw her kid splattered on the ground, his head popped open and his body parts all twisted. People were screaming and crying all around. Is that the kind of shit you wanted me to be *truthful* about? Is that the crap you wanted me to *share* with you? Well, okay, babe. Let's share."

Archer's voice dripped with sarcasm, and Josie's response came back small, shaken, unsure.

"I understand. . . ."

"No, you don't understand!" His hands slammed into the table. He was out of his chair again and out of his mind. "You don't understand how all of this haunted me. You don't understand that I'm afraid, and I don't know where to turn, and I can't turn to you because I don't want you to see what I've seen. . . ."

Suddenly Archer's massive shoulders shook with a sob. It had come from nowhere, gripping him hard, and he was ashamed. Like a blind man he felt for the chair and used it as a crutch when he sat down.

"I don't want you to save me. I want to save myself. I need to prove to you that I couldn't have hurt that boy. I would never have done that to Lexi. Never."

Josie faltered, unable to think, unsure of what to do. In this plain room she had finally heard the truth, and it had nothing to do with Archer and everything to do with her. Josie had always been removed from the horrors of losing the people she loved. Now, though, she was wading through a sea of hurt that pulled her under, suffocated her, rendered her powerless against the rise and fall of the tides of Archer's hatred and self-pity. What was she to do? Save him from the law? Protect him from himself? Turn her back and walk away because he had lashed out and wounded her? Archer's head lifted. He was spent. He didn't know what he had done.

"Can you get me home, Jo?"

She shook her head. She was numb. She whispered, "No."

As if on cue the door opened and an officer was there.

"They filed a formal complaint?" Josie barely glanced at him.

"Sure did. We just got word bail's been revoked."

Josie nodded. The door closed. She sat at the table with Archer and touched his hand, entwining her fingers in his.

"From here on out, we are lawyer and client. Do you understand?"

"It will break us, Jo," Archer murmured.

"Maybe. Maybe not," Josie said, knowing in her heart that he was right. Some truths she might not be able to live with, not with Archer by her side.

She slid her hands from under his. The cop was back. He had Archer by the arm and was lifting him to his feet, cuffing him.

Against her better judgment, against all rules of protocol, against the warning Josie had just given Archer that she was nothing more than his attorney, Josie stepped forward—not to her client but toward the man she loved.

Putting her arms around him even though he could not reciprocate, Josie touched her cheek against his and breathed in his scent. She moved slightly so that Archer could feel her body properly against his. The policeman who had him in custody would never know how intimate the moment was.

"Archer," she said under her breath.

There was nothing more. As he was led away all Josie could do was pray that she would be planning his defense, not his funeral, in the days to come.

21

"Of course I'm mad. Lord, Hannah, what were you thinking, letting a man you don't know in this house?"

Hannah sat on Josie's bed, one leg cocked under her, her head held high as Josie paced. The only sign that Josie's anger upset her was the scratching: left hand, right forearm. Though the sleeves of her shirt were long, Josie knew the skin beneath was fragile from so many years of cutting. The scratching wasn't a good sign, but that minute Josie didn't care.

"Stop scratching, Hannah. Just stop. And don't count. I can't take it tonight."

"Then don't watch." Hannah's lashes fluttered, and Josie saw just the hint of defiant green eyes. "And don't get mad because I let Jude in."

"But you didn't know it was Jude," Josie insisted. "You've never met him. This case has been in the papers, and anybody could have shown up and said they were Jude."

"I knew it was him. I have good instincts. He's not dangerous. He's just full of himself. And rich. My mother would like him." Hannah tossed her head and her long black hair rippled down her back. It was a frivolous gesture, the icing on the cake of infuriating things Hannah was doing to stake her claim to Josie's attention.

"Stop!" Josie threw herself at Hannah and took her left hand in both of hers. So tall she had to double over, Josie looked a surprised Hannah straight in the eye. "I can't worry that you're going to spiral, Hannah. I need you to give me a little payback here."

"I thought you asked me to stay with you because you wanted to help me. I didn't know I was being bought," Hannah challenged boldly.

"Oh, please." Josie let go of her hand and stood up. "You know exactly what I'm saying. Letting a man you don't know into this house is stupid. I want better for you. What I really want is for things to be normal for you, and I'm upset they can't be right now. So I'm asking you, I'm begging you, try to chill until I get through this thing with Archer. Try not to take it personally because you think I'm not paying attention to you."

"That's not what I'm doing. That's not it at all, and if you think it is then you don't know anything about me." The mattress gave a little bounce as Hannah got off the bed and stormed out of the room, slamming the door behind her.

Josie whipped around, not sure where to turn. The French doors she and Archer had hung led to the patio and the garden oasis it had taken her three months to build with her own hands. Beyond that there was the wall and the beach and the town of Hermosa and Los Angeles past that. The thought of running from her problems made Josie feel sick. She was not her mother. Josie didn't give up because life got tough or was uninteresting or there was the promise of something better just over the hill. But life was tougher than it had ever been, and something was eating away at her confidence, and . . .

"I don't usually have to invite myself into a woman's bedroom to get her to notice me."

Josie's shoulders sagged. Her chin dropped to her

chest and she chuckled pitifully. She hadn't even heard Jude open the door. He grinned at her when she looked over her shoulder.

"I'll just bet you don't, Jude. I also bet you don't get asked to leave a bedroom too often either." Josie walked by him, flipping off the light as she went. In the living room she pointed to the coffee table. "Do you want a fresh drink?"

"No, thanks. Hannah makes a strong one. She's an interesting kid." Jude sat on the couch as if he did it every night.

"The operative word is *kid*," Josie warned, and sat across from him in the leather chair. "But Hannah isn't the topic. Pacific Park is."

"Well," Jude said regretfully. "Archer really blew it tonight. Colin's making noises about filing against Archer whether or not he's exonerated. So if you want to protect him, you've got to control him."

"He's in jail, Jude. You can't get more controlled than that." Josie got up, unable to sit still while she talked about Archer. She went to the kitchen and grabbed a beer, raising her voice while she did so. "We never asked Colin for anything. I'm sorry he forfeited the bond money but it was a calculated risk. Don't worry. He'll get his day in court when Archer is out of this mess."

"I don't appreciate the sarcasm, Josie," Jude said quietly. "Colin is genuinely anguished. He wanted to help Archer because he just couldn't believe anyone would intentionally hurt Tim, but if Archer's guilty, Colin wants his head."

"Then I guess we'll just have to make sure we prove he isn't, won't we?"

Josie leaned her shoulder against the wall that divided the living and dining rooms. Jude didn't bother to argue, and she didn't much feel like talking about Colin Wren and his self-righteous, long-suffering act. She raised her beer. She took a drink. She wanted her life back, and she wanted it back with Archer. Jude sitting in her living room wasn't helping anything.

"Why didn't you just call me with whatever you turned up in the inspection, Jude?"

"I thought you might need a friend." He gave a small smile and looked sad. "But now that I see you don't, I'll just tell you what I've got; then you can figure out where you want to go from there."

"I think that's a dandy idea," Josie sniffed, her backbone stiffening. She took another drink. Pitied by a legal gigolo. How far she had fallen.

"We didn't find anything you can use," he admitted. "The harness straps on some of the stations had been replaced; it was obvious they were of varying age. Tim's was older. The locking mechanism was somewhat different from the newer ones, but no less serviceable. We'll make sure that it met industry standards at the time, but there's no reason to think it didn't." Jude stood up and slung his jacket over his arm. "Wilson and Dr. Hart suggest the ride be tested for metal fatigue, do stress tests on the harness before you go to trial."

"Don't you mean *if*?" Josie drawled.

"No, Josie, I mean when. Any chance you had to beat the prelim ended tonight, and I think you know it."

"I would have expected more fight out of you, Jude."

"I'm practical. I know when to regroup. So, I guess that's it. I'll see you in court." He took a minute. When she didn't say anything he sighed. "We were all pulling for it to go a different way, Josie."

"He is innocent, Jude." Josie stared at the floor, the bottle of beer dangling from her fingers. "Everyone is until someone proves they're not."

"Guess that's true in criminal," Jude noted. "In civil law everyone is guilty of something and there's a price to pay."

"Then let's find out what Pacific Park is guilty of and maybe it will make Ruth Alcott and John Cooper think twice about prosecuting Archer. Bring me something I can leverage." Her eyes flickered to Jude as she laid down the challenge. "I want Archer out of jail. Colin can have his pound of flesh, just not at Archer's expense."

Jude paused as he came abreast of Josie. Equally tall, equally handsome, they looked each other in the eye. Jude touched her arm. He gave it a squeeze.

"Ask for help if you need it, Josie, but don't order me around. Shooting yourself in the foot can be fatal in our business."

Josie looked down at his hand and he backed off, ready to leave. She hated that she needed his help, but suddenly she realized he had something she could use. Jude had Wilson Page.

"Okay, Jude, I need help," she said, and turned her back to the wall and faced Jude head-on. "Ask Wilson to go online. I want the plans for the east quadrant of the park during the years the Shock and Drop was in operation. I mean, from the minute it was assembled to the minute they moved it. I'm looking for camera placements in the community areas. Would you do that for me? Would you ask Wilson if he can do that online?"

"Okay, Josie. Okay." Jude stepped back. He seemed to want to say something else, to do something more. Instead he gave up and let himself out.

Hearing the door close, Max raised his head and blinked at Josie. She still stared at the spot where Jude had stood. Slowly the dog got to his feet, his hindquarters hobbled by arthritis but his spirit strong as ever. His toenails clicked on the hardwood as he came up beside her and leaned against her legs. She touched him absentmindedly, then pushed off the wall and headed to her room. Josie lay on her bed, the bottle of beer held on her stomach with one hand, her other arm cocked behind her head. Her eyes were fixed on the ceiling and her brain was filled with nothing but doubt.

There is no sound in heaven or earth that resonates in the gut like the sounds men make in prison. They are loud, constant, unintelligible; a hodgepodge of noises made by bullies and victims, supplicants and avowed saints. Some call out to friends, some holler for the hell of it, some talk, convincing only themselves of their innocence. They throw things, demand things, pray for things, and nobody pays much attention at all: not their fellow inmates, not the guards and certainly not God. Archer had heard it all before—he just hadn't heard it from the inside.

He had been scrubbed down, his clothes, keys and wallet taken away, his body checked for contraband. All this had been done with a detached efficiency Archer used to call professional. Now he had another word for it: dehumanizing. Even the guard who looked familiar as he came to collect Archer and move him past the first gate barely gave him a look. Archer was a prisoner and the guard had a job to do.

A switch was thrown. Mechanics and metal, wiring and wizardry created magic. The gate was pulled back just in time for the guard to guide Archer through it

and into a narrow hallway. They had gone only fifty
yards, but prison's instant-messaging system was tele-
graphing Archer's arrival in a wave of calls and hoots
and hollers.

A fingertip on the shoulder and Archer lurched, irritated that this guy who should have recognized him
was treating him like a normal son of a bitch. But
Archer had turned just enough to see that the guard
was quick and professional. His hand was at the ready
on the club that hung off his belt.

"Sorry, man," Archer mumbled, and clicked his
eyes forward. Another thirty feet and they reached
Archer's private accommodations.

The door was new and shiny. Two rectangular slits
were sliced out of the metal: one for Archer's eyes to
see out, one for food to be shoved in. The guard
touched him. Archer knew the drill. He stepped to
the side. A button was pushed. The breakaway of the
lock was jarring. Swallowing hard, Archer kept his
eyes forward. The door pulled back like a slow-mo
reveal: stainless-steel toilet, metal bed frame, thin mattress, desk, chair, a window that allowed no more than
a sliver of sun into the small room. Overhead lights
Archer couldn't control. No sun, no sand, no sea to
look at. This was a horror of a place, and Archer
would die here; of that he was sure.

With no recourse Archer stepped into the room. He
paused as he faced the wall, thinking he couldn't bear
to watch the door shut and then he couldn't bear not
to. The uniformed man never took his eyes off Archer.
His expression was blank but . . . there . . . was something. Archer stepped forward, hands out to his sides
to show he was no threat. His lips parted. The guard
spoke instead.

"Watch your back," he said just before the door closed tight.

Watch your back.

He knows me.

The man remembered that they had worked together. He had given Archer a bit of advice he didn't need, but the effort meant the world to him. Slowly Archer walked to the door and touched it. It was cold as ice. It sounded like the gates of hell when it opened and a coffin lid when it closed. No matter which it was, Archer was having a damned hard time drawing a breath now that it was done.

The first sob came on Josie so quick she jackknifed with the force of it, cupping her hand over her mouth so Hannah wouldn't hear her cry. The beer sloshed out of the bottle she still held, and Josie scrambled to set it aside. She grappled for a pillow and buried her face in it. She rolled and sobbed and still could not get rid of the pain.

Every arrogant belief Josie had ever held regarding her strength, her independence, her objectivity crumbled as she mourned for what she was losing. Finally, exhausted, she lay still, curled on her side, her arms wrapped around the pillow as she stopped fighting and let the tears flow down her face and into the pillow that swallowed her softening sobs.

She must have dozed, because when she opened her eyes evening had become night and she wasn't alone. Hannah was kneeling by her bed, one hand on Josie's head, patting it in gentle bursts of five, ten and twenty.

Josie blinked. She felt Hannah's touches. Josie wanted to sleep but was afraid she would never get up if she did.

"It's okay if you don't pay attention to me," Hannah whispered. "That's not why I was mad."

Josie took a deep breath, trying to find the energy it would take to engage in conversation.

"Then what?" was the best she could do.

"I didn't want you to hurt," Hannah said softly. "I was mad because Archer hurt you. I wanted to protect you. Then you'd love me, if I protected you."

Josie closed her eyes. This was a first. Someone wanted to take care of her. In the still room, Josie reached for Hannah. The girl lowered her head onto the pillow that Josie pressed against her body and her other arm reached out. Josie lifted her own hand and her fingers wound 'round Hannah's forearm. She wanted to hold tight, to let Hannah know she was appreciated if not quite loved yet. Before she could speak, Josie's fingers touched something warm and wet on Hannah's arm.

Blood. Oh, God. Blood.

Josie's eyes opened. Hannah's were closed. Josie's touch had made the girl peaceful. Carefully she closed her fingers around Hannah's arm. There was no reason to talk about the cutting, no need for outrage. Hannah had taken Josie's pain and lanced her own skin to let the sting of it run out with her blood.

They stayed like that—the tall woman, the girl with the dark skin and the green eyes. Their heads were close together; their breathing was deep and measured. They listened to nothing, felt the moon rise and watched its light creep into the room. Josie's fingers caressed Hannah's arm gently, the way she thought a mother might. When Hannah's breathing slowed and sleep was upon her, Josie let go and touched Hannah's hair, promising herself that this was her last moment of self-pity and doubt. Hannah would never hurt on her account again. Nor would she hurt for Archer.

Closing her eyes, Josie knew she could keep the first promise. It was the second one she wasn't sure of. That one just might kill her.

22

Emily Baylor-Bates was always in exactly the right place at the right time. It was an incredible talent that Josie admired in her mother. If a supermarket gave away free groceries to the twentieth person through the door, Emily would walk through, number twenty. If there was a man in heat, Emily would be there to fan the flame. If there was attention to be had, Emily would turn the corner right into it.

Josie was a little different. She worked for her good fortune, identified her strengths and honed them, made plans and executed them. It wasn't a bad way to live. In fact, Josie took pride in the fact that, when she set her mind to something, she usually figured out a way to get it. Perfecting her volleyball game got her a scholarship to USC; tenacity and brains had made her one of the highest paid lawyers in California before she decided morality should not take a backseat to money and power. And Josie kept her eyes wide open even after she decided to shrink her universe and make Hermosa Beach and Faye Baxter's neighborhood law firm her home. Bottom line, Josie liked knowing what she was walking into, unlike her mother, who preferred to open any door to a big, fat surprise.

That was why, when Josie parked in front of a low white building out in the Valley, she had a pretty good idea of what was in store for her at the Greenwood Home.

The Greenwood Home housed a maximum of thirty-five patients, all of whom had both mental and physical disabilities. The extent of those disabilities ranged from complete dependence to functional but limited independence. Tim Wren was at the high end of the scale. He had grown up in this place, and Barbara Vendy was the current administrator. She was also the easiest person to identify on Ruth Alcott's witness list, so this was where Josie started.

Tossing her baseball cap on the backseat, Josie ruffled her hair and unzipped her jacket. The weather was mild; the sun was out. Traffic had been bad on the freeway and no better once she hit surface streets. She was half an hour late when she walked up to Greenwood's entrance and through the automatic door that was wide enough to accommodate wheelchairs. Josie heard the mechanical swoosh and felt a ripple of cool air embrace her. Another swoosh and the door closed behind her. Josie's steps slowed, and she made a concerted effort not to show that she was less prepared for Greenwood than she thought.

A man paralyzed from the neck down motored along in a wheelchair powered by his own breath. A woman used one finger to type on a keyboard that translated her thoughts into the painful hesitation of mechanical speech while a nurse listened patiently. Josie could not imagine being so broken, so dependent. She nodded to the woman with the keyboard, then stuck her head in the first office she came to.

"Barbara Vendy?" she asked.

"Second office on the left." The young girl with the pencil stuck behind her ear made a motion. Then, thinking again, she looked up. "She's expecting you, right?"

Josie nodded. The girl went back to a task that involved a yellow marker, a computer printout and a ruler. Down the hall Josie passed an office with the door closed before she found the right one and knocked perfunctorily.

"Barbara Vendy?"

"That's me." The woman looked up and took off her reading glasses.

"Josie Bates. Sorry I'm late."

Barbara Vendy put out her hand and Josie took it. Her grip was as no-nonsense as the rest of her: khaki pants, open-necked oxford with the sleeves rolled up to her elbows, loafers, dots of gold in her ears and a haircut that was more for convenience than fashion. Her face was broad, kind and plain.

"No problem. Have a seat." Barbara pointed to a chair and held up a file. "I don't have much on Tim Wren, so I'm not sure the drive out here was worth it."

"I thought he lived here for most of his life," Josie said as she sat down.

"Tim was in one other facility for a while, but you're right, we had him since he was eight. I'd say that was most of his life."

She opened the file, scanned the contents and ticked off an overview.

"Difficult birth. Oxygen deprivation resulted in brain damage. Not a problem with the doctor, just one of those things. He had cerebral palsy that was managed with some of the newer drugs. Patient frustrated with his lack of physical control, and there were some socialization problems that were dicey. But then who wouldn't be bothered?" Barbara glanced up as if she expected an answer but didn't have time to wait for one. "And, for a grand finale, there was some trouble with one of his heart valves." End of story. She closed the file and gave it over to Josie. "That's all I've got."

"I was hoping to get his complete medical files so I could understand the details of his treatment. There should be no patient confidentiality problem."

"Unfortunately, I don't have the files. We usually keep patient records five years, but in this case we were asked to forward them to Lexi after Tim died. We kept this summary as a backup." Barbara pulled up her chin, and her bottom lip disappeared beneath the top in silent apology.

"Okay, I'll track down the medical records in Lexi's storage, but what can you tell me about Tim himself? I mean, what quality of life did he have?" Josie pressed.

"Mostly he was happy. Sometimes he was a handful, but that's to be expected when you have someone who is both physically and mentally limited."

"What about his relationship with his stepfather?"

"I don't know," Barbara answered with a shrug. "Sorry. I only met the man in passing. He wasn't here very often, but when he was he was courteous. I have to be truthful, Ms. Bates. I'm an administrator. I make sure nothing leaks, broken things get fixed, bills are paid and our residents have access to their doctors."

"But you did know Lexi, right?" Josie pressed. "She was coming here long before she remarried."

"Everybody knew Lexi." Barbara laughed lightly, as if just thinking about Lexi made her feel happy. "She was a lovely woman. She never missed a planned visit and came as often between those as possible. She always paid in advance and tried to anticipate everything Tim might need. She even managed to come up with money for experimental treatments and therapies. Lexi was a model parent. I wish all of our families were like her."

"Did any of it work?" Josie asked.

"No," she answered sadly. "And it never would. Only Lexi believed, and she believed like a fanatic."

"Then it was money down the drain," Josie mused.

"Not really. If it made Lexi feel hopeful then there was a benefit." Barbara cocked one arm on her chair. "But what you're really asking is, How did Lexi's husband react to all that? All I have is some insight. Sometimes one spouse resents the output of money, the time spent on useless endeavors, the emotional connection between a patient and a parent. Situations like this can be especially hard on men, and worse for a stepparent to boot. With Lexi's husband, you had it all."

She dropped her arm and put her hand on the phone.

"You know, I think maybe you should talk to one of the nurses who worked with Tim and his family. Maybe that would help."

23

"Hey, hey, Mr. Folton. Come on, now. Be good for me. There you go, man. Nice and easy now. Shit!"

The big black man threw himself across the bed and landed on top of a patient who fought like a banshee and looked like a beanpole. The black man was football-player big, and still he struggled to bind the other man's hands to the bed frame. There were grunts and groans, and it was impossible to tell who was working harder: the one who wanted to be free or the one who wanted to make sure he was not. The football player in green scrubs won the scrimmage. Mr. Folton was restrained, his energy sputtering out as the other man talked.

"Okay, Mr. Folton. Now, there you go. Now you gonna go right to sleep in a minute after that nurse get here and give you something to make you sleep. Then you're gonna feel just a whole lot better, Mr. Folton. You'll see. You'll see there, buddy. No sweat now, sir."

The man on the bed wrenched and hollered one last time. The big man reached out and put one of his hands on Mr. Folton's head as if he were giving a blessing. Josie heard a calming *shhhh* as he tugged on the bindings once more. When the man turned away he saw Josie.

"You sure ain't the nurse, but we could use you on our team," he muttered as he walked right at her.

Josie stepped back, let him pass, then followed him down the hall.

"Don't you think you ought to stay with him until the nurse does come?" Josie looked over her shoulder, half expecting to see Mr. Folton chasing after.

"He can't hurt himself now. He'll be fine until she gets there." He gave Josie a sidelong glance. "Why you so interested?"

"I'm not." Josie had to shorten her stride to keep abreast of him. "It just seemed that was a little drastic, what you did in there. You could have crushed him. Instead of tying him up, you could have stayed with him until he got his medicine."

The black man stopped and laughed with a hack.

"It's worse to let him loose, lady. He could hurt other patients who can't protect themselves. And if he couldn't get to them, he'd hurt himself tryin'. Now, if you ain't a relative, I don't think I should be talkin' to you about what's good and what ain't for Mr. Folton." The man put his hands on his hips. "And since I've been takin' care of him for 'long on about ten years now, I don't think you're a relative. And if you're from some do-good agency like I figure, then, with all due respect, I don't want to be talkin' to you neither. What I do think is you should be talkin' to the people in the office. So, 'scuse me, ma'am, I got things to do."

"Wait. My name is Josie Bates, and Ms. Vendy sent me to see you." Josie hurried after him. "I'm an attorney. I want to talk to you about Tim Wren, and if you don't have time now I'll wait until you do."

He turned around. The hard heels of Josie's shoes made harsh sounds in the quiet hall. She extended her hand. He checked it out and took his fine time deciding what he wanted to do.

"Nate Walters." He took her hand. "You here to hurt or help?"

"Help, I hope."

"You ain't gonna make Tim seem bad."

"I'm not going to do that," Josie assured him. "From what I know about Tim, he couldn't be bad."

"You got that right. He could be a handful but he couldn't be bad." Nate looked down the empty corridor, then back at her. "You want to come with me? I got a break."

A few minutes later Josie was sitting in a room full of mismatched furniture, a radio, a sink, a coffeemaker and a bulletin board covered with messages, reminders and jokes cut out of magazines. Nate sat across from Josie with his legs splayed, one hand on each knee, his dark eyes holding steady on hers as he talked.

"I take care of the men mostly, 'cause they need a strong hand. Tim started acting out right about the time he was eleven or so, and they thought he'd be better with me. He liked men, anyway. He wanted to be one of the guys." Nate chuckled, remembering his charge. "That kid kept saying he wanted to be one of the guys. Took us a month of Sundays to figure that one out. Everybody thought he was saying he wanted to be a fly. He was okay, that kid."

"But there were times he was violent, right?"

"No worse than most of them. Hit the nurses if they tried to help him when he wasn't in the mood. He tried to hit me, but I was always one step ahead of him. He never figured that one out." Nate relaxed. He clasped his hands and put them on his lap.

"Was he big enough to fight off a grown man who was trying to do something bad to him?" Josie pressed.

"Sure, he could do that," Nate answered matter-of-factly. "But you're thinking like a normal person. You're thinking if someone went at Tim would he try to fight 'em, right? That's not the way it works."

"You mean he wouldn't try to protect himself if someone tried to hurt him?"

"What I'm sayin' is, he wouldn't necessarily know about normal. Like when he was on that ride at Pacific Park, Tim may not know what was good for him and what wasn't. See what I mean?"

Nate held his palms skyward and smiled, pleased that he got the drop on her.

"Oh, yeah, I been readin' about it. It ain't like they lock us in here night and day. I got a life. I get the paper. They say that man unbuckled Tim's straps. Well, Tim might not know it was dangerous if someone did that. He probably wouldn't know that he'd fall out if he didn't hold on."

"You mean he didn't understand cause and effect," Josie suggested.

"You got it. That's it." Nate grinned broadly. "Come at him with a baseball bat and he'd probably sit there till you hit him in the head. But you try to take away his rice puddin', I'm tellin' you, you were in for a fight." Nate laughed, amusing himself with his stories of Tim Wren.

"So, since you know, how was Tim when he was around Lexi's husband?"

"Nobody knew her husband all that good. The man was hard to read. Most I can say is he didn't look real comfortable when he was with the boy."

"Was it a normal uncomfortable or an angry uncomfortable?" Josie asked.

"In this place they're about the same. Being around here makes people feel guilty for being okay. Your guy gets props for sticking to it, though. I mean, he weren't a father or brother or nothin'. Mothers have the most love. Strangers, they're polite, you know. But steps? They marry the mother or the father of one of these people, but they don't know they bought into a lifetime of misery. It gets ugly when they figure it out. Lot of marriages go belly-up because someone's got kin here."

The door opened and a small woman with red hair looked in.

"Nate. We can't get Richard into the shower. Can you come?"

Nate raised a finger and the woman ducked out as quickly as she had poked in. He put his hands on his knees as if that helped him get up. Josie stood up, too, but cut him off before he got to the door.

"But it didn't get ugly with Archer and Tim, did it? Or with Lexi?" she asked.

"Not that I saw," Nate answered, "but I ain't here 'round the clock. The only thing I really know for sure is it was a damn shame Tim's own pop didn't come down to see him, but Tim kept hopin'."

"His real father never did come here, did he? You didn't see him at all?" Josie pressed. "Balding. Glasses. Not very tall."

"Not that I know. Tim never said. I didn't see anyone like that with his mom." Nate walked around Josie, stopping long enough to pass the door to Josie after he opened it. "Tim would have told me if his pop came."

"Did Tim's mother ever say anything about Tim's real father?"

"You mean like raggin' on him?" Nate shook his head. "I ain't on intimate personal terms with the patients' families. But if you're askin' if I ever heard her say anything against Tim's pop while I was around, the answer is no. The only thing I know for sure is that woman walked a tightrope between her man and Tim. At the end she only cared about the boy. She didn't worry that her man didn't want to be here. *She* wanted to be here." Nate threw a look over his shoulder and then gave Josie another minute and a suggestion. "I gotta go now, but if you hang around till dinner, you can catch Mrs. Schmidt. Her and Tim's mom were tight. Maybe she knows what went down."

"Thanks. I just might do that." Josie was already turning away.

Nate was a step farther down the hall when he stopped and called her back. They walked toward each other. When Nate was close enough he said, "Just for the record, if your man hurt Tim I hope he fries."

As Nate went on to where he was needed, Josie took account. This was the first time she'd heard it said aloud, that cold call for blood. It had been implied in the press, reflected in people's eyes, even heard in Burt's wavering defense after Archer's second arrest. Raising her eyes, Josie clutched her bag tight, drew a deep breath through her nose and let it out through pursed lips. She heard someone holler. She heard the sounds of a television and a respirator. Things could be worse for Archer. Not by much, but it was possible.

In the parking lot Josie settled into the Jeep and called Hannah to let her know she wouldn't be home until late. That done, Josie put her head back and looked at the roof of her car and wondered if anyone would notice if she just never got out again.

Hannah hung up the phone as the doorbell rang. Following the new house rules she pulled Max close,

walked quietly toward the door, and pulled back the
white curtains on the window just enough to see if
friend or foe waited outside. With a cluck and a put-
upon sigh, Hannah sent Max packing, unlocked the
door and opened it as though she were doing a great
favor to Billy Zuni, who waited on the porch with a
huge grin on his face.

"What do you want?"

Holding the door open just far enough so he could
see her face, Hannah assumed Billy would see exactly
how unimpressed she was with his presence, how impatient she was for him to get the message. It wasn't
enough. Billy grinned wider and pushed his blond
bangs out of his eyes.

"Hannah. Hey. I told Ms. B. I'd be checking on you
when she wasn't around. I don't see her car, so I figured I'd check on you. The way I said I would . . ."

His voice trailed off. He wasn't as dumb as Hannah
thought. The fading smile, the way he moved his
weight from one foot to the other, told her he knew
when he was being dissed. Too bad it didn't make him
go away.

"The car could be in the garage, you know," Hannah pointed out wearily.

"Yeah, but it isn't because I've been waiting for her
since four and she didn't come home from work
early." Billy brightened as he bested Hannah. He was
a man on a mission and he wasn't going to give up
trying to make Hannah like him. "So, since Ms. B.'s
not home I should watch out for you, 'cause it's getting dark."

"You mean you want to babysit me?" Hannah
rolled her eyes in disbelief, and Max whimpered as if
he felt bad for Billy.

"No, no." Billy shook his head hard. "No, for sure,

I just want to make sure you're okay. Like, do you need anything . . . or anything. If you don't, I could just, like, well . . . You want me to sit on the patio and hang? I can do that."

"No, I want you to go home, Billy. Just go home and leave me alone."

"Naw, I can't do that. My mom's got somebody over and I promised—"

"Oh, Christ. I know. You promised Josie. . . ."

Hannah threw open the door and walked away. He could come in or not—his choice. Hannah went into her bedroom and shut the door. Billy just talked louder.

"So, I thought we could go to Burt's and get some burgers. I don't have any money but Burt knows I'm good for it. . . ."

Billy stood in the living room waiting for her to come back, but it was Max who came to greet him. Billy took the dog's face in his hands and ruffled him affectionately.

"Okay, we'll have dinner, dude," he whispered.

Billy changed Max's water and dug in the bag for his food. When he was done he went to the patio and picked up the hose to water Josie's plants. That was where Hannah found him.

"So, do you want to go get something to eat or not?" she demanded.

Her fingers touched the sides of the door over and over and over again, short bursts of activity that kept Hannah aware of her parameters, hiding the fact that she was nervous because Josie wasn't there. Billy didn't seem to notice; the same way he didn't notice her low slung jeans and her tight T-shirt, the choco-latey skin in between and how beautiful Hannah was even when she was annoyed. Billy didn't notice those things because Hannah had just told him that she was willing to go with him to Burt's. That made him grin again.

"Yeah. For sure, Hannah. You want to go down to the beach? It's not too cold. You know, we could sit and watch the waves for a while and then go to Burt's and then we could go walk on the pier later. They say there's going to be red tide, but I think it's too late for that."

"This isn't a date. I just want to go get dinner and then go home again and then you leave." Hannah led Billy through the house. She touched the table, the lamp and the sofa on the way out the door.

As loyal as Max-the-Dog, Billy listened to her ground rules while Hannah locked up. She walked to the end of the path three times and three times she went back to check the door. The fourth time Billy went with her, and that was enough to make Hannah stop checking. Shrugging into her hoodie, she walked at Billy's side as they crossed the street and made a right on the bike path heading toward Burt's. Billy stuck his hands in his pockets and looked around, racking his brain for something to say. Finally he hit on something they both knew something about.

"You know, maybe this thing with Lexi's kid is why Archer doesn't really take to us. Maybe it's why he doesn't like kids."

"Maybe," Hannah muttered.

"Like, what are you going to do if Archer is guilty?" Billy asked.

"I'm not going to do anything." Hannah pulled a face and looked at him as if he were a mutant. "Why should I have to do anything?"

"Hey, whoa, Hannah. Don't get mad about it. I was

just asking." They walked in silence a minute longer. Then he brightened. Another thought had come into his head. It was the answer to her question. "Because things aren't going to be good if Archer killed that kid."

"I wouldn't imagine." Hannah didn't want to use her energy to point out how really stupidly obvious that was.

She bent and swept something off the street. It was a piece of silver paper, a gum wrapper. She put it in her pocket. Even though the beach wasn't her favorite place, she didn't want to see it dirty. Maybe she would use it in a collage or painting. Besides, it gave her something to do while Billy struggled to get the conversation going.

"Yeah," Billy mused. "Josie might not want kids around anymore if Archer has to go away because of a kid. See what I mean? I don't think she'd want me around anymore because I'd remind her of that boy, but maybe Josie wouldn't want either of us around anymore. You know, because it was a kid who caused this grief. And we're about his age. You and me. Well, we're older but . . ."

Billy walked on, hardly noticing that Hannah had fallen back. When he turned to find her, Hannah blanked her expression, opened her mouth and said, "God, you're stupid."

Turning around, she stormed back to Josie's house. Billy followed her. He took no offense at her attitude. Billy knew Hannah hadn't thought about what would happen the way he had. He always thought ahead. When you figured out the worst that could happen then everything else was better. He wasn't the smartest guy on the beach, but still, he did know one thing for sure. It was a lesson his mother had taught him well. Billy Zuni knew that women liked to blame the kid when the men walked away or were taken away or were put away.

That was just a fact of life.

24

Using normal parameters Josie Bates did not consider herself an overly charitable person. She didn't collect toys for children at Christmas. She didn't pray for world peace. She didn't lunch with ladies who raised money to save anything with four legs or two fins. She never volunteered to help the sick. Yes, she had taken Hannah in, but that seemed less charity than an in-your-face necessity. That act was definitive: feed and clothe Hannah, teach her, give her an opportunity to thrive and then let her take it from there. But charity? The kind personified by truly selfless goodness in the face of unrelenting need? That was another matter altogether. Total dependency, perpetual weakness, those were conditions that Josie could not abide because it made the person on the other end of the stick seem almost godlike. And nobody—but nobody—was that good.

Maybe that was why Josie took a minute to study Mrs. Schmidt in room 217. She was looking for a sign that the woman wasn't as perfect as she seemed. Josie wanted to catch her when she faltered, see the break in her bearing that would prove this woman was as fatally flawed as 99 percent of the population. But she wasn't. Mrs. Schmidt was possessed of superhuman patience, kindness and good humor. To top it all off, she was gorgeous.

Mrs. Schmidt was willowy and ladylike. Her clothes

were simple and chic. Her face was exquisitely pro-
portioned and framed by honey-blond hair. Her
hands were graceful as she went about her chore, and
Mrs. Schmidt's voice was gentle. She didn't seem to
notice that the man in the bed did not respond to
her loving dialogue or eat the food she so carefully
spooned into his barely moving mouth or look her in
the eye.

Because she was in the presence of a truly charitable woman, Josie waited to knock until after Mrs.
Schmidt wiped her husband's mouth when the food
bubbled out.

"Mrs. Schmidt?"

"Yes." The bowl went into her lap. Her wide brown
eyes looked straight at Josie. Her shoulders were back,
her expression clear and without curiosity.

"My name is Josie Baylor-Bates and I—"

"And you're here to talk to me about Tim and
Lexi," the woman finished for her, punctuating the
sentence with a gentle laugh as she put the bowl aside
and pushed the bed table away. "Nate told me about
you. He watches out for all of us. He knows how
family members hate surprises."

"I don't mean to intrude. I can wait until you're
finished." Josie looked at the man in the bed. Her
gaze didn't linger because Nate had been right. There
was no comfortable place here for those who didn't
really belong.

"That's all right. I'm done, actually."

She leaned over her husband and took the napkin
from his chest. Working quickly but without a sense
of urgency, Mrs. Schmidt folded the napkin, said a few
words and laid one hand atop his head just before she
kissed him on the cheek.

"This is my husband, James. He's been this way

since a car accident seven years ago. I come have dinner with him every night—just in case."

"In case there's a change?" Josie asked, trying desperately to make the right small talk.

Mrs. Schmidt's bovine eyes turned Josie's way. She smiled a Sophia Loren smile.

"No, there won't be any change," she said frankly as she joined Josie. "I come every day to get my spiritual brownie points. James always said you needed to put something away for a rainy day. He meant money, but I think it's wise advice for a lot of things in life, don't you? I mean, who's to say I won't be in a bed like that someday? If I am, and if I have enough brownie points, maybe God will send someone to take care of me. So I come just in case."

"That's good advice. I wish I followed it."

They ambled down the hall, Mrs. Schmidt leading Josie with no more than a slight list, an almost imperceptible motion of her hand. She and her husband must have been fine on the dance floor.

"I wish I had before this happened; then I would have had something to draw down on. Maybe James would have just been hurt instead of ending up like that." They stopped at a glass door. Mrs. Schmidt put one hand on it and inclined her head. "Do you mind sitting on the patio? I like a cigarette after dinner."

A second later Josie was standing on a square of concrete where the patients were taken to "get air." White wrought-iron tables and chairs with sun-bleached cushions were scattered around. The umbrellas were collapsed and fastened; the summer flowers had faded and not been replaced in the three small planters. The patio was illuminated by light that filtered in from the surrounding hallways.

Mrs. Schmidt took a chair at the table in the far

corner, pulled another one up and put her feet on it. Josie sat opposite her and knew that she was privy to a ritual: a cigarette, a look up, a few thoughts about life and love and fate, then home alone..

"I miss Lexi." Mrs. Schmidt's voice was almost dreamy. There had been no prompt. She didn't look at Josie. The tip of her cigarette moved like a dawdling firefly settling near her lips before flying into the air again. Back and forth. Lazy. Thoughtless. Unenjoyable, but comforting. Then she held the cigarette away and said, "It all seems so long ago. Almost as if they were never here."

She tapped the ash off her cigarette with a deft flick. Through the darkness Josie saw her turn her head; she saw the glint of her teeth as she smiled ruefully.

"I'm sorry. I guess I miss Lexi more than I knew. I'm already getting personal, and I don't even know what you really want. Maybe just having you sit in that chair the way she did makes me miss her." She took another drag, then said, "My name is Carol, by the way."

"I'm Josie," she reiterated. "Archer's lawyer. I am sorry to intrude, but I need all the information I can get, and I need it fast."

"I can only tell you things that I observed, and it was all a very long time ago." Mrs. Schmidt raised her shoulders slightly, honest and apologetic.

"But you knew Lexi well," Josie prodded.

"I did." Carol Schmidt held her cigarette out and looked at the glowing tip as if trying to decide whether to give the habit up. She took another hit. "Lexi and I were sisters under the skin. Raw deals all around. Only someone who's been beaten up like we have could be the kind of friends we were. She called me the married widow. I liked that."

"Why did she call you that?" Josie asked.

"Because I wouldn't fool around; I wouldn't acknowledge that James would never be well and that I
was healthy and young. She didn't want me to give up
on James; she just wanted me to have a life, too. You
know, the way she did after she met Archer. I told Lexi
I was too much in love with the man James had been."
Carol took another drag, then tossed the butt into the
flowerless bed. "I didn't want to sleep with anyone else.
I didn't want to be close to another man."

"Did Lexi understand that?" Josie asked.

"Of course she did. Just look at what she was doing
for Tim. Every waking hour was spent thinking about
that boy; every spare cent was spent on him."

"But she remarried. She had a life outside of this
place," Josie reminded her.

"And she had a son in here, not a husband. That
was the difference," Carol answered.

"So are you saying that Archer was second fiddle
to her relationship with her son?" Josie asked.

"No, of course not. Lexi loved Archer fiercely, the
way she loved everyone important in her life. She
couldn't believe her luck, finding a good man who was
willing to let her do what she had to do for Tim.
No"—Carol shook her head—"Lexi was happy, and
that surprised me to no end."

"Why would her happiness surprise you?" Josie
asked.

"Because she was so bitter about her first husband.
She hated Colin for running out on Tim," Carol
Schmidt said. "That's why I was amazed at how pure
her happiness was when she married Archer."

"What about what Colin did to her? Didn't that
make Lexi bitter, too?"

"Obviously you didn't know her." Carol laughed, unaware that her comment had made Josie feel somehow small, insignificant in the face of the drama that had been Lexi's life. "Lexi always said Colin abandoned Tim; she never said Colin abandoned her. If Lexi truly loved you, you knew it. Then again, if she really didn't like you, you knew that, too." Carol dropped her feet. She put her arms on the table and fiddled with the pack of cigarettes. "I'm sorry. I suppose I should let you ask some questions instead of me just rambling on."

"No," Josie assured her, "this is fine. Everything helps. Was Lexi's relationship with her ex really that bad?"

"Who can say? I'm sure Colin had a problem relating to his son, but I don't know if Lexi gave him enough time to adjust to the disappointment of having a child like Tim. For Lexi, love had to be unconditional. When they divorced Lexi didn't want a settlement. She said it would be like a payoff; like Colin wiping his conscience clear of the way he felt about their son. Lexi was so proud and so angry at Colin."

"But she did get a settlement, and a good one at that," Josie reminded Carol.

"Oh, she finally came to her senses. She took what Colin offered. I thought it was very generous. I thought she should live in the apartment building, but she didn't. She said it would be like forgiving Colin, but I think that was a little grandstanding. Basically, she did the math and realized that the income from that building would pay for Tim to stay at Greenwood. The actual cash Colin gave her in the settlement didn't last long, though. She just threw it at people who might be able to help Tim. She really wasn't thinking straight. Some of her decisions after the divorce were good and some were just plain destructive."

Carol Schmidt sighed and she tapped the cigarette pack with one finger as if that helped her think.

"I stopped throwing money at doctors eight years ago. Figured my brownie points with God might bring a miracle but there wasn't enough money in the world to cure James. Lexi never did get to that point. I told her she should invest the money so there would be enough for Tim to live on if something happened to her. But she didn't listen. Lexi never really listened. She was like a little steamroller when she got an idea into her head, whether it was right or not."

"And Archer?" Josie asked.

"And Archer." Carol sighed. "Well, I would have bet money that Lexi had sworn off men, but Archer just caught her up. He didn't ask for anything. He was honest. That's why she loved him, and that's why I was happy for her."

"So the love was good, but how about the marriage?" Josie asked, knowing her curiosity wasn't only a matter of business.

"He was a fine man to go home to when Lexi was done here."

Josie moved in her chair. It was cold and it was dark and it was hard to hear someone else assess Archer's worth.

"Was Archer good for Tim?"

"I'd say it was a wash. He did more than most, less than some. He married Lexi even though she came with baggage. I think that's a lot." Carol traced a circle on the wrought-iron pattern of the table. "He came with her to visit for a while."

"I thought he came all the time because Tim was so hard to handle." Josie stopped fidgeting.

"Oh, no, I'm sorry. If Lexi wanted to take Tim out, Archer was always there to help her. It was the visits where they just stayed around Greenwood that he couldn't take."

"Did he say so?" Josie pressed.

"I just assumed that was the case," Carol answered. "You get a sense about these things. Just because Lexi married Archer didn't mean everything changed. She could get pretty obnoxious if she thought Tim was getting the short end of things, and that made Archer uncomfortable. Lexi would blow up and then be fine by the time she got home. She could change like that." Carol gave her fingers a snap. "It's an art when you live two lives like we do. One inside the walls and one out. You'd go crazy if you didn't adapt."

"So Lexi took it out on you when she was angry or frustrated?" Josie asked.

"Please don't put words into my mouth. She would vent, that's all. Believe it or not that helped me, too. It's like purging by proxy." Carol's brow furrowed as she remembered those times. "When Lexi got sick, though, everything changed. She was obsessed about what was going to happen to Tim when she was gone. She dragged Archer here whenever she could, hoping he would start feeling something for that boy. It almost killed her when she figured out it wasn't going to happen. Don't get me wrong; Archer tried hard from what I could see, but he didn't want anything to do with Tim."

Carol Schmidt licked her lips. There had been a catch in her voice, so she took a minute.

"There were times when she sat right here and

ranted that Archer was a selfish SOB. Then she'd break down and admit she knew she was asking for an enormous commitment from him. It was very emotional. I think what was really going on was that Lexi was so angry that she was dying and that there was nothing she could do about it. Everything was out of control. I can only imagine what went on at home."

"So, you're telling me that Archer refused to have anything to do with Tim?"

"I'm sure he didn't outright refuse," Carol said. "But I can't say positively. All I know is that it was like a soap opera. Up one day, down the next. Archer would stay away from home all night; then he would come back and beg Lexi to take care of herself. You see, he was worried about her, she was worried about Tim, and Tim was clueless. Lexi just couldn't see how she was more important than her son. She was dying; Tim was just broken. Tim would need Archer long after Lexi was gone. In her mind the whole thing was simple."

Carol got up and walked the patio. Josie knew she was struggling. She stopped. She talked.

"I saw Archer in the hall one night. He looked terrible. I asked him if he was all right. He said he would never be all right. Then he said . . ." She started to move toward Josie but stopped. Her face was in the shadows; she held on to a chair. "He told me Tim should be the one who was dying, not Lexi. He said that would make sense. I'd never spoken more than a handful of words to him before and he tells me that. It broke my heart."

Josie's gut lurched. She had known those sentiments were incriminating when Archer shared them with her; it never occurred to her that he might have been publicly vocal about his feelings here, of all places.

"Did you think he meant that?" Josie asked.

"Yes," Carol answered. "But I'm equally sure he didn't mean to threaten Tim, if that's what you're thinking. It was such an honest statement. Archer believed that would be the best thing."

Carol sat down again, warming to her subject, seeming to find some relief in sharing her thoughts. Archer wasn't the only one who lost something when Lexi died. Carol Schmidt lost a confidante, a lifeline, a friend.

"Look, Lexi wouldn't have married Archer if he wasn't a good man. Maybe Archer would have eventually stepped up to the plate if Lexi hadn't been so sick, or if she hadn't pushed him so hard and asked for so much. I just felt sorry for all three of them. You can't make anyone love a damaged person. And most of us accept that. . . ."

"But?" Josie urged.

"But I suppose I wouldn't put anything past anybody. That's just the way of the world."

Carol shook out a cigarette, held it in one hand and her lighter in the other. She was practical, honest and, suddenly, a frighteningly dispassionate woman.

"I thought about killing James. I could even have done it once. It would have been easy. The problem was, I thought about it. I had to ask if I was going to do it to end his suffering or mine. That's not something you discuss with people; it's not something you do to a helpless person. The point is, I honestly believed it was a solution. Maybe Archer thought the same thing. Maybe he wasn't chicken the way I was and he did help Tim die. It could have been his way of showing compassion."

Carol Schmidt raised the cigarette to her lips. She held it there and flipped the lighter. In the glow of the small flame, her eyes looked sultry, and with the cigarette between her lips her voice was sadly dispassionate.

"Maybe, if he did something, it would have been a mercy killing."

25

"No," Josie barked.

"What?" Carol Schmidt started as if she were surprised to still find Josie at the table.

"No," she said more quietly. "That wouldn't be the case. It's an interesting theory, though."

Josie gathered her things, distressed by what she had heard and determined not to show it. If Carol Schmidt had offered the same offhand comment to the prosecution there was no doubt that Ruth would make this a cornerstone of her case. This would make sense to a jury. This was something that—God help her—for a minute, made sense to Josie.

"I think I'd better go. It's a long drive back home," Josie said, knowing there was nothing more she needed from Carol Schmidt.

"I live close. I'll stay awhile longer," Carol answered, yet neither of them moved.

Josie knew what lay beyond the patio and couldn't imagine why Carol would want to stay. The sights and smells and sounds of the Greenwood Home seemed three-dimensional, an obstacle Josie would have to break through to leave and wash off when she got home. Now Josie understood why Archer balked at coming here. He couldn't bear all the trappings of sickness any more than she could. She glanced at Carol Schmidt, sensing unfinished business.

"Since I told the prosecutor who contacted me,

maybe I'd better tell you, too. I saw Archer get physical with Lexi. Just once. That's all," Carol said reluctantly.

"What happened?"

"I don't know all of it," she admitted. "I want to be very clear that I just walked into the room at the wrong time. Archer had Lexi up against the wall. All I heard him say was, 'Stop it, just stop it.' "

"How was he touching her?" Josie asked.

Carol's lashes fluttered. She sat up straighter and put out her hands. Her cigarette was between her fingers; a lazy plume of smoke rose into the darkness as her fingers curled to show Josie what Archer had done.

"He had her by the shoulders. He was pushing her. Sort of shaking her." Carol looked directly at Josie. "Kind of like he was pushing her back into the wall but not really doing it. I could see his knuckles were white, so he must have been holding her very tight. There was something in Lexi's expression—as if she were afraid or had just realized something terrible about Archer."

"Are you sure? Maybe she was just surprised," Josie suggested, reaching for straws.

"I don't think so," Carol answered sorrowfully. "I really don't."

"When did this happen?"

"Just before Tim's accident. Two days before. I know whatever Archer did to Lexi, it was done out of frustration. I'm positive that's all it was."

"The district attorney will try to make it sound bad; you know that," Josie advised her.

"I do." Carol smiled sadly. Her cigarette had burned down. It was nothing more than a nub in her fingers. Her voice was filled with embers, too; the last vestiges of hope that life was fair had been burned away. "And you'll make it sound like I'm an idiot who can't tell the difference between a discussion and a fight. My husband was hit by a drunk driver, Ms. Bates. That man's lawyer made James look irresponsible and arrogant. It took me years to realize that none of what happened in that courtroom was about justice. It was all about who could tell a better story."

Carol didn't bother with the last puff. She put her cigarette out in the dirt, crushing it.

"So, you see, I have nothing to do with how my recollection is perceived. It's up to you to take care of that, or the prosecutor, or the media if they're interested. I'll be a good citizen. I'll show up in court and that's the most either of you can expect, I suppose."

"The DA wants to win. The difference is, I want the truth," Josie assured her.

Carol Schmidt appraised Josie a minute longer. In the next she tapped out yet another cigarette. The last things Josie heard were the snap of her lighter and Carol Schmidt's dubious observation: "I'm sure you do."

"Oh, Roger, I wish your father were alive. Not that I don't trust you as much as he, but we were the same generation. It was different then. Men did business honorably. Now, I say something and next it's written down in a contract and it's never quite the way I say. Nobody understands the value of a handshake."

Isaac carried on while Roger McEntyre poured a drink and set it in front of him. The old man had loosened his tie. His hair seemed thinner, his face more sallow than usual. Roger knew it was no trick of the light; Isaac had had a day that would wear out any man.

"Settling on the boy who was killed three months ago isn't dishonorable, Isaac. It's good business," Roger assured him as he sat down opposite Isaac. "I don't think it was the wisest settlement. Five million is a lot of money these days. Receipts are flat and there was no fault on our part. Hillerman said we could win if we went to court. Barring that, he was sure the family would have settled for two if we held out."

"I know. I know." The old man was impatient to be talking about a problem that was put to bed. "That stupid boy should have stayed seated and he would have been fine. We could holler from the mountaintops that it wasn't our fault and we'd still look bad. Nobody wants to know the truth. Everybody wants to think we're bad people, that our business is bad. Untrue, all of it. Still, people believe what they want." Isaac took a long drink. "A jury would have settled millions more and we would have been ruined. If we waited them out on the settlement, the newspeople would make it look like we were trying to put the cheap on the price of a life. I took care of it quietly. This problem is gone away. The park needs good press now, not bad. It needs good everything now."

"The Boy Scouts are going to hold a West Coast fun day here, Isaac," Roger said. "We're tying in with all the local radio stations, giving access to television. We'll get that good press."

"I hope so." With a sigh Isaac set his glass aside and let his hand hang limply over the arm of the chair. "Greater United Parks may not want to buy my park, and if they don't acquire it then Pacific Park will disappear. I can't have that, Roger. The only thing I have is my life's work, and I don't want it to just go up in smoke, to be wiped off the face of the earth as if it never existed."

"That won't happen, Isaac. You did the right thing settling on that family before we got to court. The other thing—Tim Wren's death—that will be out of the way in six months at the outside. That's as long as we have to hang on, Isaac."

"Six months." Isaac sighed. "Six months is a lifetime when you're my age, Roger."

"It only seems that way in here, Isaac." Roger looked around the darkened office as if inviting Isaac to see what he saw. "Go into the park. Things will look better."

"You're right, Roger. You're always right." Isaac struggled to get up. Roger was ready to help but the old man made it on his own. Isaac found his jacket, put one arm in and took a minute to find the other sleeve. Finally he shrugged into it, buttoned it, adjusted his shoulders. "Still and all, I want to be sure about this thing with the Wren boy. I mean, the operator could be saying things because he's worried for his job. You know how these girls and boys can be. I'm too close to meeting my maker to have that on my soul."

Roger McEntyre walked with Isaac Hawkins to the door of the office. He had heard all this a hundred times since Archer's arrest and he would hear it a hundred more until the day Isaac died.

Wishing Isaac good night, Roger walked back to his own office. In less than an hour the park would close down. The cleaning and maintenance crews would descend like locusts to wipe away any sign that thousands of people had tromped through the park. Before they did Roger had a little maintenance of his own.

In the corner of his office, in a panel hidden in the credenza, he found what he was looking for. Turning on his desk lamp, McEntyre looked at them carefully. One sported the park's identification; the other wasn't labeled, as if the person who sent it didn't exactly know what it should be called.

Unhurried, Roger destroyed the first one and then the second. He piled the entire mess into his briefcase and he drove for two hours to find just the right place to dump it all. After that he had one more stop to make.

It was almost finished.

A few loose ends to clear up and all would be well.

"Moo shu?"

Amelia held up a Chinese take-out container and Jude declined.

"I'll stick with what I've got," Jude said, momentarily taking note that Amelia, the associate Josie had found too good to be true, looked even lovelier with her shoes off and her long legs stretched out in front of her. She obviously didn't think he looked better at the end of the day. Her focus was on business and food in that order.

"I spoke to Colin Wren again today. He wants an answer on when we'll be back on track with his case. He wants dates. He's making me nuts. He's calling every day now."

"He's a man with a mission," Jude said as he set aside his food and reached for his drink. "I've told him a million times, the minute the criminal trial ends I'll be on it. What's he think, I'm going to wait around for an invite before I get this up and running?"

Amelia shrugged. "I told him the same thing, but that's not what he's calling about. He wants to know what we have on the criminal investigation. He wants to talk to you about bringing a civil action against the criminal defendant. Colin says he has researched it and knows he can file simultaneously with the criminal action."

"Oh, Christ," Jude mumbled, and stabbed at an elusive piece of beef. "Now he's a lawyer. I swear."

"What's up with him? I've never seen anyone so antsy to get their day in court. It's become an obsession with him. Are you sure his business is solid? Maybe he needs a cash infusion and he's relying on a big settlement to solve a company problem."

"He's not going to get it by suing Archer," Jude scoffed. "And, no, I didn't check him out. Why bother? We're looking at a contingency on a Pacific Park settlement; he's not footing the bill. But Colin is going to screw us royally, Amelia. I can feel it."

Jude poked around in the little take-out box.

"Colin wanted his day in court. He was willing to post the bond for Archer just to get it faster. Now he wants us to file in civil against Archer. The press will get ahold of that and crow that the victim's father now thinks Archer is guilty. The DA will start thinking Colin is on their side. If Archer is convicted, we're left with a civil suit against a guy who, compared to Pacific Park, doesn't have a pot to piss in."

"You're going to have a heck of a time talking Colin out of doing this. He seemed hell-bent on covering all his bases, and that includes Archer," Amelia said.

"Well, I'm not about to throw all these hours down the drain for a settlement that won't pay the phone bill. Nope, we go for maximizing return on our investment, and that means going after Pacific Park. Colin is not going to muddy those waters."

"You know, he asked me if I thought Archer was guilty," Amelia commented.

"Yeah? What did you tell him?"

"I told him that he was getting ahead of himself."

"And he said?"

"He said he was tired of people saying things like that. He said, and I quote, 'Doesn't anyone have any guts?'"

"Charming." Jude took a deep breath. "I think we're going to have to remind Mr. Wren that having guts and covering his bases is going to get him squat in the long run. If he wants to be compensated for his son's death it ain't going to be on Archer's back. I'll talk to him."

"Good luck," Amelia drawled.

"I don't need it. Colin's not stupid, and I've got some information that's going to refocus him real fast. Wilson called today. The chatter says one of Pacific Park's primary insurers is going to drop them. There are two more policies but it's like a house of cards— one insurer turns tail and the other ones will, too. If that park closes down we're just one in a long line of creditors. I wouldn't mind Colin settling for the land if he could get it, but if the criminal case drags—or if Archer is convicted—the chances for a Pacific Park settlement are almost nil. Everybody else will get theirs before we can even put our hand out."

Amelia pointed to him with a chopstick, a speck of plum sauce dropping into her lap.

"You want me to call and tell Colin that?" she asked.

"God, no." Jude rolled his eyes. "I'll do it. He's getting so squirrelly I think he's going to need it to come from the top."

"And then there's the real problem," Amelia said.

"Which is?"

"Proof that he even deserves a settlement. We can't find anything that backs up his story about trying to find Tim. No letters. No phone records. We only have his word. I'm hoping to run down some of the people who worked for the management company at the time: He says he sent letters through them. If Pacific Park's people are any good they're going to put together some pretty fancy time lines that show Colin wasn't all that interested in his son over the last ten years."

"Be that as it may," Jude answered, abandoning his food, "it will have to be first things first. I'll get Pacific Park's financial information to Josie. She can make it look like they're using Archer as a scapegoat. Losing their insurance, losing out on a merger deal with Greater United Parks . . ."

"And don't forget they settled the other thing this morning. Five mil. That was a hit where it hurt," Amelia reminded him. "All of this will add up to trying to pin the blame for Tim's death anywhere but on them."

"I'll meet with Colin and lay down the law. I'm not going to eat the costs we've incurred just because he wants to play avenging angel."

Amelia wrinkled her nose as she stared into the little white box. She was listening, but they had been over the same ground a hundred times. She was weary of it. Besides, Jude was the one who had to rein in a meddling client, not her.

"All the pork is gone so I'm out of here. Want me to clean up?"

Jude shook his head.

"Naw, I'll get it. You put in a good day. Go on home and take a long hot bath."

Amelia didn't argue and wished him good night. True to his word, Jude picked through the leftovers and he put everything back in the bag. There was no answer when he called Josie, so he left a message as he cracked open a fortune cookie and read:

All eyes are watching.

Lucky him. It also listed his lottery numbers. Jude didn't believe in the lottery—he liked a challenge, but he wasn't an idiot. The fortune was another matter altogether.

All eyes are watching.

Thoughtfully he pocketed the little bit of paper and picked up the phone and dialed as he sat down again. Twirling in his chair until he was looking through the glass wall of his office at the plants on the other side, Jude was vaguely aware of his own reflection, and a bit later he realized someone was skulking in the garden beyond the glass. That someone was dressed in dark clothes. They were bending down, almost hidden by the stand of palms. Jude leaned forward, the phone pulling away from his ear. His heart beat faster even though he knew there was no real danger. The glass was thick as steel. Still, for the first time in his life, Jude wished he weren't alone. He felt vulnerable, and that was a really bad feeling.

Jude shifted in his chair, tracking the man who suddenly stood up, noticed Jude watching and raised his hand. The hand with a watering can in it. Jude's eyes went to the overalls. GERRY'S JUNGLE. He laughed aloud. Plant maintenance. God, what had he expected? Colin in the shadows? Archer, escaped and murderous?

Jude laughed at himself. *Watch your back* had taken on a whole new meaning. You just never knew who was stealing a glance, checking you out, watching. Just like the fortune. You just never knew who was—

"Hello? Hello? Who is this, please?"

Jude faced the desk. He'd forgotten about his call, but now he could hear Wilson on the other end of the phone. Frantic at first, Wilson relaxed when he heard Jude's friendly voice.

"Wilson, my man," Jude greeted him. "Sorry, I was just watching the guy do the plants in the office. Hey, listen, I know you're working on getting the park plans and financials for Josie, but this is something else. I have a message for you to put on your magic Web site. It will take a minute. Nothing to it and it might pull in some interesting information."

Jude fingered his little paper fortune and dictated as Wilson oohed and aahed, impressed with the simplicity of the plan.

"There's money in it, Wilson. Make sure you put that in," Jude directed.

Jude rang off. He dialed Colin but got the answering machine. He left a message that was less than charming. After that, he was finished for the night.

Jude crumpled the paper bag with the remains of his dinner and tossed it toward the trash. He made it on the first throw and still felt unsettled. Colin was getting on Jude's nerves with his petulant silences and now his meddling. But Jude had set a plan in motion with Wilson—a long shot at best, but no more so than getting a settlement for a guy who hadn't seen his disabled kid in ten years. If Wilson came through, Archer would be out of the mix, Jude would be negotiating a settlement with Pacific Park, Colin Wren would have his pound of flesh and they would both have a ton of cash. In the end, that was what Colin really wanted. That much Jude Getts knew because, in the end, that was what everyone wanted.

                        *   *   *

Colin played Jude's message twice. The first time
he listened; the second time he heard it.

"So, that's how it is." He pushed the answering machine back on the desk but stared at it as if waiting
for it to speak, open a dialogue, discuss the matter.

"Arrogant son of a bitch," Colin muttered. "Damn
arrogant. It's my call. My choice. How dare he tell me
there's too much time and money invested to change
course now."

Colin touched the desk. He drummed his fingers.
He wanted to smash it. But that wasn't his way. He
was more methodical, thoughtful and patient. He had
trained himself to rein in his emotions. Once or twice
he had lost control, done stupid things, hurt people,
but that was so long ago. It hadn't been easy to retrain
himself, but he had done it. That was his penance. All
he had wanted . . .

"All I ever wanted was a chance to prove that I
could be a good father. All my lawyer wants is money.
That's unconscionable."

Colin paced in front of his desk. He swiped up his
drink. The glass had sat on the desk long enough to
set a ring on the wood.

"The bottom line is truth. If Archer is guilty then
he should pay, shouldn't he? I mean, I want to be fair.
If Pacific Park had nothing to do with Tim's death
then I should just drop that lawsuit and go after the
man who is guilty. Don't you think that's fair?"

Colin blinked at Roger McEntyre, and Roger
looked back steadily. He had no idea what he was
expecting when he had called Colin Wren and asked
for a private meeting, but he wasn't expecting this.
Colin Wren was a mess. Roger opened his mouth and

chose his words carefully. It would be a pity to waste such an opportunity.

"That's always been Pacific Park's position, Mr. Wren." Roger raised his own glass and watched Colin Wren over the rim. Colin hadn't even heard what Roger said. It was time to up the ante. "Look, sir, I know how hard this has been for you, and that's why I wanted to tell you something myself before you heard it on the news."

Colin stopped pacing. He cut his eyes toward Roger.

"Heard what? Is there new evidence against Archer?"

"No, nothing like that. The district attorney has all the evidence," Roger answered kindly. "It's about the boy who died a few months ago. We've reached a settlement with his family. Five million dollars."

"Why tell me this?" Colin asked warily.

"Because, sir, we've tried to play straight-up all along. When we think there might have been some negligence on the part of Pacific Park, we admit to it. We told that to your lawyer, but he's looking for a really big payoff. I mean, it was pretty slick the way he got you to bail Archer. Makes you kind of wonder if there isn't a kickback going down when it comes to settling on your boy. The way I see it, Josie Bates and Jude Getts have been pretty cozy on this issue."

"No. No." Colin shook his head once, then twice. His hand rose up and he shook that, too. "Jude wouldn't do that. Just for money? Ridiculous. Jude didn't even know that woman lawyer before this started. I was there when they introduced themselves."

"Maybe. Maybe not. I wasn't there, of course, but I'd be curious to know how long it took him to convince her they should hook up on this thing."

"It was a long . . . I think . . . No, she was unwilling. . . ." Colin paused, his brow furrowing as he thought back to the day he first laid eyes on Josie Bates and Archer. Obviously the memories weren't good ones, because Colin didn't share them.

Roger lowered his eyes and took up his drink again, satisfied that silence was the conduit he needed. Right now he could feel it surging with the electricity of Colin Wren's doubt and pain and anger. Jude and Josie Bates were close, sharing strategies—perhaps secrets—maybe even the promise of money. Archer, accused of Tim's death, could get off. Jude was strong-arming Colin, taking the decision making out of Colin's hands. It was all too horrible to think about. Tim would be abandoned all over again for a paycheck. Roger gauged the silence and determined it had lasted just long enough.

"I just don't want to see you suffer, Mr. Wren. Those two could get Archer off even though he's guilty. And, if they do that, I'm afraid putting you through a civil trial is going to cause more hurt than it's worth." Roger set aside his drink and reluctantly told Colin the next bit of news. "Our main insurance carrier has seen fit not to renew our policy. There's no pot of gold at the end of this rainbow, Mr. Wren. I just think you should have all the facts. I don't like to see anybody get screwed, especially when it's your son that's dead."

Roger stood up. He clasped his hands solemnly and hung his head. Colin had collapsed into the chair behind his desk. Roger controlled the twitch of his mustache that hid a small smile. Yes, sir, this meeting was a surprise. Roger never imagined that Colin Wren might let Pacific Park off the hook without a fight or a settlement.

With a sigh and a somber nod Roger McEntyre left Colin Wren to stew in his own juices in a pot that Roger was almost sure was ready to boil over.

26

Archer was already there when Josie was let into the interview room. She saw the chain around his waist. Though his hands were free, his ankles were still shackled. He didn't even try to get up.

"Are you all right?" Josie sat down across from him.

"I've been better." Archer checked her out. "You look good, Jo."

"So do you, babe." The endearment felt odd because it had been uttered out of habit. It was wrong in this place so she left it behind. She would not use it again until he was free. "Are they treating you okay?"

He lifted one shoulder to show there had been moments but he wasn't going to share them. Maybe later, maybe if they were still together when this was all over, he would tell her.

"Okay," Josie breathed. She took out her notes. "Let's get to work. I brought you a suit. You're going to need time to change, and we're due in court at ten, so we've got half an hour to talk."

Josie explained the proceedings and her concerns even though Archer had attended a thousand preliminary hearings in his day. When she looked up Archer's eyes were unguarded and she saw a deep resentment that was directed, not at his change of fortune, but at her. Josie took it in but didn't react. It was what it was between them. She got down to business.

"I looked over the notes you gave me." Josie went to the second page of her notes, then referred back to the first. "You said that Lexi wasn't feeling well the day you went to Pacific Park. How bad was she?"

"She was sick as a dog early in the morning. There was pain. Exhaustion. The chemo had taken a toll." Archer recited dutifully, though it felt like he had told her the same things ten different ways already.

"And you still took her to a theme park?"

Josie pressed Archer for a crisp answer, something that would convince a jury of his intent. If he insisted Lexi go to Pacific Park when she was sick, the prosecution could argue that he had an agenda. That agenda was to get Tim to the park no matter what, no matter how ill his wife was.

"*I* was taken to Pacific Park," Archer said with overt patience. "Lexi never broke a promise to Tim. She had set the whole thing up weeks earlier. Look at the records at Greenwood. They have a log and they have to write down when one of the patients is leaving the home. Lexi made the arrangements; Lexi signed him out."

"Okay. Good." Josie was satisfied. That answer fit, and Carol Schmidt could vouch for Lexi's devotion to Tim. "Did you have any unusual interaction with Tim that day? Anything someone else might notice?"

"People took notice of Tim all the time. How should I know if they checked me out while they were looking at him? I took charge of the kid and kept him in line. I tried to keep Tim quiet. I made sure he didn't fall. Lexi walked with us. Sometimes she held his hand. Sometimes she put her arm around him. And then she got real tired. She had agreed to leave after the Shock and Drop. It was the fifth ride of the day."

Josie took notes, thinking back to the tape. Lexi

didn't look exhausted. Josie would have to work around it. Even now she had to hide her concern, because it was personal.

"Then you'd only been there a few hours."

"Three hours, maybe. Two of the lines were long. The Shock and Drop was the longest wait." Archer shrugged as if to say these details were ridiculous when the facts of the day were clear. "Lexi wasn't having fun. Tim was agitated most of the time. He calmed down later. I was glad we would be going home so Lexi could rest. When we got through the line at the Shock and Drop I fixed Tim's harness. I checked it twice. I put his hands on the holding bar. I tried to show Lexi that I was being careful with Tim, that I knew this was the last time she would have a day like this with her son."

"Don't phrase it that way, Archer," Josie warned.

"I meant because she was dying, not because I was going to take the kid out." He put her in her place with a look. "I was thinking about her, but she just looked right through me."

His voice faltered. Even now, so long after it was all over, Archer still cared what Lexi thought of him that day. Even now his dead wife's disregard hurt. Even now Archer still didn't have a decent thought for Tim Wren.

"So you went on the Plunge, the roller coaster, the Rotator . . ." Josie read her list and Archer finished it.

"The inner-tube ride and then the Shock and Drop. If I was going to kill Tim it would have been a hell of a lot easier to push him into the water at the Plunge. He couldn't swim. That would have been easy."

Josie took in what he said and ignored his sarcasm. Archer had been a cop; right and wrong were black-

and-white, and he couldn't understand why everyone didn't get it. Josie was a lawyer. She knew that the one who could make the jury see the shape of truth in the shadows of the shade won the day. She also knew not to rise to Archer's bait, but knowing didn't make it any easier.

"I've noted fifteen areas where you would have had better opportunities to hurt Tim if you wanted. But what about earlier, when you got up?"

"There's nothing that can help there. . . ."

"Humor me, Archer," she said. "We don't have much time."

He put his big hands over his face. Josie saw a cut on the back of one, a bruise on the wrist; then his hands fell to the table. He remembered the details but it was hard to speak them.

"I went for a bike ride. Lexi took her chemo and her Compazine. She liked to be left alone for an hour or so after she took those pills, so I got out of the house. Lexi showered. She called Greenwood to make sure Tim would be ready when we got there. . . ."

"Did you hear her do that?" Josie paused, her pen raised.

"I saw her list. She marked it off." Archer shook his head. "Lexi made lists of all sorts of stuff after she got sick. Lexi worried about the cancer getting to her brain, or that she wouldn't think right, or she'd forget something important. She even said she was going to write down her thoughts for Tim in one of those journals"—Archer snorted—"like he'd understand them."

"Did she?"

"Did she what?" Archer asked.

"Did she keep a diary?" Josie came to attention. This was the first she'd heard of a journal. "Do you have it? Her diary?"

"She started one but gave up. Tim wouldn't understand whatever she wrote. But Lexi thought there was going to be some Hallmark thing. She'd die and Tim and me would have Christmas and read from her journals." Archer snorted humorlessly. "It just wasn't going to happen."

"Good for you, Archer. Stick it to a dying woman."

"It's not like it sounds, Jo," Archer insisted. "You weren't there. She believed in doing what she thought was right, and I knew my limitations. No exceptions. It was the way we lived."

"But she was dying, Archer," Josie reminded him.

"Yes, she was. But *I* couldn't live if I lied to her," Archer countered. "My conscience wouldn't let me."

Josie couldn't argue with that one. She understood about conscience because she had learned the hard way. She had advocated for a woman, exonerated her of murdering her husband, only to have her client turn around and murder her own children. Hadn't Josie struggled to live with her part in that? She still had nightmares about those children. Maybe Archer was right. Brutal honesty might be the better course, but Archer supposedly loved Lexi. That should have bought her a little white lie, a peaceful death. Looking at Archer, Josie couldn't help but wonder what she would want from him: pretty lies or an ugly truth. Perhaps it depended on whether or not you believed the soul lived after death. Josie believed in the here and now, and that only memories survived death.

"Then what *were* you willing to do for Tim?" she asked.

"I was there while Lexi was alive, for God's sake," Archer barked, frustrated that Josie, who knew him so well, could not understand this.

Josie leaned over the table, not wanting to understand. She put her hand in front of him and tapped twice.

"It's not enough, Archer. We're about to walk into court and listen to Ruth Alcott make a case against you for murdering Tim Wren. I need to impeach her witnesses. To do that, I need to know what you were willing to do for that boy *after* Lexi died." Josie sat back and lowered her voice. It was flat and commanding. "I need to hear you say something that isn't so selfish, so self-centered and so righteous it sounds like you can't understand why people don't feel sorry for you when two really good people are dead."

Archer colored. His eyes registered anger, shame and confusion as Josie pushed him. The tactic was ugly and unjust if he was innocent. . . .

No, it was ugly because he *was* innocent. In these minutes before she was due in court Josie couldn't afford to think otherwise.

"I promised to pay the bills," Archer said righteously. "I promised to check and make sure Tim was okay. If there were medical problems, I'd find doctors to take care of it. When he died, I'd bury him. But I wasn't going to pretend to be his father. They're not going to hang me because I wouldn't pretend to be his father."

"They might, Archer," Josie answered.

"Then you better make them see my situation for what it was." Archer tried to stand up but the chains rattled to remind him that freedom lay beyond this door, and only the woman across the table could secure it for him. He stayed where he was and put a big hand on the table in front of her.

"Listen, Jo, there's a lot you don't know about me because we were just starting to find out about each other. You didn't know I believe in heaven, did you? And I believe in hell, too. And I believe that if I lied to Lexi, she would know that I didn't do spit for that kid after she was dead. So why don't you make the judge understand that I was trying to do what was right when I strapped Tim onto that piece of machinery."

"And what will I say," she asked evenly, "when they put Carol Schmidt on the stand and she testifies that she heard you say Tim would be better off dead? Or when she testifies that she saw you lay Lexi up against the wall in a fit of rage? You know, Lexi—the woman you loved? The woman you were so concerned about?"

Josie cut him no slack. She asked what Ruth would ask if she had him on the stand and she saw what Ruth would love to see: Surprise and caution were in Archer's dark eyes, but he covered quickly.

"You'll say that no one saw Lexi getting hysterical in that room except me. She was afraid to die. She was afraid for Tim, and she blamed me for not fixing it all. Nobody saw that. Everybody saw her being perfect and brave, but I saw her when she was scared shitless and crazy." Archer lowered his voice even further, making his directive seem almost like a threat. "And you'll say no one heard us apologize—both of us—because it was a private moment between my wife and me. You'll make the doctors at Greenwood testify that Tim wasn't the lovable retarded kid everybody wants to make him out. He hit another patient and gave him a black eye. He tried to hit me. I had to control him."

"And the other people will say you were hurting him," Josie countered.

"I was doing what a cop would do when faced with

an out-of-control mental patient. That is what it boils
down to. Lexi and those people at Greenwood never
acknowledged that Tim was mental!"

Archer slapped at the table with both hands. His
chains rattled and his face mottled with indignation.
He didn't care who Josie had been to him; right now
she was an enemy.

"Okay, Archer!" Josie hollered. She put the knuckles of one hand to her lips and took a minute. Time
was precious and they were wasting it. She pulled her
legal pad in front of her. "We're off track. What happened after you got back to your place?"

"Lexi packed the bag she was taking that day." Archer sniffed. He licked his lips. "I carried it to the car.
I was a necessary evil. I drove and paid for things and
carried stuff. It was Lexi's day with Tim. Maybe that's
why I get so upset when I think about this. I was
doing everything I could to make it a good day, Jo."

"Tell me if you touched him, Archer. Or if he
touched you," Josie went on, riding roughshod over
him.

Archer's head dipped. He flipped the cuffs dangling
from the chains like he was tossing coins and knew
he would never get heads up.

"Here's the truth, Josie; then I'm not going to talk
about it anymore. The accident happened way too
fast. Maybe Tim moved the wrong way and I thought
he needed help. Maybe I put out my hand. Maybe my
hand hit that harness the wrong way. It was like pulling your gun in a dark alley. You just do it when you
sense it needs to happen. I reached for him and that's
what you saw on the tape. Did I touch that harness
and unlatch it? Did I try to catch him because he did
it himself? I don't know, and I don't want to. It would
be tough knowing I did anything to cause that kid's

death. But if I did, there was no malice, there was no premeditation and that means there was no murder."

Josie took all this in like a professional, but her heart swelled with sympathy and understanding, and honest belief in Archer's innocence. In the next instant all that hope and faith was drained from her as surely as if Archer had lanced her wounded heart.

"Make sure they know that, Josie. Make sure you do your fucking job."

27

Ruth Alcott started the show off with a bang. Eric Stevens, ride operator on the fateful day Timothy Wren died, testified to things Josie already knew.

He noticed Timothy Wren.

Retarded people made me nervous.

Yeah, he recognized Archer.

The guy almost killed me a couple of weeks ago.

"We're talking about the day Tim Wren died, Mr. Stevens." Ruth rerouted her witness easily. "Tell us all about it. . . ."

Hot day . . .

Kid was crazy, but calmed down when he got to the platform . . .

Defendant pushed me away. Wouldn't let me do my job. He strapped the kid in. . . .

He did it and the kid fell. . . .

The kid died. . . .

Ruth smiled. She passed the witness to Josie, who managed to get Eric to admit that once, during a hazing, a safety latch had been released and the rider had not fallen to his death. He had been scared to death, but he had not fallen. Josie made Eric admit that Lexi had not seemed concerned that her husband was strapping Tim into his seat. Josie picked at Eric's recollections of that day until, finally, he testified that all he knew was that Archer had put the harness on Timothy Wren and checked it twice.

That, certainly, was not damaging testimony. What came next was a little more worrisome.

"Dr. Weber, could you describe your relationship to the deceased, Tim Wren?"

Ruth Alcott addressed her second witness. Dr. Weber was in his early sixties. A strawberry birthmark covered one side of his forehead, and he touched it as if that would help him think.

"I was Greenwood's physician for some time. I saw Tim Wren intermittently for three years. I am both a pediatric psychiatrist and pediatrician. I specialize in dealing with children like Tim."

Ruth clasped her hands and gave him a glowing smile, as if thrilled that her star pupil was performing so well.

"And what was your assessment of Tim Wren?"

"If you mean would he ever progress past the mental capacity of a five-year-old, the answer is no. If you mean was he a well-adjusted five-year-old in a teenager's body, the answer is still no. He was discouraged by his physical limitations. His mother coddled him, so there was a bit of the spoiled child about Tim. That isn't unusual in situations such as this."

"What were the limitations that frustrated Tim?" Ruth asked.

"Specifically his motor skills. He needed help dressing. He couldn't tie shoelaces. He could feed himself with a fork if the food was properly cut, but he couldn't use a spoon or a knife effectively."

"So it would be hard to imagine Tim actually opening his own harness buckle, would it not?"

"In my estimation, that would have been very surprising, if not close to impossible," he assured her.

With a "Your witness" thrown at Josie, Ruth took

her seat, adjusting her elastic pants as she settled in. The
doctor waited for Josie, seemingly unimpressed by her
height, the athletic grace with which she approached
the witness stand or her straightforward manner.

"Tim could fasten and unfasten the Velcro on his
tennis shoes, could he not?"

"Yes, I believe he had mastered that."

"He was able to unbuckle his belt, and he was
working on learning how to buckle it again, was he
not?"

"That is also true," the doctor acknowledged, but
he didn't stop there. "You must understand that Tim
learned those things by trial and error over the course
of time. He had the help of patient people who understood the steps necessary to teach him what to do."

Josie let Dr. Weber talk on. Obviously he was not
seasoned as an expert witness. He had opened a door
that Josie thought she would have to knock on a long
time before it even cracked.

"So Tim learned by repetition," she mused. "Doctor, did you know that Tim, by conservative estimates,
had been on the Shock and Drop at least twelve times
in the course of his life?"

"No, I did not." He rotated his head and touched
his collar, then drummed two fingers briefly against
that birthmark.

"Would Tim have understood how the buckle on
the harness worked if he had seen someone fasten and
unfasten it twelve times?" Josie asked.

"Objection, calls for speculation," Ruth called.

"Overruled," the judge intoned. "This witness is expert and his opinion is acceptable in this matter. Doctor, you may answer the question."

"It is possible, but not probable. If the person fas-
tening the harness did not—"

"But it is possible," Josie insisted, interrupting now that she had the answer she wanted.

"Yes, it is," Weber agreed, but still he refused to be limited in his response. "However, I doubt anyone suggested Tim take his harness off while the ride was moving. Tim had to concentrate very hard in order to accomplish anything. I doubt he could have concentrated while that ride was going."

"Then let me ask this." Josie rerouted the questioning. "Did Tim understand death?"

"Yes. Tim had a roommate who died and he often asked about him."

"Did he understand that his mother was dying?" Josie asked.

"Yes," the doctor answered.

"How did Tim react to that?"

"He was intermittently upset, then curious. The loss of his mother's hair upset Tim a great deal. Sometimes he ignored me when I tried to discuss the matter with him."

"Would you characterize his attitude as one of depression?"

"Yes, that would be appropriate at times," the doctor agreed.

"Did Tim want to go with his mother when she died?" Josie raised her voice, separating the words in the next question so there would be no mistake. "Could Tim have wanted to take his own life?"

"You are presupposing Tim's understanding of how death came about," the doctor answered coolly. "In reality, Tim would not have understood that opening his safety restraint would result in his death. The concept of suicide, or how it was accomplished, was too complex for Tim Wren."

"Do you have any more questions for this witness,

Ms. Bates?" The judge asked, tiring of this line of questioning.

Josie shook her head and the witness was dismissed. She had accomplished nothing. The judge raised a finger to Ruth who called Carol Schmidt to the stand.

Ruth didn't need to prod, cajole or threaten. Carol Schmidt told the story of Lexi and Tim in a modulated voice, holding her hands clasped loosely in her lap, doing what she had told Josie she would do—her duty. Carol Schmidt was the perfect witness, and Ruth Alcott led her through her testimony with skill and cunning that provided shadings Carol never intended. By the time Ruth was finished, it sounded as if Archer had attacked Lexi with intent to kill, as if he hated Tim, as if he would have walked over hot coals rather than care for Lexi's son after her death. And, in all this, Carol Schmidt seemed a reluctant but honest witness, a saint, a responsible citizen. Carol Schmidt was the standard by which a jury would judge Archer's attitudes and behavior.

Thank God there was no jury.

A jury would hate Josie for what she was about to do.

"Mrs. Schmidt, do you remember speaking to me at the Greenwood Home on the evening of October twenty-eighth?"

"I do," she answered, a smile of recognition faltering on her lips as Josie addressed her.

"During that conversation you told me you considered killing your husband, is that correct?"

Josie asked this without preface, and she felt dirty as she watched Carol Schmidt's expression melt into one of indescribable pain. Her beautiful face paled to the cold color of marble. Her eyes fell deep into shadows that hadn't been there before. If Josie had not surprised her, wounding her so deeply, Carol Schmidt might have defended herself. But the injury was deliberate and she had breath enough only to whisper, "Yes."

"And did you also tell me that you considered killing yourself?"

A tremor gripped Carol Schmidt. Josie was close enough to see it crawl up the woman's neck and take root in her jaw.

"Yes," she answered.

Still Josie didn't move. She would give no quarter. Josie's compassion for this woman was secondary to her loyalty to Archer.

"Did you kill your husband, Mrs. Schmidt?" Josie demanded.

"Your Honor," Ruth called in disgust.

Josie asked again when Ruth made no specific objection.

"Did you kill your husband, Mrs. Schmidt?"

"No, I did not," she said, her voice so small.

"And you are still living, are you not?"

"Yes," Carol said as if ashamed.

"And so, when you said to me that you thought of ending your husband's suffering and that you considered taking your own life, you were not speaking literally, were you, Mrs. Schmidt?"

Carol seemed to have no voice, so Josie continued on, ever more forcefully.

"And when you heard my client say it *might* be better if Tim Wren were dead, did you have reason to agree with that statement?"

"Yes."

"Did you believe the defendant meant to kill Tim Wren?" Josie's voice did not waver, and the cadence of the questions seemed to thrust Carol Schmidt into a puzzling maze of uncertainty.

"I don't know. No, I don't think so."

"Do you believe it is possible that people say things they don't mean because, on some level, there is a compassionate truth in those statements?"

"Your Honor, this is inappropriate. Mrs. Schmidt is not on trial. No foundation has been laid for this woman's expertise. . . ."

Ruth Alcott's voice trailed off into nothingness. All eyes were trained on Carol Schmidt. Her head was bowed. The judge offered his ruling gently, with great empathy for the witness and grudging acknowledgment that his decision was proper.

"You opened the door, Ms. Alcott. Proceed, Ms. Bates."

Josie asked the question again, and this time Carol Schmidt readied herself for the fight. She pulled back her shoulders. She licked her lips and raised her chin. Josie saw it and gave her a final kick, hoping to keep her down.

"Do you think it possible that there can be compassion in such statements, Mrs. Schmidt? Do you, Mrs. Schmidt? Can someone be compassionate by wishing to end another person's life because they are suffering? Or are you the only one blessed with such a moral compass?"

Josie's question hung in the air. All eyes were on Carol Schmidt. To her credit, she made it clear she would not play Josie's game.

"I'm not a philosopher or a member of the clergy," she said. "I can't answer that."

"You visit a man who is a vegetable, Mrs. Schmidt. I believe that qualifies you as an expert. So, I ask you again, can death for someone whose quality of life is severely damaged be a blessing?''

"I believe death eases suffering. I would like to see my husband's suffering end. But I know I will not be the one to end it. It is wrong to do it. . . .''

"But not to wish it, is that right, Mrs. Schmidt? The way my client wished his wife's suffering would end and Timothy Wren's suffering would end? That's not wrong, is it?'' Josie drawled as she held Carol Schmidt's gaze long enough to make the other woman lower her eyes in shame. "No more questions of this witness.''

Satisfied that she had neutralized Carol Schmidt's testimony, but feeling no better for it, Josie started back to the defense table.

"If there's love!''

Carol Schmidt nearly screamed, and Josie was stopped dead in her tracks. She turned slowly. Carol still sat in the witness chair, angry, tearful, but strong as she threw her testimony back in Josie's face.

"It's compassionate to wish for a *loved* one not to suffer. I want you to understand that. But he . . . he didn't love Tim. He couldn't have felt compassion because he hated Lexi's son.'' Carol threw her hand out in a damning gesture.

"Your Honor, move to strike!'' Josie bore down on Carol Schmidt, hoping to silence her. It wasn't going to happen.

"No, no.'' Carol Schmidt was fairly screaming. "Don't strike what I say. . . .''

"Ms. Alcott,'' the judge called, "control your witness. . . .''

"How dare you? How dare any of you try to control me and twist what I have to say.'' Carol half rose from her chair. She leaned against the witness box and begged the judge to listen. "I believe if he had the opportunity, Archer would have killed poor Tim. I don't know if he did, but I know he would have. That's the difference. He would have killed Tim if it meant helping Lexi. That's not compassion. That's selfish."

Carol's head whipped toward the judge, to Ruth Alcott. She looked at the spectators and finally she looked at Josie, and the two women faced down. Carol Schmidt's chest rose and fell, her breathing was shallow; there was a look of horror and relief on her face. It seemed as if Carol's demons had been released and would no longer plague her, because she had accused Archer of something worse than wishing. Carol Schmidt seemed almost rapturous, as if she had seen the light and her soul was free.

Stunned, Josie could not take her eyes off the witness, but she was the only one who couldn't. Everyone else looked away, shamed not only by what Josie had done but by Carol Schmidt's breakdown.

Josie felt defeated. While she might win the day, defending Archer had thrown her back to a time when winning was the only thing and people were changed as Josie cut through their lives. If Josie had any regret it was that she had lost a personal battle. Expediency had been chosen over decency, and there would come a time when she would be called to account.

"The witness is speculating, Your Honor," Josie said, undeterred. "Mrs. Schmidt, could the defendant's statement regarding his feelings about his wife's illness and his stepson's situation be regarded as compassionate? Yes or no."

"Yes." Crushed, Carol sat down, her voice barely a whisper.

"At the time the defendant made that statement, did you interpret what you heard as a threat?"

"No."

"There will be nothing else of this witness, Your Honor."

Josie claimed her seat at the defense table. Carol Schmidt's testimony had gone as she expected. The one thing Josie didn't expect was the next witness and the one after that.

28

The man who sat in the witness chair had been there before. He knew what he wanted to say, and what he had to say worried Josie beyond measure as he stated his name for the record.

"My name is Tom Ford, and I am chief of detectives with the LAPD out of the West Los Angeles Division."

"Did you ever have occasion to meet the defendant?" Ruth raised a hand toward Archer.

"The defendant was a detective under my command before his retirement."

"Did you ever encounter any difficulty with the defendant during the time of his service?"

"He was an ideal officer until approximately three months before his retirement. At that point his behavior became erratic. Some of my detectives refused to work with him until an evaluation was made."

"And was such an evaluation made?" Ruth asked.

"The defendant refused psychological counseling through the department. He also did not follow up on a promise to seek private counseling, as far as I know."

"Can you describe the defendant's behavior during those months?" Ruth hitched her green doubleknits absentmindedly.

"His general demeanor had become aggressive. He was short-tempered, angry and edgy."

"Was there specific behavior that concerned the department?"

"An excessive-force complaint was filed against the defendant," the witness answered.

"What exactly was the defendant accused of doing?"

"He was cited for using excessive force in the arrest of a sixteen-year-old boy. It resulted in the boy being hospitalized," the detective informed her.

"Was this unusual behavior for Mr. Archer?"

"Yes, it was. But it was also understandable."

"How so?" Ruth queried.

"The defendant's attitude toward the job could be traced to the diagnosis of his wife's pancreatic cancer."

"Objection," Josie called, "facts not in evidence."

Ruth took care of the matter promptly, introducing the time line of Lexi's illness and the complaints against Archer. It was a small bit of legal housekeeping. When it was done she got back to the meat of the matter.

"Wouldn't rage have been considered normal under the circumstances?" Ruth continued.

"Objection!" Josie was on her feet. "This man is not a doctor. He cannot make a diagnosis."

"Sustained. Ask again, Ms. Alcott," the judge directed.

"Did the defendant ever personally offer you any insight into his behavioral changes?"

"He alternately expressed denial and rage at his wife's condition. His anger became more prevalent as she became sicker. He became quite vocal about his situation."

"Wouldn't you expect that of a man who was facing the loss of his wife?"

"Yes, except the defendant's anger was exacerbated by his belief that his wife, while expressing deep concern about how her son would fare after her death, had expressed no such concern about him, her husband. Archer often talked about that. He thought she should be worried about him, since he was the one taking care of her, paying the bills, getting her to the doctor."

Josie cast a sidelong glance at Archer. He was rigid beside her, his jaw clenched tight so that she could see the cording of muscle that ran down the side of his neck. She put her hand on his knee—not as a sign of comfort or fealty but to gauge the extent of his agitation. It was off the charts. He was tight as a drum.

"Did he often talk about money?" Ruth asked.

"Yes. He was concerned about the expenses that were being incurred."

"Was the defendant eventually relieved of duty because of his demeanor?"

"No. He was reassigned to a desk position, was unhappy with that and finally took his retirement. I believe his wife died some three or four weeks later."

"So the defendant resigned as an officer of the law the week Timothy Wren died, is that correct?"

"That is correct," Tom Ford answered without looking Archer's way.

Ruth thanked him. Josie took up the charge, rounding her table as if she were storming the witness box.

"Sir, are you aware that the defendant's wife was a paramedic and, as such, was covered by county insurance?"

"I knew she was a paramedic."

"Then why would the defendant worry about money when his wife had catastrophic insurance?"

"I don't know the specifics of the policy," the chief answered.

"We will stipulate to catastrophic insurance coverage," Ruth said, and Josie found her indifference worrisome.

"Would you then stipulate that your assessment of the defendant's state of mind regarding money would be inaccurate?"

The man shook his head.

"No, I would not. The defendant told me directly that his wife wanted her son to undergo an experimental operation. I was informed that copays on his wife's treatment, along with the anticipated expense of experimental procedure for the boy, caused the defendant great concern. Money was a big problem. I know that for sure."

Josie began the next question but never finished. Something was wrong. The courtroom seemed suddenly odd, out of kilter, as if she were standing on the deck of a boat and had lost the horizon. Bits and pieces of information had been swirling around her like currents running in the wrong direction, picking up her tiny boat and moving it inch by inch away from the shore until, suddenly, Josie realized she was lost. She had no oars with which to row back to land. Indeed, there was no land in sight.

"Ms. Bates? Ms. Bates!"

Josie shook herself free of the mind drift. She looked at Archer, silently asking him what she was supposed to do. They were painting a picture of a selfish man, a man out of control, a man concerned with money and not with life, a man who lied by omission or silence even to her. Archer looked back at her, not with answers, but with demands. She waited for something to pass between them, but what she heard instead was her father's voice.

You are supposed to fight.

Her mother was there in her head, too.

Run away before this eats you alive.

She shook her mother's spirit away and held on to her father's. She was his daughter. If she ran, she would lose herself and her purpose and, maybe worst of all, she would be abandoning Archer.

"I'm sorry, Your Honor." Josie cleared her throat and addressed the witness. "Sir, was it your professional opinion when you reassigned my client that he was a danger to anyone's life?"

"No, it was not," he answered. "I would have relieved him of duty if I thought that."

"Was the excessive-force complaint indicted?" Josie asked.

"No, it was not."

"Thank you," Josie muttered.

Cutting her losses, she went back to the table and sat beside Archer. When he leaned toward her, whispering that he and Lexi had only talked about that operation for Tim, that he had not taken on an excessive financial burden, that his edginess was normal, that no one could blame him for that, Josie cut him off. They would discuss it later. Ruth Alcott was calling the lawyer for Lexi's estate. He didn't have much to say, but what he did say was indisputably damaging.

Lexi had a minimal life-insurance policy, but she had an apartment building in Hermosa Beach, and Tim, her son, was due to inherit after his mother's death. But Tim died first and it was established that Archer was next in line to take over that little piece of real estate.

"And how much did the defendant hope to gain?"

"Substantial income from the rental units should he retain the apartment building in Hermosa Beach and approximately four million if he had sold it at the time

of her death. Of course," the witness said, "the market
has continued to appreciate, so today the property
could realize another million and a half."

"Not bad," Ruth said with a grin, "for taking out a
retarded kid."

"Your Honor, that is outrageous!"

Josie objected to Ruth's base comment, but even
she had to admit there was something to be said for
a motive that included that kind of money. She passed
on the cross and Ruth called Mr. Hillerman, Pacific
Park's attorney.

He had been present when Pacific Park made an
offer of a settlement to Lexi. She refused any monies
despite her husband's strenuous urging that she take
her time and think about it. The defendant's wife was
adamant. All she wanted from Pacific Park was for
them to bury her son. They did so in the finest manner. No expense was spared.

Finally, Roger McEntyre was called. The day was
ending, and so was Ruth's presentation. Josie lay gasp-
ing for breath in this ring, trying to figure out how to
go down with some glimmer of hope that she'd be
back to fight another day.

Roger McEntyre narrated as the videotape of Tim
Wren's death played. He answered questions regarding the recent assault on Eric Stevens. Roger spoke
of how he feared the defendant would kill Eric Stevens the same way . . . Well, Eric was a young boy.

Josie wanted to scream at his implication and mis-
characterization. But when it was her turn with him,
Josie was all business. She approached, carrying with
her a long roll of paper.

"Mr. McEntyre, could you tell me why there are
surveillance cameras at Pacific Park?" Josie was cool,
confident and didn't impress Roger McEntyre one bit.

"They are there for a number of reasons."

"Give me two," Josie suggested, trying not to think about the hole Ruth Alcott had punched through her gut.

"The cameras provide our patrons with a sense of security. They provide a record in case anything goes wrong at the park."

"Like the video we just saw of the accident?" Josie asked.

"Yes," Roger answered.

"As head of security you must know where the cameras are located in the park."

"I do."

"You must also know how many cameras are trained on each ride," Josie challenged.

"More or less. I would have to refer to our latest maintenance records to be specific. The park is a work in progress. We are always changing things. No safety system is perfect. Our camera system is not perfect."

"Mr. McEntyre, when we spoke at Pacific Park you told me you had one tape—the one we have seen in this courtroom—that recorded the accident on the Shock and Drop the day Tim Wren died."

"That is correct." Roger nodded.

"Do you still say that, Mr. McEntyre?"

"I still say I have one tape of the accident from a camera that was focused on that piece of machinery."

"Why aren't there more, Mr. McEntyre?" Josie asked.

"Because that's all I have, Ms. Bates."

Josie unrolled the blueprint in her hand and blessed Wilson Page as she spread it out in front of Roger.

"Mr. McEntyre, can you tell me what these are?"

"They are the blueprints of the electrical schematic of the park dated from the year 2003."

"And will you identify this for the court?" Josie pointed to the blueprints.

"That is the east quadrant of the park, and the indicator stamps denote the cameras located in the area."

"And this camera in particular, Mr. McEntyre? Can you tell me what that camera was recording?"

"That particular camera recorded activity in front of the Shock and Drop."

"Were you able to see the ride itself, particularly the bottom half of the ride just at the slowing curve?"

"I don't know."

"Or you won't tell us," Josie suggested as she took away the blueprint.

"I don't know," Roger said flatly. "That camera was dismantled when we reconfigured the area for a new attraction. We extended the common area because the new ride was smaller. That camera no longer exists."

"But it was working on the day of Tim Wren's death—is that correct, Mr. McEntyre?"

"To the best of my knowledge."

"And who reviews the security tapes, sir?" Josie asked.

"In a situation such as we had that day, I would," Roger acknowledged.

"And you're telling me you don't remember if that tape allowed a view of the bottom half of a ride on which a young man died?"

"I didn't remember what was on the first one until I reviewed it again."

"Then why didn't you review the second one?" Josie demanded.

"Because there is no tape to review, Ms. Bates."

Josie's pulse quickened.

"Did you destroy that tape, Mr. McEntyre?"

Roger hesitated. His mustache twitched but his gaze never faltered.

"Yes, I did."

"Did you destroy that tape because something on it would exonerate my client?" she asked, daring to hope that this would end the matter and Archer would walk free.

Roger McEntyre tipped his head. His dark eyes held hers. She thought he smiled. Josie thought he was toying with her. She knew it when he answered her question.

"I destroyed it because that camera was on common ground. It is normal procedure at the park to keep those tapes for nine months. It is only the ride-specific videos that are kept for a couple of years. Does that answer your question, Ms. Bates?"

"Yes," she muttered, disheartened. "Yes, it does."

Roger McEntyre was excused. Those who stayed in the courtroom were silent, waiting to hear the judge's decision. It didn't take long to find out. He looked at Josie and Archer and delivered a well-rehearsed speech that changed their lives.

"The court finds probable cause to believe these charges are true and orders the defendant to appear for arraignment in department one hundred in ten days. Court is adjourned."

It was so little to say, but there it was. Archer, knowing he would stand trial for murder, didn't look back at Josie as he was led away. She didn't call after him. Ruth packed up and took off without a word to anyone, just a look of pleasure on her face and another hitch of those pants over her wide hips. Spectators lingered, looking at Josie, wondering why she had not found some point of drama, some small thing to turn this around in a blaze of glory. Wasn't this, after all, the attorney who had so dramatically defended that girl not long ago? She shouldn't have lost her edge so soon, should she? The show should have been better, shouldn't it?

Josie felt those thoughts, felt their eyes on her back as she slowly packed away her papers. She looked at the seal of the state hanging above the judge's bench but she found no comfort in it. Finally, hearing nothing, sensing the emptiness behind her, Josie picked up her briefcase and started to leave, only to find she wasn't alone.

Sitting on the farthest bench was Colin Wren. The light caught the lenses of his glasses, his hair was neatly combed, his suit was freshly pressed and he didn't move even when Josie pushed through the bar. The little gate swung back and forth, the thump echoing through the nearly empty chamber. Josie put her hand back to stop it before she walked down the center aisle. Josie thought to speak to him. She wanted to explain that there was a very long way to go, that he should not be discouraged, but Colin preempted her. He got up. He stepped into the aisle and made sure Josie was looking right at him. He turned. He left her alone.

"Jesus Christ."

Jude palmed his cell phone and closed his fist as if he could crush it. Seven months, hundreds of billable hours, not to mention his own belief that Colin Wren's suit against Pacific Park was warranted, and now this.

Biting his lip, he swerved around a minivan filled with what looked to be a dozen kids, took the turn five miles faster than he should and braked to a stop in front of Wilson's house, not caring that three quarters of the Mercedes was hanging over in the red near a hydrant. Wilson Page's neighborhood wasn't high on the list of drive-bys for the meter maid, and with the financial hit Jude was about to take, a parking ticket was the least of his worries.

Leaving his jacket, Jude slammed the car door and walked to Wilson's house, wishing he hadn't planned this work session. When things took a turn for the worse, Jude preferred the company of a willing woman with a quick wit to Wilson's, but what the hell. He was here. Jude knocked hard, rapping twice. He walked in before Wilson even had time to give him permission to enter.

"Jude!" Wilson greeted him happily from his perch in front of the huge computer screen.

"We won't be working on Colin's stuff, Wilson. Forget it. Just forget everything." Jude walked the length of the small room and back again. "Colin just called. He's dropping the lawsuit against Pacific Park. He says if Josie somehow pulls this out it won't matter, because he knows the truth. Colin says Archer's guilty as sin."

Frustrated, Jude pocketed his keys and flopped himself on the couch. It was the wrong side. He fell into the indentation that Wilson had made when he used to be small enough to sit on a sofa. That was it. Fit to be tied, Jude pushed himself up, walked past Wilson and said, "There's no sense working now, Wilson. It would be a waste of our time. I'll call you later if something changes." Jude was at the door. He had his hand on the knob and, when he opened it, he looked at Wilson. He saw the man's sympathy and his unerring devotion and his neediness, and suddenly it just pissed Jude Getts off to no end. "Get a goddamn new couch, will you, Wilson?"

29

Josie was slumped in a chair in Faye Baxter's office, dribbling her volleyball on the floor beside her. Outside Faye's office Angie, the paralegal, and yet another new receptionist dealt with the everyday problems of a neighborhood law firm. Faye should be doing the same, but Josie had appeared needing a sympathetic ear and an objective opinion.

"Jude's throwing in the towel. He told me I'm on my own."

"It doesn't sound like he has much of a choice. His client pulled the plug. What's he supposed to do?"

"Hang in there with me," Josie wailed. "Archer wouldn't be in this fix if it weren't for Jude and Colin. If the situation were reversed I'd still . . ."

One look at Faye was enough to make Josie backpedal, albeit reluctantly.

"Okay. Okay. If it looked like I was out thirty grand maybe I'd do the same thing. But it doesn't change the fact that Archer doesn't have the money to pay for the kind of research we need."

"So it's going to be hard. But you've still got a client and a trial. You're not going to do Archer any good if you're obsessed about Jude Getts."

"I'm not obsessed and I'm not sidetracked," Josie griped. "I just needed to vent. Maybe I'm not mad about all that, anyway. Maybe I'm worried that . . . Archer . . . might be . . . guilty."

Josie dribbled the ball in rhythm with her words, as if that alone would herd all those nasty emotions into a box that she could stow away. Loss of faith in Archer, in herself, anger and disappointment at Jude, worry about Hannah—Josie needed all those feelings to go away so she could concentrate.

"Give me the ball, Josie." Faye clucked. "You're driving me crazy. I can't think when you're doing that."

Faye held out her hands, but Josie palmed the treasured ball, a present from her father when she had earned her volleyball scholarship to USC. She held it tight against her stomach, a round, rubbery security blanket. Faye pulled a face, the kind you would give an unruly yet basically good child.

It was a pity things hadn't worked out between them. Faye had been so anxious to bring Josie on as a partner in her neighborhood firm. Yet Josie's commitment to Hannah's trial, the uproar it created in a firm ill equipped to handle such a high-profile case, changed everything. Faye had cut Josie loose, the partnership never materializing. Luckily, their friendship endured. They had come to an agreement that worked for both of them. Josie would pay a nominal fee to use Faye's offices and staff; Faye would use Josie's services as needed. It was an arrangement that suited them both—especially Faye. She was too old for the kind of worry Josie was bringing, but she wasn't too old to put in her two cents when it was asked for.

"Thank you," Faye said when she was sure the dribbling stopped.

"You're welcome," Josie grumbled, then added, "Sorry" before she started in again. "Jude threw me off. The testimony today threw me off. I didn't expect to win without a fight, but I didn't expect to be creamed, and I don't know what went wrong. I wasn't thinking, my reaction time was down. I didn't impeach any of those witnesses, unless you call browbeating Carol Schmidt impeachment. I was trying to reconcile the testimony I was hearing about Archer with the man I know."

"You're human, Josie."

"No, it was more than that. I was judgmental. If Archer did anything to hurt that boy—subconsciously or spontaneously or with malice—it would be despicable and he should be convicted. That's the way I felt, and that is wrong if I'm supposed to defend him."

Faye shifted her considerable weight and leaned her chin on her upturned palm. She looked gorgeous; the original big, beautiful woman.

"Well, that's a switch. Seems not too long ago you were arguing that Hannah actually had a right to defend herself against an abusive man, but you're not willing to go the distance for Archer. Not very lawyer-like of you, Josie," Faye scolded.

"Don't be ridiculous. Apples and oranges," Josie insisted. "Archer wasn't abused. He's a grown man, and he made it very clear that he did exactly what he wanted to do in that relationship."

"Really?" Faye raised a well-shaped eyebrow. "If your client was anyone else you'd see it. You think Archer's the Rock of Gibraltar because he's always there for you, but the way I read it, Lexi did a big number on his head. That relationship was awfully complicated, Josie. It sounds like Lexi was badgering him day and night about Tim. She may have been weak because of the cancer, but that woman had an incredible strength of purpose, from what I'm hearing. So Archer's sick with worry about his wife, watching her die, afraid for himself, still trying to be strong for her, and she's beating up his brain every waking moment with guilt. Come on, Josie, think about him now. You're so hurt he didn't spill his guts to you that you can't see how Lexi manipulated him. I think a case could be made that Archer was psychologically abused."

"Good defense, but we're talking about a man. It's risky. Nobody believes men can be abused." Josie picked up the ball, made to dribble, saw Faye raise a finger and put the ball back in her lap. "I was pretty arrogant, thinking I could do this for him, wasn't I? I never thought he would need a defense because I would make this all go away. Just little, old me."

Josie leaned over that ball, cradling it like a child. The pull of her brow, the pursing of her lips told Faye that Josie was lost, second-guessing everyone, especially herself.

"So retain new counsel," Faye suggested kindly. "Second-seat whoever it is, but get a little distance if you don't think you can pull this off. You owe that to Archer."

Josie turned her head and stared at nothing in particular. She thought. She sighed. She speculated.

"If they blew it, I couldn't live with myself. If they won, Archer would never look at me the same way. I'd never look at myself the same way." Josie shook her head and bit her bottom lip and swung her head around to look at Faye. "I'm missing something. I know I am."

"Then tell me another story," Faye suggested. "One that gives Archer the benefit of the doubt."

"All right. Fine." Josie took a minute to gather her thoughts. Slowly she sat up. She spoke cautiously. "At Greenwood I saw a skinny little man almost fight off a guy who looked like a linebacker." Josie paused, speaking in bullet points so both of them could hear her thoughts clearly. "So, what's the one thing everybody's always said about Tim? They said he was strong. Lexi couldn't control him. So strong and unpredictable, Archer had to keep him in line."

"Was Tim upset the day he died?" Faye asked.

Josie shook her head. "No. He was rambunctious enough for Eric Stevens to notice him in line. According to that same witness, though, Tim was calm when Archer strapped him on the ride."

"Then you have to ask yourself if Tim's outbursts were intermittent. If you could prove that his moods and outbursts were unpredictable, then you might make a case that he was causing trouble and somehow loosened his own restraint."

"That's not what's on the tape." Josie almost dismissed the suggestion but caught herself in time to think again. "They were out of the camera's range for at least thirty seconds. We know there was a huge behavioral change in a forty-five minute span when Eric Stevens noticed him. But Eric Stevens couldn't have been watching every minute. Maybe Tim went through forty-five changes during that time. Could some uncontrollable urge have changed Tim's behavior in the thirty seconds he was out of camera range?

"Maybe he had a sort of burst of activity, a sudden spasm. If he did, Archer could have been reaching across to try to stop it or control it. That's something he would do instinctively if it happened that fast."

Josie's grin grew as she turned toward that new light at the end of the tunnel. It was bright and it illuminated the stage from a different angle, revealing Archer as hero, not villain.

"Let's use a different word, Josie," Faye suggested. "How about seizure? If Tim had a seizure, he could have burst the latch as his body was thrown against the restraint. Once I talked to a woman—she was a teacher—who wanted to sue the family of a little epileptic girl. During a fit the teacher tried to help and the kid hit her just right and broke her jaw. The teacher thought she was doing something good and ended up with her jaw wired for six months. But she assumed the risk when she tried to help. So if Archer was aware of the seizure he might have instinctively or inadvertently released the restraints because it seemed they were doing more harm than good. The consequences of helping were just worse than a broken jaw."

"Whoa, Faye, that's good." Josie palmed her ball, then put it down beside the chair. "That is really good. But the instinct argument won't fly. Even instinct wouldn't drive a normal person to release that safety while the ride was moving. I wouldn't put it in front of a jury."

"Just thinking out loud," Faye said. "But Archer could have been startled by the seizure, reached across Tim and pulled that latch while he struggled to control Tim."

"Absolutely. Yes," Josie agreed. "Barbara Vendy said they sent his medical records to Lexi. I'm going to find them and have an expert review them. I should have done it before the prelim. I gotta go."

Josie took a rain check on the dinner Faye offered, and took the shortcut home. The porch light was off. Inside, the house was dark, and Josie was disappointed she couldn't count on Hannah for the simplest things. To be fair, though, it was just past dusk. Hardly the dead of night. Josie tossed the volleyball in the corner and dug in her pocket for her keys. Before she could find them, the door opened and any reprimand died on Josie's lips. Deathly pale, Hannah gripped the edge of the door. Blood stained the side of her mouth, and her hair hung in a mess over her eyes; a rope was strung around her neck.

"Jesus . . ." Josie whispered, unable to move. "What . . . ?"

"What?" Hannah said back.

"You're bleeding. . . ."

Hannah threw out her hip and flipped the switch behind the door. The porch light flared, Josie blinked and her heart began beating again. Hannah wasn't pale; she was painted white. The blood didn't just trickle out of the side of her mouth; it gushed and was as thick as ketchup.

"Halloween?" Hannah stated with the inflection of a resounding *duh*.

Max-the-Dog ambled through the doorway and gave Josie a tail wag. There was a bowl of candy on the table behind Hannah. She was just a kid ready to play her tricks on anyone who wanted a treat.

"Halloween. I forgot," Josie admitted.

"I remembered," Hannah answered.

"Well, put that bowl of candy on the porch. We've got work to do."

30

The old springs groaned as Josie raised Archer's ancient garage door. His Hummer was wedged into the left side of the garage; the right was a mountain of neatly stacked and sealed boxes. Josie turned on the wall light.

"Where do we start?" Hannah walked into the cool, dark garage. It smelled of mold and old wood. She threw her arms out and did a deliberate pirouette. "There is so much stuff in here."

"First I'll move the car. Then we start at the top."

Josie backed the Hummer out and spent too long trying to find a parking spot on Hermosa's narrow streets. She jogged back, hitched Archer's ladder off the hooks on the wall and got to work handing boxes down to Hannah.

When Hannah called a halt, Josie climbed down. The girl was surrounded by boxes, overwhelmed by boxes, almost hidden by them. Methodically Josie sliced through the tape on each of them and they began. It took no more than a cursory look to see that most held nothing of value. Archer's old case files. Unused crockery. Junk.

"What are we looking for again?" Hannah asked as she pushed aside a box and dug into the next.

"Tim's medical records. Look for anything that has his name on it, anything that says Greenwood or has a doctor's name on it. If you find Lexi's records, put them back. If you have any doubt, show me."

"Okay. Hey, Josie, look at this. This is so cool." Hannah held up a leather jacket lined with rabbit fur.

Hannah put on the jacket but Josie saw Lexi: her shape, her size, her style. She might as well be watching through the looking glass, seeing Lexi dressing to go out with Archer, Archer helping her off with the coat after an evening out. Archer making love to Lexi, whose body was strong and compact. Where Josie could match Archer inch for inch, Lexi would be gathered up and protected. She had been a little thing to wear a jacket that small, and knowing it made Josie feel big and unwieldy.

"Put it back, Hannah." Josie turned away.

"Do you think Archer would let me have it?" Without understanding that Josie could not bear looking at her if she wore it, Hannah took it off and folded it. She reached the right conclusion for the wrong reason. "Never mind. You're right. I should put it back. Besides, I don't think Archer would give me the time of day. Nothing but clothes in here. Where's the tape?"

Josie tossed the roll her way. Hannah brushed her hair out of her eyes and grunted when she lifted the box, then scurried for cover when Billy Zuni, passing through the alley, poked his head in to see what was happening.

He was on his way to Sharkeez to celebrate the day. Plastic leis had been added to his faded T-shirt. He was, he informed them, a Hawaiian pool boy. With a laugh, and a warning that he'd better not try to get into Sharkeez until he was of age, Josie sent him on his way and closed the garage door behind him, then pulled on a string attached to the naked bulb in the middle of the ceiling. It took her a second to adjust to the bright light. When she did, she found Hannah burrowing in the back of one of the stacks. When Hannah reappeared she was grinning.

"I found Lexi's purse. It's got her wallet in it and everything."

Scooting out from between the boxes, Hannah sat cross-legged on the cold concrete and pulled back the heavy zipper on Lexi's bag. Josie joined her on the floor, reaching for the purse just as Hannah was beginning to poke around. Hannah relinquished it but stayed close as Josie inventoried the contents.

"Picture." Josie took a good long look at it before handing it to Hannah.

"It's kind of weird finding this stuff, isn't it?" Hannah whispered as she took it.

"I don't know. Archer said the only place Lexi went after Tim died was to the funeral. Other than that she was at home or at Burt's. You don't need a purse to get a cup of coffee and sit on a wall to watch the beach."

"I guess. She probably just never unpacked it. Tim looks nice." Hannah shifted closer to Josie and passed the picture back.

Josie nodded. Tim Wren did look nice, and he looked flawed, and Lexi was beautiful despite the scarf that covered her bald head. She gazed adoringly at her son. One arm was around Tim's waist; in her other hand Lexi held a drink. She pulled him tight so that the odd angle of his arms seemed almost natural. What he was really doing was reaching for the water bottle Lexi held. It was a brilliant, natural moment caught through Archer's lens.

But the picture wasn't taken with Archer's camera. It was a dated, timed Polaroid. Josie put it aside, knowing it might have some significance for her defense. Hannah leaned against Josie's back, hands on her shoulders, to see what would come out of the purse next. But Josie didn't want Hannah hanging on her just then, and she braced at her touch, Hannah melted away gracefully in a well-practiced move. Disappear before you're rejected. It had been a lesson Hannah's mother taught her.

"Pills," Josie muttered. She turned a little brown bottle so she could see the label. "Oral chemo."

"I didn't know they had a pill for that," Hannah whispered. Josie didn't know much more than Hannah, but she would find out. She pulled out another vial.

"Celexa." This bottle was held up, too. "Lexi's."

"Depression," Hannah said with the confidence of an expert.

"Phenobarbital." The final vial.

"What's that for?" Hannah had moved in close again. This time Josie let her stay.

"I don't know. Pain, I imagine," Josie said as she gathered up the bottles. "These were probably the only things that kept her going."

"If she took them," Hannah mumbled. "I mean, you can't tell if she took them, can you?"

"Want to second-seat me?" Josie half joked, impressed with Hannah's observation.

"No way I'd ever want to be a lawyer," Hannah muttered as Josie opened the bottle and poured out the pills.

"Twenty left on a count of thirty on the phenobarb." She cupped her hand, poured them back in and secured the top. Josie took up the Celexa. "Almost a full bottle. She filled it a week before the accident. They should all be gone."

"Maybe she had her regular prescription at home

and these were for going out," Hannah suggested. "Or maybe she had a bottle she didn't finish so she poured them together."

"Maybe she didn't think she needed them. Look at that picture. She looks happy," Josie said with a nod to the print.

"It's fake. Nobody gets better if they have to take that stuff," Hannah agreed. "I used to toss my pills down the toilet when I thought I was all cured. Hey, what's that?"

Hannah pointed out a small black pouch. Josie opened it, touched the few things inside as she spoke.

"Lip gloss. Lipstick. Mints. Mascara."

She zipped the little black pouch up again, feeling as if she had trespassed on intimate territory. The live Lexi had painted her lips coral and then smiled at Archer. She carried mascara even though her eyelashes were gone along with the rest of her hair. The contents of the little purse made Josie feel less than a woman. She didn't color her lips or her cheeks; she didn't smile at Archer and hope that he noticed that she was beautiful. Archer never asked her to do any of that, but it didn't mean he wouldn't have appreciated the effort. Josie sighed and set aside the cosmetic bag. She didn't want to know this much about Lexi. She didn't want to know this much about herself, so she began the hunt again.

She found a plastic bottle with a mouthful of water left even after all these years. Josie dropped it back in the bag. Lexi's identification, her health card and a few dollars were inside her wallet. A small pack of Kleenex and a half-empty box of candy were there, too. Josie put everything back in the main compartment, then dug into the side pockets.

"Two tickets for the Shock and Drop." She showed them to Hannah. "Archer must have carried his own."

Hannah took them almost reverently. She held the tickets between her fingers and lowered her lips as if she were kissing the bits of paper. She closed her eyes, remembering people she had never met.

"I can feel them," she whispered.

"Then tell them to give me a clue," Josie muttered, glancing back over her shoulder.

Josie didn't need to channel through a pair of tickets to feel the deceit of that day: the forced cheer, the desperate attempt to make their time together seem normal. Lexi's pills, little bits of nothing that made her feel less of everything except love for her son. The cosmetics were packed as if she cared about freshening her lipstick. The picture attested to the love Lexi had for Tim and the thoughtlessness for herself. The water bottle that would revive her when she felt tired, or help her get the pills down when the pain came. The tickets that had been anxiously folded over and over again until they were just slivers of paper. And this . . .

Evidence that Archer told the truth, at least in this. It was Lexi's list—her plan for one perfectly happy day—written in her own hand. The writing was a little shaky but very deliberate. *Get up. Confirm Greenwood. Shower. Take medicine. Fix water bottle. Pack purse. Pick up Tim.* On and on and on the list went, making note of the rides they would take, the food they would eat, when it was time for medicine. Each little note was crossed off as the task was accomplished.

"Look." Hannah reached over Josie's shoulder, pointing at the final notation. A whimsical *The end* had been crossed out by a weak hand.

Hannah stayed still as Josie put the list back where she had found it. Before she closed the bag Josie paused, disturbed not by what she found but by what she hadn't. There was nothing to remember Archer. Lexi had not asked anyone to take a picture of them as a family. She carried no picture of him in her wallet. He was not mentioned on the list. Archer was off camera, out of mind. No wonder he was hurt. He had been little more than a servant that day—or maybe every day. Certainly Archer loved Lexi, but suddenly Josie was wondering exactly how much Lexi loved Archer.

Lost in thought, Josie had forgotten Hannah until she heard a familiar sound. The rhythmic tapping that signaled Hannah's distress. Josie looked behind her. Hannah was sitting among the boxes, watching Josie, tapping to twenty before beginning again. Josie stood up and went to the girl. Bending, she took Hannah's hand in both her own.

"Do you want to get out of here?" Josie asked. Hannah nodded. "Okay. Grab a box. We'll take some of this back to the house."

Hannah smiled, relieved and grateful. She didn't want to look through a dead woman's bag anymore. She didn't want to think about a dead boy, because, if her own mother had her way, Hannah would probably be dead, too. Happy to be leaving, Hannah took the first box she could reach but Josie stopped her.

"No, Hannah, don't bother with that one; it's too small. It won't have what we're looking for." Josie motioned to the white box, taped and twined.

Hannah tucked it back into the stack, rolled her eyes and hoisted one of the big ones. Josie took two. They passed costumed revelers headed to the bars and restaurants. The women wore rabbit tails on their tight rears, spangled devil horns in their long hair. The men wore hats or masks, and everyone was having a great time, including Josie, who talked with Hannah all the way home.

They dumped their boxes in the living room, and Max went to Hannah for a pet. She ruffled his ears and took him out as naturally as if she'd been doing it all her life. Josie was going through the mail when she got back.

"It's good to be home." Hannah sighed.

Startled, Josie looked up. Hannah called this place her home when all this while Josie had thought of her as a long-term visitor. Funny, Josie didn't mind at all, and that was big. That one word also revealed what was at the heart of Lexi and Archer's problem. In its simplest form, what Lexi wanted was Archer's promise that his house could be Tim's home.

Josie tossed the mail aside. She would not make the mistakes her mother or Hannah's mother or even Lexi had made. She would even forget Jude and Archer for a while. She was doing her best, and Hannah had just told her that was enough. Josie put her hand on Hannah's shoulder.

"Come on, I'll fix you a sandwich."

The evening came and went as Hannah talked about school and how she couldn't abide Billy Zuni. She talked about clothes and wondered how her mother was faring in prison. Her fingers tapped. She checked the refrigerator to make sure it was closed every time Josie opened it. But the manifestations of her compulsions now seemed habit rather than necessity. Through it all, they opened the front door and handed out treats until the candy was gone and Hannah went to her room. A minute later music pulsated through the closed door. Josie opened the boxes they had brought home but found nothing important in them. She would go to Archer's again in the morning.

In her bedroom, Josie watched the news, sketched out theories, tried out strategies and rerouted them when they led to dead ends, and fell asleep. When she woke the bedroom was dark, the television had been turned off. Hannah had covered Josie during one of her many trips to make sure Josie was still there, that she hadn't been left alone. Josie touched the blanket and smiled. As obsessions went, Hannah's wasn't a bad one. The thought in her head wasn't bad either. In fact, it was bordering on pretty damn smart.

Tossing off the blanket, running a hand over her face to bring the blood up, Josie got out of bed. In the living room she switched on the table lamp and rummaged through the files she had accumulated for the preliminary hearing. A second later she was sitting cross-legged on the floor watching Pacific Park's security video of Tim's death. When she was positive that she hadn't imagined what she was seeing, Josie pushed her back up against the couch, took the phone and dialed Jude Getts. He sounded sleepy. When he heard Josie's voice he was peeved. Before he could hang up Josie said, "Call Colin Wren. Do whatever you have to do, say whatever you have to say, but I want his permission to exhume Tim's body."

31

Josie sat with her legs crossed at the ankles, her head back against the wall and the rest of her body resting uncomfortably on one of the few chairs in Dr. Chow's waiting room. Though she was exhausted, Josie couldn't relax as they waited for the results of Timothy Wren's autopsy. She had hardly rested in the last weeks since her late-night call to Jude.

As Josie expected, he didn't put up a fight when she dangled a settlement carrot on the end of this new stick. Colin Wren, though, had been harder to convince. He had heard the evidence against Archer, watched the tape, seen Archer's fury in action. Colin didn't want his son's body exhumed to prove a defense theory born of desperation. Colin wanted Tim to rest in peace. That was the crack in Colin Wren's door, and Jude pushed through it. Tim, Jude said, could never rest if there was the slightest possibility that they were trying to right one wrong by committing another.

Colin had railed, he hedged, he let loose a flow of rage toward Archer the likes of which Jude had never heard. Jude listened patiently because he wanted only one thing: permission to exhume. Spent, Colin eventually gave it.

The request had been made, approved and the wheels put in motion before he could change his mind. At the cemetery Josie stood apart, leaning against a tree, her hands in the pockets of her jacket as the backhoe bit into the hardened ground. The day had been cold. The Los Angeles sky was clear, but thunderheads billowed over the local mountains. A biting wind blew leaves off the trees and tumbled them across the grass. In the distance a family decorated a child's grave with balloons and teddy bears. Josie watched, fascinated by such devotion, as if by bringing the trappings of childhood they could still play with their spirit child.

Then the backhoe strained to lift the dirt and Josie's attention was drawn back to the business at hand. Tim's last resting place was marked by a flat piece of bronze etched with his name, the date of his birth and death. Nothing more. *Tortured. Angry. Broken. Victim.* Those were not words to carry into eternity.

No one had been to his grave since he died: Archer because he had no ties to the boy, Colin because, according to him, he had had no idea that his son was dead. Josie glanced his way, wondering if she believed that or if it even mattered anymore. Josie supposed it mattered to Colin, this fantasy of his. To her it was a reminder that Archer had a wife and her name was Lexi and she was gone, too. Buried beside her son, her grave spoke more of Archer's devotion than of Lexi's life. The headstone was simple but expensive and tasteful. Two words were etched into the marble.

BELOVED WIFE.

Again and again Josie's eyes went to those words, and they mocked her. If she were to die there would be no etching on her stone. She was not a daughter. Her mother was gone to parts unknown; her father was dead. She was not a mother. The child in her home had been rescued, not born. Josie was not a wife, nor was she a mistress. She was a modern woman who loved Archer in the modern way. They shared no legal commitment, only a deep and abiding respect, a love that was tempered by the knowledge that they could both walk away if they so desired. That was not enough to earn the title of *beloved,* and she wasn't even sure they shared—

Jude came to stand beside her. He wore an overcoat, overkill for southern California, but that was Jude. He was trying to make amends for the harsh words he had levied against her when Colin decided to withdraw his lawsuit against Pacific Park. Jude asked about Archer. Had it gone well when she told him about her theory? Josie had shrugged. How could it go when your lover was sitting across from you in prison garb? How could it go when hope rested in speculation and nothing more? The way it went was that Archer was pissed, he was mean, he was getting grief inside now that he had been moved to the general population.

Josie answered Jude's question with a noncommittal "fine." It was the best she could do. Everything else was too complicated.

After that, Jude and Josie had nothing more to say to each other, so they watched Colin inch closer to Tim's grave, close enough to make the backhoe operator stop work until Colin backed off. He didn't stay gone long. It was as if he expected to see Tim, and Josie thought it was just a little bit sick to carry his fantasy that far.

But all that was days ago, and now Josie started as her foot was kicked. The present wasn't any more pleasant than the cemetery had been. Josie looked askance as Jude slid into the chair next to her, sitting so close their shoulders touched.

"I thought you said the doctor was ready to talk to us?"

Colin hadn't agreed to reopen the case against Pacific Park even if Josie's theory played out. That put Jude on the wire again. That made him unhappy, so he took it out on Josie.

"That was the message I got," she said. "I told your secretary you didn't have to be here. I would have called with the results."

"Are you kidding?" Jude sat up straighter. "Colin is about ready to jump out of his skin. I swear, we'd better get to court on this or it's just throwing good money after bad. More hours wasted."

"Good, Jude," Josie sighed, "I had almost forgotten we don't exactly see things the same way."

She crossed her arms and closed her eyes so she wouldn't have to look at Jude. In a pathologist's waiting room everything about him seemed excessive, an overabundance of all life had to offer in a place where death stripped everything away. She must have sighed again. He actually figured it out.

"Sorry," he said, and Josie felt him relax beside her. "This place gives me the creeps. There's a reason I work with money."

Jude tapped out a few notes with the toe of his shoe, then rested his forearms on his knees as he looked at his client. Josie opened her eyes and looked, too. Colin Wren was leaning against the wall outside the door. Josie and Jude could see him through the large windows that were set deep into the wall.

"He's not happy with this idea of yours," Jude muttered.

"You'd think he'd want to know the truth about Tim's death even if it means that no one was responsible," she speculated.

"You still don't get it. It's not just that his kid died; it's all those years that he was cut out of Tim's life."

"Archer didn't have anything to do with that."

"What about Lexi?" Jude asked.

"You're never going to sell me on that one." Josie stretched her legs. "The one thing we know about Lexi is that she was devoted to Tim. If Archer wasn't going to pick up the slack, then she would have every reason to mend fences with Colin. She wasn't going to die without knowing Tim was taken care of, and Colin would have been better than nothing. I think he blew her off and made it clear that he wasn't open to negotiation. I don't trust that guy as far as I can throw him, and if he's having fantasies now about what could have been, that's just too bad."

Jude cocked his head. "You've never heard that women can be vindictive just for the heck of it?"

"You've never heard that most men are idiots when it comes to responsibility?"

"That's a sweeping statement," Jude countered.

"It's a fair one, or haven't you seen the divorce statistics?" Josie waved her hand, then chuckled and put her fingers to her forehead. "Oh, my God, I can't believe I said that. I'm sorry. This is ridiculous. We could argue either side of this fence until the cows come home. Bottom line, I just don't like a guy who shows up with his hand out and doesn't care what's put in it—money or Archer's head."

Jude's gaze lingered on his client.

"I don't know. I'm not getting that vibe. I think Colin is in the early stages of real grief and that's why your theory hurts him so much."

"I don't know why this would bother him any more than thinking Archer caused Tim's death or that there had been a problem with the Shock and Drop that resulted in his death. No matter what happened, Tim is still dead. So what would it matter if he died before he fell?"

Josie warmed to her subject. She scooted forward, trying again to get Jude excited about her proposition.

"Look, Jude, I watched that tape a hundred times over, and it seems to me that Tim's eyes were closed and his body completely limp when he fell. There is every possibility he had a seizure or a blood clot, something that killed him in the second before we see him come back into the frame. A blood clot can kill you like that." Josie snapped her fingers. "Archer sensed something was wrong, reached for Tim and somehow unlatched the harness.

"Bottom line, if Tim Wren was dead before the harness opened, Archer could have yanked him off the platform and thrown Tim to the ground and legally it still wouldn't be murder."

"And if the doctor confirms that?" Jude countered. "Then Colin is the only one suffering. There will be no one to blame, and he'll be left alone with all that pain and nothing to show for it."

"Maybe all that man has in him is anger and Tim's just an excuse to let it out," Josie said as she glared at Colin Wren. "Besides, you could argue operator error. Given the way Tim looked and acted, he shouldn't have been let on the ride. It will still be a payday for Colin."

Jude put his hand on Josie's shoulder as he got up wearily. There was no arguing. Josie had made up her mind about the man, but Jude felt sorry for him out there alone. He leaned down and whispered in her ear.

"Cut him some slack, Josie. It takes some people longer than others to wake up to how they feel about their kids. Few parents are monsters, but then again few of them are saints either."

With that, Jude wandered outside. He said a few

words to Colin, who moved away a step. He didn't want a friend. Josie watched but had eyes only for Jude. His words had hit her where she lived and left Josie breathless. What would she do if her mother reappeared wanting to claim her? Would she melt into her arms, drink in her apologies, believe the repentance and absolve her of her sin? Or would she want her mother to pay for all the hurt she caused just because there was no one else who could settle the bill?

The hell with it.

Her mother wasn't coming back, so the question could never be answered.

The hell with him.

Josie shook away a twinge of sympathy she felt for Colin Wren, the prodigal father, the man who wanted to champion his son in death to make up for the sin of abandoning him in life.

Standing up, Josie smoothed her trousers and her conscience. Tim Wren was a victim who still had something to say. With that thought, the man who could interpret the language of the dead opened the door and smiled at her.

Dr. Chow, the independent pathologist, was ready to talk.

32

"Will Mr. Wren be joining us?"

Jude had come at Josie's call. Colin remained outside standing with his back against the wall, his hand held to his chin, his shoulders slumped a bit. Jude made excuses.

"This might be a little too raw for him."

"Oh, now, I didn't find anything too gruesome. I know people always expect me to go into excruciating, gory detail, but the fact of the matter is, what I do is fairly cut-and-dried. No pun intended, of course." Dr. Chow pushed up his glasses, wound the grin down a notch and looked out the window toward Colin. "Would you like to ask him again if he wants to come in? Pathologists don't come cheap."

"Thanks, but he was pretty clear," Jude assured him.

"So? Doctor?" Josie opened her hands, urging him to get on with it.

"Yes. Well. I have completed my examination of Timothy. I must say, the embalmer did a top-notch job. Timothy was quite easy to work on, thanks to the expense gone to before he was buried. Made my job so much easier." Dr. Chow readjusted his glasses again. They were square and black-rimmed and made him look very young. "I will, of course, provide you with a final report, but here it is in a nutshell.

"The death certificate lists blunt-force trauma as the cause of death and, truthfully, I have no reason to bicker with that. It is fairly standard in cases such as this where the cause seems quite obvious and there is no reason to perform an autopsy."

"So you're absolutely sure Tim wasn't dead before he fell?" Josie asked, hoping against hope that she had misunderstood.

"No, there was nothing wrong with Timothy's heart. It was strong despite a valve problem. No evidence of a stroke. But that is not to say that he couldn't have appeared to be dead, as you described to me, Ms. Bates. Timothy was definitely out of it. He had a high concentration of phenobarbital in his blood. I'm surprised he was still standing after ingesting that much medication. His reaction time would have been slow. His body would have been heavy. It would have taken a great effort for him to forcefully break through his restraints or to catch himself should the restraint break. So, yes, basically he was a deadweight, but he was by no means dead."

"I found a bottle of that drug in Lexi's purse." Josie looked from the doctor to Jude. "I assumed they were hers."

"They might have been. You'll have to ask Timothy's physician if he would have prescribed them for the boy," Dr. Chow suggested.

"Would there be any reason to prescribe those meds for Tim?" Jude queried.

Dr. Chow shook his head. "Phenobarbital is prescribed for seizures, but I saw no evidence that Timothy suffered in that manner. I would speculate that the prescription was for the mother. She might have suffered seizures if her cancer had affected her brain.

It would not be unusual to prescribe phenobarbital for that. But the question is, why was it in Timothy's system?"

Dr. Chow took a breath, pursed his lips as if he were about to kiss one of them and then began to speculate.

"I suppose there are a number of scenarios that I could testify to if you chose to examine me on the matter. For instance, prescribing the medication might have been done in an effort to keep Timothy from acting out. The drug can actually be used as a substitute for heroin. With so much in his system he would appear nearly comotose. I am appalled to think a physician would have done such a thing, but nothing about the medical profession surprises me anymore. Now, there is another option. Phenobarbital might have been used experimentally in an attempt to control Timothy's muscle spasms. I am not up on any new literature regarding experimentation with that drug, but I certainly could research it."

"I'm almost sure I saw Lexi's name on the bottle, though," Josie mused.

"And that brings us to another possibility," the doctor said. "It could be that the mother shared the medication with the boy. Self-medication is not unheard of. If she was concerned with his comfort and she, herself, had found relief using the drug, she might have given it to Timothy. I would have to question the amount administered. It was excessive. But if a layperson was giving the medication, they would have to guess at how much to give. And then that leads us to a problem. How could anyone prove how the medication got into Timothy's system now that I have proved it was there?"

"But it is your opinion that the amount of phenobarbital you found in the boy's system would have slowed his reactions," Josie insisted, wanting the doctor to be very clear.

"Oh, most definitely. Very much so. I'll view the copy of the tape you have brought me, but, given my findings, I have no doubt that Timothy was in a stupor. I can state fairly clearly that Timothy made some attempt to stop that fall, and that is incredible given the amount of drugs in his system."

"How would you know that?" Josie asked.

"There is DNA material under his nails, Ms. Bates," the doctor answered. "I scraped him and sent the material out for matching as soon as the body was delivered to me. The nail on the middle finger was broken; the material was only found under three nails on the right and left hands, so he was not grappling with someone as you would if you had hold of them; rather he was flailing as if to stop something, grasping without an equal amount of force."

The doctor motioned with his hands like a dog digging in the dirt.

"Timothy was doing this in a forward movement and it was reactive. There were varying amounts of material under each nail. If he was clutching on to someone and struggling with them, there would have been foreign matter found under the nail bed of the thumb and the other nails, also."

"Could you tell if someone was trying to stop Tim from doing something to his own harness?" Josie asked, knowing she was reaching.

"You mean was someone intervening as he tried to unlatch his safety harness?"

"Exactly," Josie said.

"There's no way to be certain, but I would say that is a doubtful scenario. If Tim had his hand on the

metal latch there would have been some sort of
scraping on the palm of the hand, some indication of
swelling or bruising if someone tried to pull his hand
forcibly away from the metal. I doubt I would have
found any foreign matter under his nails if that were
the case." Dr. Chow was using his hands again, panto-
miming as he talked. "If Tim had grabbed on to the
webbing material of the harness in order to keep himself erect or to save himself from falling, I might have
noted some kind of burn, the type of which you get
when rope is drawn through the hand. No, if I were
to testify, I would say that Timothy was scratching at
a person defensively before he died"—Dr. Chow took
off his glasses and cleaned the lenses on his lab coat
as he continued—"and there seem to be only two
choices of who that might be."

"No, Jude, I won't do it, so don't ask again," Josie
said under her breath.

Dr. Chow was gone after requesting a sample of
Lexi's DNA and Archer's in order to complete his
report. Josie made noises about getting the samples to
him but was singing a different tune now.

"Don't be absurd, Josie. Just do the test."

"No, I don't have to be sure. If it is Archer's
DNA—"

"Which it probably is unless the angel Gabriel suddenly appeared beside Tim on that ride," Jude said.

"If it is Archer's DNA then Ruth is going to argue
that Tim was making a defensive move to ward him
off, and that's as good as giving her the last nail in
his coffin," Josie argued as she made to leave. "I'm
not going to do that."

"Don't be afraid to find out, for God's sake. The
strong position is the one with the knowledge. None

of this happens in a vacuum. Ruth is going to find out exactly what went down here, and she's going to have a field day with it."

"I'll work around it. Give me some time to think about it." Josie tried to pull away, but Jude held her tighter.

"You better think fast, Josie, because if you use anything you found out today, if you even mention the drugs in Tim's system, then no judge in the world is going to stop Ruth from using whatever she can get her hands on. Ruth will argue that Tim scratched at Archer because Archer was trying to hurt him. Ruth will argue that Archer could have given that kid the drugs. Ruth will argue—"

"Tell me something I don't know, Jude," Josie snapped. She was already halfway to the door when Jude called to her.

"If we know for sure, Josie, then we can plan." She looked back as he walked toward her. "We can get ten more doctors to argue statistical error and dilute the DNA information. Juries still aren't sure what to think about DNA. If you do that, then you can play up the drugs in Tim's system, the effect it would have, given his body weight and his state of mind. Josie, think."

"I don't know what all this *we* stuff is, Jude. You opted out, remember? The only reason you were here was because you thought there was an outside chance you'd find out something that would convince Colin to move forward on the wrongful-death suit. But you forgot that Dr. Chow can't release that information without my express agreement. I paid for the damned autopsy. Archer is protected."

"Don't be a fool." Jude threw up his hands. "I don't care if there won't be a settlement on Colin. I'm trying to help you by pointing out the obvious. In the first place, Ruth is a good lawyer and she'll find some way around that privilege if it kills her—"

"And in the second place, I'll tell the prosecution anything it wants to know to make sure your client pays for what he did to Tim if that's his DNA under my son's fingernails."

33

Slowly Josie turned and looked into Colin Wren's red-rimmed eyes. She felt Jude move up behind her as if they stood two against an avenging angel. They had been so involved that neither was aware that Colin had come in, stood close, taken in every word of their argument.

"Don't give me that. You had your chance to be something for Tim. Hurting Archer isn't going to make you feel any better about losing that chance," Josie insisted.

"Don't push me, Ms. Bates. I want to know who is responsible for killing my son. Now, you have a choice. You can provide a sample of that man's DNA, or I can ask the prosecutor to get it for me."

"So you can sink Archer because it's convenient?"

"So I can know," Colin said, his voice little more than a strangled scream. "And once I know I will work to convict your client if that's the way it should be. I will then sue him for every last cent he's worth in civil court. I will try to make sure that he never sees the light of day, but, if he does, he will never have one penny to call his own for the rest of his life. I will make him wish he was as dead as Tim."

"That's not even a rock and a hard place, Mr. Wren. No matter which way it turns you've already got him convicted." Josie swung her head toward Jude. "So tell me about your client now, Jude. Tell me how sensitive he is. Tell me how this is about grief and bonding and all that crap. I think you hate Archer because he had your woman, because he didn't want your son and neither did you. I think you'd do anything to ease all that misery inside of you, Mr. Wren."

Josie stepped away. One step, then two. Backward toward the door.

"One way or another there's a payday coming for you, isn't there? But I'm not going to let it be on Archer's back because he didn't do anything. Understand me? He didn't do it."

Josie slammed through the door and didn't look back. The men watched until she roared off in the Wrangler. Jude took a deep breath. He was going to say something to Colin—he hadn't decided what—but found himself mute when he looked at his client. There were tears in Colin's eyes that kept the words from coming out.

Jude put his hand on his client's shoulder and walked him out the door. By the time he got to his own car Jude Getts felt strangely empty. Maybe the challenge wasn't as exciting as it used to be. Maybe it didn't matter that Colin wanted to drop the suit against Pacific Park and Jude was going to eat the bill. Maybe all this wasn't about winning but about knowing the truth, and that made Jude Getts uncomfortable as hell.

Archer put his tray on the conveyor belt. Lunch sucked. He'd kill for one of Burt's burgers. He would give anything to be sitting with a beer on his balcony. Instead, he was watching his back in the general population at the Men's Central Jail. No more special privileges. Archer was bound over for trial, and the objective was to survive until his case worked its way through the system. To survive, he needed to make some decisions, and one of those was if he needed a new attorney, one who—

"Ar-ch-er."

The sound of his name rose like smoke and curled around his ear. No one had heard it except him and the man who tilted toward him as they shuffled toward the yard. Archer turned his head and got a general idea of who his playmate was.

Medium height, powerful build, head shaved bald, Hispanic. One hand in sight. Archer shifted his head the other way. He couldn't see the man's other hand without turning around, and that was not a good idea. He'd be off balance. Steady on his feet meant he could dodge, weave, sidestep if that hidden hand held a weapon. So Archer toed the line, breathing in the smell of a hundred men, a thousand men, every man who had ever walked here since the place was built. He kept his senses tuned for a movement or a sound that would be the precursor to trouble.

"You Archer, right? Detective? West LA, man. Right? Right? I think I know you, man." God it was an ugly sound, a whisper that wasn't a whisper at all.

"Who wants to know?" Archer kept his own voice steady. No fear, at least none the man behind him could hear.

"Nobody in particular. Just asking. Word has it you did a kid. Not a good thing, man. My boys don't like that kind of action.'Specially from a cop. You suppose to protect and serve, man. Ain't that right, Ar-ch-er?"

The man was so close his breath licked the back of Archer's neck. Archer steeled himself. His hands were loose by his side. He was ready for anything. He picked his feet up and put them down deliberately.

How had it come to this?

He flexed his fingers.

He had done everything right. Almost everything.

Up with the right foot and down.

Balance. Balance.

Archer thought the word until it became a part of his backbone. Moving his head ever so slightly he checked out the line. Eleven. He counted eleven men in front of him, God knew how many behind, and not a one who would help him if he needed it. But if he could make it to the door and the guard. If that could happen . . .

"So, Ar-ch-er . . ."

The man behind him was closer still, his pelvis pushing into Archer's ass. Still no hands, still nothing tearing through his skin, ripping up his insides. Archer whipped his head to the side, only to catch himself. No fast moves, nothing to draw attention until he was closer to the door, the guard and help.

"Oh, sorry, man. Sorry I got kinda personal there." His friend chuckled, and then it came.

A sharpness near his kidney, a pressure that seemed unbearable. Archer stiffened and started to crumble and succumb to the fear that grabbed his gut before he realized it was a joke. His friend sniggered.

"Sorry, man. Gotta watch that. Gotta keep in my personal space."

Archer righted himself. Seven more men and he was there. He would be safe. He would ask to see Josie, who would ask for protective custody, who would—

Again. The jab.

God, he was scared.

Strong fingers, long nails.

Something in the hand? A shank?

Archer tried to move away, but the man in front

turned with a look of such utter, soulless antipathy that Archer backed off.

God help me.

"It's nothing, man." That breathy whisper again. "Nothing but a little love tap. Nothing but me telling you how it is, man. Nothing but . . ."

God save me.

"You."

A guard barked. Archer's head snapped toward the call along with every other man in the cafeteria. Archer was weak with relief. The guard was looking at him.

Thank you, God.

It was over for now. The man picked him out of the line, ordered him toward another door, away from the yard, away from the guy who recognized him, toyed with him, waited for him. He was saved for another hour, and maybe that was all he needed, because the guard brought news.

"Your lawyer wants to see you."

Some things were still going his way.

Archer opened his mouth. A lady in a white lab coat swabbed his cheek. Josie looked on with eyes as dark blue as a rough sea and a face as hard as a sheared cliff. Archer kept his eyes averted from both of them. He was angry at Josie for insisting on this humiliation, insisting on proof of a guilt he swore he didn't own. So Archer closed his eyes and let the technician work. The woman did so with little interest, eventually packaged the swabs and was let out of the interview room. Josie waited until the door closed.

"I told Colin and Jude I wasn't going to have you tested."

"Then why are you?" Archer still wouldn't look at her.

"Because I want to be sure that you were the one he was reaching for, Archer. I want to know that you were the last person Tim Wren touched." Josie's gaze was glued to Archer. She looked for any little tic of guilt, a tremor that followed a lie.

"I probably was."

"Were you scratched?"

"I don't remember. Even if it's my DNA it won't prove that Tim was trying to stop me from unlatching his harness. It won't prove he scratched me on the ride. All you're going to do is give the prosecution the chance to make this seem like proof. Is that what you want?" Archer slid his eyes toward her.

"I'm paying for the test. These results can't be released without my permission. You would have to approve releasing anything with Lexi's DNA on it. None of this is going to get into court," Josie said, and Archer found that as reassuring as Jude had.

"There's always a way around everything. There are ways to make the smallest, most insignificant thing seem big and important. Ruth Alcott is a master at that. I thought you were better than Ruth Alcott." Archer swung his head away, only to look back at a silent Josie. There it was. The final brick in the wall between them. Josie had no assurance to offer. Archer stood up. "I guess we're done?"

"No, we're not," Josie said, and motioned him down again. "I have a few more questions. Did you medicate Tim the day of the accident?"

"No." Archer answered simply.

"Did Lexi?"

"No, and I was with them every minute." Archer straightened his shoulders. "That's the truth, Jo."

"Who took Tim to the bathroom, Archer?" Josie was unmoved by the protestation.

"I did. Twice."

"Tim had phenobarbital in his blood. We found a bottle of it in the bag you took to Pacific Park that day," Josie told him. "Someone gave it to him."

Archer's dark brown eyes narrowed as he took a good look at Josie. She looked parched, as if all the moisture that made her skin glow and her hair shine had been sucked out of her. Those blue eyes of hers were shadowed and haunted, sinking into a face that was slashed to harsh planes of cheekbones, chin and brow. Her hands shook and she wasn't even aware of it. When Josie tired of waiting for him to speak, she did, and she sounded exhausted.

"Someone gave it to him," Josie said again as she got up to leave.

At the door Josie rapped twice. It opened. She looked a moment longer at Archer, waiting for the words that would make everything right.

"I already told you everything you need to know, Jo."

"What about the things I should know, Archer?" she asked with a trace of resignation in her voice.

"I've told you that, too. Believe whatever you want."

It was the last thing Archer said. He didn't even try to stop her from walking out the door.

"What do you think? Can you come down any more?" Roger McEntyre knew he was asking the impossible.

"Sorry, Roger, that's as close as I can shave it. Twenty grand is going to get the Rotator up and running like new. If I cut any corners on that thing you're going to have problems. You don't want any more problems, do you?"

Roger looked out the window of the small office and almost laughed. Blackstone Engineering had been holding the attractions at Pacific Park together for more years than Roger could remember, and they knew what another problem meant to the park. They also knew the shape the Rotator was in and they had just given Roger the bad-news bill to fix it. Of course, Roger wouldn't have to worry about any of this if Colin Wren made it official that he was withdrawing his suit against Pacific Park. Roger had expected notification by now, but nothing. Still, he wasn't surprised. Jude Getts wouldn't let a wrongful-death plum like Colin slip away so easily. So, until they were officially off the hook for Timothy Wren, Roger had to watch the pennies even with Blackstone Engineering.

They had always talked straight about the trade-off between cost and safety. Now that Pacific Park was under Greater United Parks's microscope, a huge repair fee for a major attraction would just be one more red flag. Isaac expected the Rotator repairs to come in between eight and ten grand. Twenty was going to give the old guy apoplexy.

"Roger?" Mike Blackstone was waiting. "Roger? I've got to know if you want us to go ahead. We're starting to book out for the end of the year and I can't hold you a spot indefinitely."

Roger took a deep breath and put a hand to his eyes. He felt up against it like he never had in his life. It seemed there was a whole army in his way: Colin Wren, Josie Bates, Jude Getts, the fat guy with the engineering friend. Even the dead kid seemed real these days. But he'd been up against armies before, and he would do what he had always done.

"No problem. Let's book this and get you guys started." Roger reached into the inside pocket of his coat, found his checkbook and a pen. "Just make it look good for GUP okay? They're coming back out end of the month."

"You got it, my friend." Mike watched Roger scribble out a check. He took it. His brow knitted. "A personal check for ten grand?"

"I'm good for it."

"It's not that. It's just . . . unusual. There something you want to tell me, Roger?" Mike asked.

"I want to tell you that this is between you and me. You give Isaac a bid for ten, cash my check for the other ten and we're good to go. Can you do that?"

"I can, if you say."

Mike put the check in his drawer. Together they decided on a date to start the refurbishment. When Roger left he had one more stop to make—drinks with a VP at Greater United Parks who hit the bottle a little too hard. A few choice words and that VP would go back to the office swearing that Archer was already convicted of murdering Tim Wren, that Colin Wren knew it and was dropping his suit any day and that Pacific Park was the buy of the century.

34

Southern California was back. The idea of fall blew out of everyone's head like dead leaves in Des Moines. It would be sun, sun, sun until Christmas and then some. Batteries were recharged. People moved faster through the day, ideas flashed in heads like the glint off a Porsche's bumper, kids ditched school, men took up with younger women, wives had their nails done and dried them in the sun. That was why the gate looked so good at Pacific Park. Not spectacular, but real good.

Isaac shared the news with Greater United Parks. He also shared the news that Archer was bound over for trial in the death of Timothy Wren, even though that had been reported in every media. He told them Colin Wren was rethinking his suit against Pacific Park. Happily, Pacific Park would be exonerated of any wrongdoing. There would be no settlement in young Mr. Wren's death. Greater United Parks, already knowing this from a certain vice president, was delighted to have the information confirmed, and all was well in the world of acquisitions.

"It was like a miracle, Roger. I thought they would worry because attendance was a little light, but they were happy. Truly impressed . . ."

Isaac stopped talking and walking. It was unlike Roger to be preoccupied, and it worried Isaac no little bit until Roger looked away from the phone memo he was reading.

"Yes, Isaac." Roger cleared his throat and smiled under that thick mustache of his. These moments of joy were few and far between for the old man. Roger folded the message and put it in his pocket. It would wait until they were finished.

"I'd almost given up, you know, Roger. Almost." Isaac lifted a finger and waved it as a warning to Roger never to succumb to self-doubt. "I thought this place would go the way of so many others. The Pike. Remember the old Pike?"

Isaac walked around Roger's desk, sat in a chair beside it and settled in for a chat.

"Now, there was a place. Long Beach was a big port then, you know. The young sailors rode the roller coaster and picked up the girls and got their first tattoos. It was a fine park. This is a fine park and a fine day. Did I tell you the rest of the good news, Roger? Our insurance is being reinstated, and the estimate on the Rotator came in exactly as I thought it would. Not a penny more. I know my machinery, Roger. No one can say I don't. What a good day this has been.

"Yes, Roger, everything will be fine. I can rest easy. My life's work won't disappear. Your father's fine work won't disappear."

Isaac's gaze wandered and his words drew out low as if to follow. It was something old men did. One thought led to another and another, and it always led to something sad. A friend long gone, a competitor out of business. Loneliness.

"I don't think there was ever a chance of that," Roger reassured him, startling Isaac as he did so. It was as if he had forgotten the younger man was there.

Then his expression changed and he looked kindly, gratefully on Roger.

"You're a good boy to try to fool me, but I knew we were in trouble. You're like my own son, the way you worry about me." Tears were in Isaac's eyes at the mention of the long-lost son, but they passed sooner than later today, and Isaac brightened. "And I want you to know that I have made arrangements for you, too. It will be in the contract that you are to remain in this position for as long as you like—unless, of course, you do something bad. And stock options, Roger. I'm splitting those . . . Ah, well, you'll see. You'll see what I've arranged."

There was that finger waggle again. Roger almost laughed aloud. This was like being a kid again.

Don't eat too much cotton candy.

Be careful there; watch the lead rope.

Roger, trust only those who have proved worthy. Like your father.

That seemed a lifetime ago. Roger smiled at the finger wagging, knowing that bad things were subjective. As far as Roger was concerned he had done nothing bad, and even today, this last bit of a problem, might be taken care of without his transgressing. It would all depend on that phone call he still had to make, that woman he still had to talk to. Roger tried to help Isaac wrap it up so he could get on with his business.

"I think I'll be around here a good long time," Roger assured him. "And I promise I'll keep an eye on the place for you."

"So sure of yourself, Roger? But then you're young. Why not be the cock of the walk?" Isaac chuckled. "Today, though, we're both the cocks, so you'll come to dinner and tell me all the crazy things the new owners will do. I'm not fooling myself about that. But I will remember the way it is today." Isaac tapped his head and his heart and gave Roger a wink. "Come on, Roger, let's walk the park. Nothing like a good crowd on a sunny day to make an old man feel happy. We'll ride the roller coaster like we did when you were small."

"No, no." Roger waved his hands. "I've got work to do if you want Greater United Parks to close the deal."

"Work! I'm still the boss. I say you can stop work for an hour or so," Isaac said heartily.

"All right. Give me ten minutes. I'll meet you by the coaster."

Roger gave in without much of a fight. If an hour stretched to two, what was the harm? It would make Isaac happy and give Roger time to think. The next move had to be well thought out. It might be as simple as a phone call. Or it could be as delicate as—

The sound of his office door closing brought Roger back. He retrieved the phone message from his pocket. Pity it had come through the general switchboard, but nothing to be done about that now. He picked up the receiver and dialed the number that had been left along with the short message. The phone rang three times before it was answered.

"Hello? Is Mrs. Tronowski there?"

Roger's mustache twitched with his almost-smile. He hit the jackpot. The lady herself had answered.

It took only a few minutes to reassure her that he did, indeed, have everything well in hand. Yes, he said, he had talked to the gentleman in question. The gentleman had called him, too, and she should not worry because now Roger would take care of everything. "Thank you, Mrs. Tronowski, for covering your bases.

This information will mean a great deal to the gentleman in question, I'm sure."

Ten minutes later Roger was standing with Isaac at the Perilous Peaks Coaster. The old man's excitement was catching, but for Roger it translated to a strange and subdued giddiness, the kind of feeling he had before a covert op. It had been too long since he'd had this sense of purpose, this desire to complete a critical mission. Funny how something small, some little piece of unexpected intelligence, a fleeting communication, could set a man on a road he never imagined he would take again.

". . . and pursuant to our agreement, you will cease and desist from using the name . . ."

Annoyed, Jude glanced toward the door and his secretary, who stood there waiting for him to finish his dictation.

"What?" It was unusual for Jude to be short with her, but she was an excellent secretary and didn't take it personally.

"Wilson Page is on two. He says he needs you. There's a lot of action on the site and he needs to show you something important."

"Crap."

Jude put his head in his hands and brooded. He didn't want to go help Wilson, because Wilson really didn't need any help. Jude had already told him to shut down the Pacific Park probe on Colin's behalf. All Wilson really needed was company, and he needed company because Wilson had no real life. He had no friends except for Jude, and he only had Jude because Jude was superstitious.

When they first met Jude was as repulsed by Wilson as most people were. Then, one day, Jude had an epiphany. He realized that there but for the grace of God went he, or any other successful person in this world. The same twist of fate that made Jude Getts rich, handsome and smart made Wilson smart, grotesque and needy. Wilson was Jude's fly. Jude knew that if you killed a fly for no other reason than that it was a fly, it came back in its next life as a teacher who hated your guts, a woman who sucked you dry, a boss who ran you into the ground, a client who ruined you.

So Jude did nothing to harm Wilson and, over the years, found out how little it took to be compassionate— most of the time. Tonight wasn't one of those times. He pulled his hands through his hair, sighing deeply.

"Did you tell him I was here?"

"No, I told him I wasn't sure if you had left for the day."

Jude blushed. He hated having someone lie for him.

"Tell him I'm gone for the evening with a client," he directed, needing some time to finish the pile of work on his desk.

"He'll try you at home. On your cell," she reminded him.

"Yeah. Yeah." Jude dismissed her. Everyone knew that he was one of the few people Wilson actually called, and when Wilson decided you were "phone worthy," he pursued that instrument of communication with a vengeance. Jude would turn his cell phone off.

The door closed. The office was quiet again. Jude picked up his tape recorder, only to forget what he was going to say as he fell back in his chair and swiveled toward the glass wall behind him. He had a few thoughts, and none of them were about the business at hand.

First, he pondered the plants behind the glass and

tried to remember when the guy from Gerry's Jungle had been there last. It would have been nice to see him stand up and wave.

Next, Jude wondered why he didn't just get on the phone and be honest. He was tired and busy. Wilson hadn't seen half a dozen clients, dealt with office politics, made two appearances in civil court and had to cancel dinner with a gorgeous woman. The most strenuous thing Wilson had done all day was go to the bathroom and type on the computer.

Finally, Jude thought of calling Josie. She was the one who still needed Wilson's help. She could put in a few hours of sweat with him if he really needed it. After all, Josie wasn't making the big bucks; she didn't have the caseload he did or the responsibilities he did. She couldn't even bother to call him back when all he was trying to do was help her—even if all he had to give these days was moral support.

Jude Getts turned back to his desk, clicked on the tape recorder and proceeded to dictate a new letter that outlined the ramifications of Colin Wren's dropping the lawsuit at this time. Jude was explicit: If Colin did this and Archer was acquitted, Colin would have nothing. Jude was not going to let this go without a fight. Everything else was secondary to getting his client focused again. Even Wilson.

An hour later, unable to concentrate, filled with superstitious guilt and more than his share of peevishness, Jude Getts locked his office, unlocked his car and headed to Wilson Page's house.

Nothing had changed at the Greenwood Home. People were still broken, puttering around in wheelchairs driven forward by the breath of their mouths,

words were spoken through electronic simulators, un-
ending rest was taken in beds that moved with the
touch of a button. Some of the people didn't know
where they were; others were horrified to find themselves still in this place.

Josie felt better being in Greenwood this time.
There was no overt compassion, no curiosity; there
was only the chore that brought her back, and Barbara
Vendy, an administrator who didn't particularly want
to revisit the problem of Tim Wren.

"I'm sorry to ask you to do this again, but I haven't
found any of Tim's medical records, so you must have
them. I absolutely need to know what medication he
was taking. There must be some mention of it in the
records you retained."

"Look, Miss Bates, I searched high and low, and I
haven't got what you want. Tim's mother must have
gotten rid of the files after they were sent to her.
There was no reason for her to keep them after he
died, and, in all honesty, I don't see how this is my
problem."

"It's not. It's my problem. But if I don't get some
information about who medicated Timothy Wren
there's a chance my client will be wrongly convicted
of that boy's death. I would find that hard to live with,
wouldn't you?"

Barbara was annoyed that the day was coming to a
close and Josie had laid a problem before her to which
she had no solution. And, yet, when it was put that
way, she relented. She pulled a stack of papers toward
her and shuffled through them. "I pulled everything
we had that even mentioned Tim. I just don't see anything in here about a medication schedule."

"How about other doctors?" Josie persisted. "Do

your records indicate that a private doctor was involved with him? I imagine they would have shared
their information with your staff doctor."

"No, no and no. I'm sorry." She flipped fast and
furious. "This page outlines a general diet; there are
some notes on his physical therapy. I can't even believe we kept that. There's nothing about his medical
situation except that we have a release from his
mother regarding an injury he incurred about four
months before his accident. . . ."

"May I see that?"

Josie held out her hand and Barbara Vendy
whipped the paper across the desk. Josie scanned it.
Tim Wren had hit a wall, running as best he could,
and knocked himself out. There were no contusions.
He was observed for twenty-four hours. Partially restrained. The release was signed illegibly in a tight,
close hand that veered off the signature line.

"Are you sure this is Lexi's signature?" Josie asked,
but Barbara talked over her. Her voice had taken on
new shadings. Instead of impatience Josie heard a dis-
sonant note.

"We have the final request for records from Lexi
and . . ." Barbara shuffled the papers again and looked
closer, muttering to herself. "Christ, it's so hard to
find good office help. This request is dated five days
before Tim died. Can you believe it? Doesn't anyone
ever look at a calendar anymore?"

"Are you sure the date is incorrect?" Josie asked,
setting aside the accident release.

"It must be." Barbara clucked. "We would have
made copies of his medical records, not sent the origi-
nals if he was still here. But this says that the original
records were released."

"How is a request usually submitted? Could Lexi have called and asked for them?" Josie queried.

Barbara shook her head and tossed the papers on her desk. She got up and stuck her hands in her pockets.

"She could have, but there would be a record of that in the medical administration office. We'd keep that at least seven years in case of any liability questions. Wait here. I'll see what I can find."

It took Barbara twelve minutes but, when she came back, she had more paper in hand.

"Okay, here it is. The dates match." She handed Josie a copy of the release request. "Lexi wrote to us asking for the records, and her letter is dated five days before her son died. Here's a copy of the log that shows the request was honored. One of two things happened. The girl who initialed the log was new at the time and she lasted only a few months before we had to let her go. So, if she received a request with the wrong date, she probably just copied it into the log without questioning it and sent out the original records rather than a copy."

"Do you still have the envelope this request came in? We could check the cancellation on the stamp," Josie asked hopefully.

"That's really asking for a miracle," Barbara quipped.

"Okay, so what's the other mistake that could have been made?" Josie prodded.

"Maybe Lexi made the mistake. I mean, look at that handwriting. It's uneven. Weak. She may have written the request after Tim died, put the wrong date on it and our girl just copied right off the letter without questioning it. Either way, it was a clerical error on our part, and I apologize."

"You're sure?" Josie muttered.

"Sure as I can be." Barbara shrugged. "There isn't anyone we can ask about it now."

"Do you have a forwarding address for the girl who worked here? Someplace you sent her last check?" Josie asked.

"Sorry. She was on probation, so we were paid up on the day she left. There were no benefits to worry about. Look, she was just a clerk. She didn't know the patients. She pushed papers. So now you've got it all." Barbara sat behind the desk again and picked up her pen. "There's nothing else to give you. The only other avenue I can suggest is for you to ask your client about all this."

"He didn't have anything to do with making decisions about Tim's treatment," Josie assured her.

"But he might remember which other doctors Lexi took Tim to. She may have mentioned them to him, or he could have overheard a conversation. Those doctors might still have records if they weren't advised that Tim died."

"Good thought. I'll see what I can come up with," Josie said as she stood up.

"I assume you have Internet access," Barbara offered one last hope.

"Sure."

"Maybe you can do a search. Look for experimental procedures for degenerative muscle diseases, anything having to do with mental retardation. I guarantee you, if you find ongoing studies in southern California during the time Tim was alive you can be sure Lexi tried to get on board."

"Thanks. I'll do that." Josie held up the request for the release of records. "Can I keep this?"

"They're copies," Barbara said.

"Great. Thanks again for your time."

Barbara nodded, but had one last thought before Josie could leave.

"Carol Schmidt is here this afternoon. She might be able to remember which doctors Tim saw."

Josie felt her lips twitch and her gut take a nosedive. But the face she turned to Barbara Vendy was composed; her voice was steady.

"No, I don't think she'd have anything she would want to tell me."

Colin Wren's home was very quiet. Light and heat were minimalized. Staples were in the refrigerator. He was a man of few needs, but a man passionate about the things he deemed absolute necessities. One of the necessities of life was atoning for your sins. He'd learned that late in life, but he had learned it. When loneliness became chronic, when he found that guilt kept him from new relationships, Colin Wren learned about the psychic necessities of righting wrongs. The wrong of Tim's life and death consumed Colin because it was wrapped up in all the wrongs committed against him. Lexi and her arrogance, that man she married, the solitary life she had left Colin to. It was funny that the idea of retribution against Pacific Park had been so easily put aside when Colin realized Archer was responsible for so much. Not just Tim's death, but Colin's own arid life. Yes, Archer and his macho defiance were an affront to the memory of Tim. Colin couldn't sleep without dreaming about Archer. Colin cursed the long and arduous court process. Enough had been said at the preliminary hearing to condemn Archer twice over, and yet they all played the game.

So, when he answered the phone, Colin Wren was thinking about Tim and the man who was supposed to protect him. The ringing had surprised him almost as much as hearing an excited Wilson Page who was looking for Jude Getts. Colin's laugh was dry and humorless. He almost hung up on the fat man, but a few words in between the labored breaths was all it took for Colin to listen. What Colin heard was beyond belief. What Wilson had told him changed the course of everything, and Colin needed time to think. Colin lied when he promised to track down Jude. What Colin really wanted was to see exactly what Wilson had before he called anyone—especially Jude Getts.

35

Josie made two phone calls on her way back to Hermosa Beach. The first was to Wilson Page, who had been put back in action when Jude got over his snit. She would have him do a search for medical trials that Tim might have been involved with.

As instructed, she let the phone ring ten times. That was as long as it took Wilson to get to the phone if he happened to be in the bathroom. Wilson had timed it, paced it, huffed and puffed to move his weight sideways through the doorway of the bathroom, readjust himself and get into his chair so he could speak to someone properly. On the fifteenth ring, Josie gave up and entertained the crazy thought that Wilson was out.

Out. That was rich.

Wilson couldn't go anywhere without the man who came to help two days a week. That man came on Sundays and Tuesdays. This was Thursday. Wilson should have been home. Since he wasn't, Josie dialed her own home and listened to another phone ring. If Hannah was there she might want to hear the magic number twenty. On a good day she would pick up on ten. Today must have been a spectacular day. Sullen though the girl sounded, Josie found herself grinning when she heard Hannah's voice.

"Seven rings. Are you celebrating?" Josie gave the steering wheel a click left and eased the Jeep around a stalled car and back to the freeway on-ramp in one graceful move.

"Sort of," Hannah answered. "I only got asked to design the cover for the yearbook next year."

"Very nice." Seeing that the ramp light was red, Josie braked, then accelerated as it turned green a few seconds later. She merged and settled in at sixty-five. "You don't sound too happy."

"A girl in my math class said her parents said you worked for a freak who killed kids. They said you had to be as messed up as Archer to defend him."

"What did you say to that?" Josie asked.

"I said, 'Screw you'." Hannah was short, but her anger wasn't directed at Josie; rather it was the posturing of someone who had just realized words had a lot in common with sticks and stones.

"I would have preferred something more intellectual, but I'm assuming that got the job done." This was a far cry from the girl who was going to quietly pay for the sins of her mother. *Good girl.*

"I know," Hannah answered. "It wasn't real creative, so I said her boob job sucked, too."

"There we go. Give her something to think about." This time Josie laughed outright. She found her opening, merged into the fast lane and kicked it up to eighty.

"Are you coming home now?" Hannah asked.

"I am, but then I'm going over to Archer's place. There are still a lot of boxes to go through." Josie raised her voice. At the speed she was going the inside of the Jeep was like a wind tunnel.

"I can help." Hannah's offer was too fast, too anxious. She didn't just want to help; she needed to help. Hard work would keep Hannah from trying to dig the bad-boob-job girl out from under her skin with a razor blade.

"Great," Josie said. "Any messages?"

"Faye wants to know if you need Angie for anything."

"Call her back and tell her thanks, but no." Josie refused the offer of Faye's paralegal as she kept her eyes on the stream of cars ahead. True to form, LA traffic was slowing for no apparent reason.

"Oh, Jude called. He said Wilson might need help with something and to call him."

"I already tried. Wilson didn't answer."

They talked a little longer. Hannah would have dinner ready and then they could start to work. When the call was done, Josie turned her baseball cap around, since the long-hanging sun had finally dipped beneath eye level. She gauged the flow of traffic. It didn't look good. In half a mile Josie decelerated, going from eighty to twenty-five and finally to gridlock. Nothing to do about it. Los Angeles was on the move and it seemed like every car in the city was feeding into the 405.

All except one; the driver of that car was already at his destination, wanting to get his work done before night fell.

Wilson Page was terribly sorry he had missed that call.

He shouldn't have gone to the bathroom. He should have an answering machine. He had software that could be activated and turn all three of his computers into answering machines, but he hadn't bothered with even one. So few people called that the idea of needing something to record a voice message seemed ludi-

crous. Everyone Wilson knew "talked" to him on the
computer. When they laughed they used acronyms or
little smiley-face icons, and it didn't matter what they
looked like or how they sounded. When they said,
"CYA," they meant through the computer. All of
them were just pixels on a screen; no need to interact
when you didn't want to. No need to put a happy tone
to a voice that didn't really sound happy at all.

Of course, there were days when Wilson missed the
sound of a voice other than his own. He heard his
own often enough as he talked his way through the
day, and he didn't much care for the conversation.

*Good morning. Good morning, Wilson. You're not
dead.*

*My, that was fine. Excellent way to start the day.
Getting out of the chair. Standing up on your own.*

*Hungry? Yes? Why, yes, I am, and only three in
the* A.M.

And then there were conversations like today: little
chats about his health and losing weight and the awful
wheezing that came because his lungs and his heart
could not bear the load they carried.

Perhaps a little less for lunch, Wilson.

Walk faster, Wilson.

Lift your arms, Wilson.

This body—it hadn't been the same since he'd gone
to Pacific Park with Jude and all his new friends. The
outing had been too much for a man as large as he
was now. Even getting to the phone was too much.
Well, that wasn't altogether true. Truth be known, he
didn't try too hard to get to the phone when he felt
off his stride. Wilson didn't like the conversations
when the words people spoke only sandwiched the
ones they wanted to say.

If they said, "Aren't you feeling well, Wilson?" they

meant, *Well, what would you expect, you hunk of blubber?*

If they said, "You should have yourself checked out," they meant, *You're going to die, boyo. Sure as shootin', death is lean, mean and you can't outrun it.*

If they said, "You really must watch out for yourself. You never know what could happen," they meant, *It's only a matter of time. They'll bury you like a horse. They'll send you to the glue factory. We're not talkin' dust, Wilson; we're talkin' a whole pile of dirt when you start disintegrating.*

Unless, of course, it was Jude on the phone. Jude never talked between the lines. Jude just took things at face value, and that was why Wilson adored him. That was why Wilson worked so hard for Jude, charged so little and sometimes actually called him just to talk. Sometimes Wilson asked Jude to stop by on one pretense or another because he liked to look at a man who was as handsome as Jude and he liked to listen to a man who was as smart as Wilson himself. In fact, Wilson Page dreamed of being Jude Getts in the same way a farm girl stuck in the middle of nowhere dreams of becoming a movie star. It would never happen, but it was a great dream.

Yet early this afternoon he had called Jude for real. Yes, indeed. He couldn't wait for Jude to check his e-mail. Wilson wanted to hear the pride in Jude's voice when Wilson told him what had come down the pipeline. He wanted Jude to congratulate him for making three real phone calls, for standing up to the people who needed to be stood up to. Jude would be so proud that Wilson had been a man.

But Jude wasn't in and Wilson's excitement abated. The time in the bathroom had convinced him that nothing was as important as getting to his chair and sitting quietly. He had worn himself out by taking the bull by the horns and calling those people. Now if the phone rang, so be it; Wilson was going to take care of himself.

Then he realized it might be Jude ringing him up. If he could get to the phone he could ask Jude to come sit with him until the panic passed. Wilson reached for the receiver and put his mitt of a hand on top of it with every intention of calling Jude's office again, but before he could, Wilson fell asleep.

He dreamed of himself as a thin man even though his subconscious was aware of the sound of his wheezing and that his lungs weren't filling properly and that his heart was pounding against the walls of his chest. That heart was pounding and knocking like an engine. Knocking and . . .

Wilson opened his eyes. He was still heavy with sleep, but he chuckled nonetheless, because now that he was awake, Wilson discovered it wasn't his heart knocking at all. There was someone at the door, rapping the way Jude rapped. Not exactly that way, but it was a confident sound, a let's-get-this-show-on-the-road sound. Wilson blinked at the clock. It was early. Perhaps Jude had gotten his message and come from wherever he had been. That would be like Jude to leave something important just to check on Wilson.

"Come in."

Wilson called out, only to find himself coughing and catching his breath, holding a Kleenex tight to the lips that almost disappeared in the fat of his face before he got out the second word. He turned his head as best he could. He wanted to greet Jude properly. But the coughing persisted, and all Wilson Page could see through the tearing of his eyes was a pair of fine shoes and gray pants that broke perfectly on the vamp.

"Jude," he wheezed.

Wilson Page looked up and smiled his exhausted smile, only to find it ending in a deep intake of breath that never quite made it to his poor beleaguered lungs.

Darn.

Just when he needed a breath the most.

36

Three men stood on the landing outside Wilson Page's place. Another waited by a car. Two more were huddled inside the front door.

" 'Scuse me. Hey, do you mind?" Josie raised her voice, but it was her height that got her noticed.

The men in the doorway stopped talking, looked right at her, then took another second to really see her. Their brows were furrowed with worry; the edges of their mouths and eyes twitched with nerves. They had been speaking in whispers. One finally found his voice.

"Are you a relative?"

"A friend," she answered sharply.

"He had a lot of good-looking friends," one of the other men muttered, eyeing Josie curiously, wondering what on earth she had to do with a man like Wilson Page.

"Look, just let me through, okay?" She put her hand on his shoulder to move him aside but he pushed back halfheartedly.

"I don't know. It's kind of tight in there. We've got stuff to figure out. Maybe you should wait until . . ."

The suggestion of what Josie might do was lost as Jude Getts called to her.

"Josie. Josie."

The men were distracted. Josie saw her opening and plowed through. She was in Jude's arms before anyone could stop her. Josie closed her eyes, unable to look at the mountain of white cloth that covered Wilson Page's dead body. When she tried to step away, Jude held tight to her arms as if to reassure himself that Josie was alive and well.

"I got here as fast as I could," she said quietly. "I was caught in traffic. I'm sorry, Jude. I'm so sorry about Wilson."

When Jude didn't let go, Josie talked faster, searching Jude's beautiful face. His hair still waved back from a perfect brow, but that megawatt smile was gone, the high color in his cheeks had drained, the crackle that was the essence of Jude Getts had flatlined.

"It's okay," he interrupted, his hands shaking her and tightening on her arms. "You made it. I've been here awhile. They . . . I don't know how . . . I don't know . . ."

"Jude," Josie said firmly, but he didn't hear her.

"I mean nobody knows what to do . . ." Jude ran on. "This is such a bizarre situation. Wilson had called and I blew him off and I felt bad. I called . . . no answer . . . I felt so guilty. I found him just like that. In his chair . . . I leaned down and said—"

"Jude . . ." Josie pulled back, but Jude stepped with her.

"Don't you see? If only I had—"

"Jude!" Josie forced her arms out to the side, breaking the hold he had on her. Startled, Jude jerked upright, his mouth opening in surprise before pulling tight with annoyance. Josie lowered her head, her voice. She put a hand on his shoulder. "I'm sorry. You were hurting me. Come on. Come with me."

She led him out of the room, past the four men who discussed the problem of moving Wilson. Josie

walked faster. Jude did the same. Josie hoped he
hadn't heard the men talking about Wilson as if he
were an unwieldy piano.

She stomped down the ramp that had been built to
the side of the steps to make it easier for Wilson to
get out of the house. She strode across a lawn that
was half-brown from lack of care, and past the man
who lingered near a paramedic unit. Jude followed
with a determined step, his eyes down as if he were
rethinking an opening statement even as he was
headed into the courtroom.

They stopped under the canopy of the big, waxy
green leaves of a magnolia tree. Josie was by the thick,
rough trunk. One foot rested atop a root that snaked
out of the ground then ducked back in again like some
subterranean creature that didn't like the look of the
upside world.

"You okay?" Josie stuck her hands deep in the
pockets of her jacket, her baseball cap still firmly in
place. She looked away from Jude, a coward in the
face of such pain and loss.

"Yeah. Thanks."

Jude lied. He kicked at that thick root, stepped on
the rupture as if he could push it back into the ground.
When he couldn't change the configuration of the tree,
he tried to figure out how he could have changed the
outcome of the day.

"If I had talked to Wilson when he called I would
have heard that he wasn't doing well. I could always
tell. I always got my doctor over to see him when that
happened. If I had just answered the phone and heard
his voice I would have known. I could have done
something."

Josie didn't bother to argue the point. She had
played the *if only* game a thousand times and there

never was a winner. *If only* she'd stayed in Hawaii with her father he wouldn't have died alone. *If only* she'd been a better child her mother would have stayed home. *If only* she had seen through Linda Sheraton-Rayburn sooner, Hannah would never have endured jail and a trial for murder. *If only* Josie had asked Archer the right questions when they first met . . . Well, that might not have changed anything.

"What happened? Do they know yet?"

"He was sitting in his chair and he died." Jude shrugged, turned on his heel and walked a few more steps. "His heart gave out or he suffocated under his own weight or he choked on something."

"Will they do an autopsy?" Josie asked, trying to channel his grief as best she could.

Jude shook his head and pulled one hand through his hair. He seemed dazzling in the dark. Every stray ray of light caught a plane of his face or a glint of gold in his hair or the pain in his eyes that was brittle as hard candy.

"I don't see any reason to. I mean, he's so big"— Jude turned away slightly—"so damned big they don't think they can get him on a table. I should have been here for him. I should have . . . done something."

"We do what we can at the time. We do our best, Jude."

"No. I never did my best for Wilson. I used him . . ."

"He worked for you . . ."

"He thought I was his friend . . ."

"You were his friend; I saw it. That is not even in question." Josie's impatience slowed the flow of self-recriminations. Jude thought about his next objection, and when he offered it, it was done solemnly.

"Then why didn't I make him lose some of that

weight? I had enough money to send him to any fat farm in the world. I could have paid to have his stomach stapled. It would have been chump change to me."

"Hey. Come on." Josie put her back against the trunk of that stately tree and one foot up against it. "Wilson had issues, Jude. I hardly knew him, but I could see that. There were reasons he ate so much and cut himself off from the rest of the world. You couldn't have turned that around if you'd devoted your whole life to him."

"But I could have tried."

"Bull." Josie's head swiveled toward the street, then back to Jude. "Jude, you can't change what someone is at the core. My mother left me as suddenly as if she had sat down in a chair and died like Wilson. I couldn't change that."

"But I could see what needed to be fixed," Jude insisted.

"And I felt what needed to be fixed with my mother. And I loved her, too. But, Jude, no matter how much we loved those people, or liked them, or sympathized, or admired or whatever you want to call it, we would never have been able to fix them. Nobody's that powerful. Not even you."

"So we just say what the hell, that's another one down?" Jude walked up and down in front of her, tangling fiercely with the knot in his tie. It wouldn't come loose, but he still struggled with it.

"Don't put words in my mouth. Just don't do that."

Josie pushed off the tree, ready to walk away. Instead she changed her mind and caught Jude on the next pass. He didn't want to stop, but she insisted, putting her hands on his shoulders until he stayed still. Josie Baylor-Bates put her fingers on Jude Getts's tie.

She loosened the knot, working it down until she slid it from under his collar, then stashed it in his pocket.

"I'm sorry you lost a friend, but it wouldn't have changed anything if you'd been there when it happened."

"He wouldn't have been alone, Josie," Jude pointed out sadly. "That's what would have been different. Wilson wouldn't have been alone."

"He wasn't, if that makes you feel any better." Simultaneously, Josie and Jude faced the coroner's man. He had come up so silently they hadn't noticed. "Sorry to break in, but there's a kid inside. He says there was someone with your friend tonight, probably right around the time he died."

37

"Is that him?"

"Yes."

Jude eyed the shroud-covered Wilson. All plans to move him had been curtailed. Yellow tape was strung across the entrance to the house, designating it a crime scene. All the people who had once been there were gone, replaced by a detective, a forensics team, a uniformed cop and a photographer because of this person—this boy—with the long blond hair whose name was David Gibson. His eyes were almost hidden by a thatch of Prince Valiant bangs. He was wearing the blue shorts and white shirt of a Catholic school uniform, and he had cried foul.

"I never saw him for real. Think I could look under the sheet?" David asked, shaking out his hair like a puppy in from the rain.

"Trust me. I don't think you want to see him for real now," Jude said.

"Let's get out of here. We don't want to contaminate the scene any more than we already have. Come on." Josie put her hand on David Gibson's arm and cocked her head.

Josie, Jude and David Gibson—CheezeWiz to his friends on the Internet—ducked under the yellow tape, walked quickly down Wilson's ramp, went past the magnificent magnolia and settled in Jude's Mercedes: David in the back with Jude, Josie in front, swiveling around to look at them. The overhead light was on. It was warm. It was quiet. David had given his statement to the police, Jude had been questioned because he was the one who found Wilson, and now Josie and Jude wanted to hear for themselves what David had to say.

"I was really freaked. I can't believe he's dead." David head-banged to music only he could hear. "I figured something was wrong, but I didn't think it was anything like being dead."

"Let's start at the beginning," Josie suggested. "First, how old are you?"

"Twenty-two. I just turned twenty-two." David blinked his liquid blue eyes once, then twice as Jude and Josie exchanged skeptical looks. David dug in his pocket for his wallet. "No. I really am. I can show you my ID." He whipped a wallet out of the pocket of his navy-blue shorts. "See. Twenty-two. I just look really young."

Josie checked out the ID while Jude checked out the real thing. Skinny as a rail, as near to emaciated as a healthy human being could be, David was as pale as if he lived in a cave on nothing but bread and water.

"What's with the St. Paul's polo shirt? The whole uniform thing?" Jude raised his chin and gave the ensemble a once-over.

"Nothing." David shrugged. "I just haven't grown since I got out of high school. I don't want to throw good money away on clothes. I mean, have you ever worn this stuff? Catholic school uniforms are like iron, man. The shorts stand up by themselves. I've got three pairs of these, one pair of long pants, ten shirts and a sweatshirt. At my personal rate of wear, the amount of physical activity I participate in, the number of times I do the wash, the pants should last me another ten years if I maintain my current weight. The shirts aren't so good, though. Four years on the outside. But that's okay."

"And you don't feel just a little strange wearing that in public?" Josie asked as he put his wallet back into his pocket.

"Ah, you're assuming I go out in public." David raised one finger high, an elfish grin on his face, as if it pleased him to stand so far outside the norm. "That's why it took me so long to get here. Since I usually have no reason to go out, I have no reason to have a normal means of transportation. It took me a couple of hits before I found someone who would lend me a car. Then I had to find out where Wilson lived and that took almost forever. It was weird. Usually I'm really quick with that kind of reference search, but I think I was just freaked and that's why I wasn't working to full capacity."

"Okay, you're here. Take it from the top, starting with how you know Wilson," Jude suggested, his patience already wearing thin.

"Geez. Let's see." David put a long finger to his chin while he calculated. "I was fourteen and having some trouble with my calculus, I went online to get some help and there was Wilson. He was cool. Totally awesome. He helped me out with the calculus, and then I saw some of his sites and those were so cool. Totally awesome."

The head banging stopped as quickly as it started but the story was seamless.

"Then Wilson got me a job testing software and, instead of going to college like my parents wanted, I just work on my computers. You know, I pick up some gigs here and there to pay the bills, but mostly I play chess—mostly against the computer. Wilson and I talked when we couldn't sleep. He had it worse than me, though."

"Do you mean you talked on the phone or on the computer?" Jude asked, impatient for real information.

"The computer," David scoffed, looking at Jude as if he were from outer space.

David pulled back his shoulders, his neck lengthened, he moved his head from side to side.

"Hey, I really need to get back to my place. I need to let everyone know about Wilson, don't you think? We'll have a wake online."

Jude took a deep breath, the sound of which filled the car. Josie was stunned. David was oblivious. The guy was living in the Matrix and she had thought it was just a movie.

"First things first. Why did you think something was wrong about how Wilson died?" Josie asked.

"I was actually testing out a new firewall. You know, feeding in some of my own viruses to see how quick I could breach the thing. Anyway, I switched over to my other PC to check in and see who I could talk to face-to-face. . . ." His shoulders hunched once again and the fingers of his hands intertwined.

"I thought you said you'd never seen Wilson," Jude interrupted.

"Not in person. I saw him through a Web cam. Wilson was mammoth," David informed them with an astonished blink. "I could see his face and some of his shoulders. I mean, those things don't exactly give you a panoramic view. If you're at the computer you're up pretty close to the camera."

"But you can see into Wilson's apartment?" Jude asked.

"Sure. I've seen you a hundred times." David smiled. "I've seen you slip a couple of bills under Wilson's books on the desk. That was funny. Wilson was always so surprised when he found that money. He'd sign off so he could order some of those lemon cakes he liked so much. You wasted a whole lot of money on Wilson. He was rolling in the dough. He contracted with half the software companies in the country. Wilson was a genius."

David looked at Josie, pleased with himself for a minute before that smile faded and that hair shook again. David's fingers, nails bitten to the quick, clutched at his bony knees. Josie saw the notes to himself etched onto his forearm with blue pen. He was still an adolescent, growing up without a handle on the passage of time, a Peter Pan who lived on the fairy dust of bits and bytes.

"Anyway, I was looking in on Wilson and I see this other guy in his house. I thought it was you"—he gave a nod to Jude—"but it wasn't. This guy's suit wasn't as nice as yours, but it was okay. I wasn't paying a whole lot of attention. I saw his back. I saw him leaning over Wilson's big chair."

"Could you tell what he was doing?" Josie asked quietly.

David shook his head earnestly and this time the hair stayed put.

"No. He just leaned over Wilson kind of like this." David contorted his skinny body but it did nothing to jump-start Josie's imagination. "Then I see him walk into the other room. Then he comes back again after about four minutes. When that guy went into the bedroom I thought that was strange. Nobody ever goes into the bedroom at night, not even Wilson."

"And you didn't see his face?" Jude prodded.

"I told you, it was getting dark, and Wilson's camera setup isn't exactly state-of-the-art, so the range was limited. I told him he should have upgraded," David said matter-of-factly. "Anyway, I saw this guy's chin. I saw his shirt, his tie, the suit. I saved a couple of images but I don't know how clear they are. The scary thing was, this guy was working Wilson's machines. Nobody has ever touched those computers but Wilson, and then this man just works them like he owns them."

David sat back. He raised his hands and widened those baby blues and shook his hair out. He was finished. The end.

"How long was this guy in the apartment?" Jude asked.

"Best I can tell, ten minutes. Not long."

"Did you hear anything?"

"I can't hear. It's a Web cam, not a sound system. We just had the picture and we'd IM—"

"What's that?" Josie rearranged her long legs. The right one was going to sleep. She wanted to get out and walk around but knew the privacy inside the car was better.

"Instant message," David explained patiently. "You know, real time. We'd type the same way we're talking right now. Wilson always had the camera going. He had a nice smile." David shifted in his seat and finally raised one hand to fiddle with the collar of his boy's-school shirt. "Anyway, when Wilson didn't come on after this guy left, I knew something was up. I tried to call even though I knew Wilson wouldn't like it. I watched and he didn't even move when the phone rang. I was really freaking. I tracked down his address, I called the cops—and that was a weird experience, man, calling the cops—and I found a car and came

here. I only came because I didn't want the police at
my place." David wiped the palms of his hands on
those made-of-iron pants of his. "It's good to know
I'm not agoraphobic or some such thing. I was a little
worried about that."

David continued talking, speculating about his socialization, when Josie touched Jude's knee.

"They're leaving."

Jude and David Gibson looked in time to see four men
wheeling Wilson down the ramp toward a flatbed truck
that had just pulled up. A smattering of neighbors had
gathered. They pointed and talked among themselves
while the men in charge of Wilson's body struggled.

"Jesus Christ," Jude muttered angrily, and threw
open the door.

Josie let him go. No one could transport Wilson in
a dignified manner, but Jude wasn't in the mood to
understand that as he stormed toward the men. He
stopped them, and Wilson's huge body tipped, almost
falling off the furniture dolly. Two men—one on either
side—shored the body upright while the detective,
calm and businesslike, reasoned with Jude.

David Gibson's eyes widened beneath the shock of
rope-thick hair. He was enthralled with real-life drama
but content to watch from the sidelines as it played
out. He didn't really know Wilson, after all. He didn't
know the sound of his voice, or the way Wilson lum-
bered instead of walked. David didn't know how gra-
cious Wilson could be or how kind Jude was. Yet
there were some things Josie would bet David did
know. She leaned over the seat in the Mercedes and
tapped David on the shoulder. He fairly jumped out
of his skin at the contact.

"David, can you get on Wilson's computers and tell
us which files were deleted?"

"Sure I could, but I don't think that's an option."

Josie looked where he looked. Other men were coming out of the house, hauling out Wilson's computers easier than they had the man himself. Josie's heart sank. The computers were being confiscated, each one of them impounded. It would be a public servant rifling through the drives to search for clues to criminal activity, not Wilson's friend. Josie wouldn't be the first to get the information on those machines; Ruth Alcott would.

Disappointed, Josie faced forward, crooked her elbow on the window ledge and put her head in her hand. So much for grand ideas and interesting strategies. Whatever it was Wilson wanted to talk to Jude and Josie about was now lost. It would take weeks, perhaps months, for Ruth to turn over everything she found. With a click of her tongue, Josie's hand fell to her lap and then went to the door handle. She was about to get out of the car when David's head popped between the seats. That lush mess of blond hair hung over the console as he turned his head sideways so that he could look at her.

"You know, I could look on my computer. I mean, Wilson and I, we were networked through two of his computers. I can access all the stuff he gave me from my place. What do you think? Would that help?"

Josie turned her head, narrowed her eyes and gave David a look of chilly regard for not pointing this out in the first place. The look of disdain was wasted on him. She pulled her lips back. Hardly a smile, more an expression of the effort it took to keep from screaming.

"Yes, David. I think you could say that would help."

38

Josie was on all fours pushing aside papers and boxes and more paper as she followed the ringing. Finally she found the phone, answered it and listened. A few *uh-huhs* as she sat back on her heels and the call was over.

"Hannah," Josie called as she tossed the cordless. Hannah caught it and put it back on its station, listening to Josie talk while she crawled back to where she had been working. "That was David Gibson. He found another sixty e-mails that our mystery man deleted from Wilson's files. He's forwarding them to my computer. Would you go and get them? Print them out and bring them here."

Hannah stood up and brushed at her jeans.

"I need a bath," she complained as she surveyed the boxes littering Josie's living room. "Archer needs to clean out his garage more often."

"Archer needs to get home before he can do that," Josie muttered.

"And I'm beginning to think we're going to have to hire a staff to track down all these leads," Jude piped in.

He swung his legs off the sofa where he had been lying for the last two hours reading through hundreds of leads that had poured into Wilson's computers after he had asked to hear from anyone who had been at Pacific Park the day of Tim Wren's accident. Someone had killed Wilson, and that someone had deleted any recent communication about Pacific Park—or so that someone thought. The Web site was still up and running, the chat rooms were still functioning and Wilson had shared an avalanche of information with David Gibson.

"Did you find anything?" Josie settled herself in front of one of Archer's boxes and drummed her fingers on the top.

"Not yet." Jude stretched his arms high above his head. "I'm going to get a drink. Want something?"

"No. Thanks," Josie said absentmindedly, thinking for a minute before opening the box and digging inside.

She dropped her glasses onto her nose again as she rifled through a pile of papers. Max-the-Dog nuzzled her back, got a thoughtless pet for his efforts and moved on. For two days Jude had made Josie's place his own. His perfectly pressed shirts and three-thousand-dollar suits had been discarded for jeans and a sweatshirt. Colin was hibernating, seemingly out of the picture for good. For Jude it was all about Wilson; for Josie it was Archer. For both of them it was even more than personal loyalties. They sensed they were closing in on something important—something important enough to kill for—and Josie was grateful for the help.

"I think I've got something," Josie called, and held up a report. Jude poked his head out just as Josie put it aside. "Never mind. Just information on Lexi."

She picked up more medical reports. Lexi. Lexi and more Lexi. Archer had kept everything having to do with her, but Josie couldn't find anything having to do with Tim. Finally she found the billing records from the Greenwood Home.

"I think Archer just dumped this stuff all together after a while," Josie muttered as she looked at the stash. "I don't know why he didn't just get rid of it. Look, receipts from Greenwood are stuck in with Lexi's blood-work reports. Here's a menu from El Burrito Junior. I swear, I don't know what I thought I was going to find. . . ."

Josie took off her glasses as Jude walked back into the living room.

"You're looking for Tim's medication reports," he reminded her. "I'm looking for something that will tell me what happened in Wilson's apartment. It's all tied together, Josie. All of it."

He took a drink: scotch and water. He had brought his own aged-a-billion-years scotch. She provided the water.

"At least we know it had something to do with Pacific Park, since only those files were deleted from the computers. The question is, was it the money I offered for information on Tim or something having to do with Pacific Park's other problems that put Wilson in harm's way? It's possible someone could have just taken exception to something Wilson posted on the general Web site. Whoever deleted those files didn't exactly do it with a fine hand. Anything in the file with the words Pacific Park in it was dumped. I don't know how we'll cull through it all on our own."

Josie had her glasses back on again. She listened to Jude because there was nothing really to say. She had listened to him read the messages retrieved from Wilson's deleted files. Josie's favorite was from the woman whose son and grandson had been at Pacific Park the day Tim died. They had come out of the bathroom just in time to see Tim plummet to the ground. For a nominal fee she would be happy to produce her grandson, now ten, to discuss what he had seen. If no money was forthcoming the woman threatened to sue for the irreparable psychological damage caused by dredging up this horrible incident on the Internet where any young, impressionable child could see it.

They had sent that message to the round file.

Josie was half thinking about all the crackpots who had responded to Wilson's plea for information, Jude was musing over the sheer volume of information and Hannah was waiting for the printer to stop printing when something caught Josie's eye.

"Something interesting?" Jude knelt down, setting aside his drink as he did so.

"Curious more than anything," Josie mumbled. "Look at this."

"It's a canceled check made out to the Greenwood Home." There was a shrug of uninterest in his voice.

"No, look at the date," Josie insisted, glancing over her shoulder, glaring at him with those sharp blue eyes of hers when he didn't get it. "This check was canceled days before Tim died. It was returned to Lexi three days before the accident, Jude."

"And Lexi probably issued another one. Who knows why it was canceled?"

"No," Josie persisted, one hand patting a stack of papers, the other shaking the canceled check at him. "I've put all the receipts in order. They're all here. If a check had been reissued a letter would be generated acknowledging the payment just like all the other payments."

Josie dropped the hand holding the check. She twisted her neck, eyed the stack of papers, acted out her thoughts.

"Two odd things happened in sequence, The Green-

wood Home received a request for medical records
from Lexi dated five days before Tim died. The administrator blamed it on a secretary or on Lexi mistak-
ing the date on the letter. Fine." Her head swiveled
back to Jude. "I would accept that. I would. But not
in conjunction with the deliberate act of canceling a
check. You have to call the bank to cancel a check,
Jude."

"And then you write another one. Archer probably
tossed the receipt in a box once the replacement was
cashed. It's a no-brainer." Jude stood. He picked up
his drink. The ice tinkled in the glass.

"I don't think so. What time is it?" Josie strained
to see the clock on the desk.

"Four thirty," Jude announced. Josie sat up, rustling
through the papers around her.

"Where's the phone, Jude? I'll call Greenwood's
accounting department. You get on the other line and
give the bank a call. I want to know if Lexi canceled
this over the phone, in person or online. I also want
to know if they still have the records of her other
transactions and if they can tell me if this amount was
reissued to Greenwood."

Josie found the phone but hesitated before she dialed. Jude was still lounging in the doorway, sipping
his drink, looking like he felt sorry for her.

"Come on," she ordered. "There's still time. Here's
the check number, Jude. It's not like your place, you
know. I don't have a dozen associates to help."

"You sure you want me to do this?" Jude asked.

"Stop with the twenty questions. I'm tired. Hannah's tired. I imagine you're tired, too. Please, just
call the bank before they close. Please."

"Okay, but I could find out that Archer was cleaning house and making plans," he warned. "Archer

could have signed her name, sent the letter and canceled the check."

"Then he did, Jude, and I'll work around it. Defense attorneys do it all the time." Josie's fingers hovered over the dial pad. "I'm not kidding myself, Jude. I won't be okay if it comes down to Archer, but right now I don't care what we find. I just want to know who canceled this check and when they did it. Now, please, go call."

"All right," Jude said softly. "All right."

When she didn't change her mind, Jude took the check, but before he could do as she asked, Hannah appeared. She held up the printouts and said, "Hey, you guys, I think this is something important."

39

Josie was awash in a wave of peace. It had come over her the minute she looked at the "something important" Hannah had found in David Gibson's transferred files. Though she didn't know the true importance of the e-mail, she understood that it was significant. She made the contact that night, responding to the e-mail, waiting for a response in return, and finally, the next morning Josie actually spoke to the woman who knew what had happened to Timothy Wren. The answer to what happened to Wilson Page would take a bit longer, but it would come.

In the last week Josie and Jude had traveled to a small town seventy miles outside the city limits of Los Angeles. They had met the woman, watched her children run in and out of the house, sipped the tea she had offered and listened to her story about Pacific Park. Hers wasn't the last piece of the puzzle; it was the first. All the little bits and pieces of motive, opportunity and means that had passed through Josie's hands, entered her mind, created questions in her heart and soul, fell into place. Until that moment, the information they had was like so many blue cardboard puzzle pieces, meaningless until put together properly to create a glorious and detailed sky.

For five long nights Josie and Jude put their heads together and laid out the evidence, followed the trail and kept their own counsel. Archer was kept in the dark; Colin was not contacted. Hannah walked on egg-shells. Max watched as the two worked feverishly. When they finished, when they had the forensics report, when they had confirmed who had canceled the check and who had requested the medical records and who had been in Wilson's apartment, Josie called Ruth Alcott and requested a meeting.

She was put on the calendar the next day. Josie had hoped for the next hour, but she took what was offered. The night before the meeting Josie pretended to sleep. She kept her eyes closed and her breathing steady to fool Hannah, who, in recent days, had taken to looking in on her not once or twice, but six or seven times before she was convinced Josie was okay. When Hannah's door remained closed, Josie left the house and walked to the Strand. The Mermaid Restaurant was locked up tight in the wee hours. Burt was long gone home. The town slept, sheltered from the wet cold of the Hermosa night. Only Josie was out.

She put up the hood on her sweatshirt and walked north toward no particular destination. She looked at nothing and yet was aware of everything: the halo of mist surrounding the streetlights, the silence that was broken by the sound of waves up close and sirens in the distance in another city. The ocean smelled of salt and creatures. It rolled in and touched the sand as it always had, then rolled away again as it always had. She passed the pier and kept her eyes forward, the sweatshirt hood a blinder so she wouldn't look too long at the desolate stretch of concrete. If she did, Josie would think seriously of going to the end and walking right off. It would be better than facing Archer with what she knew; it would be better than staying silent and living with what she knew.

And yet . . . and yet . . .

There was this peace when she stood in front of Archer's old pink building that once belonged to Lexi and before that to Colin. It was November now, full-blown winter by the beach, and Josie let thoughts drift through her mind like the wispy morning fog.

Josie thought about mothers: her own, Hannah's, Lexi. Josie couldn't help but think of Lexi and the way she loved her son and how Archer never could. He just never could, and that failing, in the end, was at the very core of what had gone wrong.

Josie thought of Jude Getts. He had been so kind when all was said and done. Josie appreciated that. She appreciated him. There were moments when she wondered what they could have been together if things had been different. Then those moments were gone. Soon Jude would be gone, too.

And there was Hannah, wise beyond her years, who hadn't been surprised by the truth. She understood that underlying passions led to unspeakable acts. She had put her arms around Josie and Josie had let her. It embarrassed her to think of it now. She wished she could have told Hannah how much she appreciated the effort. Instead, Josie stayed in that girl's arms for no more than a minute, but it was a moment unlike one she had ever experienced. She would have liked to have shared it with her own mother. But Hannah had been there, Emily wasn't, and Josie had stood in Hannah's embrace, unable to say—

"Josie. Josie."

Impatiently, Ruth called to Josie. It took a minute but finally Josie composed herself and apologized with a curt, "Sorry," to the people around the conference table. She shot a glance over her shoulder. Roger McEntyre looked back, his expression a mix of curiosity and admiration. She knew the reason for this meet-

ing had piqued his curiosity, but what did he admire?
The answer didn't matter. Josie didn't care. He was
here, as were Ruth and Jude, and that was all that
was important.

"I'm ready."

Josie pushed in the videotape. There was a click
and a mechanical sigh as it settled itself.

"This video was shot by Mrs. Michael Tronowski.
She and her husband and their children were behind
Archer, Lexi and Timothy Wren as they waited in line
for the Shock and Drop on the day of Tim's death."

Enough said.

It was showtime.

Mrs. Tronowski was a decent videographer. The
camera was steady, lingering where it should, panning
over the crowd when she was bored, focusing and closing in tight on anything she found interesting. Mostly
Mrs. Tronowski found her children interesting, but
Lexi, Tim and Archer were caught in every frame.
Archer's impatience with Tim's antics was barely con-
cealed. Lexi offered her son water, candy, a hug. He
pulled away. Archer grabbed Tim's arms. They could
see him speaking harshly to the boy.

"Play that again," Ruth directed.

Josie did as Ruth asked. They all watched Archer
discipline Tim, holding the boy's arms tightly to his
sides, Archer's face turning scarlet with irritation.
Ruth looked smug, as if this were proof that she had
the moral high ground. Dutifully, Josie played the
scene twice, then moved on.

"I can show you this next part, but it's disjointed.
Mrs. Tronowski thought she turned off the camera
when she hadn't. She starts filming again in a minute."

The high whine of fast-forward filled the room; then
the tape began to play again. The first frames caught

the shuffle of feet. They heard a jumble of sounds: a garble of voices, the child closest to the camera asked to go to the bathroom, the woman said it was too late and, finally, Mrs. Tronowski's motherly cheer rallied the troops as they inched toward the Shock & Drop. The camera panned the line.

We're almost there. One . . . three . . . eight more . . .

She counted the people in front of them.

There was a redheaded girl making out with her dark-skinned boyfriend. A big bald man escorting three children. There was Archer, hands in his pockets, uninterested in everything. Behind him, seemingly disconnected from everyone including Archer, stood Lexi and Tim.

Lexi's arm was around her son's waist. Her head lay against his shoulder. Suddenly Tim rolled away from his mother; his head lolled sideways, then back. For a split second his unfocused eyes looked directly at Mrs. Tronowski. His arms hung down loosely even as his body jumped with involuntary tremors and twitches. Lexi pulled him back to her and, as she did so, she looked directly at the camera, too. She looked raw and hard and turned away when she realized the camera was on her. Tim jumped once, his head did that wave movement, and his legs dipped so that he seemed to be collapsing. Lexi whispered something to him and clutched him tight. She held him up, that big boy.

Her big boy.

It was their turn at the Shock & Drop.

Eric Stevens was on tape, motioning them forward. Archer spoke to him. Eric shook his head. Archer put a hand up. He moved Eric out of the way without any real force. Archer tended to Lexi's son. He latched the safety harness—twice—without looking at Tim. Mrs.

Tronowski tired of the people in line and turned her camera up and focused on the Shock & Drop.

Oh, look.

Archer, Lexi and Tim came into view.

So high.

They were almost at the top. A long way. Mrs. Tronowski hit a button and the camera adjusted for a close-up.

So fun.

Lexi touched Tim's face. She said, *I love you.* All three jolted as the platform reached the top, engaged and then . . .

Oh, my God! Oh, my God!

Recording a memory, Mrs. Tronowski caught a murder on tape.

Shooting straight up, her vertical view of Tim and Lexi and Archer saw what Pacific Park's horizontal camera had not. Yes, Archer's hand shot out and grabbed at Tim's harness. Yes, Tim's hands came down on top of Archer's. It was hard to tell how much force Tim used, or whether Archer was scratched, or whether Tim, in the state he was in, was able to make a good-faith effort to save himself. So much was unclear except for one thing: Each of them seeing this tape knew who released the safety on Tim's harness.

Lexi.

Her hand had shot out and pulled back before Archer even turned his head. This was what broke Josie's heart. A mother—Tim's mother—had sacrificed her son in one, quick, definitive movement, and the implication of all that entailed sent a chill through the room.

"Oh, Jesus," Ruth breathed.

Josie played it again and couldn't shake the feeling that watching this was like looking up a woman's skirt.

Straight on all you saw was the skirt; looking up you
saw the underpinnings, the forbidden stuff, the titillat-
ing reality of the human form. Mrs. Tronowski had
lifted the skirt of Lexi's psyche to reveal the desperation of the human spirit: a dying mother so terrified
that her son would be alone after her death that she
sent him on before her. They would be together in
heaven. God would not blame a mother for taking
care of her child. God would not be that cruel.

Lexi could not look at what she had done; Archer
watched because he could not believe what he was
seeing. He had only sensed the movement, reacting in
that split second as Tim fell. Poor Archer had not
seen how it happened, only that it did happen. It was
a matter of perspective: moral, physical, psychological.
The perspective of one silent witness over another;
one camera telling the truth it recorded, the other
telling the truth as it was.

"Jesus," Ruth said again, and then cleared her
throat. Back in character, her voice bold now. "So it
was a mercy killing."

"No, it wasn't," Josie said flatly as she rewound the
tape. "Lexi committed premeditated murder."

"The woman was dying," Ruth argued, unwilling to
point the same finger of guilt at a woman and mother
that she had at Archer. "She was worried about her
kid. Her mind was gone. Tim wasn't in any great
shape himself. It was a mercy killing."

Josie punched eject and the tape came to her like
a well-trained dog. She held it against her middle as
if to keep sickness away.

"She knew exactly what she was doing," Josie said
again as she looked across the table and gave a heads-
up. "Jude."

His coat was unbuttoned and, when he stood, it fell

open so that the flash of the silk lining could be seen. Today he wore a tie the color of blood. His breast pocket was glued to his shirt by starch and a meticulous maid. His suit was black. It was Jude in all his glory, and yet it wasn't. His expression was guarded so that no one would see the deep and enduring sadness this exercise had caused him. Josie and Jude had talked, argued and speculated but, in the end, they had come to the same conclusion: Love had gone terribly awry, and people they cared about had been caught in the wake of one woman's premeditated action. Wilson was dead; Archer was close to losing life as he knew it. Jude handed everyone an overview of the facts. They would leave no question that the victims were the people they loved.

"The killing was premeditated, and carried out despite the fact that Tim Wren was generally in good health. Lexi killed her son because she was arrogant enough to believe that, without her, his life wasn't worth living."

Jude looked at Josie, saw she was settled and let her take over.

"Our independent autopsy showed that the problem with Tim's heart was manageable," Josie began. "For all intents and purposes he was healthy and could live a long life. Dr. Chow could make no decision regarding the quality of that life, but that was not for him or Lexi to say.

"Lexi requested Tim's medical records be released to her five days before his death. They were sent out by a clerk who didn't check on Tim's status and were subsequently destroyed."

There was a rustle of pages as everyone followed Josie's lead and turned to the next page.

"Page two," she intoned. "Three days before Tim's

death, Lexi received a form letter from the Greenwood Home and the attached check. A stop-payment had been issued seven days before that. We can document a pattern of payment for Tim's care until that day. When Lexi could, she paid in advance for fear that Tim would somehow suffer if she was ever in arrears. Yet, on this date, Lexi deliberately stopped payment on the check that would have assured Tim's care for the next three months, because she knew he would not be returning to the Greenwood Home. Greenwood expected a new check to be cut. When Tim died, they didn't follow up.

"Page three." Again the rustle of paper. "A report on the water bottle we found in the bag Lexi carried that day shows phenobarbital is evident. That is the same drug found in Tim's system when he died. The drug subdued him during a forty-five minute wait so he wouldn't make a scene. The doctors believed Tim did not understand cause and effect, but Lexi knew better than to assume. She medicated her son as a precaution. If he had struggled or fought her off, Archer, at the very least, would have known what she was trying to do. We have the bottle from Lexi's bag, a Polaroid of her holding that bottle as she stood next to her son that day and Mrs. Tronowski's video that shows Lexi making Tim drink from that bottle at least twice.

"Page four," Josie went on. "A copy of a list Lexi wrote. Please note that she carefully marked off everything that she had done the day of Tim's death, even going so far as to write 'the end' as the final postscript. Certainly, there is no greater evidence of her premeditation."

Josie turned the pages back. She clasped her hands atop them and looked at Ruth Alcott.

"We were working backward. All the little pieces

of information on Lexi and Tim made no sense until we had Mrs. Tronowski's tape showing a different angle of the incident. Once we had that, everything else fell into place. You don't have a case against Archer. You never really did."

"We indicted on good faith," Ruth objected.

"You indicted because someone put a bug in your ear." Josie had no trouble with the accusation. "You indicted because it was sensational and John Cooper gave his blessing to help out an old friend and you couldn't resist something as juicy as this."

"We'll drop the charges; your client will be out this afternoon." Ruth pushed back her chair, unwilling to take the blame for any of this. "But be clear. I don't have the time to indict people just for the fun of it, and I don't do favors, even for the DA. Indicting your client was a mistake—a bad one, but a mistake nonetheless."

"Then maybe you should rectify it," Josie suggested. "Investigate Pacific Park. They're the ones that used you, and Mr. McEntyre should be the first one you look at."

"What's she talking about?" Ruth snapped as she looked Roger's way. "Mr. McEntyre?"

"I don't know," Roger answered.

"Then let me fill you in. I'm talking about obstruction of justice, tampering with evidence and, if our eyewitness and the fingerprint evidence holds up, we are also talking about the murder of Wilson Page. Pacific Park is knee-deep, and I think it starts at the top," Josie said.

"Isaac Hawkins knows nothing about security issues," Roger answered without a trace of emotion.

"What are you talking about?" Ruth demanded, but Roger had eyes only for Josie. He dared her to lay it out, and she obliged.

"Mr. McEntyre knew about this tape two years ago because Mrs. Tronowski forwarded a copy of it by registered mail to the head of security at Pacific Park. The signature card was signed by Roger McEntyre. I imagine the second camera on community grounds caught exactly the same view as Mrs. Tronowski, or at least something close to it." Josie pushed a Xerox of the signature sheet toward Ruth. Jude supplied an electrical schematic of the park with the cameras highlighted. "Mr. McEntyre never told anyone about either tape."

"Is that true?" Ruth asked, her face ashen. "You knew all along that Tim Wren's mother was responsible for his death?"

Roger didn't answer and his gaze never wavered. Ruth wouldn't let it go.

"If you had this tape, why did you lead us to believe that Ms. Bates's client had committed the crime?"

"I was doing my job. I was protecting the park," Roger said. "Two simultaneous wrongful-death cases would have put us out of business."

"But that doesn't explain what happened two years ago," Ruth insisted. "You had the original tape. You could have proven that Pacific Park wasn't culpable. You wouldn't have had to pay out a dime."

"That's bullshit and you know it. The company pays. It always does even if they didn't do anything." Roger looked around the table, daring anyone to contradict him. "Besides, why even bring it up? The boy's mother wasn't going to make a fuss, so why should I tell anyone she killed her kid in our park? It wouldn't look too good to point a finger at a dying woman no matter what was on that tape."

Roger McEntyre shook his head as if he had just realized he was surrounded by idiots.

"Within three hours I had reviewed and confiscated the park videos. I didn't get the Tronowski woman's tape until a month after the accident. Then Tim Wren's mother was dead. I had the tapes in the safe and I figured that was the end of it."

Roger looked back at Josie and Jude.

"Unfortunately, I made two mistakes. I believed no one would even think about the second camera once the grounds were reconfigured, and it was my assumption that Mrs. Tronowski had sent me her original. Once I destroyed those tapes I figured everything was taken care of."

"But why implicate someone else? Why let an innocent man pay the price for something his wife did?" Ruth demanded.

"Mr. Getts is a fine lawyer," Roger said, his mustache twitching with a wry smile. "I couldn't take the chance that he would convince a jury that the boy's father deserved compensation from Pacific Park. The only way I could be positive we wouldn't be held liable was to make someone else responsible, someone unrelated to the victim. Isaac Hawkins would have insisted I tell the truth if he knew what it was. I couldn't have that."

Roger adjusted his jacket. He looked around the table and everyone looked back, waiting to hear the rest of his story.

"It was a calculated risk, pointing the finger at her client"—Roger raised his chin toward Josie—"but I had to take it. Best-case scenario, he's acquitted and all he lost was some time. Worst case, he gets sent up. Simple as that. All I did was turn the attention away from the park. You all took it from there."

Roger sat back, but Josie and Jude knew the story wasn't finished.

"You forgot one thing. Wilson Page," Jude said.

"Jude, be careful," Josie warned, not wanting to tip their hand before all the evidence had been turned over to the DA.

"He killed Wilson," Jude whispered. "The camera was on."

"What camera? Who in the hell is Wilson Page?" Ruth demanded. Josie looked her way, but she caught Roger's gaze and finally understood his admiration. He liked a worthy opponent.

"Wilson Page was a friend of mine," Jude answered. "He ran a Web site investigating Pacific Park. We found this tape because of him."

"He was a problem," Roger admitted.

Jude spoke over him.

"He was my friend. I asked him to put out the word that I would pay to talk to anyone who had seen exactly what happened at Pacific Park that day. The promise of money brought in a thousand people looking for a quick buck. Wilson called me the day he died to tell me he had hooked up with Mrs. Tronowski. When he couldn't get ahold of me, he called Colin Wren and told him what he had. Colin wanted to see for himself. He got stuck in traffic and never made it to Wilson's place. He didn't want anyone to know about what Lexi had done either. If I had to guess, he probably still loved her in some weird way or he still blamed Archer for pushing her so far and wanted him to pay."

"And what does that have to do with me?" Roger asked, baiting Jude and enjoying it.

"We have a witness who saw you through a Web cam hooked up to Wilson's computer."

"Really?" Roger raised an eyebrow. "And someone

saw me kill your friend? They identified me, is that it?"

"Not yet. The witness saw a man in Wilson's apartment. He can describe his clothing, the shape of his face," Jude said.

"That doesn't sound like much," Roger said.

"The man who caught sight of you on that camera was able to digitally enhance the image. It's not the clearest, but it will be enough when coupled with the fingerprints we found in the apartment. Guess you made another mistake when you thought we'd just accept that Wilson died of natural causes."

"That's not exactly heavy evidence," Roger said, ignoring Jude's taunt.

"Then how about this? Wilson called you, the same way he called me and my client," Jude said triumphantly. "What did he say, Mr. McEntyre? Did Wilson ask you to come clean about the tape? Did he do the right thing and warn you so that you would be prepared when all this came out? Wilson would want to give you a fighting chance. But, you see, Wilson didn't use the phone much, so your number stands out like a sore thumb on his telephone records. The call to you lasted eight minutes. You'll want to talk to a lawyer before you tell us exactly what was said in that eight minutes."

Jude pushed a piece of paper toward Roger McEntyre.

"I also have this. The e-mail Mrs. Tronowski sent to Wilson telling him she had a copy of the video and that she re-sent one to you so that there wouldn't be a mistake this time. How's that for some interesting information, you bastard."

"That's enough, Jude," Josie warned him before

turning her attention to Ruth Alcott. "We'll send everything we've got, and it's a whole lot more than you had on Archer."

Josie touched Jude's shoulder. It was time to go. Ruth could sift through it all, and she could deal with Roger McEntyre. On her way out Josie dropped a card in front of Roger.

"You may want to give this to Isaac Hawkins. Colin Wren may not be pursuing his suit, but you'll be hearing from Archer."

Roger picked it up. He toyed with it, flipping it slowly between his fingers. Josie could hardly stand the sight of him, and his nonchalance turned her stomach. Roger was so composed, so unrepentant. He had killed one man and tried to condemn another to a life behind bars. Josie grasped the back of his chair and the edge of the table and cornered Roger McEntyre.

"What kind of man are you?" she demanded.

Slowly, Roger turned his head. The card had stopped spinning. He held it up so Josie could see it even though their eyes were locked.

"I'm a man of faith, Ms. Bates," Roger said. "I had faith you'd get him off. I just didn't know it was going to be at my expense."

Jude walked Josie to her car.

They had arrived separately, knowing they would be headed in different directions when the day was over. Josie unlocked her car, giving Jude a minute. She had seen him wipe the corner of his eye in the elevator, heard him sniff back the sorrow he carried over Wilson's death. Josie understood what he was going through because she carried something, too. She just didn't have a word for the knot of emotions in her gut. Relief, guilt, anguish, love and even shame that she had thought Archer capable of the crime of which he was accused were a jumble inside her. It would take a while to unravel it all. She couldn't help but wonder what she'd have left when it was done.

"So." Jude put his hand on the hood of the Jeep and patted it like an old friend.

"So." Josie opened the door and palmed the key. She tossed her briefcase in the backseat. When she faced him, she smiled.

"We were good together, Josie." Jude chuckled. "We could burn a swath through this town if we hooked up for good."

"Are you offering me a job at your place or do you want to hang out under my shingle?"

"Your place is a little modest, don't you think? Besides, I've got the staff. I even have more than two phone lines. What do you say?"

"I say let's file it under M for maybe. Right now I've got a couple of things to take care of."

"Archer?"

She inclined her head as if to ask, *What else?* It was the only thing left. Josie lingered, though she shouldn't have. She owed Archer a face-to-face, and yet she put it off because she was afraid to find out that she had lost him in all this. Maybe she had even thrown him away.

But Jude didn't catch on. Always the optimist. Always the man on top. He said, "Archer's a lucky man, Josie. He had a great lawyer. He's got a good woman."

"Yeah, well," Josie said quietly. "You'll let me know about Wilson's funeral?"

"Absolutely. David Gibson's putting out the word. He says the computer crowd is actually going to come."

Josie put her hand on Jude's arm. There was nothing more to say, and Archer was waiting.

"Good then." Jude pushed off, leaned over and kissed her on the cheek. "You change your mind, you let me know."

"You'll be the first, Jude." Josie swung herself into the Jeep.

She rolled down the window and put on her baseball cap. The Jeep's engine turned over. She threw it into gear and started to pull out of the parking space, but Jude was in the way. When she put her head out the window to ask him to move, Jude seemed startled. Then that glorious, megawatt grin of his was shining right on her. He stepped back, but before Josie could pull out completely Jude put his hand on the car door.

"You know I lied, don't you?"

"Really?" Josie said. "About what?"

"I like short hair. I like it on you."

With that he stepped back. He was still watching Josie Baylor-Bates when she took the turn to the exit that would put her on Temple Street not too far from Men's Central Jail, Archer and the hardest good news Josie would ever have to deliver.

40

"It looks good. Really good, Hannah."

The dining room that had once been blue was now a subtle blend of white on white on white: Navajo overlaid with pearl and sponged over with bright white. It looked like a fresh snowfall or the sands on the beach in Ixtapa. Josie's mother's hula-girl plates would be rehung, cracks and all. Hannah finished dabbing at one corner, then admired their handiwork.

"I told you it was the right way to go. You just didn't have any faith in me as an artist." Hannah sniffed.

"I did. I swear," Josie objected. "I just didn't know if I had enough faith when it came to turning over a whole room in the house. What if you thought red would look real nice?"

"Then it would have looked nice." Hannah tossed her hair over her shoulder, still posturing like a normal teenager but happier than she had been in months. Josie was home, school was okay, her psychiatrist wasn't a monster and she was even glad Archer was back if only for no other reason than it made things seem normal. Still, Hannah wasn't going to let Josie know exactly how relieved she was that Josie liked the room. "I was worried you wouldn't get the hang of the technique and I'd have to do it all myself."

"Well, how about if I leave you to clean up the

mess by yourself. I told Archer I'd help him with the garage. He wasn't real happy with the way we left it."

Josie grabbed a rag off the floor and wiped the paint from her hands, keeping her eye on Hannah just in case she was skittish about being left alone. If Hannah was concerned she didn't show it.

"Is he going to keep all that stuff?" Hannah asked as she gathered the brushes and sponges.

"No. He knows he has to let Tim and Lexi go." Josie worked on a streak of bright white paint that had dried and crackled on the side of her hand. "Where's the turpentine?"

"Here." Hannah stretched, holding out the can, then sinking to the floor, sitting cross-legged as she looked at Josie. "You never told me how Archer took the news about Lexi?"

"Hard."

Josie pulled a chair out from under the tarp and sat down, abandoning her cleanup, remembering everything about that meeting. She told him straight. No trying to soften the news.

Lexi killed Tim.

Archer didn't flinch. He took the blow deep inside.

It was a long time before Archer touched Josie after all was said and done. When he did, Josie thanked God. They were together again. A little tougher under the skin, a little wary, mourning what had been lost, but willing to put things together again.

"He took it hard, Hannah. He loved Lexi a lot," Josie said.

"As long as he understood. I'd really be pissed at him if he didn't understand that Lexi did what she thought was right," Hannah mumbled, and Josie couldn't believe her ears.

"Lexi killed Tim because she was selfish, Hannah,"

Josie explained, surprised by the girl's empathy. "Lexi wanted too much from Archer and expected too little of the rest of the world, so don't go making a hero out of her."

"Is that what Archer thinks or is that what you think?" Hannah challenged.

"It's what I know," Josie insisted. "Hannah, she made a list, she closed accounts, she put the medicine in the water. That means killing Tim was a premeditated act, and that means it was murder."

"What did Archer say about the list and stuff?"

"He didn't say anything, and I didn't ask," Josie said. "Archer's in shock; he's in denial. He loved her. That's what Archer will remember. If he tries to rationalize all this, he'll tell himself it was the cancer. He'll say she wasn't in her right mind."

Hannah put one of the brushes in a bucket of turpentine and worked it like a butter churn. In the quiet, Josie could almost hear Hannah thinking, trying to unlock the mysteries of mothers and their children. Finally Hannah asked, "Do you think Tim would have missed his mom when she died?"

"I think so," she answered.

"Okay," Hannah mumbled, and the brush went into the turpentine again and again. Hannah's lips moved as she counted. Josie drew her back into the discussion.

"Look, Hannah, Tim wouldn't have been alone when Lexi died. The thing to remember is that the people at Greenwood would have taken care of him. If Colin had any real interest in stepping up to the plate he could have. I do understand that Lexi felt alone, but that doesn't give her permission to take a life. If it were me, I would have begged Colin, I would have bribed him to take care of his son," Josie tossed the rag toward Hannah. "Bottom line, I think they were both screwed up. Colin and Lexi took selfishness to a high art, and Tim was just a damaged kid caught in the middle."

"So was Archer screwed up too because he loved Lexi?" Hannah challenged Josie, still wanting to find Archer culpable. In her mind no woman was the root of all evil—men shaped them; men created the situations that made women choose everything but their children.

"Maybe he was." Josie shrugged. "He does seem to be attracted to women who come with a heck of a lot of baggage, doesn't he?"

"You don't have baggage. I've got baggage," Hannah objected, abandoning the paintbrush in the can as she looked for another one. Anything to keep her hands busy. "You're just neurotic about your mother. Lexi was just more in love with her kid than any mother you or I ever met. That's why you can't get your mind around what she did. But I can. I think the way Archer acted made Lexi look for another way out. I think Lexi didn't want to go to heaven without her son if nobody on earth was going to take care of him."

Josie stood up and swung one long leg over the seat of the chair. She walked into the living room, found her sweatshirt and zipped it slowly while she listened to Hannah rationalize the death of Timothy Wren.

"That's a very romantic idea," Josie said kindly, but it was her responsibility to be honest with Hannah, since so few had been truthful before her. "I don't know about heaven, but I do know that there are laws: man's law and the moral law, and both of them are clear. You don't take anyone else's life. Period."

"Not even when there's no one who will really care

about you? Not even if your life sucks big-time because you're retarded and sick and all that stuff?" Hannah asked, her exotic green eyes growing darker as she tried to sort out her feelings. "Maybe if Archer had wanted Tim just a little bit—the way you wanted me just a little bit—then things would have been different. Don't you think Lexi would have made a different decision if Archer had just given an inch?"

Josie was tiring of the debate. She had a history with Archer; Hannah didn't. Josie had a father she admired, a lover she respected, and Hannah had neither respect, love nor admiration from any of the men who had passed through her young life. Hannah didn't have to believe what Lexi did was wrong; she just had to accept it. Josie put her fingertips atop Hannah's curls as she passed. For her part, Josie didn't want to believe that maternal instinct could be so strong that a woman would rather kill her child than leave him to an unknown fate. If she believed that, then her own mother shouldn't have walked away, and poor Billy Zuni's mother shouldn't shove him away, and Hannah's mother . . .

"I think we should have a party to celebrate how great this room turned out." Josie changed the subject as she reached for the door. She turned to look at Hannah still sitting cross-legged on the floor, surrounded by paint cans and tarps and brushes. Her face was pinched in contemplation; her hands were busy.

"You're not going to answer me, are you? Archer could have stopped what Lexi did, couldn't he?"

"I don't know, Hannah, and neither do you. If Archer knew what really happened, he blocked it out. Tim and Lexi are dead. Colin is still alone and feeling guilty that he left his son to Lexi. Roger McEntyre will go to jail for killing Wilson and half a dozen other charges. Ruth Alcott will keep doing what she's doing. Pacific Park will stay in business, and all I really care about is playing some volleyball, helping Archer put his life back in order and you cleaning up this mess."

She opened the door, but Hannah had one more thought.

"Do you think Archer will blame you because you were the one who found out about Lexi and—"

The door closed, leaving Hannah to speculate to Max-the-Dog and clean up the paint and brood about all the questions that torture a young mind. Josie jogged down the street. Thoughts of right and wrong, Lexi and Tim, and Colin peeled away from her as she ran. Josie thought a little about Jude and missed him. She couldn't change the way the world worked and she didn't want to. Her crusading days were long gone, and home was Hermosa Beach, quiet and comfortable even though the sun hid behind a cloudy sky.

Josie blew past Burt's, saw that business was good and decided to make Archer settle his legal debt by taking her to dinner when they were finished with the garage. He needed to be part of the town again. Josie ran past a house under construction and admired the brickwork. She turned off the bike path, circled around Archer's building and found him in the garage just where he said he would be.

"Hi."

Josie stepped around some boxes and over a basketball to get to him. She kissed the top of his head before planting her hands on her hips, catching her breath. Archer wrapped an arm around her legs.

"You're out of shape, Jo."

Archer raised his face to her. He didn't smile but she saw it resting there in his dark eyes, that old level playing field she loved so much. Now, though, there was a long scar on one brow to remind her she wasn't perfect, that she had doubted and he had paid for it.

"I could still take you down." She laughed and stroked his hair.

"If that's a proposition it will have to hold."

"Guess I'd better pitch in and help if I'm ever going to get any quality time with you."

"You've got energy to spare. Drag all that stuff out to the Dumpster." Archer gave her butt a pat as he let her go.

"You're sure you want to get rid of all this?" Josie kicked through the mess, hefted the first box and looked over her shoulder.

"Yeah, babe," he answered without hesitation.

Josie didn't ask again. Once all this was gone, the wounds would heal faster. Josie made four trips to the Dumpster and was headed back for a fifth, but, as she bent down to gather up some stray papers, she realized something was wrong. Archer was still in the corner, but now his shoulders were slumped, they trembled, and Josie heard the heartbreaking sound of weeping.

Carefully, quietly, she picked her way through the memories of his life with Lexi and knelt down beside him. This had been coming, Archer's moment of overwhelming honesty, and Josie was glad she was here for him. Josie was about to speak, about to let him know all would be well, when she realized this was not an expression of relief, nor was he lamenting his lost wife. Archer was weeping because he had been injured anew, and the wound was deeper than any before it.

In front of Archer was the white box that Josie had rejected as being too small to hold anything of importance. Now it was open, and Archer had taken a stack of papers from it. He held them tight against his chest, and when Josie took hold he pulled them closer still. Josie pulled harder, silently insisting that he let go.

When he did, she lowered herself to the ground beside him, but Archer didn't want to be near her. He got up, walked to the door of the garage, raised his arms and held on to the top of the open door as his head hung low. Josie looked long enough to reassure herself that he was not leaving before she smoothed the papers and started to read. Unable to believe what she was seeing, Josie shuffled through one letter after another after another again. Her eyes moved but her mind lagged behind. She pointed at the words as if to sound them out and understand the meaning.

Dear Lexi . . .

Oh, God.

I'm sorry. . . . Please, just tell me where Tim is. Let me see him. . . .

Damn you, Lexi.

Please, I was wrong. . . . I won't bother you . . . let me see my son. . . .

You bitch.

Please, Lexi . . . Please.
                                    Colin

Josie's head fell back.

You manipulative bitch.

She stared at the naked beams of the ceiling. That old fine line. It was here in these letters. Colin had told the truth. He had tried to find his son, but his pleas could not break Lexi's bitterness, and Lexi's hurt had no room for Colin's repentance. Archer loved a woman who was a liar, and Tim died because she was cruel.

Josie let the letters fall to the ground. Twenty of them. Maybe more. Remorseful letters that begged for forgiveness. They had been forwarded by the company that managed the apartment building—the only way Colin knew how to get ahold of his ex-wife. The letters were addressed to Lexi Wren; some used her maiden name. Colin didn't know she had remarried. Lexi used Archer, hiding behind him, not wanting to be found.

Josie went cold and let her head fall forward. What had she done to Archer? How could she have insulted such an honest man, questioned his motives and integrity, painted him with the same brush with which she painted her own mother?

Then and there Josie made a promise. She would make it up to him if he would let her. Josie would give Jude these letters if Archer would allow it. They would prove Colin Wren deserved to be compensated for the loss of his son. Love and affection had not only been lost; they had been willfully denied by a woman Colin had once loved and Archer adored. Colin wouldn't have a case against Pacific Park, but he would be vindicated.

Gathering up the letters, Josie put them in the box and sealed it. Finally she looked at Archer. Lexi had used him and Colin and even her own son. She had sucked the life out of three good people before her own was snuffed out.

Women could be so cruel.

Getting up, Josie went to Archer. She put a hand on his shoulder. It wasn't enough. He didn't move. Josie wrapped her arms around him.

"All of it was a lie, Jo," Archer whispered.

"I know," she said back.

After that Josie Baylor-Bates put her cheek against Archer's back, closed her eyes and fell silent.

Read on for a sneak preview of

PRIVILEGED WITNESS

by

Rebecca Forster,

coming soon from Signet

The half-naked woman came from the penthouse—she just hadn't bothered to use the elevator. Instead, she stepped off the balcony eleven stories up. Her theatrics kept Detective Babcock from a quiet evening with a good book, a glass of wine and some very fine music. Detective Babcock didn't hold a grudge long, though. One look at the jumper made him regret that he hadn't arrived in time to stop her.

Beautiful even in death, the dark haired woman lay on the hot concrete as if it were her bed. Her arms were out, one crooked at an angle so that the delicate fingers of her right hand curled toward her head; her other arm lay straight so that her left hand was open-palmed at her hip. Her slim legs were curved together. Her feet were small and bare. Her head turned in profile and her eyes were closed. The wedding ring she wore made Horace Babcock feel just a little guilty for admiring her. She carried her age well, so that it was difficult to tell exactly how—

"Crap, I think I felt a raindrop."

Babcock inclined his head. His eyes flickered toward Kurt Rippy, who was hunkered to the side of a pool of blood that haloed the jumper's head. It was the only sign that something traumatic had occurred here. It would be a different story, though, when the coroner's people turned the body and packed her up. Her brain might fall out. When they cut off the yellow silk-

and-lace teddy at the morgue, lay her face up, naked, on a metal table, they would find half her head caved, ribs pulverized, pelvis broken from the impact of her fall. How glad Babcock was to see her this way. Elegant. Asleep. An illusion.

Raising a hand toward the sky, he checked the weather. Even though the day was almost done, it was still hot, and he could see that the thunderheads that had hovered over the San Bernardino Mountains for the last few days were now rolling toward Long Beach. Pity tonight would be wet when the other three hundred and sixty-four days of the year had been bone dry.

"Are you almost done?" Babcock asked, knowing the rain would wash away the blood and a thousand little pieces of grit and dust and things that Kurt needed to collect as a matter of course.

"Yeah. Not much to get here. I bagged her hands just in case but she looks clean."

Detective Babcock bridled at the adjective. It was too pedestrian for her, hardly poetic.

She was pristine.

She was beautiful.

She was privileged.

She was a lady who was either going to or coming from something important. She was going or coming alone because no one had run screaming from the penthouse, distraught that his or her loved one had checked out of this world in such a manner. The traffic on Ocean Boulevard had slowed but not stopped as the paramedics converged on the site, sirens frantically wailing, until they determined they were too late to help. With a huge grunt Kurt stood up and rolled his surgical gloves off with a little snap.

"That's it for me. I'm going to let them bundle her

before we all get wet. I hate it when it's this hot and it rains. Reminds me of Chicago. I hate Chicago. . . ."

Babcock moved away. The medical examiner's people moved in. They would deal with the body and he would not watch.

Just as it began to rain, as the last vestiges of blood were being diluted and drained into the cracks of the sizzling sidewalk, Detective Babcock walked across the circular drive, past the exquisitely lit fountain of the jumper's exclusive building and went inside. There was still so much to do, not the least of which was to talk to one Mr. Jorgensen, the poor soul who had been making his way home just as the lady leapt. Old Mr. Jorgensen, surprised to find a scantily clad dead woman at his feet, had made haste to leave the scene as soon as the emergency vehicles arrived. He probably couldn't offer much, but a formal statement was necessary and Babcock would take it.

He rode the elevator, breathing in the scent of new: new construction, new rugs, new fittings and fastenings. Babcock preferred the Villa Riviera a few buildings down. The scrolled façade, the peaked copper roof, the age of it intrigued him the way new never could. He got out on the third floor and knocked on the second door on the left. He waited and waited, hearing nothing. Eventually, the door opened and Babcock looked down at the wizened man with the walker.

"Mr. Jorgensen? I'm Detective Horace Babcock." He held out his card. The old man snatched it.

"It's about time you got here," he complained and turned his back. The thumping of the walker was swallowed by the lush carpeting but the acoustics of the spacious apartment were fine. Babcock heard the old man's every mumble and word. "Haven't had my dinner yet. Have you told her husband? Bet you can't even find him to tell him. He's in Los Angeles somewhere. Giving a speech or some such nonsense. Should have been all over the news by now so I figure you haven't told him yet."

"No." Deferentially slow, Babcock followed the old man but something in his voice seemed to annoy Mr. Jorgensen, who stopped just long enough to flash a look of pure disgust over his shoulder.

"You don't even know who she is, do you?"

"The jury finds Kevin O'Connel guilty of assault with intent to kill and awards Susan O'Connel special damages in the amount of one hundred and fifty thousand dollars and general damages in the amount of one and a half million dollars. We further find that the assault was committed with malice and award Susan O'Connel five hundred thousand dollars in—"

"That's crap! That's just fu—" Kevin O'Connel shot out of his seat. Instantly, O'Connel's attorney grappled with him while the judge gave warning.

"Go no further, Mr. O'Connel."

Josie heard the scuffle, heard Kevin O'Connel curse his attorney for not doing more and heard him fall silent as the judge threatened contempt and incarceration. It was quite a scene and it didn't seem to interest Josie one bit. She pushed her fountain pen through her fingers, then did it again, concentrating on that so the court wouldn't see an unseemly grin of satisfaction. She was pleased that she had come close to ruining Kevin O'Connel. He deserved worse. When the clerk spoke again, an appropriately grave Josie Baylor-Bates gave the woman her full attention. Another five hundred thousand in punitive damages was awarded.

Now she did smile, beaming toward the jury as they were dismissed with the court's thanks. The judge left the courtroom. Josie packed up her papers. It was over. Susan O'Connel was a rich woman on paper and Josie was ready to do everything she could to make sure Susan collected. Wages would be garnished, the retirement account cleaned out, and the house Susan and Kevin had shared would be sold so Susan O'Connel could get what was coming to her. Josie had made sure that Kevin O'Connel would surrender his car, his boat—she'd have taken his toothbrush if she could have. He wouldn't have a pot to piss in and Susan O'Connel would have enough money to live anywhere in the country. Every time Kevin got a little ahead, Josie would be there with her hand out on behalf of her client.

It had been a very good day and it wasn't even noon.

Picking up her briefcase, Josie reached for the little swinging gate but Kevin O'Connel put his hand on it first. He held it, looked Josie in the eye, then pushed it back with a cool loathing that was meant to intimidate. It didn't. Josie walked past him down the center aisle and out the door.

From her height to her confidence, Kevin O'Connel hated everything about Josie Baylor-Bates. He hated that she won. He hated that she stood taller than he did. He hated that she dismissed him when she put her fancy little phone to her ear. He knew who she was calling and that pissed him off royally.

When she pushed open the doors to the hall, Kevin O'Connel was right behind her. It appeared he was trying to maneuver around Josie but stumbled instead and knocked her off balance. Her phone clattered to the floor, her arm went out and she steadied herself against the wall before bending to pick it up. Before she could touch it, the phone was snatched away.

"Sorry. Guess I better look where I'm going," he teased.

Josie reached for the phone but he held it back like an evil little boy who had pinched a hair ribbon. Slowly he put the phone to his ear, smiling all the while.

"Good news, Suz. You got it all, babe. Everything and then some. Enjoy it while you can."

Kevin O'Connel must have liked what he was hearing. There was a glint in his eye. His smile was gleeful until suddenly he held the phone away from his ear.

"She hung up," he said in mock surprise.

"Push me again and I'll bring charges for assault. Hand over the phone or I'll have you arrested for stealing. Say one more word to your ex-wife and you'll go down for stalking. If you were smart, you would quit while you're ahead."

"And you better think twice before you let me see your bitch face again," he hissed as his rough and handsome face came close enough for her to feel the warmth of his breath. "I don't go down that easy. Tell Suzy she's got one more chance. She can come home and everything will be fine. If she doesn't, she won't get a penny and I'll fuckin' take you both down. I swear, I will."

"The only way Susan will ever look at you again is over my dead body, Mr. O'Connel."

Josie had enough. She put out her hand for her phone. The man pulled back and with a laugh held his fist high, let it unfurl and dropped the phone at her feet.

"Oops," he said flatly though it was obvious his delight knew no bounds.

Josie lowered her eyes, then brought them up again. Kevin O'Connel was still smirking, waiting for her to bend down and get it. He could wait until hell froze over. She wouldn't spend one second at his feet.

"Think about what you said." Kevin O'Connel warned. "That dead body thing . . ."

"Excuse me?"

Surprised to find that they weren't the only two people in the universe, O'Connel stepped away, and both he and Josie looked at the lady who had bent down to pick Josie's phone off the floor. That was all the time it took for Josie to get curious. There was a good two grand on the woman's back, another couple hundred on her feet. Not exactly the type who would stop to pick up something a stranger dropped; not exactly the kind of woman you found prowling the San Pedro courthouse. She stood up and Josie had the impression that she smiled.

"I think this belongs to you."

She held Josie's phone out on the palm of her hand like a peace offering. Josie took it with a barely audible thanks and her eye on Kevin O'Connel, who was backing away. With a cock of a finger he shot Josie an imaginary bullet filled with hatred, arrogance and warning. Then, with a laugh, he turned on his heel and walked away, leaving Josie and her Good Samaritan to watch.

"He doesn't seem very pleasant," the woman muttered.

"He isn't," Josie said. With a quick "Appreciate it," Josie walked away, keeping her eye on Kevin O'Connel's back.

There was a lot to do so Josie didn't give the woman in the expensive suit another thought as she got Susan on the phone again. But Josie didn't walk alone. The woman in the bright blue suit, the woman with the fine leather shoes and the in-your-face jewels, started down the hall, too. Too close to simply be going the same way; too far to be noticeably in Josie's orbit.

As Josie spoke to Susan O'Connel, she flung open the old wood and glass doors of the San Pedro court-house and walked through, absentmindedly holding it for the woman behind her.

Josie was reaching for her keys and her sunglasses when she felt a hand on her arm.

"Josie Bates?"

"Yep," Josie answered. She glanced first at the hand that touched her, noting the obscenely large emerald ring, and then she looked at the lady in blue who had been on her heels.

"I wonder if I could take a few minutes of your time?" She offered a smile and followed up with an invitation. "Perhaps lunch? It's already past noon."

Josie inclined her head. She had sworn off this kind of client long ago: the kind with more money than good sense, the kind you usually found in Beverly Hills or the Palisades, the kind who had a different sense of justice than the rank and file. This one looked to be bad news. Like a high-priced car, she was sleek, high-maintenance and tuned to the point of a silent, powerful, itchy idle. If Josie let her, she would press the gas and Josie would have no choice but to go along for the ride. So the trick was to get out of the way before the flag dropped.

"I have an office in Hermosa Beach."

Josie reached for a card but the woman put out her hand again. Josie moved to avoid the contact and tried to shake off the sudden chill that tickled the back of her neck. She had the sense that something was amiss here but it was vague and she couldn't get a handle on it.

"I'd like to talk to you today. It's very important," the woman insisted in a voice as subtly deep as her perfume. "It's personal matter. There's a place not too far from here where we could talk privately."

"Look, I'm sorry, but that's not the way I work. If you've got a problem, call my office. If it's something I can help you with I'll let you know; if it isn't I can offer a referral."

"No. I need to talk to you," the woman whispered, unwilling to be gotten rid of. "It's about Matthew. Matthew McCreary."

Those were the magic words. Josie Baylor-Bates was mesmerized, hypnotized, her eyes unable to leave the other woman's. The lady came close again. This time both hands reached out and took Josie by the shoulders as if relieved a long search was over.

"I'm Grace. Grace McCreary. Matthew's sister."

Josie shook her head hard. A tremor skittered up her spine. She stumbled as she tried to free herself. The woman in blue tightened her grip as Josie whispered:

"You're dead."